BLOOD LIONS

THE BELL TRILOGY #3

STEVE BRADSHAW

BLOOD LIONS©

1st Edition 2015

2nd Edition 2016

FOREWING MYSTERY/THRILLER ©

ISBN: 978-1-948059-55-8

Library of Congress Cataloging-in-Publication Data

BLOOD LIONS/Steve Bradshaw

Printed in USA

BOOKS BY STEVE BRADSHAW

The Bell Trilogy
Bluff City Butcher
The Skies Roared
Blood Lions

Evil Like Me

Serial Intent

ACKNOWLEDGMENTS

I owe my sincere thanks to my family for their unwavering support and my friends for their continued encouragement in writing of The Bell Trilogy. I give special recognition to my beta-readers and valued critics for helping me hone my writing skills. I dedicate BLOOD LIONS to my early readers, those very special few that took a chance on a new, mystery/thriller author. Thank you for taking the journey. I hope you will always remember. It is the readers that keep my creative juices flowing. It is for you that I write.

THE BELL TRILOGY

Is an utterly plausible genetic solution for life extension woven into a heart-pounding epic battle between good and evil . . .

The Bell Trilogy chronicles a family of great privilege harboring an unimaginable secret and dream that turns into a global nightmare. Elliott Sumner, a world renowned forensic pathologist, struggles to rectify his abandoned beginnings and innate gifts when unexpected paths cross. The serial killer hunter meets the genius psychopath of Memphis urban legend and discovers a secret to life people will kill for. He must protect the greatest evolutionary leap for mankind.

BLUFF CITY BUTCHER – Book one begins with Elliott's chilling, forensic pursuit of a genius, psychopathic serial killer. The heart-pounding hunt for a real monster uncovers a century old mystery and sinister plan with profound, world implications.

THE SKIES ROARED – Book two enters the unfathomable realms of wealth and power where a secret society seizes control of a genetic breakthrough. Stealth armies on an evil mission and an unstoppable killer lure forensic sleuth Elliott Sumner onto a horrific blood trail that crosses three continents. While hunting the deadly force and navigating the startling twists, Elliott must find answers to an utterly plausible threat to mankind.

BLOOD LIONS – Book three is the masterful conclusion to the Bell family nightmare. Shocking pieces of the ill-fated puzzle fall in place. Elliott Sumner and his unlikely allies must secure, formulate, and disseminate the Medino biogenic compound or the greatest evolutionary leap of mankind is lost. Sinister forces seek control waging a secret battle. In the end Elliott must embrace a real monster and call upon his innate gifts to prevail.

For more information on **The Bell Trilogy** *books, visit author website at*

BLOOD LIONS

Primary Characters

Bell, Albert	Billionaire Patriarch
Bella, Alberto	Gilgamesh COB
Duncan, Adam	Psychopath
Gregory, Maxwell	PI Retired CIA
Mason, Carol	Investigative Reporter
Medino, Enrique	Geneticist
Medino, Marcus	Son of Enrique
Sumner, Elliott	Forensic Pathologist
Wilcox, Tony	MPD Homicide Detective
William	Butler

Supporting Characters

Ali, Mobuto	Gilgamesh Board
Armstrong, Robert	Gilgamesh Board
Bates, Henderson	Shelby County Medical Examiner
Bolivar, Francisco	Gilgamesh Board
Cottam, Henry	MPD Deputy Chief
Duncan, Betty	Mother of Elliott, Adam, Jack
Flanders, Jean	Geneticist
Harris, Alex	MPD Homicide Detective
Henley, Dirk	Gilgamesh Twin
Henley, Glenn	Gilgamesh Twin
Masher, Bentley	Bodyguard
Sorokin, Kim	Geneticist
Stark, Leo	Geneticist
Stubs, Robert	Geneticist
Tanner, Boris	Bodyguard
Vanlandingham, Vince	Geneticist
Wade, Collin	MPD Director

"Do not try to fight a lion if you are not one yourself."

African Proverb

PART ONE
PROVOCATION

ONE

His cell vibrated—UNKNOWN CALLER. He took it anyway. The voice was new and the warning old; he had heard them all before. But this time, if it was true, he could not go on.

Elliott focused. He would remember each word, each pause and inflection. It lasted twenty-three seconds, then the caller was gone.

He punched speed dial—Tony Wilcox, Memphis Homicide. Tony picked up immediately. Elliott was direct. "Have you heard from the DCPD?"

"Shit . . ." Tony swore under his breath. Elliott had to hear about it just seconds after the proprietary information reached the MPD. *I need time to* . . . "Elliott, I want you to slow down. Where are you? Your place, of course. I'm coming now." *Don't do anything, goddamn it . . .*

Elliott heard enough, what he could not bear. He dropped his cell and fell to his knees.

"Elliott!" Tony yelled. *Don't do this. Please, just give me some time to . . .*

Leaning against the sofa, his heart beat in his throat and ears popped. He gasped for air, and then he puked. Elliott stayed down digging his fingers into the carpet as his demons stirred. They would have their way with him soon.

"Elliott . . . Elliott?" But Tony was now lost somewhere between the sofa cushions. Nothing more he said mattered. "Elliott, don't . . . Listen. We need to talk. I'm coming now." He grabbed his coat and ran down the hall of Memphis police headquarters. His car sat out front. He could get to Elliott's in five minutes, but it would be too late.

The door was open. Running to each room Tony called his name. Then he saw the vomit next to the sofa, and the overturned lamp. And he found Elliott's cell phone.

Seven hours later Dr. Elliott Sumner sat on the edge of a bed in a cheap hotel somewhere in north Arkansas off I-40. The rain let up. An empty bottle of scotch laid on the floor, another half-empty on the nightstand. For the first time in hours he found himself in familiar territory—alone, drunk, and ready to end his miserable life.

He looked into the barrel of the .357 magnum and rationalized, *one hollow-point will take off the back of my head, and it will be done.*

She was supposed to go to New York City for only a day, he cried inside, *not D.C. We talked about it. I did not know what we were up against, not this time. But they knew we had it in our possession. They had to have it—to control it. But it is too big. It would change everything. Oh God, I didn't believe it possible. It is too much for anyone to bring into this world.*

He looked into the cracked mirror on the wall across the dismal hotel room. Like the time before, he stared at the haggard, tormented man and he saw the pain and a way out. Elliott slid the carbon steel barrel into his mouth and wrapped a finger around the trigger. He closed his eyes.

I don't want to live forever . . . He pulled.

ONE MONTH EARLIER

The Memphis Tribune
MPD Find Heads on Mud Island
Carol Mason, VP Investigative Reporting

Memphis, TN April 14, 2010: Decapitated heads on poles around a campfire were found by Memphis police in the early morning hours today. Following an anonymous phone call, world-renowned forensic pathologist, Dr. Elliott Sumner, and Memphis Homicide Detective, Tony Wilcox, were first to arrive at the scene on Mud Island.

On an isolated bank along the Mississippi River, human heads were on display atop poles configured in a semicircle around a small fire. Memphis police, County Sheriff's Office, and FBI were called in. Air, water, and ground searches are underway as the disturbing multiple-homicide crime scene is investigated by the medical examiner and CSI. Officials closed the north end of Mud Island to the media and public.

Unnamed sources close to the investigation say the ritual-like display included heads that had been frozen for several weeks. "We have a dangerous killer—or killers —out there and need to move quickly," Detective Thompson said. "There's a lot of evidence to work through that may connect to more deaths." Dr. Sumner and Detective Wilcox were unavailable for comment.

Mud Island is not new to horrific events. There were two in the last year. The legendary Memphis serial killer known as the Bluff City Butcher confronted Sumner, Wilcox, and Shelby County Sheriff G.E. Taft on October 17, 2009. The alleged BCB escaped with injuries and resurfaced at the residence of billionaire patriarch Albert Bell on December 23, 2009. The BCB died attempting to escape.

Some believe the BCB is alive—that he survived the traumatic incident at the Bell mansion witnessed by over a hundred guests attending the Bell Christmas Gala. Over fifty Memphis police and county sheriff deputies were called to the scene. They surrounded the mansion. Impaled on a rooftop spire, the Butcher died before reached by paramedics.

Later, the BCB's true identity was revealed to be Adam Duncan, the biological son of patriarch Albert Bell, and the brother of Dr. Elliott Sumner and president of the LIFE2 Corporation, Jack Bellow—deceased. The three sons born in 1968 were separated at birth. Albert Bell swears to have no prior knowledge of their existence until the night of December 23rd when informed by phone.

MPD Director Collin Wade commented on the current Mud Island case and its unnerving similarities to the numerous BCB homicide cases. "This heinous crime is the work of a very sick person. The Bluff City Butcher is *not* a suspect because he is *dead*. I know because I was there the night he died. Any further speculation about the BCB is a waste of our time and a distraction from

serious efforts to find those responsible for these deaths."
Efforts to identify the victims found on Mud Island are
underway.

TWO

"For in that sleep of death what dreams may come."
William Shakespeare

"Appears you've had an eventful evenin', Mr. Bell." The tall, lanky silhouette in the doorway stood over the coagulated blood, the light from the hall reflecting off the red-brown pool seeping into the grain of the polished wood floors. Five pints, maybe more, soaked through the cracks and would stain the ceiling below. The blood belonged to one of Alberto Bella's bodyguards—the first to die in the study the night after the heads were found on Mud Island.

The wiry man knelt down. He leaned in as if talking to the corpse moved hours before. "Cut ya from the base of ya spine to the center of ya shoulder blades," he said. "Knife moved through ya body with great force and accuracy." He turned his head in Albert's direction. "I'm told, don't ya know." In the dark by the dead fireplace Albert sat with a glass of scotch.

The man stepped over the blood pool and walked to the desk at the other end of the study. "Medical examiner said the blade of that butcher knife *bisected* every organ in its path—the liver, kidney, heart and lungs. Got the four big ones with that big ole' knife . . ."

He stopped. The light from his cell phone lit his face, an African American wearing a uniform. He scrolled squinting at the small screen. "Let's see, *bisected*. Had to ask what it meant. Made a note. Not a word ya hear much in my line of work. Here it is. Bisected is to cut or divide into two equal or nearly equal parts. What kind of thing can do that from behind a man?"

The light went out. "Think that's significant. Don't ya agree, Mr. Bell? Cut four organs nearly in half in the dark from behind. Clipped half-dozen ribs up close to the spine like a hot knife in butter. Then severed the spine with a sharp twist at top of that upward sweeping motion—left to right. Strong! Our killer's left-handed. Bet a month's pay." Albert felt the man's eyes on him, but stayed silent.

"Yes sir, the ME said instant hip and knee lock. He's a big un, too. 310, 320 pounds of solid muscle standin' in that there doorway five seconds before he dropped like a big ole' tree. Instant paralysis. Probably tried to stand. Fell over anyway. Bet dead before he hit the floor. The one wielding the butcher knife was not your average killer. Nope, he was not. This one's got special skills. Skills we just don't see often round here."

He used his cell as a flashlight this time, moving the glow along the front of the desk and down to the floor. Albert turned his head enough to watch the light move from the desk to the blood-soaked Persian rug where Alberto Bella died.

"So this is where Mr. Bella met his maker. A knife, a fist, and part of a man's arm in the old man's chest poking out his back. You don't even see that kinda stuff in the movies, not unless there's a zombie around or somethin'. It had to be one awful thing to watch . . . you bein' a few feet away just standin' there and all."

Albert looked down. He didn't see the man pointing to the empty chair on the other side of the desk. "Had to be tough, watchin' a stranger kill your grandfather like that." He got to his feet. "Seems excessive, don't you think?"

Albert touched the glass to his lips. He cocked his head, swallowed the last of his scotch, and reveled in the numbing effect. Staring over the rim, he tumbled a single ice cube in his mouth waiting for the uniformed black man to complete his elaborate setup. They each had their own ritual, their way of working up to the *gotcha* moment. This was Albert's third cop tonight. It would be his last. He eyed the half empty bottle of scotch waiting to refresh his glass.

"Excessive for the average killer." Wiping his hands on his handkerchief, the uniformed man moved across the dimly lit room to the sofa opposite Albert. A covey of police entered the study. With a wave of the hand, he stopped them in their tracks. "Everyone can leave now. I'll finish up here." The badges disappeared in the hall without a word. Albert gripped his empty glass and their eyes met for the first time.

"You okay, Mr. Bell?"

"I've been better."

"I have an update on your son."

Albert sat up. "What do you know about Elliott?"

"He's at The Med. Ran into some complications, but the docs guaranteed me . . ."

Albert's eyes narrowed. He lost his breath even though he tried to prepare himself for any bad news. "I'm not interested in your guarantees. I should be at the hospital. They took him out of here hours ago. You should be worried about your boss."

"Director Wade's in critical condition. I am worried about him, sir. They couldn't do much for him in the ER but stabilize.

He's not strong enough for surgery. The doctor says they can't get to the bullet easy. Risk of paralysis. They'll take their time."

Albert set his empty glass on the table, leaned forward and held his head pushing his fingers through his thick, silver hair. He waited for the next move on the chessboard.

"I'm Henry Cottam, deputy chief, Memphis police."

"I know who you are," Albert said with his head still buried in his hands.

"I'm sorry. I would have remembered meeting you, sir."

"We didn't meet. You're second in command. You're taking over for Collin Wade."

"Well, yes . . . until the director's back on his feet, of course."

The dark blue uniform was flawless, starched and creased. It fit him perfectly. The badge captured the scant light in the room. It gleamed like his brass buttons and the bars on his shoulders and metals on his chest. Albert prepared for the impending inquisition. He studied Cottam through his fingers.

You look like your picture, he thought. *The one the mayor brought by a month ago. Part of your vetting process—seeking my opinion. But you wouldn't know about that. Mayor said it took a year to get you inside, a twenty-five-year veteran cop on a beat stabbed five times, shot three, and in more "educational fights" than most cops would allow without pulling a gun. You're a patient man, and always the last one standing. You don't know the mayor wants you at the helm. He never liked Collin. But now here you are. Let's see what you can do.*

"You've been through enough tonight, Mr. Bell. We've been crawling over the mansion since eight o'clock. Let's make a deal. I gotta take care of my paperwork, and I know you have some questions and want me out of your hair."

Albert turned a shoulder. "I've already spoken with Detective Turner and the interim medical examiner. I've lost count of the blasted CSI people running around here asking a thousand questions. I suggest you do what leaders do, rely on your people to do their jobs and leave me alone. I'm not up for this relentless interrogation."

"I understand, but . . ."

"Clearly you don't." Albert leveled a stern look at Cottam. "I need to get to The Med."

"First you need to talk to me. Then you can leave."

"I'm a victim here. This is police harassment. Do I need to call in legal counsel, Mr. Cottam?"

He's not going to be pushed into talking. Maybe a different approach will work. "That won't be necessary, Mr. Bell. I understand your position. And yes, I will speak with Turner, the ME, and my CSI team." He sat on the edge of the sofa. "I'm not here to interrogate, Mr. Bell."

"Then don't get comfortable. Goodnight, Mr. Cottam."

"I plan to see this case through, starting with you. I'm in charge now."

"Yes you are, until Director Wade returns."

"To do my job, I must understand what happened here tonight. I value the opportunity to speak with key eyewitnesses, and your home is a crime scene."

Albert turned to him. "Or what?"

"Or we go downtown—holding cells, lawyers, interrogation rooms, and a very long night. One way or another, we're talking, sir. If you just work with me, we can be done soon."

Albert sat up. "Where's Detective Wilcox?"

"Unavailable. Detective Turner was closest when the call came in. That's why he was first on the scene."

Albert crushed the last of the tumbling ice cube between his teeth.

Cottam got it. "Okay—truth. Detective Wilcox was downtown in one of those holding cells I mentioned. He was detained for internal matters I'm not at liberty to discuss."

"It had to do with Mud Island, the heads on poles found early this morning. Elliott was there. He told me all about it."

"I don't know what Dr. Sumner told you, but Detective Wilcox was implicated along with Dr. Sumner on a procedural matter. There was a misunderstanding."

"I see." He dropped fresh cubes in his glass, poured scotch to the rim, and sipped. Albert looked up again. "Collin came here tonight with warrants for our arrest. It was something to do with the removal of a paper from Mud Island. Paper attached to one of those heads."

"Correct," Cottam replied. He glanced at his watch. "A very bizarre scene on Mud Island."

"I've heard nothing more on the matter."

"Let's just say Director Wade had a moment of clarity—in the ER—before he passed out the last time. In his *fist* was a piece of paper with your name. That's what he came here to get earlier this evening. Dr. Sumner had it in his possession."

Albert leaned forward. "Elliott gave it to Collin just seconds before the shooting started. Collin had it in his hand when he got hit and went down."

"Unlike the other papers attached to heads on Mud Island, yours was empty."

"And what—pray tell—does that mean?" Albert asked.

"Names, dates over many years in several countries. It's very early in the investigation, but we believe we're looking at several hundred cold cases—unsolved or suspicious deaths. It appears the dead men on Mud Island were involved."

"What do you mean—suspicious deaths?"

"Questionable suicides, unwitnessed accidents, unsolved homicides, and disappearances."

"Is there some significance you found this on Mud Island? Memphis?" Albert questioned.

"We don't know. The heads were on display to draw attention."

"Doesn't take a brilliant detective to figure that out." Albert downed his drink. "And Collin Wade thought Elliott, Tony, and I were involved?"

"We don't know what he was thinking. Maybe know more when he can talk."

"You said he had a moment of clarity?"

"Yes. From the gurney he ordered all charges dropped and Wilcox reinstated." Cottam touched his chin. "He saw something here tonight that changed everything."

Albert turned to the empty fireplace. *Surely they'll revisit that decision when and if they connect the Gilgamesh dots,* he thought.

"I don't know if you are aware that Dr. Sumner has a very liberal consulting agreement with our city. He has enormous freedoms with regard to all investigational matters."

Cottam glanced at his watch a second time. "MPD needed his help to find the Bluff City Butcher. Dr. Sumner had certain stipulations. The city capitulated."

"What kinds of stipulations?"

"Dr. Sumner can remove something from a Memphis crime scene without prior approval or explanation."

"Then the warrants for our arrest are bogus."

"That would seem to be a correct conclusion, Mr. Bell. And for that reason, I am confused. You see, Director Wade was well aware of Dr. Sumner's contract yet he acted on this matter. I believe when I find out why, I will know what happened here this evening." Cottam tilted his head, assessing Albert. "Tell me what happened here tonight from your eyes, Mr. Bell."

Albert stared at the ceiling and ran his hand over his face. He turned to Cottam. "We were at my desk." He waved over his shoulder, almost spilling his drink.

"Excuse me. Who was at your desk?"

"Elliott and Carol Mason sat to my left, Max Gregory to my right. Then Collin Wade appeared in the doorway. His presence was unexpected. He came into my study unannounced." Albert dabbed his mouth with a folded handkerchief. His hand trembled. "Conversation ceased. Collin crossed the room, walked up to the front of the desk and served his warrants; plopped them right down in front of us."

"Did he explain the warrants to you and Dr. Sumner?"

"No. He said Elliott and I were under arrest. When I started to examine the documents, he demanded Elliott give him the paper. Called it a 'vellum' strip. Elliott paused. I'm sure he too was set back by the director's aggressive behavior."

"And he gave the paper strip to Director Wade at that time?"

"Yes. Maybe within twenty seconds of Collin asking for it." Albert's glass stopped half way to his lips. Cottam could hear the ice cubes rattling against the crystal. Albert was frightened.

Cottam waited. He studied him. "Then what?"

Albert blinked several times. "The first god-awful explosion." He winced.

"A gunshot?"

"Yes." Albert leaned toward Cottam. "That's when Collin got shot." Albert's eyes froze. "I watched the blood soak his shirt. His face was white as snow. His eyes—he just stared back at me. He collapsed. Dropped to his knees, and then face down on the floor."

Cottam let Albert relax some, let the vivid images that now haunted him begin to recede. "Who shot Director Wade, Mr. Bell?"

"The man in the doorway shot him. The man holding the gun did."

"And who was that, Mr. Bell?"

Albert shook his head and looked at the floor. "There were

two more explosions. Elliott was hit next." Albert looked up in a daze. "Hit him in his right shoulder. The blood filled his shirt before any of it sunk in. Then the second explosion came—loud. Elliott was hit a second time. Hit in his left shoulder. God, he was falling backward. He was trying to stand but . . ." Albert closed his eyes. "I thought he was going to die right then. Why are you making me go back over this again?"

"Please, this is the last time. Go on Mr. Bell."

"Carol caught Elliott as he was falling. She guided him to his chair. Elliott didn't move after that." Albert set down his glass and held his head. "Blood was everywhere." He looked at his hands, the traces of blood still there from touching Elliott's chest later, as he was loaded onto the ambulance. Right before they rushed him to the hospital.

"Were both men shot by the same person, Mr. Bell?"

Albert lifted his head distraught, reliving the dreadful moment. "Elliott was bleeding to death. Carol was doing all she could, but she couldn't stop it. I just stood there. Everything happened so fast."

"Mr. Bell, tell me who shot Elliott Sumner and Collin Wade. Who was holding the gun? Who did this, sir?"

"*You* know *the shooter, Cottam*," he yelled.

"I must hear it from you."

Albert leaned back into the sofa. He grabbed his scotch and took a long swallow then tilted his head back to stare at the ornate plastered ceiling. "My grandfather, Alberto Bella, shot Director Wade and Elliott—three bullets, three hits."

"Are you *absolutely* sure, Mr. Bell? Is there a chance you could be wrong? You said it happened fast. It's been a long night. Even now, talking to me, you're hardly with it. Maybe you don't remember correctly. Is that possible, Mr. Bell?"

"*No*, Mr. Cottam. I am certain. I know my own grandfather. After he shot Collin and Elliott, he walked to my desk with the smoking gun in his hand. He put it in my face. He was proud of himself. Damn happy. Even bragged about shooting them."

"What exactly did Alberto Bella say to you?"

"He said policemen always got in the way of him doing business. Said that's why he shot Collin Wade. And then he said he was in no mood for heroics. That's why he shot Elliott. He also said he didn't intend to kill either one, he just wanted my full attention."

"Those were his words . . . wanted your full attention?"

"Yes. I suggest you ask Carol Mason or Max Gregory if you care to check my accuracy."

Cottam paused. He was changing direction. "Is it true Alberto Bella is alias Rudolph Kohl?"

"Yes. That information has been shared recently."

"Really. One and the same?" Cottam scratched his head again. "If that were true, your grandfather would be how old . . . at least one-hundred-fifty years?"

"Actually, he would have been a hundred-sixty-five this year, according to him." Albert took another swallow of scotch. "He's what they call a 'supercentenarian', one of the few in the world who live beyond a hundred-fifteen years."

"Supercentenarian? Never heard of that."

"It's quite the topic within the Bell family. There are thirty people in recorded history that have indisputably exceeded the 115 mark. Some claim to be much older, but records are not adequate to validate. Personally, I believe it is folklore folly."

"If you think it is folklore folly, how do you explain your grandfather, here, tonight?"

"My grandfather claimed he changed his identity to avoid talking about his age. Said it was a fruitless exercise, too distracting from the more important things in life. He said his longevity is an odd rarity. Personally, I question the dates. Immigration records in the 1800s are woefully inaccurate.

Perhaps he came to America a much younger man than the documents state." *Maybe that'll give him enough of a bone to chew on a long while.*

Cottam tapped the side of his nose. "Okay. I will accept that for now."

"Anything else?"

"Why was he here tonight, Mr. Bell?"

"My grandfather?"

Cottam sighed. "Yes. Why was he here tonight?"

"Other than to shoot two innocent people, I don't know."

"I find that troubling. He shot Director Wade and Dr. Sumner and then turned the gun on you. You're tellin' me you don't know why?"

"That's correct."

"Your supercentenarian grandfather, with all his great wisdom, entered a secured compound unannounced, shot two innocent people and turned the gun on you. Do you really want to stick with your statement?"

"My grandfather has always been an unpredictable man."

"Did he appear to be angry? Or was he shooting people for some other reason? Was he looking for something?"

Albert finished his scotch, set the empty glass on the end table and smiled. "You think I'm withholding information, Mr. Cottam?"

"Respectfully sir, yes I do."

"My grandfather was a very wealthy man, a multibillionaire. He lived a life of great privilege. Got what he wanted when he wanted it. Nothing was beyond his reach. He was a very powerful man with a much longer life experience. Frankly Mr. Cottam, I stopped trying to understand my grandfather many decades ago."

"Then why was he here tonight, Mr. Bell? He got your full attention for what?"

Albert tilted his head to the ceiling and closed his eyes. "Alberto was just about to talk. His mouth started to form his first word, but then . . ."

"But then what, Mr. Bell?"

"I remember his gun in my face. He cocked it. His mouth opened. I thought the eccentric, old man had finally snapped—lost all his marbles. He shot two people for no reason and now he was going to shoot me."

"Then what happened?"

"There was a god-awful groan, it came from somewhere down the hall."

Cottam's lips tightened. "A groan like someone in pain?"

"Gut-wrenching. We all turned to the sound, even Alberto. Someone stood in the doorway."

"Who was it, Mr. Bell?"

"I thought Alberto's bodyguards—a large, dark, menacing figure."

"Did you say bodyguards? *Plural?*" Cottam pulled out his notepad and fanned through.

"Had two with him all the time." Albert opened his eyes. "Didn't know where those groans came from. Was it the bodyguard at the door or someone else somewhere in the house?"

"Tell me about the one in the doorway." Cottam kept checking his notes and flipping pages.

"He started to sway a little left and a little right. Then he fell into the room. It was rather startling."

Cottam stopped on a page and dragged a finger. "I have note of only one bodyguard."

Albert ignored Cottam's comment. "After he fell into the room, there was another dark figure in the doorway."

"Did you recognize this second figure?" Cottam asked.

"No. But Alberto did. He started shooting at him. Shot three times and missed three times."

"You're telling me your grandfather successfully shot the length of this room, hit Dr. Sumner in each shoulder, and missed a closer and larger target three times?"

"That's right. Maybe your CSI boys can explain it. They dug bullets from my wall across the hall. I'll bet the same bullets you take out of Collin and Elliott."

"You said he missed three times. They only found two bullets in your wall."

Adam was hit. "Don't know about that either. That dark figure crossed the room and got to Alberto before the trigger got pulled a fourth time."

Cottam made a note. "How did that man in the doorway kill Alberto Bella?"

Albert rubbed his eyes. "A knife. My grandfather got stabbed in the chest. He dropped his gun and collapsed where your people found him."

"Who killed your grandfather, Mr. Bell?"

"It was dark and happened fast."

Cottam closed his notepad and sat up straight. "Your stories match Miss Mason's and Mr. Gregory's. I've not yet spoken with Dr. Sumner."

Albert brushed his sleeves and sat up. "*Truth* is often consistent, Mr. Cottam. Now if you don't mind, I need to get to the hospital." He started to stand.

"You know what I think . . . ?"

Albert leaned back. "No. What do you think, Mr. Cottam?"

"I think the three of you are interfering with the investigation of a multiple homicide."

"And I believe *your imagination* is working overtime, Mr. Cottam. You are new."

He smiled. "I could charge all three of you."

"I don't think you will."

"Oh, why's that?"

"Forensics are too compelling."

"What are you saying?"

"I'm saying the city prosecutor will look at this case. He will see Alberto Bella held the gun that shot three people. The survivor, unaccounted for tonight, was the one with a knife that went up against my grandfather's gun and saved your director's life and three others in the room."

"Still, you three are holding back. You're obstructing justice. I could arrest you."

"One day your director will be able to answer your lingering questions to your satisfaction. You won't arrest me tonight."

Still, Cottam pushed. "Director Wade was unconscious when the man in the door entered the room and stabbed Alberto Bella."

"Not true. I'm surprised you run with such an assumption. I never told you that."

"Can you prove to me he was conscious, Mr. Bell?"

Albert smiled. "Collin kicked Alberto's leg the third shot. May have made the difference—why he missed the man charging him."

Cottam shook his head. "Two were slain by this unidentified man. He must answer for that."

"From where I sit, the only crime he committed was leaving the scene after stopping the real killers in the room. He left before we could thank him. You make this far more painful for the victims than necessary. We survived. Our failure to identify the man who saved our lives is not a criminal offense. It's just something *you* want to know." Albert wiped his mouth with his handkerchief. "There's no crime here except what my demented grandfather and his bodyguards did to innocent people."

Cottam relaxed his shoulders for the first time. "It's in your best interest to involve the Memphis police department."

"The dangerous people are dead. I've told you everything I

know. Hopefully the two innocent people live tonight. There's nothing more to this. We're done here."

"You say the dangerous people are dead?"

"Alberto and his two henchmen."

"*Two* henchmen? You mean bodyguards?"

"Yes. Alberto introduced me to them in January—Bentley Masher and Boris Tanner. Looking back now, I should have paid much closer attention, asked questions."

"Do you know for a fact both men were here tonight?"

"Yes. Mr. Masher stood at the door. He's dead. I saw his body. Mr. Tanner was with Alberto and Masher in the beginning. He left after Alberto shot Collin and Elliott, I assume to cover the flanks. God knows what else they had in mind tonight."

"There was no Boris Tanner listed among the dead or injured." Cottam pulled out his notepad a second time and flipped through the pages inches from his nose under his light.

Albert retrieved his empty glass. His ice cubes were almost gone. The bottle of scotch on the end table was now empty. "They said three were dead. I assumed Mr. Tanner was one."

Cottam slid his notepad into his pocket and held his two-way radio to his mouth.

It was too late . . .

THREE

B oris Tanner stood in the dark behind Cottam's sofa.

A stiff gust swept across the balcony, opening the French doors. The wind moved through the study, lifting papers off the desk and pushing a painting off the wall. Albert turned to the crash and watched the framed canvas flip and slide across the wood floor. When he turned back, he saw Alberto's other bodyguard. Tanner's giant fist delivered the fierce blow to the side of Cottam's head. The chief director slumped over like a rag doll and slid off the sofa to the floor. Albert watched Cottam's body twitch and then nothing.

Albert got to his feet and went behind his sofa. Now there were two between him and Tanner. "Stop this. It's over," he ordered. "Alberto is dead. Masher is dead." Albert backed away. "Too many have died or been injured tonight. There's nothing more for you to do." Albert pointed to Cottam's lifeless body. "He could still be alive. We may be able to save him if we get help now. You don't want to kill this man . . ."

Tanner had fifty pounds and five inches on Masher. "Give up to authorities," Albert said as he continued to retreat into the study. There was no one to help. All had been dismissed by Cottam. And William—if he wasn't already dead—could be anywhere in the sprawling mansion unaware of the new peril Albert faced in the study. He too had had a long night.

Tanner watched Albert's eyes as he nudged Cottam's body with a foot—nothing. He moved the sofa like a toy, it now blocked Albert's path to the door. Tanner's hands were clenched into massive fists. He pounded his thighs twice and moved forward with muscles flexed in his blood stained shirt.

Albert had two options; the balcony was one. But he would not survive the fall. The second was the gun in his desk. But he remembered CSI had taken the gun for a ballistics check. Albert was defenseless, except for the sterling silver letter opener in the top drawer. He could try to keep the desk between them for a while. *No*, he thought. *Tanner can outmaneuver me. His fists are lethal weapons.* Backing up, Albert looked at Cottam. *My God. You killed him with a single blow.*

Nearing the balcony doors, Albert looked over at his desk. *It's gotta weigh a half a ton. But you could push it to the wall with little effort. It would bring you great pleasure to crush me and watch me die. The balcony is where I must go.*

"Tanner. Think about this. You don't need to kill me. Your employer is dead. Alberto Bella is dead. You have a choice. You can leave."

Tanner's face stayed flat and empty, his eyes black and cold. Then he smiled and outstretched his thick arms, further limiting Albert's chance for escape. Tanner forced Albert to the balcony as the gap between them narrowed. The back of Albert's shoe met the granite step. He tripped. He caught himself and faced reality as he backed onto the balcony.

It was bathed in sliding shadows and floating moonlight. Albert passed through the layers of light and dark as his end neared. He would be forced to jump to a certain death. But the familiar boyhood smells folded over him like a warm blanket. The stench of blood and gun smoke that hung inside the study was absent from the balcony.

Albert's life was over. He would die with a lifetime of unanswered questions, all of which led to the final moments. He would leave unable to complete his ultimate mission, the one Willie Starnes had delivered in the small, leather box—the secret to life Dr. Medino wanted to give to the world. The secret Gilgamesh sought for a century and was unwilling to share.

One last time, Albert looked over Tanner's bulging shoulder at the desk and chair where he spent countless hours, the place where a billionaire cotton merchant managed a dynasty, and where Albert learned he had sons Gilgamesh had taken from him forty years ago, the secret society of the very wealthy behind all the killing and led by his demented grandfather.

I remember the day, December 23, 2009, on the speakerphone from Dallas. You had important news. It couldn't wait, Max. Elliott sat across from me. Adam held a knife to Elliott's neck. Adam was there to kill us, manipulated by Gilgamesh. They thought they had Medino's research, the biogenic solution for life extension. They thought they didn't need us alive. But everything changed that night . . .

"You die tonight, Albert Bell," Tanner puffed through hideous teeth as he approached the balcony doors now only twenty feet away.

That night, Max, you told me I had sons. Albert backed another step. *You said Adam and Elliott are my sons. We thought Adam was a monster, a serial killer, but he was not. He was fighting a stealth war, stopping Gilgamesh from killing Dr. Medino and taking his discovery.*

Tanner stopped at the doors to savor the moment. Albert's eyes moved to his desk. *In the top drawer is Dr. Medino's portable hard drive, his research, his secret. Elliott must take it to the world without me.* His eyes returned to Tanner as he approached. Albert could not outmaneuver the giant man. *I will not give you the satisfaction of hurling me off my own balcony—I will jump.*

But Tanner stopped at the edge of the balcony. Albert watched his smile fade and fists tighten. He watched Tanner's eyes—they were no longer on him. Then Albert felt hot breath on the back of his head. A hand rested on his shoulder. Albert turned. *Adam. It's you!*

He loomed above Albert in the moonlight, the son he barely knew, the so-called Bluff City Butcher, the one who had put an end to Alberto Bella and more than a hundred Gilgamesh soldiers. He saw Adam's lip up, snarling, his brow down, and his eyes filled with rage. Time slowed. Sound faded. Albert's heart beat hard as Adam moved him to the side.

The commanding voice came from deep within the study, out of Albert's view. "Don't move, Tanner. I will shoot," Cottam barked.

Tanner's eyes stayed on Adam. Muscles tensed. Tanner leaned forward to lunge onto the balcony to battle Adam. But Cottam shot his gun and Tanner dropped to one knee holding his thigh, and his eyes stayed on the balcony and the infamous Bluff City Butcher.

Adam moved forward one step, his muscles bulged rock hard, and a sheet of sweat glistened on arms with the dried blood of Masher and Bella. Albert stepped in his way and held his hand on Adam's chest. He whispered, "Wait . . ."

Tanner got to his feet like a wounded bull, injured but furious and determined.

"I said *don't move.*" The order came from the dark recesses of the study but was closer this time. Albert leaned over to see, but still Cottam was out of view. Albert could not know he was on his feet rubbing his head and moving from the fireplace toward the balcony doors. He could not know Cottam's gun was leveled on the man that knocked him unconscious. Tanner never looked over. He started to leap onto the balcony a second time. The second shot rang out.

"Damn! Nobody ever listens," Cottam grumbled. Tanner dropped to the floor with a booming crash and gurgling squeal.

Albert pushed Adam's massive chest, holding him back. He felt his son's heart pounding like that of a wild animal; one on a hunt, or fiercely protective. "Go son. Now."

Adam's brow eased and his face softened. He went over the side, easily absorbing the fall his father would have not survived. When Adam landed, Cottam rounded the corner, his gun sweeping side to side to avoid another painful ambush. Still holding his head he checked Tanner with a foot and backed onto the balcony. "You okay, Mr. Bell?"

"Yes. How's your head?"

"Hurts like hell. Who were ya talkin' to out here?" he asked eying the mound named Tanner.

Albert ignored the question. "Will he live?"

"Maybe. Damn that hurt." Cottam rubbed his head, holstered his gun, and glanced back at Albert. "Gotta get my radio." As he ran back in the study he yelled back, "Don't think I hit any major arteries. Hell, he'd be dead by now if I did."

"Where'd you shoot him?" Albert asked.

"Buttocks," he yelled from somewhere in the study. "Best place to stop these muscle guys."

Tanner groaned and started to get to his feet. Cottam appeared over him, gently pushed Tanner back down, and patted him on the back. "You keep moving around you're gonna bleed to death." With a half-smile, Cottam looked back at Albert. *Tanner's nowhere near dying but he doesn't know it.* "We don't need any more trouble tonight, son."

Cottam's radio crackled alive. "Cottam here. I need an ambulance and backup, Bell mansion. Pronto. Got a loose end with a few holes in 'em. Could be more surprises, so hurry." He slapped cold steel around each fat wrist.

"Mr. Tanner, you're not going anyplace," he said as he eased back onto the balcony.

He saw Albert leaning over the railing. Cottam walked up behind. "Now, you gonna tell me who you were talking to out here?" He scanned the grounds tracking Albert's distant gaze.

"Thought it was my time to go," Albert muttered.

Cottam weighed the words. A warm breeze brushed his face. "And?"

"I was talking to someone very important to me." *Did I just say that? It's gotta be the scotch, or adrenaline, or just relief. I'm not thinking straight.*

"Who?"

Albert searched for a fix. "Ah . . . Someone I've recently gotten to know." *Adam saved our lives. He's not a monster. My grandfather's the monster. Gilgamesh's the monster. Besides, everyone believes Adam's dead. Why bring him back? For what purpose?*

Cottam leaned in, rubbing his jaw. "Someone you've recently gotten to know?"

"I ah . . ." *We have something important to do. Elliott must survive his wounds and Adam must stay in the shadows. It's the only way.*

Cottam slid his gun into his holster and snapped the strap. "I already know *who*, Mr. Bell. No need to say anything else."

"What do you know?" Albert asked as he watched Cottam point to the stone wall surrounding the estate. *You can't see Adam out there. You didn't see him from the fireplace, the angle. It was impossible.* Albert scanned the stone wall. *Where are you son?*

"You were talkin' to the *big man*," he said.

Albert turned to Cottam's finger pointing into the sky. "The big man," Albert said.

"It's okay. I get it. I'm not real religious either. I've been to the edge few times in my life."

"Been where?"

Blue lights and sirens broke over the crest, swarmed the grounds, and closed on the mansion for the second time that night. Cottam patted Albert's shoulder and returned to Tanner. On his way in he boasted, "*God* was with us tonight, Mr. Bell. Guess I need to talk to him some, too."

Albert sighed. "Yes, Mr. Cottam. I believe you should." He watched him kneel down and grip Tanner's massive shoulder. "Is he alive?" Albert yelled.

"I think, but I'm not a doctor. Don't really know how long he's got. This is one of those times can't do much to help." He leaned closer. "Son, I need for ya to talk to me before ya die."

Albert looked to the night sky. He squinted to the southwest stretch of the stone wall fifty yards away. *Where's the place I go when I was a boy? The crack in the armor. The only place in the Bell fortress I could scale—a collection of rock edges making the perfect ladder. I was young. Back then, all I wanted was to escape the God-forsaken life of repulsive privilege.* He cocked his head over the side and squinted. *Maybe I can see you. You'll be a large shadow in the dark. You don't have your father's physical limits. You can go over the wall anywhere, the other side just thick woods and trails. Go back home to the catacombs.*

Growing up, Albert's family often spoke of the manmade tunnels under the city, built in the 1800s. He always wondered if they came this far to the east. Now he wondered if Adam used them to move undetected in Memphis.

Alberto spoke of a network of underground rivers crisscrossing the county created over eons beneath the ever-changing terrain of the Mississippi River Valley. You said they were hundreds of feet down—navigable routes. I wonder if it is what Adam uses. Maybe they connect to the catacombs.

"Mr. Bell?" Cottam called from the study.

But Albert found his son. Adam was the shadow on the wall. Then he was gone. *I have a feeling I'm going to see a lot more of you . . .*

Police cruisers slid to stone-throwing stops in the courtyard. The dust cloud climbed to the balcony. Car doors flew open and orders were barked. Rifles, handguns, and dogs scattered. Light beams shot across manicured lawns, up granite walls, and in old oaks. Badges filed into the mansion as an ambulance and fire truck exploded over the ridge barreling down the drive. The Bell estate would never be the same—people had died

"Mr. Bell, my people are here."

Albert came back to the present. "I see that."

"You're free to go. I know you want to get to the hospital."

"Yes. Thank you."

"Mr. Bell, please don't leave Memphis. We may want to talk again. That's official."

"I have no plans to leave, Mr. Cottam."

"Good." He turned back to Tanner and leaned close to his head. "You hurt anyone else? Don't tell me a lie. You're in enough trouble. Lies *now* are more serious. Hurt someone, you go to jail. They die, you are put to death in the state of Tennessee, son." Tanner blacked out.

Albert stayed on the balcony, his eyes drifting to the desk and antique globe lamp on the corner. It was a gift from Alberto—given fifty years ago. Its meager glow in the dark room now reached his grandfather's blood pool.

You were once a good man, an honorable man, a man I admired. You built an empire. You had more money than you could ever need, but something changed. Your philanthropic endeavors, your dreams, they turned into a twisted obsession, lies, and death. You wanted it all, Alberto. It killed you and your memory in the end . . .

Police filed into the study with flashlights and guns out. Paramedics followed. Cottam waved. "This man needs you, boys." Cottam got to his feet. "My people, search this mansion and grounds. I want eyes in every room, closet, nook, and cranny. Climb every tree. Look under every bush. Walk the wall on both sides. I want to know if anyone else is here. We didn't do such a good job last time. *Now go!*"

But nobody moved, not even the interim director, Cottam. Albert Bell stepped from the balcony into the study. The revered billionaire patriarch nodded. He used much of his fortune to benefit the community, and everyone knew it. Now Albert Bell was buried in a family tragedy that seemed to get worse by the moment.

They stared in silence as Albert stood at the balcony doors, the moonlight falling on his back. But they could not see the patriarch's eyes locked on the sparkling brass handles of the top desk drawer. He turned to the room, brushed his sleeves, straightened his tie, and walked through the frozen crowd into the hall.

It's time . . .

FOUR

"Confidence is the feeling you have before you understand the situation."
Mark Twain

"You're Marcus Medino." Carol's eyes moved from the stranger to Elliott as the door closed behind her. She crossed the dimly lit room holding a cup of chipped ice and damp washcloth.

The stranger nodded and did not move.

Carol stopped at the foot of Elliott's bed. She fought off the urge to gag from the thick smell of antiseptics and floor wax. Marcus got to his feet, pushing back his hair and straightening his crumpled shirt. Sliding hands into his jeans, he looked down at his shoes.

With each realization Carol's heart beat a little faster. Elliott's shoulders were wrapped in blood-stained bandages. His arms were strapped onto white plastic boards clamped to the bed railings. A tube came out his nose and was pinned to the collar of his hospital gown. It drained a hideous, dark fluid. She heard it bubbling over the side of the bed. A bulging bag of blood with a fat, maroon tube went into one arm, and clear Ringer's lactate went into the other. Elliott looked dead, an alien being in a sea of flashing lights and bleeping monitors.

She closed her eyes and bit her lip. She looked at Marcus. "No one is talking." Her voice broke. "Tell me the truth. Is he going to . . . ?" She would not say the word.

Marcus cupped Elliott's wrist and looked at his watch. "Is he going to die? No."

"But, he's lost so much blood. God, I couldn't make it stop. He was in my arms . . ."

Marcus squeezed the bag of blood. She watched him slide fingers down the tube to Elliott's arm and examine the inserted needle beneath the blood-stained bandage. "This is the last unit he'll get. His volume's been restored."

"But he looks . . ."

"You're seeing the aftermath, his body reacting to the trauma of major blood loss." Marcus lifted Elliott's eyelid and swept a penlight. Elliott's pupil contracted. Marcus repeated on the other eye.

"He's settled down. He's resting, healing." He turned to Carol's wide eyes and frozen stare. "And yes, I am Marcus."

"Nice to meet you." Carol's eyes did not leave the man she loved. "He was hurting. He tried to hide his pain, lying in the chair unable to move. After Alberto Bella shot Collin Wade in the back, shot Elliott immediately. We didn't see any of it coming."

"So it *was* Alberto Bella?" Marcus went to the window and raised a slat. "That man is a monster," he muttered. "He hunted my father most of his life . . ." When Elliott stirred, Marcus turned back with eyes of admiration on the man who saved his life just weeks before.

"In the study after Elliott was shot, he was in and out." She touched his hand. "You kept fighting to stay with me."

Elliott settled, comforted by Carol's voice. Marcus turned back to the window and open slat. "Alberto Bella could have killed him if he wanted to."

"Why would you say that?"

Marcus returned to the bedside. "He shot Elliott in both shoulders. The bullet severed the subclavian artery lateral to the ascending thyrocervical trunk. Not just once, but two times, the right and left shoulders. That bullet path is the most ideal route to neutralize but not kill a person. Yes, it is a very painful site, but low risk for long term damage."

"But so much blood everywhere."

"Arterial bleeds can be frightening and usually are fatal— without intervention. Not so much with the shoulder or upper extremities. There's more time." He straightened up. "I'm certain Mr. Bella only intended to knock Elliott down. He did not want to kill him. Guess Alberto Bella did not see Elliott as a long-term threat anymore. I find that to be somewhat interesting."

"*Interesting!* His injuries are interesting to you?" Carol exploded.

Marcus had the presence of mind to act embarrassed. "I didn't mean to be insensitive. Like you, I'm trying to understand all of this."

"Fine. But, why shoot him in the first place?"

"The Bell triplets have been unpredictable since birth. They've confounded Alberto's quest to control biogenic secrets for immortality. Two of the triplets are dead. The fact that Alberto allowed Elliott to live tells me he was confident in achieving his lifelong quest. He no longer saw Elliott as a threat. I can only conclude he came to the Bell mansion for my father's research on an encrypted hard drive. Somehow he discovered it was there. Once he had it in his possession, he saw nobody as a risk. His lifelong mission was a reality."

"How can you be so sure about Elliott's wounds and Mr. Bella's intentions?"

"I read the medical chart. The wounds—zero bone, cartilage, or nerve damage. Only soft tissue and limited vascular trauma. All repaired successfully. Mr. Bella knows how to use a gun, a highly decorated marksman."

"Elliott told me about you. I have an idea why you know so much. But some of your information must be flawed. Alberto was not a good enough marksman to stop Adam."

Marcus jerked his head up. "Adam? Adam Duncan? But he is dead."

She touched the washcloth to Elliott's cheek as if she did not hear his reaction. "I assume you are a medical doctor."

"Yes." He noted the obvious dodge. He would let Carol chose her time. "But like my father, I lived in a laboratory. I'm research focused."

"Genetics, like your father?"

"Of course . . . biogenics."

"What else did you see in Elliott's chart?"

"What you know I saw," Marcus said. "What you know they don't understand."

"Tell me what you think I know and they don't," Carol said.

"Elliott's recovery, he's ahead of schedule. Let's just say in three hours he's where they would expect him to be in three days to a week."

She tugged and smoothed the sheet. "Anything about that in the medical chart?"

He smiled. "You mean, has he attracted undue attention? No. But he's got them scratching their heads."

"How do they explain it?"

"They can't. Since they can't, they do what doctors do—rationalize. They assume Elliott's injuries and blood loss were less severe than initially thought. In their world, the human body is not capable of rapid repair. There are known parameters. Anything outside must be explained another way. Modern medicine has not seen anyone like Elliott Sumner."

"You know about him," she whispered, only her eyes lifting.

"Yes, I know about him, the Bell family genetics." Marcus leaned into Elliott's face and studied twitching muscles. "And this NG-tube will come out soon. Doesn't need it anymore."

"What's it for?"

"Helps get rid of the internal garbage—blood in stomach, wound seepage, various body secretions." He followed the tube and knelt by the bulging plastic bag on the side of the bed. "Almost a liter. Incoming is clearing up—all good."

"You're saying I don't need to worry?"

"You can stop worrying. And I also know about you, Carol Mason."

"You do, do you?"

"You're the head of investigative reporting for the Memphis Tribune. You have a Pulitzer for work on the west coast. Albert Bell brought you here—a collaboration. You met Elliott shortly after your first experience with the Bluff City Butcher."

She reached for Elliott's arm, the only area without bandages, tubes, or dried blood. It was warm and comforting.

"Sounds like this one's been talking about me again."

"I'm close to Elliott, Miss Mason."

She efficiently moved her long blond hair behind her shoulder. "What're you doing here, Marcus? Shouldn't you be hiding somewhere?"

Marcus reeled back like a teenager caught joyriding in the family station wagon. "I heard on the radio. They said there were shootings at the Bell mansion. Police and a forensic investigator were among the injured. I knew it was Elliott." Marcus took a deep breath, reliving the moment.

"It's not safe for you here, out in public. People are hunting you like they hunted your father. Nothing's changed, Marcus."

"Elliott's the only one I trust now. I've been on my own since my family was killed. Things started to close in on me. Elliott found me, brought me here. I could not sit in the catacombs waiting and wondering."

"I covered the crash—December 22—two years ago now. I joined *The Tribune* that September."

"I lost everyone that night." Marcus closed his eyes. "There was a banquet honoring my father, his research accomplishments." He turned to Carol. "The LIFE2 Corporation. It was late. They were driving home. For a long time police said a one car accident. I knew then someone ran them off the road. Gilgamesh finally got him . . . and my family."

"I'm sorry, Marcus."

"My mother, sister, brother, and grandmother were in the car. That didn't stop them. They were going to kill my father that night. Like I said, Elliott saved my life. I trust him."

"How did he save your life?"

"Nashville. The Patterson House."

She rolled her eyes. "Guess he was saving that little story." She gently slapped his arm. "What happened at the Patterson House?"

"I left the lab on Vanderbilt campus. Late as usual. Noticed a car in the parking lot—a shiny, black Mercedes. It was out of place. I pick up on aberrations, inconsistencies, things that don't belong. Looked like four suits just sitting there."

"Okay, that's odd." Carol placed the washcloth on Elliott's forehead.

"I would expect Gilgamesh to be stealth. Come out of

nowhere and grab me. These guys were obvious. When I neared the car their heads dropped in unison."

"I'd be suspicious."

"Wonder why they didn't just jump out and get me then."

"Believe me, there was a reason."

"Yeah, people were walking around and cars pulling out."

"There you go."

"My father told me Gilgamesh would come for me if anything happened to him."

"They are a determined group." She placed ice shavings on Elliott's lips.

"It'd been a few years since my father's death. Nothing happened. I felt safe. Convinced myself I was no longer a threat to anybody."

"You wound up at the Patterson House that night?"

"Right. It's where I met Elliott, at the bar. He said if he found me, Gilgamesh could. Said it was time for me to leave Nashville— time to hide. Said things were about to get intense."

"How did Elliott save your life that night?" she asked.

"In the mirror behind the bar, he saw their car parked across the street. Said don't turn around, did I know anyone with a black Mercedes. I told him about my earlier experience. Next thing I'm doing is taking off my coat, hanging it on my chair, rolling up my sleeves, and heading for the bathroom. That's what Elliott told me to do."

"Nice touch, leave your coat. He wanted you to exit out the back?" she said.

"Exactly . . ."

"He paid the bill and went out the front door like he didn't know you?"

"Yes. Guess he was pretty certain they'd not recognize him with the beard. After Nashville, he told me he had something to do in South America. Guess he came back early."

"And how'd you two get out of Nashville?"

"I ran three blocks, through restaurants and down alleys, and he picked me up. Then we were off to Memphis—the Brent catacombs—my old stomping grounds."

She touched Elliott's cheek. "This man sure does have a habit of showing up with danger."

Marcus nodded. "Doesn't surprise me. He is always calm. Seems to know what to do—the associated risks, options, and has great timing. A minute later, things could have been ugly."

"How'd you get here tonight? Were you seen?"

"I'm Mexican. Borrowed a lab coat with a name tag, grabbed a rack of tubes, stethoscope, and someone's reading glasses. I blended in great. No one saw me come up here."

"Are you that sure? They know you're with Elliott, now. Probably have video of you guys at Patterson House and getting in Elliott's car a few blocks away."

He rubbed his head. "I guess I'm in denial. I want this to be over."

"It's just beginning. Your father's work is landmark. Some very bad people still want it."

"And are more motivated to find me."

"They need to capture or eliminate the son of Dr. Enrique Medino," Carol whispered.

He raised the slat. "You're right. The mind goes crazy places when you're alone in those dirt tunnels a week."

"What are you looking at?" Carol asked.

"A car . . . it's parked on the street under a tree. Been there a while now, but people are not getting out. They are in suits and ties, like before at the Patterson House."

"Is the car running?"

"Yes. I see the exhaust."

"You need to go now," Carol ordered.

"I know. But before I do, tell me about my father. I know you met him. We did not speak at the end. For a year. A stupid argument."

"I met him at a charity dinner, the Bell mansion. It was two days before he . . ."

"Was killed . . ."

"I'm sorry, Marcus."

He lifted the slat. "Please, just continue."

"Albert Bell introduced us. Your father attended on behalf of the LIFE2 Corporation. He spoke about the Ossi2 project—their first product."

"Biogenic cartilage regeneration."

"At the time, we failed to grasp the significance of it all."

"Let me get some clarity here. You failed to grasp the significance of the biogenic breakthrough, or you did not grasp the significance of Ossi2 as a decoy product to establish the LIFE2 global distribution network for a life extension breakthrough?"

"We missed both. Today, I can appreciate the decoy strategy. It makes a lot of sense to setup a global manufacturing and distribution capability in advance of releasing a world-changing technology."

"Jack Bellow is the genius behind the LIFE2 business strategy," Marcus said.

"And your father, the breakthrough." Carol joined him at the window. "Their lives were in great danger the moment their secret got out."

"Father was a brilliant man, a genius no doubt. His focus was always genetics, his life in a laboratory. Jack Bellow was the consummate business entrepreneur, the visionary and perfect partner. Right or wrong, they started LIFE2 with a plan . . . and now they're dead. They paid a great price. Was it worth it?"

"I don't know. Extending lifespan seems wonderful, but there is always a downside."

"That is what we argued over before my father was killed. I told him the Ossi2 product would be viewed as a major threat by the entire medical industry. It would change their world. The Medical device companies would go out of business. Hospitals would go under without the revenue from orthopedics. I said Ossi2 should be eased into the world. If not, desperate people will do desperate things. My father refused. He said the world must know everything."

"I did a story on medical advances, weighing the good and the bad. That explains why he wanted to talk with me that night at the Bell mansion. Your words did have an impact, Marcus."

"What story? I did not see it."

"I wrote about the LIFE2 cartilage regeneration product. If it works, the $40 billion a year joint replacement industry would evaporate. The new biotechnology would eradicate osteoarthritis —the number one disease in the world. Although it would have an incredibly positive effect on millions of lives, there was also an enormous downside—the death of an industry that would put millions out of work. My series was an attempt to start a dialogue on the impacts of any breakthrough. How do we weigh impacts? What drives adoption?"

"Any change in human lifespan impacts everything—the planet, environment, the limited resources, economics, laws, and even religion. It also increases threats. Covert interests like Gilgamesh will stop at nothing to control it," Marcus said with his nose in the blinds.

"Those who live longest can control the world."

"An older society would have more knowledge, experience, and more access to the world's limited resources. They could wait for adversaries to die and take what they wanted. Seems like these world changing possibilities should be weighed . . ."

Carol left the washcloth on Elliott's forehead and fidgeted

with the bindings pinning his arms to the bed rails. "Can we take these off?"

Marcus left the window. "Not until he's conscious. We don't need him pulling tubes out and creating new problems."

"I don't like any of this," she said.

"Where did your conversation with my father wind up?"

"After an hour I agreed with him, Marcus. Advances cannot be suppressed. No one has that right. The world will decide. Either we evolve, or we stay where we are. We are given the ability to solve problems, to make decisions, to choose. We should do that freely."

"I see." Marcus closed his eyes. "Genetics consumed my father. Navigating the uncharted territory took all of him. His judgments in our world were often poor at best."

"Are you referring to his organ and tissue harvesting practices?"

"Yes. I don't care if Adam Duncan killed Gilgamesh soldiers sent to kill them. My father crossed the line when he used their body parts in his research—tantamount to Igor and Dr. Frankenstein."

Carol held back a smile as Marcus returned to the blinds. "May I suggest you cut your father some slack? I'm not justifying what he did, but I understand *why* he did it."

Marcus shook his head. "It was wrong."

"Your father could not stop a psychopath from killing. And Gilgamesh would not stop sending trained assassins. It was the perfect storm."

"My father kept it from me because he knew it was wrong. He did it anyway."

"Adam protected your father because he was a good man, Marcus. Although I spent just one evening with him, I feel he did all he could to stop Adam. Dr. Medino was a gentle man, a non-violent person. He cherished life and dedicated his to increasing the miracle of life. Using tissue from an assassin's corpse was his way to get some good out of a terrible tragedy."

"Adam Duncan was not as crazy as people think," Marcus said.

"He's a dysfunctional psychopath. When Adam gets angry, he turns into a monster."

"That is a small part of Adam Duncan," He mumbled peeking under a slat.

"Your father tried to help. Adam protected him."

"Still, I have a problem."

"If your father found a secret to immortality, he will be remembered in human history as the most important man to ever live. His name will join those of Galileo, Newton, Da Vinci, and Einstein. He will be the father of the greatest evolutionary leap for mankind. Marcus, I am certain all the greats had their shortcomings."

"Since the age of ten, I washed beakers and test tubes and tissue culture flasks. I can calibrate complex laboratory instruments in my sleep. I've loaded a hundred miles of data in my father's computers and taken care of mice and rabbits, frogs and fish, clams and snails, and bacteria cultures. As I got older, I did endless calculations with my father's bizarre rules and formulas. I wrote reports to be loaded in secret files and shredded later. I swept the floors and took out the trash. I did it all, Miss Mason."

"And what is your point, Marcus?"

"Not until after medical school did I get it . . ."

"He wanted you with him, Marcus. You were always going to finish his work."

"He always knew he would not make it to the endgame." Marcus raised the slat more. "And we have a problem. They're getting out of the car now. They are the Nashville guys." Marcus backed away from the window. "And one just looked up here."

FIVE

"A mouse never entrusts his life to only one hole."
Titus Maccius Plautus

"I think we'd *all* best get out of here now."

Carol and Marcus turned from the window. Elliott's eyes were open. "We don't have a lot of time. Marcus, disconnect me."

"*Elliott!* My God. You're awake!" Carol ran to his side and kissed him and studied his face. "You lost so much blood. You've been shot, Elliott. Should you even move?"

Marcus did not hesitate. He disconnected IVs and clamped the drain tubes hanging from Elliott's shoulder. "I mean, is it safe? Should you even try?" Her voice cracked.

"Those men have plans for us far more hazardous to my health." Elliott sat up. "Get my clothes. I'll dress on the way." He paused on the edge of the bed.

Carol looked back from the closet. "Elliott, can you walk? Let me help you."

He smiled, his face gaining color. "You know I'm a fast healer. Let's go." He got to his feet.

The nighttime hospital corridor was dim and empty except for the nurse station a dozen rooms away. The three went the opposite direction, Elliott stepping into his pants and slipping on his shoes as they moved along the wall. When commotion broke out at the nurse station, they turned into a nearby storage closet to wait it out. Marcus stayed at the door. He leaned out to watch. Carol helped Elliott finish dressing, managing dripping drain tubes like they were delicate fuses connected to a bomb ready to detonate.

Marcus watched men in suits explode onto the floor holding guns high. One shouted orders at the nurses. "It's them, the men in the Mercedes. They have guns. They're . . ."

A nurse broke from the chaos and ran toward them. "She's coming this way—shit! She's trying to . . ."

A man tackled her and started beating her. He stopped. She was unconscious. He grabbed her foot and dragged her back.

"What's going on?" Carol whispered as Elliott pushed his arm into a shirt.

"They control the floor. I don't know how many. Now a man's ripping a sheet and passing strips to someone I can't see."

"They are tying and gagging," Elliott said.

"Two are pointing guns at the people."

"They can't do this long," Carol said. "Doctors are on rounds and visitors and lab people are running around the hospital. These floors stay busy 24/7."

"They've got a guy on the elevator," Marcus said. It's not going anywhere."

Elliott stood up. "This is not good. We need to think about getting out of here."

"Got two coming our way. They are looking at room numbers. Now they're going to your room, Elliott."

"They are Gilgamesh, I'll bet," Carol muttered.

"Okay, they see it's empty and are in the hall again. They're talking on phones and looking around. Okay, they are checking all the rooms now—two guys. One goes in and the other stays outside. All the other guys are down at the nurse station. Still got one guy holding the elevator doors. He's getting off. Okay, looks like he turned off the elevator. The room checks are coming this way."

Elliott put his hand on Marcus's back. "The door across from us is an exit. We need to take it, one at a time, to buy time. "Carol, you go first. Go down a few floors and find a supply closet. Hopefully you'll get lucky—a change of clothes, scrubs, a lab coat. Something less becoming." He winked and Carol grimaced.

"The good news is I don't think they'll be looking for you, Carol. I want you to leave out the emergency room. From there, go two blocks east to the blood center. Wait in the shadows of the south side parking lot by the morgue. We'll pick you up there."

"Always a fun date, doctor," Carol quipped as she got next to Marcus at the door like a runner starting a race. "See you boys in a bit." She reached back and patted Elliott's hand that rested on her shoulder. She tucked her hair in the back of her shirt. "I'm ready."

"When I open the door, do not look. Just go. You have three seconds to cross and get out the exit." Marcus watched and then opened the door. Carol flew across the hall. The exit door closed slowly. She was gone.

"Marcus, you are next." Elliott stepped up to the door expecting Marcus to move over.

"No. I'm not going first. I have this door thing down. You'll just screw it up, Elliott. And anyway, you need more time than me to get out of this hospital, old man."

"I don't have time to argue, Marcus. They'll be here in less than a minute."

"Then listen. You know my way is more logical—no heroics. It just makes better sense."

Elliott pondered. "Okay then. You are right. Meet me at the doctor's parking lot on the west side of this place. We'll drive out of here together."

Marcus nodded, leaned an eye and whispered. "*Damn!* He's just staying in the hall, looking around as the other guy goes in the rooms. Now what . . . ?"

"They know we are on the floor. We wait for an opportunity."

"*Oh no* . . . !" Marcus closed the door. They stood in the dark. "I think one saw me. He's coming this way." Elliott locked the door.

The door knob rattled. Marcus backed into the closet. A key ratcheted into the knob. The lock popped. The door opened. Light poured in, finding Marcus standing at the end of the closet with his head down and back pressed against stacks of folded sheets. The man raised his gun and stepped inside. Marcus dropped to his knees. Elliott came from behind the door wielding a steel bedpan. The door closed when the metal met the intruder's head. The hollow *bong* stayed in the closet. Then all was quiet again. Elliott opened the door a crack. Their intruder was tied in sheets and gagged, face down with Marcus sitting on his back.

"Is he out?" Elliott asked as he leaned out the door.

"Yup." Marcus reached down for the carotid. "He's alive. Man, I did not see that coming. You're full of surprises. Your arm moved like lightning—just a blur like Adam."

"I don't think so, Marcus. We've gotta leave together now."

Marcus jumped up. Elliott grabbed a folding chair, opened the door, and they charged across the corridor and out the exit. As Elliott inserted the chair between the door and the stair railing, they heard feet shuffling.

"They're looking for their associate. Let's go," Elliott said.

They picked up Carol in a red S-Class sedan Mercedes-

Benz. Driving east on Madison Avenue, Marcus sat at the wheel wearing a black cowboy hat, horned-rimmed glasses, and oversized blue blazer. Elliott lay low—out of view—in the backseat wearing hospital scrubs. Carol, in a white lab coat with her hair tucked in a surgical cap, leaned over the seat touching Elliott's side.

"You okay back there?" Marcus asked.

"Going to be," Elliott slurred. Their recent escapades had drained what little he had.

"Two bullets, five units of blood, stitched shoulders, I'd say it's a miracle you're still awake superman." Carol could not hide her concern.

Marcus turned off Madison onto North Belvedere. He kept it at thirty in the right lane. "So far it looks like we're alone."

"And whose idea was the red Mercedes?" Carol asked as she took off the lab coat and paper hat. "Seems it could attract unwanted attention . . ."

"That would be me," Marcus beamed. "Elliott's not the only one around here with taste and special talents."

"You just had to go cherry red. Wasn't there a less conspicuous model to hotwire?"

"Tell the truth Marcus," Elliott poked.

"I could have hotwired any one of them. I do have the particular skill set. However, this Mercedes was the first one we came upon."

"And the keys were in the ignition."

"*Really?* Who does that anymore—leaves keys?" Carol checked her watch.

"Doctors," Marcus said. "Anyway, I was drawn to the dark tinted windows—stealth."

"They're gonna be watching the Peabody, Carol's place, and my condo. Let's go to Albert's." Elliott seemed to struggle with his words. He was talking with eyes closed. "Maybe things have settled down out there. A big place. Good security."

"The Bell mansion, are you sure about that?" Marcus challenged.

Carol reached back and touched her finger to Elliott's lips before he could respond. "No, he's not sure. He's a tad delirious at the moment."

She watched Elliott sink into the seat. His shoulders were bleeding again. "Marcus, we need to get somewhere close. His shoulders need attention."

"I saw that too, but where?"

"We can't go to the Bell mansion. We need a place off the grid, something nearby. Let's go to Tony Wilcox's place. It is close, Mud Island. The last place these people are gonna look is a Memphis homicide detective's residence. It is too risky. And it could be knowledge they wouldn't have."

"Okay. We need to get him some place safe."

"Actually, this Nashville armada is here for you, Marcus. They're not looking for Elliott or me. I'll bet their orders haven't caught up to the current state of affairs, Alberto Bella being dead and all."

"They're after me?" Marcus sighed.

"It's not so bad. Would be worse if they were hunting Elliott. They know his hiding places." Carol looked for a street sign. "Okay, we need to get to Island Drive. Tony lives on a street named Down River. Don't know the address, but will recognize it."

"Detective Wilcox, I've heard about him. Guess it will be good to be with someone with a gun. At this hour he should be home, too."

Elliott stirred. "Better chance that he's not. People get killed at all hours. He's never been one to let others handle his homicides at the front end."

"What do you mean, the front end?" Marcus asked.

"I got this Elliott—you rest," Carol ordered. "Tony is MPD's top homicide guy. He got into the habit of showing up at every homicide in the city when they were hunting the Bluff City Butcher. Tony collaborated with Elliott over ten years. They got close. Dead bodies in Memphis did not move until Tony and the M.E. said they moved."

Elliott interrupted. "When I was in Memphis, Tony held death scenes until I got there."

"That's all we need, another alpha male on the team," Marcus mused.

Elliott chuckled into a cough. "He's a colorful guy. You'll enjoy him."

"If you like cussing," Carol quipped. "And if he's not home, we may need you to climb to his balcony to let us in."

"Or you can draw upon your hotwire and lock-picking skill sets."

"Let's try ringing the doorbell first. I find that often works best." Marcus smiled turning off Poplar onto North Front. They approached Willis Avenue. "It's like riding a bike. Still know my way around the bluff city."

Carol turned to the window and took a clearing breath. Her next words were for Marcus, words he had to hear before they got too far into the night. Marcus needed to grasp the much bigger picture. Carol had to know if he was going to be part of the solution or excess baggage.

"This has been a significant twenty-four-hour period. Seven Gilgamesh board members were found dead on this island and their Chairman was killed just hours ago. Gilgamesh has been devastated, severely crippled. From the beginning, the secret society of like-minded billionaires has been run by the twelve-member board."

Marcus stared out the windshield.

"Alberto Bella went to the Bell mansion tonight to get your father's hard drive." She watched Elliott's face with each passing street light. He opened his eyes. They exchanged the look that said much more. "Jack Bellow had it delivered to Albert for safe keeping."

"So my suspicions were right, my father's portable hard drive is at the Bell mansion?" He turned onto Island Drive north. "I'm surprised he did not just shoot everyone and take it."

"Alberto Bella coming personally was an atypical display of aggression," Elliott said.

"More like desperation," Marcus said.

"He was not taking any more chances. This time he would not be denied. Gilgamesh pursued your father's research for decades."

Marcus stopped the car at the quiet intersection. The moon reflected off the Mississippi River a hundred yards away. They could go right or left. For the few seconds they took in the peaceful night. "I don't know where he lives."

"Take a right on Island Place and another on Fleetsbay."

"Marcus, do you remember Willie Starnes?" Elliott asked.

"The night watchman at LIFE2. My father liked him a lot. Spoke of him often. He trusted that man as much as he trusted Jack Bellow."

"Willie Starnes was also a longtime friend of the Bell family. There's more to him than we have time for right now."

"My father wanted to tell Mr. Starnes I was his son," Marcus said. "You know, brag some—the proud father thing. But he could never show his feelings because of our situation—keeping me under wraps to protect me and his secret." Marcus wiped his eyes and gripped the wheel with both hands. "He did tell Mr. Bellow about me—the only one." He stared straight ahead. "Sorry for all that memory lane stuff."

"That's okay. You sacrificed a lot. You miss your father."

"Excuse me. We need to stay on this road until I tell you different," whispered Carol. Marcus nodded.

"Before Jack died, he gave the hard drive to Willie with instructions."

"What instructions?" Marcus asked.

"Willie was to hold onto it until the spring, until things settled down to make sure he was not being watched. After Jack was killed, Willie left the company—retired. Three months later it was time to pass it along."

"Take Fleetsbay." Carol looked back. "Are we being followed?" Marcus slowed. The lights approached. "Stay down Elliott." They watched in silence. It passed, turned, and disappeared.

"Willie met with Albert in March. He delivered a brown leather case with the hard drive. Albert was to hold onto it."

Carol injected, "We're getting close. The instructions—simply stated—recruit Elliott to complete their mission. Jack and your father want Elliott to take the biologic worldwide or . . ."

"Or destroy it," Marcus finished the sentence.

"Not only do I question whether life extension is even possible—biogenics or no—I'm perplexed as to why Jack Bellow and Dr. Medino are so hell-bent on Elliott," Carol said

"We've talked about this," Elliott said with a gentle reminder tone.

"You met Jack twice in your life. Both times it was a murder investigation and before you knew you were brothers. You met Dr. Medino at a stockholder meeting—once! Why they want you to take on this incredibly dangerous mission is beyond me."

"That's going to be one of those unanswered questions. Jack and Enrique were smart men. They must know something I don't."

Carol turned back around in a controlled huff. "Marcus,

we're here. That two story brick on the right." He pulled into the driveway as Elliott sat up in the seat and looked around.

"Turn out your lights and let's park over there." Marcus eased onto the grass, crawled into the dark between the condos and turned off the car.

"Okay. Before we go anywhere, I have something to say, and a question." Marcus turned to both holding up his hand. "My turn first." They nodded.

"My father knew Elliott from birth. He followed *you* and Jack throughout your lives, but never overtly. He would not put you at more risk than you already were—Gilgamesh was always watching. And he did not tell Jack who you were. Right or wrong, he felt it wasn't his place. My father was very involved in his research and the Bell triplets.

"A few months before his death, he told me about you. He said if anything happened to him and Jack, I was to find you. You would know what to do. He said you were the only man who could finish this or destroy it if it would endanger the world.

"That all said, you were not a casual selection. My father observed over a lifetime. You are the one my father and Jack wanted. My only question is, how can I help you now?"

After a long, reflective silence Carol and Elliott looked at each other and turned to Marcus. "Are you kidding?" Elliott said. "How can you help me?" Elliott rubbed a painful shoulder with full knowledge it was bleeding. "Marcus, I appreciate all that but I know nothing about biogenic life extension research. I have not been in a lab for a decade. I'm a forensic pathologist. I chase bad guys. You worked with your father most of your life. He prepared you for this. You know his research, his data handling systems and encryption methods. You know formulation techniques, and his biogenic jargon. You know the way he solves problems in a laboratory, the way he thinks. No. You need to step into your father's shoes, Marcus. He prepared you for this moment. This is about the Medino legacy. I cannot accept this responsibility."

Marcus nodded. "The hard drive is only a part of this, Elliott. There's security software and passcodes. One wrong move and everything is lost. Then, if we're lucky, there's formulation and production and distribution to the world without being killed along the way."

They sat in silence. It was impossible. Then Marcus chuckled. "Now I see why my father made me take so much IT in college—database management, set theory, predicate logic, RDBM, and extensible markup language. I could go on."

"Please don't," Carol teased. "We've got a lot to work through. I suggest we get inside and take a look at Elliott's shoulders." Headlights turned onto Down River Drive. They lowered in the seats and watched the dark sedan slow in front of the Wilcox condo.

SIX

The dark sedan moved down the road. The brake lights flashed at each house. "I don't think you'll need to scale anything, Marcus," Elliott whispered. They watched the car pull into a driveway a few houses down.

Carol tried the front door. Elliott reached under the mailbox for a key.

"We need you to lie down." Carol went to the kitchen. Marcus got Elliott to the sofa. They kept the room dark—only the half-moon for light.

Marcus lifted bandages and examined Elliott's shoulder wounds. "We need to stop this bleeding," he yelled to Carol. "Find a couple of plastic bags or towels and ice. I need two setups."

Elliott drifted off as Marcus cleaned and bandaged surgical wounds. They each took a shoulder with a cold compress and watched lights pass by the front windows. The gravity of the moment sunk in.

"Seven hours ago Elliott's heart stopped in the ER at The Med," Carol whispered. "I talked to Dr. Alan Hansen—he refused to give up. Said his use of the defib paddles was commensurate to bringing Frankenstein to life. The dosage of adrenalin he injected into Elliott's heart was well beyond protocol. After looking at Elliott's vitals, he had a hunch Elliott could handle it."

"The Bell triplets are unique people," Marcus said.

"They transfused three units of blood while Dr. Hansen worked on bleeders in the hallway. He would not lose one second moving Elliott. Thirty minutes later, his heart was beating strong and his color was back. No one was saying it out loud, but they were wondering how any man could come so far so fast? They've seen a lot of miracles at the regional trauma center, but nothing like Elliott. His vitals were better than normal an hour after he died." Carol rubbed Elliott's cheek. "Dr. Hansen said they kept him listed as 'critical condition' because no one recovers that fast."

"What the hell's going on down here?" Tony descended the stairs in his underwear holding his gun and rubbing his scalp.

"Jesus, Mason." Then he saw Elliott. "Holy shit! Now what's happened? And why the hell are you here? No. Don't tell me. Goddamn Gilgamesh is after your asses." He leaned over Elliott. "Bleeding again?"

Wilcox went to the front windows and looked out setting his gun on an end table.

"Always good to see you, Tony," Carol said with an edgy tone. "He will be fine. I'll explain later." Tony turned back. She pointed. "This is Marcus Medino."

Tony squinted still scratching his head. "Well I'll be a son of a bitch. You must be related to the Dr. Medino of LIFE2."

"He's my father."

"Holy shit . . . I couldn't write this story."

"Where have you been the last twelve hours, Tony? Your best

friend almost died tonight. Do you live in a vacuum? Don't you cops talk, watch TV or listen to a radio?"

"Whoa now. Slow this all down." He pulled a pair of jeans off the back of a chair and stepped into them. "I've been in a holding cell all damn day—they kept me isolated. Brought me home a few hours ago . . . like a goddamn fugitive from justice. I had no contact with the outside world since the shit hit the fan on Mud Island. It seems they did not like your boyfriend taking shit from a multiple homicide crime scene. They got me on video looking the other way."

"I heard all about it," Carol said.

"Hell, I am still under house arrest—they posted my brethren on the doors. I've been captive in my own home since eight o'clock. Started drinking bourbon then and fell asleep on the balcony until something woke me up—a car in my backyard. I knew there was no damn road back there, just the Wolf River. Thought I was dreaming. Or maybe it was a damn motorboat late at night."

"You're rambling, Tony."

"That was us, Mr. Wilcox," Marcus said. "We hid the car between the condos."

Tony stared at Elliott. Although he wouldn't say it out loud, he worried about him. Saved his life many times over the years. Loved him like a brother.

"Tony, there was a shooting at the Bell mansion tonight. Director Wade was shot."

"Wade shot? That explains why nobody was talking, and I saw Cottam walkin' around."

"He was shot in the back," Carol said. "He's at The Med in critical condition."

"And Elliott shot in the shoulder—anywhere else?" Tony asked.

"He was shot in both shoulders."

"Both? What the hell is that all about?"

"Elliott was in critical condition, too. He lost a lot of blood."

"Then what the hell's he doin' here? He should be in the goddamn hospital."

"We were forced to leave ahead of schedule."

"Shit to hell. Okay. First, who shot everybody?" Tony barked as he shook his cigarette pack.

"I'll tell you everything. Just sit down and calm down. We need you level headed and sober if you're gonna be of any help." Carol took the other ice bag from Marcus. "Put on a pot of coffee. I've got this." He jumped up and went to the kitchen.

"Fine. Tell me what the hell's goin' on, Mason." Tony popped a cigarette in his mouth. He would sit when he was damn ready. The type A personalities often clashed.

"I'm giving you the edited version," Carol said as he stood defiant. "Because you're so damn smart and we need to stay alive." Tony did not move.

"Around eight o'clock Alberto Bella shot Collin Wade in the back at the Bell mansion. We were meeting in the study. Alberto then shot Elliott—to neutralize him. I'm told he could have easily killed Elliott if he wanted."

"Why was he there in the first place?"

"To get the Dr. Medino hard drive, the one we all talked about for a year."

"So the damn thing does exist," Tony muttered.

"Yes it does. His breakthrough research is on that hard drive," Carol said.

"I'll be damned. Albert Bell had it in his possession all the time."

"Not really. He was given it recently—another story, another time. Suffice it to say it is still in Albert's possession. Alberto Bella was killed moments after shooting Elliott. Bella's bodyguard was killed, too."

"Don't tell me, with a butcher knife?"

Carol looked over her shoulder and whispered, "We've not been talking about the 'whom', but *yes*. Adam showed up. If he hadn't, we'd all be dead, Tony. He stopped the mayhem and left before Memphis's finest arrived."

Tony lit and sucked his cigarette as he sat down. "I'll bet that was one sight to behold. That man's one scary mother . . ."

"Focus, Tony. And yes, it was unbelievable. Adam dodged two bullets shot at him point blank. He leaped thirty feet across the room and stabbed Alberto Bella as the third shot was fired. Adam was hit in the chest, but it didn't seem to bother him." She wiped Elliott's arms with the damp cloth. "I don't know how that's possible."

"You know Elliott's gonna be fine, don't you?" Tony said.

"I do," Carol replied with knowing eyes. "He's incredible too."

"Okay," Tony said, blowing smoke. "Now, tell me why you ditched the hospital."

"Gilgamesh showed up. We believe they're hunting Marcus."

"There's a surprise. You mean they're not hunting Elliott? Why Marcus?"

"He's capable of continuing his father's work. Gilgamesh did not know Dr. Medino had a living son until recently. They located him at Vanderbilt. So did Elliott. He found him first."

"This group in Memphis has orders to terminate Marcus?" Tony asked.

"We think. Marcus has been hiding in the catacombs, a place familiar to him. He pretty much grew up there helping his father."

"Enrique's backup plan, I'll be a son of a bitch." Shaking his head, Tony butted out his cigarette as Marcus entered the room with a coffee pot and four cups.

"You know I can hear in there," he said. They ignored his comment.

"So you're Dr. Medino's son." Tony took a cup and held it out.

Marcus poured. "Yes. His son and only family survivor. And I know Adam Duncan is alive, so you don't need to exclude me from that discussion."

"How do you know?" Tony asked.

"Miss Mason inadvertently mentioned it at the hospital. It's difficult to talk about any of this stuff without Adam coming up." He poured her a cup and set it on the table within reach. "Adam was very close to my father, like a son. I saw him often."

"It's not that we don't want to share with you," Carol said.

"Then what?"

"He's a complicated part of a century-old puzzle we've been trying to solve. Now, people think he's dead. Best we keep it that way."

"Hell, I hunted the bastard a decade. He almost killed me last year—a real goddamn monster." Tony rubbed the twelve-inch scar on his belly reliving the memory. "I watched him pop out of a fat set of chains like they were nothin'. I was cornered, sure he was gonna finish the job, pull off my arms like hot turkey legs." Tony paused to light another smoke. "Shit, he didn't. Then I find out Gilgamesh had set me up with the guy. Adam thought I was a secret Gilgamesh employee and MPD insider. The man hates anything Gilgamesh."

"I'm happy you figured that out," Marcus said.

"Well, I just started to get it figured out about a week ago. He is one mean character, but he is not the serial killer we all thought he was."

Marcus sat down on the hassock next to Tony. "We're safe now, right?"

"If Gilgamesh is hunting you, they know you're with Elliott, and Elliott knows me. Just a matter of time before they come snooping around here. That car of yours, parked between Johnson's and my place, is a big goddamn give-away. We need to move it."

"By the way Tony, we did not see police outside. Are you sure you're being guarded? There's no one on the street and no squad cars. The whole island is quiet."

"They left around midnight. I was feeling no pain when one came on my balcony and told me the director made a mistake—about me—all had been forgiven and forgotten. At the time, thought I was dreaming. Guess I wasn't. Think Wade's gonna make it?"

"Don't know. He's in a coma. Bullet next to his spine," Carol said.

Tony jumped up and held out his hand. "Give me the keys." Tony moved the car into the garage and parked his Tahoe in the driveway facing the road for a quick departure. When he returned, Elliott was sitting up sipping coffee.

"Hey Tee. You got any scotch around here?" Elliott smiled with a wince.

"Sure, buddy."

Elliott turned to Carol. "I need something a little stronger."

She patted his leg. "Get four glasses, Tony."

"I heard Carol bring you up to speed," Elliott said with a little more strength.

"Glad someone did. Hate being the last to know anything."

"We all need to lay low. I have some things to do. When I know more, I'll get us together. Maybe then Albert's place will be the best place for us to meet, except you, Marcus."

"Thought the goddamn nightmare was over," Tony said into his glass. "Hell, with most of the Gilgamesh board members dead on Mud Island and now their chairman dead too, maybe after a few days this'll get to the rest of the clan and they'll give this shit up."

"The worst has yet to come, Tony. The stakes are too great," Elliott said.

"Give us the *big* picture." Tony lit another smoke.

"I'm confused at the moment."

"Try. You know more than you think."

Elliott sipped his scotch. The three watched. "You're right about some things. Seven board members are dead. We saw their heads on poles on Mud Island. Tonight their chairman died. Albert was the only Gilgamesh board member they kept in the dark from the beginning. That leaves three on the run. They may try to pick up the pieces, continue on their mission"

"Go after Medino's immortality shit? What do we do?" Tony asked.

"Albert must lead the effort to dissolve Gilgamesh—their international network, and all strategic alliances. He must expel the 200 members and take control of the financial assets."

"We need to stop the three rogue board members," Carol said.

"Tony, when you get back to the station and dig deeper into the Mud Island cases, you'll pull in the FBI. These are dangerous, sophisticated killers on the run. They are resourced like a small country, desperate, and motivated. The success or failure of law enforcement's international hunt will decide our collective fate and much more."

"The people looking for Marcus are running in the dark," Carol said. "Gilgamesh is in disarray. We need to make it through the night so they can catch up with their own bad news. Maybe their plans will change, they will see this as over."

"We'll stay here tonight. Let the word get out," Elliott said. He finished his scotch and set the glass down. "Marcus, we need you to stay in the catacombs."

"I'll need someone to drop off some food once in a while. Not grilling any rats."

"Carol goes back to her place in the morning. Go to the *Tribune* as if nothing happened. You may be off their radar. I want to keep it that way. But keep your eyes open."

She nodded. "And what about you?"

"I'll stay with Tony a while and then head back to my place in a few days. I need to stay close to the Mud Island investigation and missing board members. MPD is ground zero for what will be an international matter. The massive volume of cold cases coming out of this will bring in the FBI, CIA, and Interpol. I hope to gain perspective on the state of the Gilgamesh organization and what we can expect."

"What about Dr. Medino's hard drive?" Carol asked.

Elliott turned to Marcus. "We need to get it in your hands as soon as possible. It needs to be in a safe place in the catacombs until we figure out what we have and what we can do."

"This is not going to stop. You're going to discover that my father's research is *real*." Everyone turned to Marcus with sobering looks on their faces. "It needs to get to the world or be destroyed." He shook his head. "Right now you don't need to believe. But I do ask that you behave as if you have the genetic solution for continuous cell replication—immortality. We have the fate of the world in our hands."

"Shit, no pressure. Don't know if I like you yet, Marcus Medino," Tony quipped.

"The storm gathering gives us no room for miscalculations." Elliott held up the scotch. Three glasses moved to the bottle in the dark living room.

The Memphis Tribune: MPD Director Shot at Bell Mansion: Possible Failed Home Invasion

Staff Reporter / April 15, 2010

Memphis, TN April 14, 2010: Around 9:00 p.m. at the estate of billionaire Albert Bell, two were killed and several injured in a suspected home invasion. Among the injured were Memphis Police Director Collin Wade and world-renowned forensic pathologist, Dr. Elliott Sumner. The names of the two dead at the scene are being withheld.

Shot in the incident, Wade received a single gunshot wound to the back and was taken to The Med in critical condition. Sumner was shot twice in the upper torso and was also taken to The Med in critical condition and later upgraded to serious. Two unnamed Memphis police officers injured at the scene were treated and released.

Maxwell Gregory, private investigator for the Bell family, Carol Mason, the VP of Investigative Reporting for this newspaper, and Dr. Sumner were meeting with Albert Bell in an upstairs study when the shootings occurred. The Director of the Memphis police was also in attendance on police matters not provided with news media.

"Director Wade arrived moments before a man appeared in the doorway and shot him and Dr. Sumner. The whole incident happened very quickly," said Gregory.

Details on the injured and property losses related to the suspected home invasion are closely guarded along with information gained from the inspection of the scene by CSI and the M.E. office. "We have a lot of work ahead to determine what happened here," said Deputy Chief Henry Cottam, interim MPD director. "I encourage the news media to avoid speculation."

Tragedy is not new to the Bell estate. On December

23, 2009, the infamous mass serial killer, Adam Duncan (aka the "Bluff City Butcher") held patriarch Albert Bell and Dr. Elliott Sumner hostage. The Bell estate was surrounded by Memphis police and Shelby County sheriff deputies. Duncan died trying to escape, impaled on a rooftop spire.

PART TWO
RESURRECTION

CAPE TOWN, SOUTH AFRICA
2 WEEKS LATER

SEVEN

"It is our illusions that create the world."
Didier Cauwelaert

They found the dead man sitting in the first pew, a wooden cross hanging upside-down above his head. It didn't take long for word to get out, yet the locals weren't surprised. It was more proof the old Dutch church on Devil's Peak was possessed. The Djinn.

When the South African sun drops into the Atlantic, terra firma winds slide between Devil's Peak and Lion's Head and roll into Cape Town. Over eons, the relentless blasts shaped the terrain of the Western Cape and ate away ancient structures, leaving piles of rubble and forgotten memories. Locals found it peculiar that the stone church on Devil's Peak, erected in the 1700s, seemed untouched by earthly forces.

The day after they found him, the coroner ruled cause of

death idiopathic cardiomyopathy. Whispers floated through the towns around Devil's Peak. They had heard it all before, and the police would not get involved. Here, attracting attention to oneself could be hazardous to one's health. Everyone knew that.

The locals were familiar with the long medical term. It was part of the urban legend. It meant the victim's heart stopped for no known reason. This was number six. Since 1974, one has been seized every six years. Scared to death, or worse, suffocated by the hand of a demon.

Perched on a rock ledge near the base of Devil's Peak, facing Lion's Head, the stone church seemed to float above the thick, tangled canopy of South Africa. There was only one path to its battered, oaken doors a half-mile up—a treacherous climb. But the perilous journey through razor-sharp brush infested with poisonous snakes and flesh eating insects, would be far more inviting than the impious sanctum of the Dutch djinn that loomed above.

Legend had it early Dutch settlers believed they could deflect the scourges of humanity with the help of God. The stone church was never meant for worship—it served as a holy shield to protect the Cape Town denizen from evil spirits. And for more than two centuries, through the grace of God and the powers of the modest stone structure, their prayers were always answered. Each spring spiritual leaders confirmed the absence of demons in the commonwealth. There were no evil possessions or eerie hauntings or voodoo hexings. No pestilence. No famine. And there were no truly unexplainable events until one fall day.

Everything changed on the 17 of October, 1974. On that dark day, it is said, *evil* moved into the stone church on Devil's Peak. The wrathful minions—denied entrance for over two centuries—overwhelmed the holy shield. Although their passage into the Western Cape remained blocked, the Dutch djinn were strong enough to claim the structure.

It was said demons moved into the stone walls. They were allowed to take over the very core of the building because only there was the place untouched by human hands. From their new home, the resident evil harvested its ration of souls in the cape.

The first corpse was forgotten. He too had sat in the first pew beneath an inverted cross, a young man's heart stopped for no known reason. The next to die was found the same way, both on an October 17, six years apart. The third death on Devil's Peak shook the locals the most. Now three dead, the same official cause, same day, same place. Too much to be coincidence. The third death was when the legend of the Dutch djinn took hold.

Each victim had climbed the foreboding path. Each had mocked local superstition and the legend. Their foolish dismissals had gotten them killed. Witnesses said it was as if their souls had been sucked from their bodies, leaving empty vessels with terrified gazes frozen on their faces.

After the third victim, the place was deemed off limits to locals. Few would visit the historical site again, unless on a dare.

Number six was found by adventurous tourists unaware of the legend. After their exhausting climb, they sat in the back of the abandoned church watching the back of a man in the first pew. It wasn't long until they noticed he never moved. Suspicious and concerned, they called for help. But instead of paramedics, the church was soon surrounded by the Cape Town police hunting a serial killer and taking no chances.

Attempts to communicate with the man on the front row were to no avail. Reinforcements were called, tear gas canisters were deployed, and the SWAT team stormed the church. When the smoke cleared, the mountain of maggots and the putrid stench brought the siege to an abrupt end. Nose plugs and latex gloves quickly replaced body armor and semiautomatics.

The coroner completed the inquest and ruled manner of death "undetermined". He ruled out "natural" and "accidental" causes, but could not eliminate the possibilities of "homicide" or "suicide", even though there was no trauma and a negative toxicology screen.

The deceased was found five days after his death. Eyes and mouth were open and dry, and the face a pulsating roadmap of oozing sores and red and blue lines on marbled skin. Well beyond "rigor mortis". "Livor mortis" patterns revealed the body had not been moved. His pants were stained—urine, sweat, crusted feces, and decomposing tissue fluids. Insects moved in and out of each orifice, and indigenous snakes nested laying their eggs in his rectum.

As the sun climbed the South African sky, the horrible details found their way into the whispering community below. But the suspicious footprints on the dust covered floor—destroyed by police storming the old, Dutch church—were lost. And the rare substance used to incapacitate a victim—that dissipates hours after injection—was not detected by the medical examiner's tox screen. And, they did not detect the potassium derivative that targets and paralyzes the myocardium, or the small gauge needle entry point under the left arm. It would be lost among the tiny wounds of foraging insects or sunk into the hideous soup of decomposition.

The trap door beneath the altar also went unnoticed. And the source of the unnerving, upside down wooden crosses remained a mystery. Expensive hydraulics, a stainless steel elevator, and a thirty-foot shaft into the core of Devil's Peak were expertly hidden. The secrets were secure, cut into the mountain over decades, debris dispersed over a thousand nights. Secrets were intact.

The legend of the Dutch djinn was crafted over thirty-six years. Only six had to die in a haunting manner. There could be no outsider interference. There could be no security breaches.

No one would see the honed chambers beneath the old, Dutch church. No one could know about the sophisticated information technology and the genetic research laboratory and the global communications systems. Gilgamesh backup facilities would soon be operational.

EIGHT

"Better three hours too soon than a minute too late."
William Shakespeare

Dyersburg, Tennessee

The weather was rapidly deteriorating, and his shoulder wounds were feeling the change in atmospheric pressure even though almost healed. Under any other circumstances Elliott would have rescheduled. Today it was not an option. The meeting came about in a peculiar manner. If he did not go, the opportunity and timing for the new information would be lost. He could not let that happen. Elliott accepted the risk of *unfamiliar territory* and *unknown players* again.

He left Memphis well in advance of the midnight meeting at the Garrett farm. Departing at 7:00 p.m. to the obscure destination southwest of Dyersburg on Highway 181 should get him there around 10:00 p.m., two hours ahead of schedule.

The meeting site had no obvious relevance—vacant property for years. The abandoned house and empty barn were used for farming equipment storage. The thousand fertile acres backing up to the Mississippi River were worked by a co-op out of Wichita Falls. Elliott's research found they sent people to the Garrett farm location on a seasonal basis to plant and harvest corn and cotton. Other than an occasional inspection in between, the farm was uninhabited.

Elliott also learned the Garrett family of four disappeared in 1998. A two-year investigation went nowhere. They were never heard from again.

His early arrival objective would give him a chance to get a look at the lay of the land, and to position for an advantage. However, there were no guarantees his mystery guest would not already be there. And the declining weather did not help. Twenty miles outside of Dyersburg Elliott ran into an unexpected obstacle. The true oddity on the crest came at the worst possible time—two burgeoning twisters. They were moving up Highway 181.

When they touched ground, the twisters centered over the road with their massive tails sweeping fifty yards to each side. Elliott watched trees uproot and telephone poles snap like toothpicks, and transformers explode raining sparks like the Fourth of July. He still could not turn back—the meeting had to happen. Slowing and keeping his distance, he followed their northwest trek, waiting for them to slide off the road into the surrounding fields or to be sucked back up in the clouds. Any attempt to pass was suicidal, the tails too unpredictable.

Of all places, the swirling twisters stopped in front of the Garrett farm, where they melded into one monstrous vortex. Elliott watched as nature's wrath hovered and churned above Highway 181, growing larger and more menacing by the minute.

It seemed to dare him to take a chance. Maybe if he could cut around the west edge of the black chaos, a sharp left onto Garrett's drive would work. The maneuver would put him at his destination early, as planned.

After battling fifteen miles of stiff winds and dodging raining debris, the car was close to overheating and shutting down. If Elliott waited too much longer, he could be more vulnerable once stranded. The spewing funnel could reverse course at any time, but a retreat was never an option and Elliott's window of opportunity was closing. If he did not get onto the Garrett farm first, his only advantage would be lost. The meeting could decide his future course—Elliott had to go.

Leaning low, he could see part of the entrance to the farm at the edge of the swirling rage. If the funnel did not move for just a few seconds, he could slip by and fishtail onto the gravel drive. If the tornado moved even five feet to the west, the outcome would be disastrous. Elliott made the decision. Gripping the wheel he floored it and the car lurched forward like a bull out of the gate.

The surge dropped off in seconds as the torrent pushed the car. The front end lifted off the ground as he neared the edge of the black vortex—and then there was an unexpected lull. The front end of the station wagon sat down and Elliott regained steering traction. He veered back onto course and would cut a sharp left as planned.

Mud, hay, rocks, and sticks pelted the car in exploding waves of black water in a black world. Sandblasting and crushing blows hit the car. A hollow groan encapsulated the battered station wagon and the windshield cracked. The roof buckled and passenger door collided with something big enough to change the floating car's trajectory. Out the driver's side window the edge of Garrett's drive came into view. Elliott had to guess where it met the highway. An error in judgment or imperfect execution would crash the car into the water-filled culvert, where he would sit injured, unconscious, or dead, only to be further decimated by the swirling monster.

All he could do was push down the gas pedal and cut the wheel sharp. Nothing else mattered as it became clear his plan was flawed. But there was no turning back. Now survival was his only focus, the power around him was enormous.

The gravel spray on the undercarriage got more intense as the car spun into position, now shooting rocks into the swirling nightmare of a thousand invisible hands. The battered station wagon moved like a toy as it was picked up and bounced about. Elliott's ears popped in the wet darkness and sounds became muffled. He lost all sense of orientation.

The wounded car descended. It exploded from the turbulent blackness upside-down and crashed through the Garrett's wood fence. Before landing in a dead cornfield, the demolished station wagon flipped over and touched down on all four tires fifty yards from the giant. Elliott hit the ground with the steering wheel in a death grip, finally out of reach. He struggled to control the wild pile of metal as he careened through cornfield stalks. After blazing a hundred-yard trail, Elliott spun to a stop on the gravel drive with the giant spitting trees behind.

Garrett's barn was straight ahead, and the blinking engine lights were no encouragement. Elliott would get out and walk if he had to, but for now he would not stop pushing the old station wagon. He accelerated, gaining more distance from the tornado in his rearview mirror.

The broken, mud-laden car had rotten cornstalks stuffed in its grill as it limped down the gravel drive dragging a bumper. Elliott could only smile as he leaned out the window; both side mirrors were gone. Now only the parking lights worked—the others had been shattered long ago. Straight ahead an old house and barn sat on the dark horizon—for the moment he could breathe again. Then his thoughts moved to the meeting he had agreed to. Like the time he met on the roof of the Peabody Hotel, he had to take a chance. People had died that night. He had escaped. He was lucky.

NINE

"Hell is empty and all the devils are here."
William Shakespeare

Dyersburg, Tennessee

His station wagon reached its limit, whining and coughing and limping along. The three-quarter moon broke from the wall of storm clouds when Elliott broke from the tornado's grip. Now the dark and boiling chaos lived in his rearview mirror and the soft, gray, quiet world sat before him. The glassy sheets of gray and white crossing the gravel road came into focus. The rising water silently swallowed everything—now it wanted the road.

Floods kill more than tornados, he thought as he forced the crippled station wagon forward. *And this water is rising fast. I need to cross now. In minutes it will be impossible.*

After breaking from the killer winds, Elliott realized the collateral damage could be even worse. The swirling, muddy water swallowed the land and ate his road. The mud and gravel under his tires turned into soup. A track of corn stalks folded as another new river pushed through the Garrett farm. In seconds all traction would be lost.

If I stop now, the water will overtake me. I'll be swept away like another dead tree—the Mississippi feeds on these rainstorms. The barn is my only refuge—the highest ground. Elliott patted the dash. *Give me one more miracle.* He pushed the accelerator. The station wagon lunged forward looking for power. Rooster tails fanned, shooting fifteen feet on each side, quickly swallowed by closing waters. The Garrett farmhouse and barn got closer. *This is like a cheap horror movie,* Elliott thought as he tried to imagine what waited for him in the old barn. But he couldn't take his eyes off the abandoned farmhouse in near collapse—the broken windows, and rotting clapboard, and crumbling chimney, and splintered pillars, and missing shingles.

Why such a dark, morbid place? The Mississippi River Valley is the most fertile farmland in the world. This farm, like the others around it, should be prosperous. Something's not right.

With a white-knuckled grip he battled the elements as the tired wagon sunk deeper and the engine spewed smoke and cold, muddy water climbed the hot exhaust manifolds. Elliott held the wheel hard right to offset the stiff wind and strong water pushing him off the road. He held his foot to the floor and eyes on the high ground as everything under him melted away.

The river reclaimed the land. The storm had its way, Elliott never in control. At a hundred feet he watched the barn door slam closed. At fifty feet the engine died and the car flew forward like a dying meteor. Elliott needed to slow and stop to avoid a collision—the door was still closed. He pounded the brakes—

nothing. He tugged the steering wheel—nothing. At twenty-five feet from the looming structure, the car electrical system died. Elliott lowered his head and braced for impact.

I'm dead . . .

He raised his head and opened his eyes in blackness. Seconds later the giant structure took shape a few feet away. *Is that a combine . . . ?* he wondered, wiping mud from his forehead and eyes.

The broken hay bales sat on the hood, and crushed bales were between him and the combine. They had stopped the station wagon from torpedoing an enormous immovable obstacle. Then a flash in the rearview mirror caught Elliott's eye. The barn door swung open and a lightning bolt crossed the sky. Thunder shook the barn, and the rafters whined.

The door had to have opened at the last second, he thought. Sitting in the dead vehicle inside Garrett's barn, his eyes adjusted. Now he could only admire the old structure, his refuge from the storm. *This barn endured many storms over many decades. I'm safe, but am I alone . . .*

Elliott blinked his way back into reality, looking around the inside of the dark barn. *My grand entrance does not seem to have attracted a welcome committee,* he thought as he checked for injuries—not a scratch. *I'm sure they would have met me at the car.*

He slapped his cheeks and shook his head. *I survived a tornado and flood. I can't believe it. Next, I have an ill-advised meeting with another mystery man. Is three times a charm . . . ?*

Holding the barn door ajar, Elliott watched the rising water swallow the rest of the gravel road. Pelting rain already erased his tracks into the barn. In the distance he could see the burgeoning tornado move up the highway as if it had lost interest in Elliott and the Garrett farm. Scanning his immediate surroundings with cold rain on his hot face, he took a closer look at the old farmhouse south of the barn. The abandoned two-story sat in dead weeds and stick trees. *I wonder what your real story is. What happened to the Garrett family? And why is this property connected to Gilgamesh . . . ?*

Highway 181 was dark, and the flood waters claimed most of the Garrett farm. Now, the island with the house and barn were only accessible by waders or boat. Elliott secured the barn door with the rope loop left off before, and returned to the tired station wagon. *I need to push you out of the way somewhere . . . maybe a dark corner behind the combine will do. I can use some hay bales and the old tarp, and then cover my tracks on this dirt floor.*

After he moved the car to its resting place and disguised it, his thoughts went back to the swinging barn door and rope off the hook. *The wind didn't do that. Someone's been in here before the weather—but why? These cornfields are fully grown and dead. Not harvested. Not worked. This place has been on its own since the fall. Why would someone come into this barn? And why is there a worn path in the dead grass to the house . . . ?*

Elliott had received the odd text message at five o'clock the day before his trip to Dyersburg. He had been alone in his condo reviewing Dr. Medino's inquest—the medical examiner's autopsy and Shelby County Sheriff's accident report. He knew Medino's execution meant Gilgamesh possessed the biogenic secret to immortality; they no longer needed him around. But why did Alberto Bella want Medino's research hard drive? And why didn't he kill Elliott that night?

When his phone had vibrated across the table, Elliott jumped from the documents splayed across the table and his troubling questions to the cell phone screen. It was an unknown number. He opened the message. The words were all caps. The first two got his attention.

GILGAMESH RESURRECTION. YOU, ALBERT BELL, AND NUISANCE ASSOCIATES DIE FIRST. ONLY YOU CAN STOP THIS NOW. MEET ME AT GARRETT'S FARM—HWY 181, DYERSBURG. BARN. MIDNIGHT. ALONE. ONE CHANCE.

At 10:37 PM Elliott positioned the last bale hiding the station wagon under the tarp. It could be found with some effort, but he had few other options. With a fistful of hay, he covered his tracks in the barn and searched for a place to hide. Multiple escape routes and a high vantage point would be ideal. He wanted to assess his unknown texter before making a commitment.

He found wooden rungs on the outside wall in a stall serving as a catch-all—deep piles of bushel baskets, empty barrels, coiled hoses, scrap lumber, and broken farm implements. After navigating the broken and rusted debris, Elliott climbed to the underside of the loft thirty feet above. The open trapdoor was partially blocked by a bale of hay. He leaned out from the wall and poked his head through. The loft—marked by moonbeams streaming through holes in the roof—ran half the length of the barn. He could see more bales and nondescript clutter. Elliott had to clear access, but his angle and reach from the rungs made the effort questionable. As he attempted, the barn door opened. He backed away from the opening and melded into the rafters with his upper torso pressed against the web-laden beam and his legs hugging the wall. All he could do was watch the large man close the door and look around the barn. He then turned back to the door and put his face to the crack—Elliott was stuck.

You seem certain you're the first here? Guess my tracks outside are gone. You think you're alone. Are you waiting for me? Elliott's heart pounded and leg muscles tensed as he clung to the wall and underside of the loft. Looking down, he saw his feet stuck out. If the man looked up, he might be seen. *But you seem very sure of yourself . . . or you're not very bright.*

With the scant moonlight finding a way into the barn, Elliott could see the man's pants were wet above the knees. His boots were covered in mud. *You parked on the highway and waded out here? Are you watching for headlights? You're an hour ahead of schedule.*

The large man turned as if he heard or remembered something. He leaned over and looked deeper into the barn, but never up. Then he took a few steps into a spray of moonlight that cut a line across the floor. It washed down his torso. *My god, you're as big as Adam, and built like him too. You're certainly not a negotiator. You are an enforcer!* He stood almost seven feet and had to weight more than three hundred. His short, thick neck balanced his big head on broad, bulbous shoulders, and his long, brawny arms hung with a slight bend and fists.

Not exactly a friendly stance, Elliot thought. *Although I haven't seen much, the way you turn and move, you appear to have Adam's agility too . . . unusual nimbleness for a man your size.* Elliott eased down a rung for a better look. When his foot settled, the door rattled and opened. The big man turned and stood firm with his legs spread and knees bent.

The door opened and light entered first. A skinny, old man in coveralls holding a lantern followed. His light poured over a twenty-foot circle and onto the boots of the stranger. "Who are you?" he asked with a high pitched, demanding tone from someone unaccustomed to danger. The towering figure stayed at the edge of the light in silence.

"You hear me fella? What're ya doin' in this barn? Ya gettin' outa the weather or up to somethin'?" he asked with even more vinegar. "Or, ya with that dang co-op? Thought that deal was over last year." He rubbed his chin and stepped closer. "They never did anything with the corn this year. Hate to see a crop go to the crows. Guess this flood pretty much finished it off anyway."

The old man rambled on, oblivious to all the signals. He stood there talking with his pant legs stuffed in his waders and a battered straw hat pushed back on his head. His shirtsleeves were rolled above his skinny, muddy arms and white, boney elbows.

This is not gonna be good, old man. You're not supposed to be here. Stop talking, turn around and leave—please. Elliott clung to the rafter, too far away to do more than watch.

The old man stepped closer. "You're a big 'un, ain't ya? Talk to me, mister. What in the hell are ya doin' out here ta-night and whattaya doin' in this barn?" He raised his lantern.

For the first time the big man let the light hit his face. *You don't care if he sees you. Okay. Are you going to say something?* Elliott saw the empty eyes and flat smile.

"I'll call the sheriff, if ya don't tell me your name and what you're doin' in here, mister. This is private property. Nobody should be here without permission."

Elliott reconsidered intervening. Maybe if he said something, he could avoid the old farmer's impending bloody nose. But there could be more Gilgamesh soldiers coming, and now it was clear the Garrett Farm was not a meeting site, it was an execution site.

This old fellow poses no threat to Gilgamesh, Elliott reasoned. *He—unknowingly—could even be employed by them—his job to watch over their Dyersburg asset. This wouldn't be the first time someone went into an old barn to get out of the weather. It's a harmless thing, drifters and people stranded for one reason or another. It's easily explained away. Sure, the old guy's going to complain and threaten and talk your ear off, but he'll leave if you just say you needed a place to wait out the storm. No reason to stir things up.*

The big man closed the barn door and threw the rope over the hook. He turned to the old man and cocked his head, the light in his face. The old man stood firm with his lantern high as the big man raised a hand to his chest and opened his mouth to talk. The farmer leaned closer. "What ya doin' latchin' the barn door, mister. You've got some nerve."

It happened too fast. It made no sense.

Like a rattlesnake strike, the hand shot out and gripped the old man's neck. He lifted him off the ground with a muffled *crack*. The old man's legs went limp and the lantern dropped to the dirt floor.

Holding him above the ground like a sack of rotten fruit, he kicked dirt on the smoking lantern. And with a single stomp, he crushed the metal frame, shattered the glass, and smothered the flame. The barn returned to darkness and empty shadows as the smell of kerosene moved across the barn. He stopped below Elliott and tossed the lifeless body onto the pile, like another piece of junk, and returned to the crack in the door like nothing happened.

Now, Elliott could do nothing but wait for his chance to escape. In a broken and nauseous state, he clung to the wooden rungs knowing his slightest movement could be his last. Like the old man, Elliott would be no match for the animal sent to the Garret farm.

Music broke the eerie silence—Black Sabbath, "War Pigs". Elliott watched the killer pull a cell phone from his pocket while keeping his eye to the crack. The words got louder and were chillingly relevant; *"Generals gathered in their masses . . . just like witches at black masses. Evil minds that plot destruction . . . the war machine keeps turning."* The music stopped.

"Señor Bolivar," he said. "Yes . . . This is Dirk Henley. I got the message. I am here now. I wait for the doctor."

Francisco Bolivar, Elliott thought, *you're one of the three surviving Gilgamesh board members hiding from international law enforcement agencies. You ordered my termination? The Gilgamesh Resurrection is real! My God . . . a world is hunting you and you still want me!*

Dirk Henley spoke in a deep, scratchy voice. His sentences were fewer than five words indicating he was all business or not very bright. "No. I wait here. He will come."

Elliott held the wooden rung for an hour before the call from Bolivar came. His shoulders were sore and legs numb and hands trembling. The twisted angle interfered with blood flow. Without relief soon, he could fall. Climbing down—closer to Dirk Henley—was out after witnessing the man's cold-hearted talents. Going into the loft was his only other option, but it had its problems too. The hay bale covering the opening had to be moved. The distance to the opening from the ladder put Elliott in an awkward position and reduced his leverage. And moving the hay bale could reveal his location.

Henley continued to speak on the phone with his eye to the crack. "There was tornado. No cars. No tracks. Area flooded. I wait . . . eliminate problem."

Elliott reached out with one hand on the rung and the other pushing the hay bale. Loose straw and dust rained down. Henley jerked around, his phone still pressed against his head. Elliott had a larger opening. He reached up and felt the floor—it seemed solid. He poked his head through to his shoulders and stretched out his arms on the loft floor. When he went, he would need to leave the ladder and rely on his shoulder strength—were his wounds healed enough? He lowered back to the ladder to locate Henley.

He was standing directly below. Elliott froze. Henley studied the combine. He walked around it and pushed over the wall of hay bales Elliott constructed. After they toppled down, Henley pulled off the tarp. He pounded the station wagon and whipped around. His eyes climbed the wall into the rafters and stopped on Elliott's outstretched body thirty feet above . . .

TEN

"The devil can cite Scripture for his purpose."
William Shakespeare

Cape Town, South Africa

"This place is abominable," Francisco Bolivar said in perfect English cradling his hat in his lap. He prided himself on his ability to speak with no accent, something his family demanded since childhood. Much of their wealth and investment opportunity resided in America.

He sat rigid on the edge of the cold, wooden chair to avoid the filthy back slats. He spent far too much money on his suits to stomach their interaction with the filth of a dust-laden pew meant for peasants. As the other two shivered in the silence, Francisco brushed the shoulders of his black pinstriped suit and dug for his white handkerchief.

"I do believe this floating South African debris is getting the best of me," he complained. "I'm certain it is intent on completely sealing my nasal passages."

Through wet eyes they watched the old Peruvian execute a disgusting trumpet-blow, one accomplishing little more than damage to an eardrum. Francisco wiped his nose and discovered he had an audience. "Excuse me." He neatly folded his linen and pocketed it.

"I've never liked this place, Mobuto," Francisco announced.

Armstrong couldn't sit any longer. He jumped to his feet and went to one of the tall, narrow windows on the southwest side of the old church. Armstrong, the youngest of the three surviving board members, had no prior knowledge of the place, unlike Mobuto and Francisco. Leaning his nose to a cracked window pane, he watched the line of taillights move from the base of Devil's Peak toward Cape Town.

"Thank God," Robert Armstrong said. "I never thought they'd leave."

Mobuto ignored Armstrong's comment and scolded Francisco. "Mr. Bolivar, we not here for de comforts of me homeland. We here for other reasons."

Mobuto Ali, the oldest and wisest of the three, did not move when he spoke. Even at the age of seventy-eight he maintained the stature of an NFL lineman. The flickering candle on the altar could only find his eyes. They moved atop the large mass in the pew, eyes darting around the room like a foreboding predator looking for prey. Like Francisco, Mobuto understood their lives of privilege were over if they failed to complete the mission.

"Okay, gentlemen. Let's not get sensitive," Armstrong said from the window, not knowing the two elders were too cold-blooded to get sensitive about anything. "It's been a long day. Mobuto, can you tell me what Cape Town is saying about this place?"

"They talk about de djinn . . . de legend."

"The story we planted is still going around," Armstrong gloated. "Good to hear. Another objective accomplished. I guess nobody's gonna wander up here for a while, now that they have another body to stir up their imaginations."

"De people frightened," Mobuto mumbled. "They do not understand what happen here. De myth, de homeland folklore . . . fills void."

"You know they can see the light from this candle," Francisco said. "Is it really necessary?"

"Many have de telescope. Talk about glow in old church," Mobuto said. "Talk about shadow moving in window. Legend strong. De light and shadow make more question. Think djinn."

"You sayin' they can see things up here all the way from Cape Town?" Armstrong asked as he backed another step from the window.

"If look with telescope, they see," Mobuto said. "You stay away from window."

"I suppose the occasional glow and shadow in the window helps the legend we've fabricated over the years," Francisco said with a sour look as he brushed his shoulders with a white handkerchief and eyed the room with disdain.

"An occasional dead tourist and upside-down cross keep people away," Armstrong teased. "Like Mobuto said on the way out here, it is working as intended. I can stand here all night."

"*No*," Mobuto snapped. "Our face in newspaper now. We hunted men. Someone look up here with telescope, they see you. They come."

"Although they believe in this dreadful legend, I agree with Mobuto. We need to stay clear of windows." Francisco sneezed.

"May I just say I've never supported killing anybody in this old church," Armstrong said.

Francisco smiled at the youth avoiding responsibility. "We're all in this deeper than six bodies, Robert. I'm sure you've not forgotten the TEA program."

"I was not a part of that either," Armstrong shot back.

"You knew about the ordered terminations. That makes you culpable. It is as if you did them yourself. From the beginning, the program logged 1,076 terminations. You know as well as me every Gilgamesh board member knew about TEA except Albert Bell. Keeping Bell in the dark had strategic reasons. Robert, you were in the countless debriefings. You did not stop $T\ E\ A$. So please, do not now pretend to be innocent, sir."

Mobuto spoke under his breath. "You frightened. We alone now. We on island. We decide what happen next. You eat fear or fear eat you."

Francisco smiled. "What my good friend says is correct, Robert. This is the endgame. We are Gilgamesh now. The rest of the board is dead. Our chairman is dead. There is no time for fear. We must complete the mission."

"We stop Albert Bell." Mobuto proclaimed.

"Why?" Armstrong asked.

"He's not our friend," Francisco said. "And he knows too much about Gilgamesh's global operations. Now he will do all he can to expose our international networks and crush everything we built over the last hundred years. Albert Bell must be eliminated very soon."

Armstrong continued to struggle with the TEA program and his culpability. His fear would not be under control for a very long time. "Alberto Bella made everything sound vital to achieving our goal," he said. "Each time I heard about someone targeted for termination, Mr. Bella spoke about them as a threat, or they exposed us in some terrible way, or their elimination was necessary to advance."

"Regardless of reasons, people were killed and you approved," Francisco said.

"Still, I was not directly responsible for killing anyone."

Mobuto smiled. "Alberto keep record, big mistake."

Francisco got to his feet and brushed his hindquarters. "The authorities can connect eighty-six murders to Mobuto and me. Although you have not killed or ordered a kill, you are complicit. There is no way to get around it. If we are captured alive, you will die a horrible death in an electric chair with us, Mr. Armstrong. "

"You're enjoying this, aren't you, Mr. Bolivar?"

"Actually sir, I find the whole topic a waste of my time. You've yet to grasp the enormity of the moment. We have but one path to returned riches and immortality—or we die miserable deaths. The sooner you get it, the better your chance to avoid the latter."

"Francisco right," Mobuto said. "We have path. We resurrect Gilgamesh and de mission."

Armstrong looked out the edge of the window. If he pushed, he would be eliminated in his sleep—another exposure risk. He could not hide his fear, so he changed the subject.

"It is quiet out there," Armstrong said not knowing their eyes were on him in a new way. "Mr. Ali, does Cape Town believe the djinn responsible for all six found dead in this church? Do you believe we still have time for the next steps?"

Mobuto picked up the conversation with renewed emotion. "Yes. De locals blame djinn for more than six. They give credit to djinn for missing people of de Cape Town."

"Surely the police don't buy that," Francisco said.

"Does not matter what they think. De police got no answer for many hundred missing each year. De people put de mystery in djinn pile. That what locals believe."

"How long have we owned this place?" Armstrong asked.

"1955. All hundred-twenty acres. The church came with the property, right Mobuto? You were involved in the site inspection and made recommendations to the subcommittee."

"Yes." Mobuto closed his eyes. It was almost two in the morning and he was weary of the questions. Mobuto's head moved to the battles soon to come.

"Can the property be connected to us?"

Mobuto kept his eyes closed. "De records at provincial capital misleading."

Francisco spoke with authority because he orchestrated the purchase by the subcommittee. "The property is deeded to a Peter T. Frederick, a wealthy businessman with England addresses. Peter never existed. The fictitious character died a fictitious death a few years ago. Management of Mr. Frederick's estate got assigned to our *preferred* legal firm." Francisco watched Mobuto doze off, his enormous body balanced on the old, wooden chair.

"That would be Benton, Carlson & Associates?" Armstrong asked.

"Yes. International tax law experts. The real estate deal ran through numerous shell companies to confound those who would endeavor to sniff around.

"Our dead Mr. Frederick is the owner of record with no connection to Gilgamesh. There were five involved in the acquisition. Mobuto and I are the last standing. I can assure you, we are invisible in this transaction."

"I hope you're right," Armstrong said leaving the window and sitting by Mobuto.

"We've operated in a stealth mode for a very long time. Gilgamesh invested a great deal to keep this place as uninteresting as possible."

Mobuto opened an eye. "We safe on Devil's Peak."

"I don't see any 'No Trespassing' signs or fencing. The djinn legend, do you really believe? Is it enough to keep people away?"

"Yes. No sign. No fence. No guard." Mobuto closed his eye. "Keep people away. Good."

"Mobuto speaks with accuracy. We know the convincing haunting does the job well," Francisco mused.

Loose window panes rattled, the oaken doors whistled, and broken louvers in the empty steeple moaned as the three settled back and waited for the critical phone call. Access to the secret chambers deep beneath the church, and the activation of the IT and communications systems required codes. They would be provided, but outside standard protocol to avoid Albert Bell and his efforts to dissolve all Gilgamesh operations. The two hundred members were being summoned to Memphis—the three board members had only a few safe contacts left.

All subversive activities were now delicate operations. The resurrection of Gilgamesh in the eastern hemisphere would proceed according to an unpublished plan. Specialized, contracted agents and hidden facilities and furtive resources defined their future. Now, the GICC access codes were all they needed in the Dutch church.

Police had removed the wooden cross, but they left the fat candle on the altar behind. Now it flickered in the cold church catching the breath of the three billionaires. They were unfamiliar with basic human discomforts—failure, sacrifice, and surrender were incomprehensible concepts for men possessing everything they wanted their entire life. For them, the last seventy-two hours were pure hell.

The three planes touched down ten minutes apart on the makeshift runway, a remote clearing in the South African bush. A waiting, nondescript car would take them to a specified drop site near Devil's Peak. From there Mobuto would lead—he knew his homeland and the secret Gilgamesh operation better than anyone. Within hours, they stood in the gnarly woods a hundred meters from the church and Cape Town police. Mobuto ordered the early sacrifice claiming conditions warranted moving up the six-year ritual. This time, the October 17 date was not important, another kill by the Dutch djinn necessary. It would attract the attention needed to heighten fear in the region. It would remind locals and tourists the legend lived. It would further secure the site on top of the new Gilgamesh headquarters.

The three board members disappeared the night the seven heads of their brethren were found on seven stakes, the night on Mud Island when law enforcement obtained detailed information on a century of killings. The horrific accounts were incriminating. After Alberto Bella died in Memphis, the three remaining board members went on the FBI, CIA and Interpol most wanted lists.

When a branch tapped the window, Armstrong pinched the flame . . .

ELEVEN

Dyersburg, Tennessee

Elliott exploded through the hole into the loft and stacked bales of hay over the opening. With aching shoulders, he took his first steps into the dark and tripped. Down on a knee, he felt for the obstacle—a pole. *Something I can use.* He lifted it, but one end stayed on the floor. He ran his fingers down the wood shaft and stopped at metal. He felt it. *An axe!*

With his newfound weapon, he moved forward like a blind man. Not knowing other access points, and unsure of his footing, he found a wall and moved deeper. Henley could be climbing the rungs, not far behind. He had one objective—kill Elliott Sumner.

Another wave of storms pounded the barn from all directions, a relentless force pulling at the roof. The fingers of moonlight were replaced with rivulets of water. Wind and rain made it impossible to hear. Deaf and blind, Elliott felt his way. He poked and scraped by the splintered boards and rusty nails swiping cobwebs off his face. *I'll be lucky if I don't get tetanus.*

"Dr. Sumner," said the taunting, raspy voice from the dark,

maybe by the covered hole. "I just want to talk about our deal." Henley's anger leaked from each word. Elliott kept moving.

"Dr. Sumner, we must talk. Gilgamesh is resurrected." His voice trailed off.

Are you moving away . . . descending the rungs? Elliott wondered. *Do you have another way up here?* Now time mattered even more. *Sure. Right. I'm going to talk with you, deal with you. I just watched you kill a man for nothing.* Elliott resisted the urge to yell back profanities. His focus had to be on getting out of the barn. He needed to move as fast as possible.

Quiet minutes seemed like hours. Elliott shook more cobwebs from his hair and stayed along the wall as he tried to make sense of it all. *Why do Jack and Dr. Medino believe I can take their breakthrough to the world? I never signed up for that. Immortality, the fountain of youth, it's all a pipe dream—genetics or not. It's nonsense. I know medicine and the limits of the human body. It is preposterous to think there's a way to live forever.* He stopped and listened. *Gilgamesh is a victim of their lamebrain dreams.*

He bumped into another bale and stepped over. *This nonsense should have stopped when Alberto Bella died. It is his obsession. Why are Bolivar, Mobuto, and Alexander refocused on this warped mission? They have enough money to hide the rest of their lives.*

Elliott bumped into a wall. He felt around. *Could there be another room up here? Or is this some kind of partition?* He ran his hand up to the low ceiling. *Goes to the roof. Who knows, maybe there are stairs I missed?* He inched along another ten feet and reached the end of the wall—an opening. Standing very still, surrounded by whining wind and sprays of rain through a hundred cracks, he leaned into the opening and squinted into the darkness. Elliott attempted to make sense of the shadows in the dark. And he needed to avoid any moving.

"Well, look who we have here."

Elliott froze.

The iron hand crashed down on Elliott, knocking him to a knee. The hand clamped onto the top of his head, each finger digging into his skull. In excruciating pain, the hand pulled Elliott to his feet and then off the loft floor. Like the dead farmer, a death grip trapped Elliott. Then he remembered the efficient twist and the cracking of the old man's neck.

"Hello, doctor," Henley said as he tightened his fingers on Elliott's head.

Elliott reached up to pry the iron fingers loose, but his attempt failed as the rest of the familiar shape stepped out of the black and filled the opening in the wall. Hot, rancid breath poured into the room. Another massive hand clamped onto Elliott's right shoulder and squeezed him into submission. His tender wound screamed.

"You're no genius, Doctor Sumner," he said with his face inches away. Henley wore the same flat smile before he killed the farmer. "They said you not come. I said you come."

Elliott closed his eyes.

"Look at me, Doctor Sumner. I want to see your face when I crush your skull and your genius-brain squirts out your ears and nose. I want you to watch me . . . or I will hurt you slow," Henley said as he tightened his grip on Elliott's wounded shoulder.

"*No*," Elliott yelled holding his eyes closed, the axe handle in his left fist, the iron head resting on the floor in the dark.

"You say no?" Henley laughed.

This is my only chance, Elliott thought as Henley's distraction loosened his grip. *Another second is too late*. Elliott jerked and popped his head loose of the iron claw. He threw his left shoulder forward with all his might and pulled the heavy iron axe into motion. It moved with all the force he could muster. Flying through the dark in a wide arc, he kept the blade horizontal to the floor and at the estimated level of Henley's knee.

Will the rusted blade be sharp enough to inflict injury? Elliott worried in the split second it took to reach Henley's leg. *Will I have enough momentum to penetrate, or will it bounce off and hasten my death?*

Elliott watched the axe meet the outside of Henley's right knee. It sliced into his pants, and the blade went deep into the joint cavity. Blood and synovial fluid sprayed. Elliott understood the medical consequences—the severed ligaments and crippling destruction of the petallofemoral tendon, and excruciating pain. The injury would eliminate weight bearing.

The gut-wrenching cry of the wounded predator further confirmed Elliott's success. Henley dropped to the floor with the axe blade firmly implanted and the wood handle in the air. Elliot was loose. He fell backward and rolled to his feet and scrambled out of reach of the flailing arms of the monster. Stumbling over hay bales and obstructions in the dark loft, Elliott ran to the other end of the loft. He looked over the side at the dirt floor thirty-feet down.

Returning to the hole in the floor to go down the wooden rungs took him back to Henley. When the bloody axe flew over Elliott's shoulder, and the wood handle brushed his hair, he made his decision. The fat crossbeam twelve feet away had to do. If Elliott could reach it, he would be free of his executioner.

But does Henley have a gun . . . ?

The hideous sounds of his pursuer got closer—the gasping and scraping and grunting. Elliott backed up and surged forward launching off the loft's edge. He cleared the twelve-foot span. His chest crashed into the side of the crossbeam, where he clung like a bug hitting a windshield. His shoulders were tender, lungs empty, and muscles spent. And his hold slipped off the grimy layers of barn dust.

Elliott swung his legs side to side to build momentum. He harnessed the end of his strength into throwing a leg high and out over the beam. With his eyes closed he felt the pressure of the beam slam the inside of his thigh. Elliott locked and pulled up and over. Exhausted he lay on his stomach with his head on its side and watched Henley stumble from the shadows to the edge of the loft. He smiled at the grimace on Henley's face when he dragged the bloody leg into view.

"You're not getting out of this barn alive, Doctor Sumner."

With contempt Elliott just stared at the cold-blooded killer.

"You don't like me, do you?" Henley sat on the edge. He touched his bloody knee and winced. "Just a little scratch," he said with his face screwed.

"How long have you been working for Gilgamesh?" Elliott asked.

"Gilga who . . . ?" Henley's smile showed black gaps in yellow teeth.

"Your conversation with Francisco Bolivar . . ."

"So what," he boomed picking at his wound.

"If you are so certain you will succeed tonight, why not talk to me. I'm a dead man."

Henley stayed with his knee . . . thinking.

Elliott sat up, his legs straddling the beam, and inched back toward the south wall. No benefits from Henley seeing him move. Elliott could not stay trapped on a beam forever.

Henley lifted his head without the eerie smile. Like a used wax candle, his jowls sagged and brow drooped. "We were born there, me and my brother, 1975. They learned from their mistakes with the Bell triplets, 1968."

Elliott watched blood stream down Henley's knee to a growing pool on the dirt floor in a moonbeam. "You better tie something around the leg."

"Glenn's not nice like me. Back there, he would snap your neck fast. He'll be here soon."

That's a helpful piece of information. "So you two are a genetic experiment like us."

"What you doin' over there. I see you movin'. You're still stuck on that beam and going nowhere."

Elliott reached the wall and got to his feet. He steadied himself and leaned back. "I'm avoiding you . . . and a little afraid of heights," Elliott said. *Maybe that'll be enough.* He felt the wall and found a loose board he could work looser.

"Do you know why Mr. Bolivar wants you to kill me?"

"Alberto Bella," Henley shot back. "You killed him. You need to pay for it."

"That's a lie. I had nothing to do with it. Alberto Bella shot me the night he died. I was unconscious, in no condition to kill anyone. I saw him holding the gun on his grandson—Albert Bell. Someone else stopped him. Not me."

"Why should I care what you say?" Henley said.

"Because this isn't the first time they've come after me. They killed my brothers, Adam and Jack. Gilgamesh has been hunting me for more than a year." Elliott worked the board loose as he spoke. "You should care about what I say because you're like us. One day they will come for you and your brother."

"Why would Gilgamesh do that? We do what they ask."

"Because we are different. We have genetic gifts. We are a threat to them. Like you, I was an asset for forty years. Now I'm a liability. They send people to kill me. They've decided I'm a problem. All I've ever done is my job as a medical examiner. I didn't even know they existed until a few months ago.

"One day you and your brother will be on their list. Nothing you do or say will change it."

The barn door opened. Elliott looked down from his perch. Another large man came inside, Dirk Henley's twin.

"Dirk, where are you?" he barked.

Before Dirk could pull his eyes off his bloody wound, Elliott forced the rotting board loose from its rusted nails. Yet to be discovered by Glenn Henley, Elliott pushed the board aside creating an opening wide enough to slip through. He poked his head into the pounding rain to see what waited below, but could see nothing. He ran the options in his mind. His shoulders were bleeding and strength zapped. He could not stay on the beam. He could not make it easy for the Henley twins. Elliott's only chance was to leave the barn and take his chances—now.

Anticipating a crippling landing, Elliott thought the fall took forever. But when Elliott hit, he sank in mud up to his knees. Pleasantly surprised, uninjured, and alone in the dark rain, he struggled to break free—the Henley twins only seconds behind. Elliott pulled his legs from the sucking mud as escape routes came into view. Rising water surrounded him. He had to leave the high ground, where death was certain. Elliott had to face the raging storm to have any chance. The twins would look east, expecting him to swim to Highway 181, his only route to Dyersburg, a population center, and safety. Elliott chose west and the Mississippi River.

He waded into the black water flowing over dead cornfields. Enormous shadows came and took him away—they too were victims of the storm. The uprooted and twisted trees were piled high. Elliott clung to the limbs of the sliding debris, and climbed onto a massive trunk where he could lie, wounded and exhausted for his ride to Memphis.

Drifting away and in the flashes of lightning, Elliott watched Glenn Henley run to the south side of the barn. Then Dirk Henley limped into view. They looked west and went east to the water's edge. As the mountain of debris slid into the powerful river, Elliott watched the twins wade into the water toward Highway 181.

No one was stupid enough to go near the Mississippi River during a flood . . .

TWELVE

Although more than a year had passed, no one would forget the cold, December night at the Bell mansion when they met the most horrific serial killer in the country.

Although Elliott had set up the eight o'clock meeting two weeks earlier, he had not yet arrived. The others entered the opulent, second-floor study of the Bell mansion on time. Each politely acknowledged the patriarch, and each turned an eye to the French doors and infamous balcony. Even now their hearts raced, but not a word would be spoken. The feeling lasted seconds, the walk from the entry to the leather chair and Albert Bell's hand. On the way, the nine-foot French doors loomed and the chilling memories flowed.

He stood like a statue in opened doors, his menacing silhouette in swirling snow and long, leather coat flapping, and fat knife in his left hand. The Bell Christmas Gala was in full swing, a hundred guests . . . the kind of 'impossible' that challenged the beast of urban legend.

He came to kill again, but this time his presence was discovered too soon. The Bell mansion was surrounded and guns stormed the room—the psychopathic killer would be stopped at last. Onlookers froze in terror—the dark authority between the French doors would not relinquish control. He stepped from the red snow and his blood-stained coat lifted in the wind. He pulled the doors from the hinges and threw them across the room with freakish might. Then the Bluff City Butcher turned and exploded off the balcony into the night.

The meeting would begin in fifteen minutes. All were present, except Elliott. Max Gregory had arrived first, Albert's longtime friend and contracted PI. After the April invasion of the estate left two dead and four wounded, Max and his retired special ops associates moved into the mansion to provide around the clock security.

Memphis Homicide Detective Tony Wilcox had arrived next with G.E. Taft, the retired Shelby County Sheriff. Carol Mason, Director of Investigative Reporting for the *Memphis Tribune*, arrived last. Although she too relived the horrific December night with the Butcher in Albert's study, unlike the others the encounter was one of several—and each could have been the last.

"Very unlike Elliott to be tardy," Albert said.

"I've been unable to reach him for twenty-four hours. When he's not responding to calls or texts, he's on the trail of something," Carol said. She took a seat on the leather sofa across from Albert, and she saved a place for Elliott.

"Bet that irritates the hell out of ya," Tony chided.

She smiled. "Not really." William appeared with a chardonnay on a silver platter.

"You're favorite, Miss Mason," he said while handing her a napkin and eying Tony.

"Thank you, William." She checked her phone and held it in

her lap. "It does worry me some, but not any more than my unplanned adventures worry him."

"Of course," Max said. "Dr. Sumner is no stranger to danger, and you have a history replete with intrigue and risk, if I might say so." Max looked for William. He picked up the bottle of Vodka, threw a handful of cubes in a glass, and poured. "Where does William keep the lime wedges, Albert?"

"In the dish next to the bottle of vodka, my good man. You're the best PI in the business, but like me, you struggle most with things under your nose." The room chuckled and looked at the clock above the mantle.

"What are we doing here anyway?" Tony asked.

"Excuse me, Albert." Max took a swallow and rolled his eyes. "Maybe we could begin without him? Elliott's quite capable of catching up at warp speed."

"Yes he is, but I prefer we wait. He is pivotal to the topic under discussion . . . and he did schedule the meeting." Albert checked his watch again. "I'm sure he'll be here soon."

G.E. pulled out a white handkerchief and blew. Wiping his nose and fixing his handlebar mustache, he looked up surprised to see he captured the room's attention. "Excuse me." He stuffed the white wad in his pocket and pushed his glasses back up the bridge of his nose.

"Jesus Sheriff, you could break a vessel and bleed to death." Tony smiled alone.

"Are we gonna talk about that immortality stuff, the biology thing . . . genitals?"

"Genetics, not genitals," Tony said, choking on smoke.

"Sheriff, you mean biogenic life extension. Genetics," Carol said.

"Right—immortality stuff—Mr. Alberto Bella's big dream."

"The thing that killed the old fart," Tony chided.

Max ignored the shot and said, "That man turned a dream

into a nightmare. Gilgamesh pursued immortality for a hundred years. Guess they had nothing better to do with their time and money."

"And rumor is Dr. Medino rang the bell before they killed him," Tony said.

G.E. cleared his throat. "After Dr. Medino got run off Austin Peay, and after Jack Bellow got killed, I thought all that secret research disappeared."

"Isn't LIFE2 goin' under, Albert?" Max asked.

"'Hibernation' is the correct term."

"Like a damn bear in the woods?" Tony mumbled.

"Similar, I suppose," Albert said. "In business a company in hibernation slows spending, lives off existing capital reserves until better times prevail. It is like a bear, waiting for spring and an opportunity to eat again."

"Are we getting close to this evening's topic, Albert?" Carol asked.

His face did not change as he put his mouth to his glass of scotch. "I'll let Elliott answer that one when he gets here, Miss Mason."

"We may never know if Dr. Medino found the genetic on/off switch for life," Max sighed.

Tony flicked his butt into the fireplace. "I don't mean to rain on anybody's parade, but people living three or four times longer is just wrong. It creates a ton of damn problems for everyone. Nobody should be messing with that crap."

"What do you think the average life expectancy was in the 1600's, Anthony?"

"Hell, Max . . . I don't know. Sixty years?"

"Thirty-two, sir."

"That can't be right." Tony lit another. "You're making that shit up."

"Max is right. I've done the research. Did a story on this some time ago." The men watched Carol cross her long, shapely legs and pull her hem to her knee. It did not reach. Wandering eyes popped back up when she cleared her throat.

"There were reasons people died young, Tony—no refrigeration led to food spoiling and food poisoning. The lack of penicillin or antibiotics led to death by infection. Drinking water and sewage were not always separated—need I explain? No anesthesia, thus limited or no surgeries. Even the concept of sterilization was new. No blood transfusion. Shall I go on?"

"I get it. But we're talking about a very different world now."

"Are we now, Anthony?" Max said. "Allow me, Miss Mason. I dare say if you were alive in the 1600's, Anthony, you would be one of those with your proverbial head in the sand when someone told you one day you could live into your seventies, the life expectancy today. That is more than twice the norm only four hundred years ago."

"Not me, Max. I'm an open-minded guy."

"Anthony, in the 1600s you would not know refrigeration was going to be invented. You would have no concept of antibiotics, anesthesia, surgery, or the benefits of a blood transfusion. If you succumbed to a nasty accident on your small farm, you bled to death or died from a raging infection. There was no FDA to keep your loving wife from poisoning you with spoiled mutton."

"Funny, Max. What's your point?" Tony sighed

"Like today, you do not know about or understand the significance of biotechnology, genetic engineering, cloning, nanotechnology, cryogenics, and the global merging of the sciences. Today very smart people are talking like never before—the melding of expertise. Computerization is making many things possible. We are working in *terabytes*, one trillion bytes of information."

"Max, this planet can't handle a growing population that lives forever," Tony rebuked. "Overpopulation is already a goddamn problem. Take a look at crime in major cities, overcrowding is unmanageable. There's a lot of people starvin' in the world, Max. How are you gonna feed people living hundreds and hundreds of years?"

"Excuse me, gentlemen," Carol said. "A little factoid—the world population has been falling since the 1960s. Experts project this decline may level around 2050. This drop in population is more of a problem than stability or growth—widespread labor shortages lead to failed economies and riots and more. Most believe life extension is the only way."

"So you're in favor of immortality?" Tony said under his breath.

"I don't think anyone's talking about immortality," Carol said. "Personally, I doubt we are anywhere near extending lifespans to a hundred or so quality years."

"I agree completely," Elliott said strolling into the study.

THIRTEEN

All heads turned. "Sorry I'm late." His eyes found Carol first. "I assume we're debating world impacts of biogenic life extension—should we or should we not. Am I right?" He reached for her. "Hello, Miss Mason."

"Elliott, where have you been?" She met him halfway with an embrace.

"Ain't love grand," Tony said.

"Wilcox, hold your tongue boy," G.E. ordered, the father Tony never had.

Albert smiled, not yet accustomed to having a son, especially one he admired before he knew. Now his paternal instincts were taking over. With the elation, he assessed the bruises and cuts, and he noticed the limp immediately.

"Hello, Albert." They shook hands with a firm grip.

"Elliott," they looked deeper than most. "You're safe. That is good."

"Lately, seems always a bit of a challenge." Elliott sat next to Carol and rested his hand on her stunning knee. They intertwined fingers and squeezed.

"Now we can get started," Max said. "The floor is yours, doctor."

Elliott's smile faded as he made brief eye contact with each person in the room. "We have unwanted guests in west Tennessee."

"Don't like that tone, doctor." Tony handed him the perfect scotch on the rocks—vital knowledge gleaned from a decade of hunting the Bluff City Butcher.

"And, they are not fond of the people in this room." Max and Tony pulled their chairs into the circle. Everyone sat pensive, except Albert. Pain is the only emotion he can't hide.

"I came here from my condo, got back from Dyersburg this morning. For now, let me just say I took an unplanned trip on the Mississippi River."

"There were tornados and floods in Dyersburg last night," Carol said. "Did you say you took an *unplanned trip* on the Mississippi River?"

"To be precise, more in than on . . . And Tony, the old station wagon you loaned me, it's no longer operational. I had to leave it up there. It's in a barn."

"Damn, Elliott. I borrowed that wagon."

"Guess you lost your cell phone, too." Carol pushed.

"Didn't lose my cell phone. It got wet."

"And what, pray tell, took you to Dyersburg?" Max asked.

"Opportunity to obtain new information on the status of Gilgamesh."

Albert asked, "What did you learn?"

"I can say without a doubt the three surviving board members are very busy."

"They're hunted by everyone on the planet with a badge," Tony said. "These three sons of bitches are responsible for a lot of dead people—damn *T E A*."

"Anthony's referring to FBI, CIA, and Interpol. They've

tracked the three to Cape Town, South Africa. I will expand on this later. Please continue, Elliott."

"That would be helpful, Max." He leaned forward on the sofa, choosing his words. "I received a text yesterday at five—an unknown number. The message proposed the meeting, Dyersburg, a remote area."

"A specific location provided?" Max inquired.

"Subleased farm on US Highway 181. A little research took me to a co-op out of Topeka. I suspect a Gilgamesh shell. Five-thousand acres nestled five miles southwest of Dyersburg along the Mississippi. The text gave me a time—midnight."

"Unprofessional, stupid, or planned," Max scoffed as one experienced in clandestine events.

"I attempted to get to the Garrett Farm early—maybe an advantage. A couple of tornados got in my way."

"Why not go another day?" Carol said.

"It was a one or done thing. I had to go. The text said I could stop the resurrection of Gilgamesh. A deal would be proposed."

"Risky goin' it alone . . . but, I get it," Tony said.

"Before I continue . . . Max, you found Gilgamesh files on the 1968 genetic engineering project involving Adam, Jack, me. Did you find evidence of any other such research?"

"There was one similar, but . . ."

"Similar, but what?"

Max struggled up and out of his chair. Rubbing his long, thinning white hair, he dug deep in his pocket for loose change to jingle. When he reached the fireplace, Tony passed him a lit cigarette. They were an odd pair—one brilliant and introspective, and the other street-smart and extroverted. Somehow they found common ground.

"Thank you, Anthony," Max muttered. He turned his blank face to the others as if he forgot he was not alone. "Oh yes, similar but . . ."

"Genetic engineering . . . research and experimentation similar to the Bell triplets," Elliott pushed. All eyes returned to Max.

"Now that you mention it, there were twins later. I believe 1975."

"There were Gilgamesh twins, Max?" Albert sat up for the first time. "Did you not feel it important to mention? Am I involved?"

Flustered, Max stumbled into an explanation. "No, Albert. You were not involved in any way. Honestly, it did not seem important at the time of discovery."

"Gilgamesh twins, not relevant," Tony boomed. "Are you *shitting* me, Max?"

"Gentlemen. Please. At the time, the catacombs produced a treasure trove of unthinkable information on an hourly basis. We were focused on stopping Gilgamesh and hunting a serial killer across Europe and South America. I might add my personal attentions were fully committed to keeping Dr. Sumner alive."

"That is true, Albert," Elliott whispered. "Thank you for that, Max. I am here tonight because you were in my corner."

"Hindsight is always 20/20, people," G.E. barked. "Max is right. We were swimming in Gilgamesh files. Damn catacombs under the Brent mansion were full. I lost two deputies down there." He took off his glasses and cleaned them on his shirt sleeve. "Easy to forget, we've been chasing our tails a long damn time."

"Go ahead, Max. Tell us what you remember about those twins."

"It was seven years after the Bell triplets. There were only a few references to genetics. No neonatal or postpartum testing notes. The babies were delivered by staff personnel in a county hospital. They went home with mother and father like everyone else." Max scratched his head lost in thought.

"Goddamn Gilgamesh," Tony grumbled with a cigarette hanging in his lips.

"I recall we looked for the parents." Max pulled out his cell and turned away.

"Where are you going with this, Elliott?" Carol asked.

"It depends on Max."

He closed his phone and faced the group. "We dropped the ball back then. The parents of the twins were never located. A loose end not followed up on."

"Bet those Gilgamesh pricks killed 'em," Tony said.

"But you're saying back then. Your initial investigation of the twins concluded they were not like the Bell triplets, right?" Carol asked.

"I recall the summary statement in the twins' file. It reported success with a donor screening SOP. Our medical consultants said it was the same protocol used in any fertility clinic today."

"Thirty-five years ahead of the rest of the world," Tony said. "And that's not counting gene splicing and playing around with eggs and sperm."

"Did anything jump out?" Elliott asked.

"Yes. One thing. A notation . . . 'Adam-plus-one'." Max lit a cigarette and tossed the match in the fireplace.

"I may be least qualified in the room to comment on this one," G.E. said. "But, maybe those 1975 twins were like Adam Duncan with one more asset."

"Or it means they have two Adams," Tony mumbled.

"Or its code for something unrelated," Max said. "I put my people back on this just now."

Elliott leaned in. "How often did 'Adam-plus-one' appear in the file, Max?"

"I recall the pediatric document was around fifty-thousand words. It appeared maybe a hundred times."

"The frequency tells me it's important. We need to find out why. Can you get a file copy?"

"Is morning soon enough?"

"Perfect."

"Is it possible we have two more Adams running around?" Carol asked.

"Two more Butchers . . . psychopathic killers," Tony grimaced.

Elliott leaned back on the sofa and the room waited for him to speak. When he did, a chill in the air entered the study. "Adam is viewed as a Gilgamesh failure, but make no mistake Alberto liked his skill sets. Alberto did not like the lack of control. It is possible the '75 twins have Adam's assets plus one—control."

"The perfect soldier," Carol said.

"What takes you there, Elliott? Do you know something?" Tony asked.

Elliott looked into space, eyes honed, nostrils flared. Carol saw his temple muscle ripple. "Elliott, you can tell us." She squeezed his hand. He blinked back into the study.

"I met the twins last night."

"They were in Dyersburg?"

"I was with them in the Garrett barn, surrounded by rising water."

"My lord," Albert sighed. He took a swallow of scotch.

"They are like Adam, but bigger. Seven feet and three hundred pounds. They are genetic engineered mesomorphs."

"What the hell is a mesomorph?" Tony asked.

"A muscular body build characterized by prominence of structures arising from the embryonic mesoderm—muscle, bone, cartilage, subcutaneous tissue, skin."

"So, they are two big muscular bastards," Tony muttered.

"And I must assume superior intelligence, although I did not see it last night. My brief encounter did not give me enough. I spent most time with Dirk Henley. I saw Glenn for a few seconds. When he arrived, I needed to go."

"Tell us about Dirk Henley," Max said.

"Dirk killed a man last night. He tried to kill me."

"Why am I not surprised?" Carol leaned on his shoulder.

"Tell me you killed the bastard and escaped. I won't tell the cops," Tony sighed.

"I did not kill him. I'll tell you about the man Dirk killed later. Right now, what I learned is important to our survival."

"No more questions. Let Elliott speak," Albert said.

"I managed to get to the designated meeting site an hour before my hosts. I had enough time to cover my tracks, check out the place, and almost get situated.

"Dirk Henley came into the barn. He did not look around. Just stayed at the door with his eye to the crack. I watched from the rafters. He pulls out a cell phone. Says hello to Francisco Bolivar."

"Francisco is one of the three surviving board members," Albert injected.

"I remember Bolivar's vellum strip, *T E A*." Tony loosened his tie and sat on the arm of the sofa. "Bastard killed thirty-seven people."

"You boys didn't tell me about the TEA. You keepin' it under a bushel basket?"

"TEA stands for 'threat', 'exposure', and 'advance'. Gilgamesh board members eliminated people to protect their mission. Each of the seven dead board members found on Mud Island had a vellum strip stapled to their neck. It identified the victims the board member ordered terminated. We and the FBI are investigating. They are cold cases or missing persons."

"How many?" G.E. asked.

"1,233 . . ."

"My God in heaven."

"Kayne Duncan went on his own mission when he thought they killed Adam. Kayne forced confessions out of each board member, and then killed them," Elliott said.

"Never did find Kayne," Tony said. "But that's another story for another time."

"The three surviving board members are allegedly responsible for eighty-three TEA kills."

"Some of these cold cases are frozen solid—go back to 1924."

Albert set his glass down, his gold ring tapping the rim. The subtle chime drew everyone's attention. He smiled, quieting the glass with a finger. "Francisco Bolivar and Mobuto Ali are dangerous men . . . my personal observation over the years. They're joined by Robert Armstrong, who according to the vellum strips has no kills. However, Mr. Armstrong's behavior suggests to me he is as bad as the others. Cleverer."

"Why cleverer, Albert?" Elliott asked.

"He hides his cold heart behind a reclusive, billionaire persona. When we were told of Bernardo Kuzma's terrible death, Mr. Armstrong was in the room with others. I happened to glance in his direction. The man could not contain his elation. He struggled to hide his joy over another's fate."

"That's low life," Tony said. "People like that are missing something."

"A sociopath," Max mumbled.

"It explains why a billionaire runs with killers?" Carol asked. "After hearing about the TEA program, I'm sure he's as complicit and dangerous as any."

"Gilgamesh resurrection, I'd bet the farm he's as loony as they come," G.E. said.

"Their first objective is to terminate the people in this room," Elliott said.

Tony touched his gun. "That's no goddamn surprise. Let 'em try. We know who they are this time around."

Carol touched Elliott's arm. "And you are at the top of their list," she sighed.

"Actually, Albert and I are at the top of their list. It depends on which one of us gives them the best opportunity first."

"That's just wonderful," Max said with as much sarcasm as he could muster.

"Albert, please share with the group the other two board members."

"Mobuto Ali is a survivor. He has been on the board since 1949. Briefly, he is an uncompromising pragmatist, and possibly another sociopath. Mobuto is a very big, strong, and smart man. He is calculated, determined and quiet. I suppose he would have no problem hunting the people in this room, he is a big game hunter."

"Wonderful," Max muttered.

"Mr. Ali's primary residence is Cape Town, South Africa. I have not seen him for many years . . . a combination of my lack of involvement, and his reluctance to leave his homeland.

"Francisco Bolivar is an organizer. He resides in Peru. He is an American-educated man, speaks our language well. The most important thing to know about this man is he managed the inner workings of Gilgamesh—global communications, IT, and networks. And based on what we've heard about the Gilgamesh stealth army of trained assassins, I suspect he oversees the operation. Mr. Bolivar has high ranking military experience and led the merging of the Peruvian Investigative Police, Civil Guard, and Republican Guard in 1988."

"And what is Robert Armstrong's expertise?" Elliott asked.

"Biogenic research . . ."

"Cut me a break," Tony groaned, flicking his cigarette butt into the fireplace.

"I would expect Mr. Armstrong to know the status of all

Gilgamesh research endeavors, the scientists, employees, and contracted agents."

"I'm sure he knows the Henley twins as well as Francisco," Elliott said.

"It's safe to say these men have the knowledge to resuscitate Gilgamesh," Albert said.

"It appears Elliott's recent travels across Europe are still misunderstood by a few. I don't believe these men appreciate you my dear man. I'm certain you are the proverbial stick up their hindquarters, doctor."

"Not one of your better metaphors, Max."

"And sir, I am surprised they bungled the Dyersburg job."

"Alberto's death and the dissolution of Gilgamesh did not bring an end to the nightmare. Has the security at the Bell estate been adequately refortified?" Elliott asked.

"Max and his people are on the grounds around the clock," Albert said. "But my greater concern is for the other people in this room."

"Carol, please move into the mansion until this is under control," Elliott suggested.

"Yes, of course. An excellent suggestion. This place is enormous and well-guarded. Your safety and privacy easily provided. You are not safe alone, my dear."

"Thank you Albert, but no. I'll be fine. I refuse to allow these people to control my life. As Max said, this time will be different, we know who they are and what they are trying to do."

"I didn't think you would take us up on this. I don't like it, but understand." Elliott turned to Tony and G.E. "Will either of you take my advice for additional security?"

"Nope," they responded in unison.

"Seriously," Tony said. "We need these scumbags to lead us to them."

The door to the study opened. A head leaned inside. "Excuse me."

"Please, come in," Max said.

Holding an ear piece, the large man in a suit entered the study. His other hand held a gun pointing down and his eyes moved to the open balcony doors. "We have a breach. Please get down . . ."

Security crossed the room to the picture window behind Albert's mahogany desk. They watched him go to the edge and lean an eye. Three of their rifles fanned out from the mansion. From the window he said, "Mr. Gregory, Interpol captured a person of interest—a Gilgamesh executive officer, picked up in London by Scotland Yard. He's being held without explanation."

"Do we have a name?" Albert asked.

"Stephen Grendel."

"I know of Mr. Grendel. He is a Gilgamesh global IT officer," Albert said.

"Trenton, why heightened security?" Max asked.

"After receiving the Grendel information on secured lines, two things happened sir. First, the law firm of Benton, Carlson & Associates contacted the Yard and informed they represent Mr. Grendel, and left explicit instructions their client was not to be engaged without council."

"Okay, he has representation," Max said.

"BC&A is a Gilgamesh firm," Albert inserted. "Premier, international tax law experts used by many of the members, I've been told."

"We thought it notable BC&A would be en route, at four o'clock in the morning London time, for a small matter. Also, it appears the law firm received instructions from one of the three Gilgamesh board members."

"You have our attention. And the second area of concern?" Max pushed.

"One hour ago a private plane touched down and immediately departed Memphis International Airport. We received video, sir. Four armed men jumped off. There was an event, sir. We believe they're coming here."

"What kind of event?"

"The airport police met the plane on the runway—an unauthorized landing. There was gunfire and casualties—not them. The unidentified plane took off next to a commercial airliner and headed south hugging the river. The unknown plane disappeared. Disembarking passengers are missing. They are in the Memphis area, armed and dangerous."

"And you think they're coming this way?" Max inquired rubbing his chin.

"Possibly, sir. This is a precautionary effort at the moment. Our last Interpol transmission talked about covert touchdown at 20:48. That coincides with the MIA event and associated with a code—RG1B."

"RG1B . . . ?" Max parroted as heads turned back to the security agent.

"Resurrection Gilgamesh, first operation, second rendition," Elliott said. "This is an effort to rectify the Dyersburg failure. They are coming for all of us now."

"A bit desperate, don't you think?" Max said.

Tony unsnapped his gun. "Desperate or determined, either way it's ballsy. These three idiots are learning from the past. If Gilgamesh had gotten rid of all of us early, maybe Bella would have won."

The glass on the French doors exploded. Trenton clutched his chest. Blood flew. Tony dove over the sofa and took him to the floor. Then more explosions followed. G.E. and Max slid off their chairs, G.E. with a grazed left shoulder. Elliott pulled Carol and Albert to the floor. They moved low toward the alcove and fireplace, as bullets filled the room and pelted the walls. Paintings fell and the one lamp on Albert's desk shattered. A continuous barrage echoed across the manicured lawns of the Bell estate.

On the floor they watched the French doors. This time, the terror entering the Bell mansion had no face. As broken glass and splintered wood rained down, Elliott took care of the wounded agent. G.E. and Tony crawled to the balcony doors with guns out.

Albert turned to Elliott. "This is all about who controls the biologic. They think we have Medino's research. They think we hold the answer. We need to find out what we have."

Elliott pressed his hand on Trenton's shoulder wound. He reached over and put Carol's hand on the chest wound. "Keep pressure here, please." He looked at Albert as they waited, unsure. "I need to get the hard drive to Marcus." He saw the others' eyes on him. "Who wanted us to have this hard drive?"

"Jack Bellow," Max said as the others nodded.

"My brother was a smart man. He built four biotech companies before he was thirty-five. If Jack walked away from everything to be with Dr. Medino, it is significant. We must find out what we have, and never allow Gilgamesh to get it."

"I agree completely," Albert said.

"If we possess a genetic solution for immortality, we have a responsibility to take it to the world. If we cannot do that, we must destroy it to protect the world. Jack and Enrique believed this from the beginning. They got this far. Now it is up to us."

More bullets sprayed into the room. "Do you have a plan, Elliott?" Carol asked.

"It is taking shape. I know this time we cannot allow Gilgamesh to set the agenda. If we get out of this mess, we take it to them. This time they are the hunted."

Bullets ripped through the leather sofas where they sat minutes ago. Heads dropped to the floor. They waited, unsure.

I hope it's not too late . . .

8,454 miles from Memphis, in honed caverns deep beneath

an old, Dutch church on Devil's Peak, Francisco Bolivar sips a tall glass of Cabernet, waiting for IT access codes. Once received, he will activate the global override and regain control of the Gilgamesh stealth network. In London, a highly paid IT Officer holds those secret codes and sits in jail awaiting the services of Benton, Carlson & Associates—the matter described as a misunderstanding and temporary inconvenience. Francisco learns RG1 fails in Dyersburg. Unlike prior leadership, the three board members agree aggressive and decisive actions at all times. Francisco immediately authorizes RG1B, lethal penetration of the Bell estate—targets Alfred and William—to be followed with the pursuit and elimination of Sumner, Wilcox, Taft, Gregory, and Mason. Robert Armstrong instructs a TEA hit squad to locate and terminate Dirk and Glenn Henley . . .

FOURTEEN

"I can confirm the three are in Cape Town, South Africa . . ."

Max sat at the end of the long table in their new location after the attack. He pulled a small, brown leather notebook from his breast pocket and thumbed through the pages like a mad scientist with his nose inches away.

"Here we are . . . May 5th. Three arrivals—22:29, 22:37, and 22:48—Cape Town International Airport, private jets. Each deposited a single passenger on the tarmac and departed. Planes leased. Dead ends, obviously."

After the shooting stopped, they were moved to one of the three dining rooms—the one without windows. Trenton sat in an ambulance on his way to Baptist Hospital for stitches. Other than small cuts from broken glass, and bruises from diving to the floor, there were no other injuries. William and Spyglass associates handled the Memphis PD investigation and cleanup upstairs. The shooters would remain unknown—they only left a few hundred shell casings in two locations triangulating Albert's study. The meeting was resumed with a new sense of urgency and purpose.

". . . And you know all this, how?" Tony asked, fidgeting with his lighter.

"My people working with Interpol. We have target cities, of course," Max shot back.

"Did they see all three clearly?" Elliott asked.

"Positive IDs. Cape Town. All three on video. Biometric analysis." Max flipped a page and dragged a slow finger. His body swallowed the dining room table chair like a Kodiak Bear on a bicycle. Although not an obese man, the retired CIA counter intelligence operative wore XXX-Large. Always impeccably dressed, organized, and the consummate PI, there were growing signs of slippage—the open fly, the missed button, dropping of relevant details, and the falling off the logical investigational path.

"In our target areas we're watching airports, trains, buses, properties of friends and associates, favorite restaurants, and the usual. We've been doing this since April and will continue until the three are apprehended. It is a long shot, but worth the go."

"What're your primary target cities?" Tony asked with a skeptic tone.

"Mr. Armstrong resides in Seattle, Francisco Bolivar in Lima, Peru, and Mobuto Ali resides in Johannesburg, Cape Town, and Durban, Africa. We will maintain surveillance in those five cities indefinitely. Again—a long shot operation."

"Why do you keep saying that? It's routine. We catch a lot of people that way," Tony said.

"He's factoring in a combined net worth of nine-point-two billion," Elliott said.

Max smiled. "The point-two means *two-hundred-million dollars*, Anthony."

"More than enough money to disappear forever—I get it. Not typical bad guys."

Max set down his notepad and smiled. "But, we do have them in Cape Town."

"We can assume they know about Mud Island and the vellum strips linking them to multiple killings," Elliott said. "Alberto had a day to talk with his board. I think we can assume they know we have Dr. Medino's hard drive." He poured scotch into two glasses and slid one to Albert.

"Their faces are all over the media and they have robust bounties on their heads," Max said. "This should make their lives a bit more difficult."

"There's a reason they went to Cape Town," Elliott said. "What do we know?"

"Cape Town—Mobuto Ali's digs. Why fly big-ass, private jets into a city being watched?"

"Has to do with the resurrection," Carol said. "They need to regain control."

"Why is Cape Town important to Gilgamesh?"

The Bell patriarch, normally the most confident and dominant figure in the room, sat in silence at the end of the long table entangled in tragedies and puzzles now defining his life. Lost in a sea of doubt, he knew nothing for sure. Over the last six months he had discovered he had three sons forty years ago. People had died horrible deaths in his home. His grandfather had turned out to be a monster—he had watched him die at the end of a butcher knife. Now, Albert possessed the small leather box and possible secret to life. If true, it would change everything. But if it fell into the wrong hands, it would redefine humanity. The powerful few would reign over the universe. The powerless masses would be their slaves. The evolutionary leap to immortality that could allow man to master the universe could also launch the final wars of mankind. Overwhelmed with his inability to see the world around him, Albert backed away from the strengths that once defined him. He blamed himself for his blindness and poor judgments.

As heads turned, Albert took a deep breath. He had not spoken since the attack in his study, and now he had something he wanted to say.

"It is at times like this I wish I were a better man." He twisted the family ring on his finger. "I will explain." The room was still. For them, he was still the revered Bell patriarch.

"I have never had an interest in the follies of the wealthy," he said, his hands together on the table before him. "Growing up with unimaginable wealth presented me with a world few will ever know, one where every dream is possible. Although my father attempted to indoctrinate me to the ways of the privileged, my instinct was to reject all of it. For me, that world was unnatural. I believed I had earned nothing. Therefore, I deserved nothing. I was not special." His eyes lifted with an exhausted smile. "I ran away often. I hungered for truth. I left seven times. Each time I was found and brought back here. This is my prison.

"My behavior was unacceptable to Father. Rejection of the family heritage jeopardized the Bell dynasty. Soon I realized my deeply held beliefs did nothing but fuel an endless battle with my father and Alberto—the always-present grandfather."

Albert stood and pushed his chair back. Without intention, his stature projected a powerful presence. "I was to be the next Bell patriarch. I was the first born male of my generation. I was the new blood. All was preordained. My life's path was set."

Raising the glass to his lips, Albert looked through the archway into the next room and out the distant windows. Flood lights poured over the grounds, reaching the eight-foot stone wall he once believed protected him from a monster. *You did not stop my grandfather, the real monster. And you did not stop the Gilgamesh soldiers. No walls exist to stop an evil world . . .*

"What did you do, Albert?" Elliott whispered.

"I stopped running. I stopped sharing feelings. I put my beliefs in a place no one could see. I found it easier to cooperate. It ended the battles. They left me alone. That day I learned to keep my private life inside. That day I learned to live two lives."

Your life is not different from mine, or Adam's, or Jack's, Elliott thought.

Albert turned back to the table and the waiting eyes. "I made the decision. I accepted my destiny, but then my father died. Gilgamesh became a part of my life. I did as I was told, as I was expected. I was not strong enough to reject it all. I was embarrassed, a club for billionaires, a ridiculous secret society of pompous fools with an absurd mission—immortality. I could never connect with starry-eyed dreamers given so much yet wanting even more . . .

"My father died in a plane crash, 1956. A terrible day. I was twenty-four when anointed the next Bell patriarch, the blood lion. I was given my father's seat on the Gilgamesh board, one of the twelve managing a portion of the assets of two-hundred billionaires from all around the world, people hoping to live forever. I never took any of it seriously. That was my mistake. I attended few board meetings. When I did, I paid little attention until the very end.

"Alberto called the emergency meeting in March. He was quite disturbed Gilgamesh board members were being killed. And he was convinced Elliot was their executioner. You were always in the vicinity. I explained it was absurd. My son is a forensic investigator. He is on the trail of killers. And I learned that day they were hunting Elliott—their reason to worry."

"Alberto knew Elliott was not a killer," Max said. "He used the death of board members to justify the elimination of a Gilgamesh problem. Elliott got too close."

Albert nodded. "There was a motion—find and terminate Elliott Sumner. I could not believe it. Who are these people? I've never witnessed such abominable behavior in my life. Alberto thought he had nothing to lose. They spoke openly for the first time—an order to kill a man. I expressed my severe disapproval and left the room. Later I heard the motion passed. That is when I understood everything. Gilgamesh believed it held a God-given right to do whatever they deemed necessary to achieve their objectives. They are above the law, and out of control."

Albert walked over to Elliott. They watched his shaking hands settle onto the broad shoulders of his son. "Gilgamesh has taken everything from me and hurt so many. I stand here tonight unable to find the words. Elliott, I am honored to be your father. You are the son any man would be proud to have. I am sorry I cannot be of help at this critical time. I am ashamed of my blindness and stupidity. I don't know how I could be surrounded by such evil and not know for so long. And I am now ashamed I walked away with little knowledge to stop it."

Elliott got to his feet and turned to his father.

"You must not be ashamed, Albert. I pray I have your inner compass—it is true. Throughout your life you have been surrounded by great wealth, power, and sinister forces, yet you have navigated the dark abyss and prevailed. You accomplished all this without the benefit of truth and a guide. There is a *good* inside you worth more than any treasure on earth, a good I only hope you've passed to me. If it were not for your strength of character and commitment to seek truth to expose wrongs, we would not be sitting in this room tonight. Without you, Gilgamesh would have prevailed."

"Elliott's comments are accurate as usual, Albert. You've got nothing to be ashamed or sorry about. I am here because of you. Thirty years we've known each other. I've not known another man with more integrity rooted in the simple notions of truth and honor, right and wrong, and good versus evil. Albert, my dear friend, you cannot remember what you do not know. Gilgamesh is a complex and secretive entity. You can trust when I say there are other ways to get these scallywags."

"It's that simple, Mr. Bell," Tony said. "You were never one of them. You've been victimized all your life, and you survived. There are other ways to get these bastards."

"I'm looking at two of the most important men in my life." Heads turned. Carol smiled. "You are why I'm here, too, Albert. We can prevail. We have an opportunity to effect good in the world. Yes, we face great risk. But you have made this time possible. Without you, we would not be here. It would be over. And I know your son, with your help, will get us the rest of the way. Elliott is a real problem for Gilgamesh. Let's get to work."

Elliott held his father's shoulders. "Let me try something. Lost memories can be found."

Albert nodded. "What would you like me to do, son?"

"I want you to think back to an experience, a conversation or event. Think about times spent with Alberto, as your grandfather and as the chairman of the board. Think about his words, odd or notable comments, and phrases he used. Think about ideas he expressed, or tried to sell. Think about those statements out of place, those that struck you as aggressive. Think about times you felt a conflict with what you knew to be true and what Alberto tried to make you believe. This simple process can trigger lost memories. They will jump forward in your mind."

Albert sat down. He closed his eyes. The others leaned forward to watch the man they all respected. Albert said under his breath, "I think I understand."

Elliott spoke hypnotically. "Go back Albert. Go to times spent with individual board members. Think about conversations with Francisco Bolivar, Mobuto Ali, and Robert Armstrong—the casual conversations can reveal a personal agenda or give you important information otherwise not shared. Think about times together on trips or business events. Did you observe arguments? Were there disagreements? Were there emotional outbursts, dropping of guards?"

"I think I have a . . ." Albert opened his eyes and looked at Max. "Did your people follow them from the airport into Cape Town? Maybe a name of a street or location can help."

"Very good, Albert. Max please."

"Sorry, gentlemen. We lost them on the twelve mile stretch from the airport into town."

"They lost you, ya mean?" Tony jabbed. "How the hell does a stretch limo lose CIA operatives? I'll be damned. Were your guys on mopeds?"

Max shrugged off the accurate comment. "They had an elaborate ground game, Anthony."

"Why the hell didn't your people have one?"

"As you know, initiating surveillance can be tricky. We had no idea where they would pop up or when. It is quite challenging to cover every scenario at every location."

"Don't forget the fourteen-second window," Elliott said.

"Correct. Most subjects lost disappear in the first fourteen seconds. They have the advantage of timing and multiple entry/exit points in all situations."

"That's a weak-ass excuse, Max. You should demand more from your people."

"Their level of precision reflected their true capabilities, Tee. I'm sure the failed Dyersburg operation was not typical Gilgamesh," Elliott said.

"Damn, Max," Tony mumbled. "We gotta do better. We can't let them slip away."

"Actually, we lost them a few times," Max muttered.

"Now you're just messin' with me," Tony said.

"We found them at the four-minute mark and lost them again seven minutes from the airport. It was near Devil's Peak. We found their vehicle abandoned, except for the driver. He took a bullet in the back of the head."

"Bastards didn't want to leave a trail."

"On our thermal imaging cameras—a flyover—we picked up hot images in an old church at the base of Devil's Peak. There is only one trail up. A treacherous climb, I'm told. When our people got up there, the place was empty."

"You sure it was them?" Tony asked.

"No. We are analyzing the images in DC as we speak. They could be hiding up there."

Tony got to his feet. "That's where we'll pick up a trail. We need to fly out tonight, Max."

"Anthony has a point. Leave now and we are there tomorrow afternoon. We need to be aggressive, Elliott. They're in Cape Town, up to something."

"*Information,*" Albert exploded and jumped to his feet. The room watched him walk tight circles. "That's it. Information. The GICC."

"What is GICC," Elliott asked.

"Global Information Control Center . . . there were three. Alberto wanted redundancy."

Max flipped a page in his little book and started writing, his long gray hair touching the table. When he spoke strands lifted and floated back down. "ICCs are quite common practice today. Large enterprises have their mainframes where all company data is stored and maintained. They have duplication sites—backups— to cover the primary site in case of compromise: fires, tornados, floods, earthquakes, and other disasters."

"Like cyberspace shit—viruses and your basic hackers."

"Yes. Gilgamesh would have an enormous volume of information to maintain. They are a hundred-year-old organization, a global enterprise, and a stealth operation. The volume of data in terms of years, languages, and complex codification must be immense."

Albert sat down. "My grandfather kept everything. The catacombs are the tip of the iceberg. There are mountains of boxes overflowing with documents. They digitized everything over the last decade. I heard about it and thought it a ridiculous waste of time and money."

"I suspect Alberto was not concerned about natural disasters," Elliott said. "He wanted the ability to neuter a GICC falling into the hands of competition. It has always been about keeping proprietary science from enemies. Where are you going with this, Albert?"

"The primary GICC is in Memphis. It's somewhere in the catacombs under the Brent mansion. I'm sorry, but I have no idea where."

"Can the primary be disabled by a backup GICC?" Elliott asked.

"Yes. Your initial comments are correct. Alberto wanted that ability."

"Where are the other two?" Carol asked.

Albert pushed his hands over the table spreading his fingers as if grabbing for answers. "I recall Moscow. Wait. Removed in 1997. Bernardo Kuzma lost Alberto's trust. To avoid internal strife, he told the board he was relocating it to South America, a better opportunity for Gilgamesh future growth—Lima, Peru."

"Well that's just great, South America. That can't be good for us. Someone said Senior Bolivar was the IT seat on the board."

"Alberto never put one in Peru. He made excuses for delays. People eventually forgot. Alberto trusted Francisco less than Bernardo. That GICC system was brought to Memphis and dismantled for security purposes. I don't believe it was ever going to be reassembled."

"Good, we've now accounted for two GICC's. Where's number three," Carol asked.

Albert shook his head. "It's in Cape Town. That's what I remembered."

"I'll be a son of a bitch. Good for you, Mr. Bell."

"That's why they are in Cape Town," Elliott said.

"That GICC is a few passcodes away from being operational." Albert said.

"We need to move on this now," Max said, closing his little leather book.

"To stop the Gilgamesh dissolution process, they must regain control of their global information network. It is the heart of their strategy."

"They will shut down Memphis as soon as they can," Carol injected. "Mr. Grendel, the Gilgamesh IT Officer sitting in a London jail, is a major factor. He has new passcodes."

"Max, your people need to keep Grendel tied up. We must keep Benton, Carlson & Associates away from him as long as possible. Those passcodes must not get to Bolivar."

"GICC gives them everything they need to restore their veiled global operation. They'll draw strength from the roots of the dying organization," Carol said.

"The takeover of the Gilgamesh brain means they don't start over. They hit the ground running." Max punched numbers on his cell and leaned under the table.

"They get control of the global network, contacts, resources, and key operational structures."

Max popped up sliding his cell in his pocket. "Our people can be ready for Anthony and me to be in Cape Town tomorrow."

"And Albert, you and I need to find the Memphis GICC," Elliott said.

"We need to put up a firewall ASAP," Carol said. "I know some qualified IT people."

"Albert, what's the status of the Gilgamesh dissolution process?"

"It will take a year to complete. Membership has been notified. They're not complicit. All 2,000 backed away after learning about the *TEA* program—kill lists managed by board members and their chairman. We'll have a meeting in Memphis to discuss R&D project redeployment and frozen capital assets. A large portion will go to a foundation to benefit families of *TEA* victims."

"We have a mountain of those cold cases to solve," Tony said.

"Gilgamesh HR roles and corporate partnering files are in the hands of the FBI. People like Detective Wilcox will be rounding up members of the stealth army. Insiders will be identified. Useful information is coming out of the catacombs every day."

"What about facilities and research?" Max asked.

"We've identified 124 facilities around the world, mostly shell companies responsible to develop and protect proprietary biotechnology. Most employees have no knowledge of Gilgamesh. Separating the innocent from the guilty will be an arduous task."

Max cleared his throat. "Before I forget, our people will delay Mr. Grendel. Seems the Yard had a system failure. Can't locate the Gilgamesh IT officer. Been misplaced. Maybe transported to another facility by mistake. Could take a while to sort things out."

"Excellent. How long do we have?"

"Twenty-four hours safe side, thirty-six a stretch. They're quite displeased with Gilgamesh. The TEA initiative is a most disturbing revelation. More than a hundred Englishmen were terminated over four decades. Accounts for many of their nagging cold cases."

"We must avoid a GICC shutdown in Memphis. They will be an even more formidable force to reckon with," Elliott said.

"They are cold-blooded killers determined to complete their twisted mission," Max said.

"Elliott's right." Carol closed her notebook. "They have nothing to lose. No hierarchy. They can move fast. They're focused. Desperate to succeed where Alberto Bella could not. We have already seen they don't plan to take their time."

Elliott stood. "Okay. Tony and Max go to Cape Town. Carol, work with Scotland Yard. Keep Mr. Grendel under wraps as long as you can, maybe some convoluted US extradition process or something. And we need your best IT people at the Brent mansion tomorrow night. Get them there and have them wait on the front porch. Albert and I are going into the catacombs. We're gonna find the GICC. We'll need to install shields and if possible, shutdown Cape Town before they shut us down."

Tony pulled on his coat. "Let's go, Maxi-Man."

Max rolled his eyes and straightened his tie as he got up from his chair. "Lovely." He pocketed his leather notepad and pen. "I suppose there's no other option."

"You'll survive." Elliott winked. Everyone stood at the table.

"Before we take off in all directions, I didn't have an opportunity to tell you why this meeting was scheduled in the first place. We were thrown off the agenda."

"And . . ." Tony sighed.

"Everything we're dealing with is connected to one thing—biogenic immortality. If it is real, if Medino's hard drive holds the answers, we must act before Gilgamesh."

"It was delivered to me with very specific instructions from Jack and Enrique," Albert said. "They want Elliott to take this to the world. If Gilgamesh or other self-serving entities get it, the repercussions would be global and devastating."

"It must be available to everyone. If that's not possible, it must be destroyed," Elliott said.

"We all agree," Max said and all others nodded in agreement.

"Tony and Carol have met someone pivotal in our mission. I honestly don't know how we could even go forward without him. Dr. Medino has a son. He was hidden from the world. He is the last surviving Medino. Marcus is a doctor. He worked side by side with his father in the catacombs."

"This is great news for us," Max said.

"Albert. We need to get his father's hard drive to him as soon as possible . . ."

FIFTEEN

A private jet landed every nine minutes over a twenty-four-hour period. Discrete travelers stepped into waiting limousines and were whisked away. Although the Memphis International Airport is a superhub, the surge in luxury aircraft traffic caught everyone off-guard, including the local news media —and no one was talking.

"Hello. I'm Chris Martin—Channel 8 Action News—coming to you *live* from Memphis International Airport—testing one, two, three." He pushed his hair off his forehead and rubbed his front teeth with his finger. "Ready when you are." He looked over his shoulder at the line of idling, black, stretch limos. Standing outside "Arriving Flights" holding the microphone, he waited. The flood lamps popped on. The tally light started to blink. The cameraman made his final adjustments, zooming in for a Martin close-up with the limos.

He held up a fist. One finger, two fingers, and three fingers . . . "Go," the cameraman whispered.

"Chris Martin here—Channel 8 Action News—coming to you *live* from Memphis International Airport. Hello everybody.

"They started to arrive yesterday morning—Learjets, Dassault Falcons, Gulfstreams, Beechcrafts and Piaggio Aeroes— the finest modes of transportation money can buy. And we have just confirmed these private jets have been landing at the Memphis International Airport every nine minutes over the last twenty-four hours, sometimes two touching down at the same time on different runways . . .

"The surge in air traffic is taking our airport to its limits. I'm told by air traffic control making room for this additional volume is a real challenge. Memphis International is not only one of the busiest airports in the country with commercial airlines connecting from all over the world, but it is also a major hub for Federal Express.

"By my unofficial count, one-hundred-and-fifty private jets not here yesterday are parked in Memphis, Tennessee. Who are these mystery guests, and why are they in our city?

"We do not have names, but our research has revealed they are some of the wealthiest elites coming from all parts of the world. We have confirmed originating cities include Cologne, Dubai, Paris, London, Tel Aviv, Sao Paulo, Seoul, Tokyo, Hong Kong and Moscow, to name just a few.

"Channel 8 Action News has been asking the questions, pushing for the answers you want to know, Memphis. Something is happening in our fair city. This unfolding mystery, surrounded by a wall of silence, has our attention." The camera zoomed out. Martin pointed to the line of limos along the curb. "I am looking for answers, Memphis. These motors are running. Drivers are in position to receive their passengers. Maybe someone will talk to us . . ."

Martin moved toward the limos, the camera followed. "Although we've yet to identify an event, there seems to be a concerted effort to be in Memphis by tonight. Whatever is happening here is going to happen soon." He leaned into the lens and whispers. "I will stay on this story Memphis. I will solve this mystery and share updates the moment new information breaks."

Martin spotted a potential interview. He approached the driver standing at an opened limo door. He wore a black suit, narrow black tie, and Burberry cap, and held a finger to his ear, his eyes locked on the bank of glass doors and escalator inside the terminal. Martin whispered again to the audience, "Let's see if we can get this driver to tell us why he's here . . ."

"Excuse me, sir. Chris Martin here . . . and you are *live* on Channel 8 Action News. The tristate area is watching. Maybe you can help us out. We are curious. Who is visiting our city today. Can you tell us why you are here, sir? Who are the travelers in need of services? Who are you picking up?"

Martin pushed the microphone into the driver's face. He squinted into the light without a word or change in facial expression. Then he looked down at his watch.

"Excuse me sir. Can you just share a few words with us? This is *live* TV."

The driver walked away.

"Sir, I understand you cannot give specifics on clients," Martin said with mounting desperation. "Surely you can talk to us in general terms. Are you providing transportation services for visiting royalty? Maybe a sports franchise or business? Or is a production cast coming to town for an upcoming performance at the Orpheum, or Tunica, one of the casinos? Is it the entertainment industry—music or theater?"

The driver glanced back, pulled out a cigarette, and stuck it in his mouth. The camera followed him until he disappeared behind the limo, and then panned over to Martin's confused face for the close-up and exit. Martin's fake smile had to salvage another embarrassing moment on live TV. *This should screw my ratings . . .*

"Well there you have it—more stone-faced silence wrapped

around this bizarre mystery. No one is talking, not even the hired help." His fake smile grew as he leaned closer. "I'm going to get to the bottom of this, Memphis. More at ten. I am Chris Martin, Channel 8 Action News, at Memphis International." `

Lights popped off. "We're good," the cameraman said collapsing his tripod and grabbing his cords. Martin lit a cigarette, loosened his tie, and strolled to the edge of the routine traveler flow from baggage. He took his ire and frustration to an out-of-the-way cement pillar.

Moments later Martin felt a tap on his shoulder. The stone-faced limo driver that had ruined his segment stood there with an unlit cigarette hanging out of his mouth.

"Great," Martin sighed. "What . . . ? Lighters in your big-ass limo on the fritz?

"Hey man, sorry. Couldn't talk on camera. Get my ass fired."

It made sense immediately. Martin should have considered the reality. "Guess we've all got our rules." He gave him a light.

The driver stayed at the pillar. "It's kind of *weird*, though. I mean, what's going on and all." He sucked long and Martin watched the thick smoke roll through the man's yellow teeth.

"Weird? That's an odd choice of words."

"Off the record . . . ?"

Martin joined him in the shadow of the pillar. "I do not reveal my sources," Martin said. "I don't want to know your name." He looked around. "Something big is going on. People normally in the know are not talking. It's like they're scared of something or somebody. I may be the only reporter in the city that thinks this is a big deal."

"There's secret shit goin' down tonight. They're keepin' it on the down-low. Most of us know nothin'. We're just supposed do our jobs and shut up. No one tells limo drivers shit. But we're like the fly in the room. We see and hear a lot of things, man."

"Tell me what you've pieced together." Martin shook four

Marlboros out the hole of his soft pack and slid them in his pocket. He passed the pack to the driver. It did the trick.

"I've been pickin' up these rich dudes for ten hours straight, sometimes out here and other times on the tarmac next to their friggin jets. Curbside is for rich pricks forced to fly commercial. No room at the hanger, man," he quipped.

"Who are these people?"

"Don't know. We get a number, no names. I'm waitin' for number 1423, American Airlines out of Nashville, a rich Arabian guy."

"So you've picked up others like him?"

"About twenty in the last ten hours. I've been listening to them talkin' on their cells and to their bodyguards in the backseat. They talk their own language. I miss a lot. But I get some shit too. These are some serious rich mothers."

"That's obvious," Martin muttered.

"I'm talkin' the 'B' word. It's the same in every tongue."

"And what's the 'B' word?"

"*Billion*, man . . . These billionaires are talkin' about getting some of their investment back, clearing their names, and shit like that. The meetin's gonna happen tonight."

"You know when and where?"

"Late. The pyramid on Mud Island. Place's been rented."

"That holds twenty thousand. It's too big for a secret meeting. I don't think there's twenty-thousand billionaires in the world."

"They don't need to fill it up, man. They want a place isolated from us peasants and crooks."

Martin scratched his head. "You're sure about the pyramid?"

"Easy enough to check. Follow the limo train tonight. Can't hide a migration that big."

"I guess even rich people have a right to get together without being bothered."

"That's all I've got, mister. Thanks for the smokes."

Wish I knew why they're getting together, Martin thought. He lit another smoke and leaned against the pillar. *This is big and I'm the only one covering the story. Could be my ticket out of this bush market.*

"Gotta go. My Arab's comin' and they don't like waitin' on American scum."

"'Weird' was the right word," Martin said.

The driver stopped. "You know, there's somethin' else. Somethin' they all said. I understood it in all languages. They said the same names."

"You got names?" Martin asked. *This is the lead I need to break this wide open.* The camera man closed the van doors and whistled. Martin waved him off. "Go ahead. What names?"

"Two names. They said Albert Bell and Elliott Sumner, the forensic guy in the news all the time, the one who got the Bluff City Butcher. Gotta go, man." Martin watched the driver return to his limo and take his position next to the open door.

The short, gaunt, elderly man with the well-cropped gray beard, black thawb, and dark sunglasses emerged from the sliding glass doors oblivious to surroundings. His face locked onto the backseat of the stretch limo, his next controlled environment and isolation from the hordes. Close behind, a dark skinned, bulbous skyscraper appeared. The white panama suit and white chafiye with an exploding star above the center of his forehead pushed through the crowd spreading a stern grimace to all that dared to look his way. He carried a brown alligator briefcase chained to his wrist. His white-knuckled fist dared anyone to think about touching it. The bump in his coat and bulges on his inside calf were guns and a knife. When his black, marble eyes found Martin, they widened. His head rotated on the thick neck like a well-greased turret gun.

Martin melted into the shadow of the pillar and dropped his head pretending to read a text on an invisible cell phone. *Oh God.*

Who are these people? When he looked up, his nose stopped a foot away from the brown face in the white panama suit.

"*Why* you look?" The harsh voice fit the cold eyes and hand in coat.

"Excuse me?" Martin squeaked. The brown man leaned six inches from his nose and the eyes narrowed beneath a dipping brow.

Martin struggled to open his constricting throat. His words eked out in a variety of pitches. "I'm not looking at anyone in particular. I'm a TV news reporter doing a story." He pointed to the Channel 8 van. When he turned back, the panama suit had vanished and a limo door closed.

He had two hours before the next airing. Martin had to change clothes. His pants were wet.

SIXTEEN

"Doubt is a pain too lonely to know that faith is his twin brother."
Kahlil Gibran

"They built the Brent mansion, the first Bell mansion in the midsouth, in 1930. I came along two years later," Albert said as he followed. Elliott led the way into the large drainage pipe located in the middle of the woods in north Shelby County. Minutes after the sun went down they knew it would be pitch black soon. Albert pulled out his flashlight and hit it a few times on his palm. The beam showed little promise of a long life.

"We're three-hundred yards north of Brent," Elliott said as he moved deeper into the eight-foot diameter pipe. Damp cement changed to bone dry at thirty feet and there were no signs of life —not even spider webs. Elliott did not miss the scuff marks shoulder high on each side of the cement arc, nor did he miss the large boot impression in the creek by the pipe entry.

"I don't remember much about the old place. Father wanted

to move to east Memphis. He built it in 1950. I recall Alberto staying behind. Lived alone a while. Didn't see much of him until Father's death." Albert shook his flashlight. "Should have put new batteries in this."

They went deeper at a steady pace. Elliott's light bounced left and right as they straddled the arc of the pipe. The hollow thud of their boots echoed as sounds from the entry faded.

"He sold it to Trenton Brent in the '70s. Brent died in 2002. Estate settlers gave the place to the county seven years later. I guess it lost its appeal. Or it could be location. I recall when Alberto decided to move to Europe. We could never use his name. He became known as Rudolph Kohl after the staged death in 1925. He didn't want his age to be a topic."

"Didn't it strike you as odd, him living so long?"

"I had no way to explain it. I remember reading about supercentenarians, people living well into their hundreds. Nobody really understands it. I never gave it any more thought, except that maybe Alberto got his birth date wrong."

Elliott stopped marching and turned to Albert. "After we resolve the GICC matter, you and I must talk about this. I must understand this phenomenon."

"I'll tell you everything I know, if it will help."

Elliott resumed the trek deep into the pipe. "Marcus Medino said he and his father spent a lot of time in the catacombs—between here and a private lab in Davidson County outside Nashville . . . I believe a barn on their farm. This site was for harvesting tissue and organs."

"I cannot justify such loathsome behavior, regardless of the situation or lofty purposes."

"Gilgamesh sent trained assassins to kill them. You would think after a few dozen corpses they would get the message—Adam is an unstoppable, killing machine. Instead, they kept at it. Dr. Medino rationalized the macabre situation. He couldn't stop

Adam or Gilgamesh. And, he needed fresh human tissue for his research."

"Adam—the one-man army—fought the secret war most of his life," Albert mumbled as he struggled with the reality his son was a serial killer. "I wonder, if he had had a life without Gilgamesh, would he kill anyway?"

"I don't know the answer to that one, Albert. I do know Adam has some level of control—he did not kill us in your study. The question is how much control? We may never know."

"He has killed so many over his life."

"Tony said recent findings confirm many kills attributed to Adam were the work of Gilgamesh. He did not kill random, innocent people, Albert. He killed Gilgamesh soldiers."

"I suppose they had to promote the BCB legend to keep people looking for him."

"They were relentless, their strategy now clear. Gilgamesh needed all the help they could get. The legend kept law enforcement in six states working for them, hunting their nemesis."

Elliott aimed his light down the pipe. "We're getting close." The undetectable, seven-degree incline took them thirty feet underground; the pipe was never intended for drainage purposes.

"So this connects to the catacombs under the Brent mansion?" Albert asked.

"Yes. There are seven. They're laid out like spokes of a wheel, with the Brent mansion the hub. Documents found in the catacombs confirm there were multiple portals into the catacombs—the one time Gilgamesh headquarters."

"Right under my nose," Albert sighed.

"We're here." He moved his light over the mold-laden brick wall at the end of the pipe.

Albert's cell phone chimed. "It's Max. Should I take it?"

"I can't believe you get reception down here. Go ahead.

Could be important." Elliott turned back to the wall. *We're gonna need all the help we can get to find the GICC.*

Marcus gave him the sequence. He counted the bricks—seven from top center, five right, and three down. He pushed with his open palm. A half section of the wall released. He pushed harder with his shoulder. It scraped open. Cold, dank air rushed out and a moldy stench filled the pipe. Elliott went inside, reaching back and pulling Albert. He then slid the wall back into place.

They walked ten yards in the dark, Elliott moving a slow beam inspecting the dirt room for a connection to the catacombs. The man-made cavity, symmetrically honed from rock-hard dirt, had a seven-foot ceiling held up with a patchwork of rotting boards. Clusters of fungus hugged the random damp spots. Support beams were draped in dust laden cobwebs. The smell of the ages seemed to hang in the stale air.

Albert pocketed his cell and said, "Max and Tony are in Cape Town. They're about to climb Devil's Peak. It's almost two in the morning for them. Max says they slept on the plane."

"Good, any other news?" He asked, fiddling with the troublesome flashlight.

"Carol had some success. Mr. Grendel continues to be misplaced. The Gilgamesh lawyers are contained—they are livid." Albert looked away and rocked on his heels.

"What are you *not* telling me, Albert?"

"What makes you think I'm not telling you something?"

"You're rocking on your heels. I do the same thing."

"Fine . . ." Albert stopped rocking. "Your mother is in the states—New Orleans. I did not want to discuss it right now. I was going to tell you after . . ."

"Betty is here! I told her to wait until I could assure her safety. She agreed."

"I know *what* you told her."

"Albert, she must go back. It's much too dangerous coming out of hiding now."

"Betty has been running all her life, Elliott. She's done running."

"This is suicide. We must find her, explain the situation—the three Gilgamesh board members focused on killing all of us this time. We must send her back, Albert."

"It's not going to happen, son."

"She knows too much. They will kill her." Elliott put his hand on Albert's shoulder. "She told me everything in Arequipa. She was a willing participant. Betty was on their research team. They won't let her live."

"I know all about that, Elliott. We've talked, too. In the beginning Betty was young and naïve. Gilgamesh sold her on the merits of their groundbreaking, surrogate maternity program, a major step forward in obstetrics in the '60s . . . and commonplace today. She was selected because she tested as the ideal vessel to receive the seed of a Bell patriarch."

"I know, but . . ."

"Elliott, your mother was manipulated by Alberto. She didn't tell you he played the role of devoted grandfather helping a desperate grandson. He said I had a rare genetic problem that made it near impossible for me to ever father a child. My only chance was the perfect match of egg and sperm, and the perfect womb. He said they tested thousands and she was the only one who fit the profile. Alberto sold her by convincing her I would commit suicide if I could not have a son . . . and the great contribution she would make to help others like me. The truth, it was always about finding the biogenic solution for immortality."

"I know that too, Albert. But . . ."

"She believed everything. She signed all the legal documents allowing the procedure and agreeing to secrecy and anonymity. But something happened Alberto failed to consider."

"What," Elliott asked.

"Betty and I fell in love. And never underestimate the power of a mother to protect her babies. Betty left us because it was the only way all of us could live. Her only leverage was the contract, the most damning evidence. If revealed, it would bring down Gilgamesh. Alberto failed to consider the ramifications of that legal document going public. They were so busy binding Betty Duncan that they revealed an illegal operation exposing eleven board members with eleven signatures."

"I wondered why they didn't follow through with their plan to euthanize Adam at birth—the defective progeny. Betty took control in Pecos."

"She had to release you and Jack so she could take Adam and give him what Gilgamesh never would. They relocated to Carrollton, Texas. We both know what happened there."

Elliott sighed. "Adam didn't kill those people in Carrollton."

"I thought . . ."

"Gilgamesh did. It was all about the birth of Kayne. They feared another Adam in the world more than the damning documents Betty held over their heads for thirteen years. Alberto Bella sent his minions to Texas to kill Adam, Kayne, Betty, and witnesses."

"Instead, they ran into Adam," Albert said under his breath.

"Adam killed for the first time. He was protecting his mother and newborn son."

"We've all been manipulated masterfully," Albert said. "It has to stop now."

"Bolivar will kill her, Albert. She is an even greater threat today."

"It is no different for you or me." Albert saw Elliott's eyes in the scant light. They were somewhere between anger and pain.

"Son, I don't expect you to like this . . . Your mother is taking an enormous risk. But I do expect you to respect her right to make her own decisions. Betty is a smart lady with much taken from her in life. I worry too, but I support her decisions and will do my best to . . ."

"To protect her," Elliott said as he rocked on his heels.

"She will stay at the mansion. We have increased security. You need to know your mother, and I need to be with the woman I love."

"I guess we could use more help dealing with Gilgamesh."

Albert wiped his eyes with a neatly folded handkerchief. "Is Marcus Medino meeting us? I certainly hope you have a plan to find this GICC needle in a catacomb haystack."

Elliott tapped his flashlight. The beam fell in Albert's direction and stopped above his left shoulder. A dark figure took shape—the head touching the rotted, ceiling boards.

"Are we on our own down here?" Albert asked pocketing his soiled handkerchief.

"I think we're getting some help."

Albert's eyes slowly climbed Elliott and stopped. He remembered that look.

"Your other son is here . . ."

SEVENTEEN

"Adam's here?" Albert whispered.

The glow of Elliott's flashlight washed over the broad chest and touched the edges of Adam's chiseled jaw, cheekbones, and brow. The black, marble eyes devoured light like a panther hunting at night.

Elliott approached cautiously, still unsure. "I see Marcus made contact . . ."

Albert touched Adam's rock hard chest below the torn hole in his black leather coat. Adam's eyes dropped but his head did not move.

Elliott saw the hole, too. He opened Adam's coat and shined the light. "May I?" Adam gave a single nod. The blood stained, cotton shirt had a matching circular tear. "This is from Alberto's gun. He did hit you."

Adam blinked once.

Elliott passed the flashlight to Albert, unbuttoned Adam's shirt, and leaned in. "I've never seen this before," he muttered. "Not even with me." Without leaving his point of view, he reached back and lifted Albert's light an inch. "Please hold it right there, if you would."

Pink skin surrounded the silver disc smaller than a dime. "Don't move, Adam." With eyes locked Elliott pulled a small leather case from his coat. The zipper yelped. Inside he had everything a forensic investigator could want at a death scene—scissors, tweezers, a scalpel, magnifying ruler, Q-tips, eye-dropper, thermometer, ampules of alcohol and formalin, gauze squares, surgical tape, needles and surgical thread, and an assortment of small plastic baggies.

"What is it?" Albert asked.

With tweezers Elliott gripped the edges of the metallic disc that protruded a quarter-inch from Adam's skin. "It's a .38 Remington slug embedded in the pectoralis major." He rocked it. "I'm breaking skin adhesions. It's been there a while." With his free hand he passed Albert one small plastic baggy. "Hold it open for me, if you would."

"Certainly. I'm not a doctor, but before you start yanking things out of Adam's chest shouldn't you give him pain killer?"

Elliott's eyes jumped to Adam's. "You okay?"

Adam blinked twice.

"We're good. Not gonna be anywhere near his pain threshold." Elliott pulled and rocked the slug. "Remember the third shot, Adam closing on Alberto?"

"Oh God, yes. I will never forget it. Adam was on top of Alberto's gun when it fired. I thought he was . . ."

"The last bullet did find him." A clear, pale-yellow drop of serum rolled from the wound down Adam's chest as the slug loosened. "This is like pulling a molar."

"But he didn't . . ."

"Although most of that night's still a blur, I remember seeing the bullet hole in Adam's coat. I told him. He said it was not a problem for him. Now I think I know why."

The slug broke free. "There she blows," Elliott said triumphantly.

"That doesn't look like a bullet to me," Albert said as he dropped it in the baggie.

"Bullets change shape when they make contact. Analysis of projectile deformation is an art. This one ran into a wall of meshed steel." He smiled at Adam.

"I don't understand," Albert pushed. "How does a bullet stop on a man's chest? You and Collin were shot with the same gun, the same bullet. Both of you had to be rushed to the hospital. You almost bled to death, and Collin's paralyzed, clinging to life."

Elliott's eyes stayed on the wound. "The bullet did not penetrate the chest muscle." He pressed the surrounding skin. "Adam's body is rejecting the bullet like a sliver in a finger. The bullet wound is almost healed—slight inflammation and no infection." Elliott rinsed the wound with a few drops of alcohol and taped gauze.

"Are you saying his chest muscles are like meshed steel . . . like human armor?"

He pocketed the baggie with the slug. "That's exactly what I am saying." Elliott squeezed Adam's shoulder. "You're gonna live." One corner of Adam's mouth moved up.

"I'm very confused by all of this," Albert said.

"Just another gift, compliments of a clandestine genetic engineering program," Elliott teased. *I wonder what others you possess, and what we share.*

"What kind of *gift* stops a bullet?" Albert asked.

"Without a detailed analysis, I can only make an educated guess."

"I need to understand. I must get my head around this new world I'm entering."

"I'll dispense with the medical jargon, and try to explain what you just witnessed. The effectiveness of any muscle is determined by the type and nature of the tissue fibers involved, and the intensity and timing of recruited strength. I suspect Adam's muscles are comprised of unique type II—fast twitch—fibers with high concentrations of actin and myosin optimizing tensile strength. In other words, they are capable of producing enormous, contractive forces."

"And that made his chest muscle impenetrable?"

"Like biologic Kevlar, but there's more. Muscles are not contracted all the time, only when they are called into action. The speed necessary to react to an incoming bullet is so excessive it tells me Adam's skeletal muscles are able to function without conscious thought. His sensory nerves collect information—like a bullet is coming—and without conscious thought his brain sends commands to the involved muscles in milliseconds."

"And that's different from everybody else?"

"Yes. Very different. And I suspect there's even more going on. Like most things in our world, the human body is complex. We don't understand a lot. Adam and I are new territory."

"That's what genetic engineering is all about?"

"Yes, to enhance biologic expression through genetic manipulation. But more often than not, outcomes are unexpected. We have some planned enhancements, but most are unplanned: unmeasurable IQ, eidetic memory, acute senses, ESP, and more. If it were all predictable, Adam and I would share all genetic gifts. We don't. My muscles don't stop bullets, but we both recover from traumatic injury rapidly. And there are gifts we have not yet discovered."

Elliott turned back to Adam. "You all right?"

"Yes," he said in a low, firm voice, lips and eyes still.

"Good. I like a man of few words." He patted Adam on a deltoid. "And our gifts come with strings, another topic for another time."

Albert turned to Adam. "You've lived down here a very long

time—your home, I know. Maybe a change one day. You do not need to live alone in these cold, dark tunnels. When you are ready, Adam, I hope you will consider my home. It is your home now."

Albert knew his wish was a long shot, but he had to begin the process of bringing Adam into the world or he would lose him again.

Adam's face did not reveal thoughts. He said, "This is good for me . . . now."

Uncomfortable with the awkward moment, both Albert and Elliott looked down.

"Is my mother coming here?" Adam asked.

Did Adam ask about Betty? Does he have feelings, or is he curious. "Your mother is coming to Memphis," Albert said. "She asked for you, Adam. She wants to see you." *Maybe you can have a normal life. Maybe you are not forever lost in a world I will never know. I must be patient, but I must always pull him forward —I'm his father.*

"Betty has been hiding most of her life, like you, Adam."

"Does she know Kayne is dead?"

"She knows. It is very hard for her," Albert whispered.

"And she knows who killed Kayne," Elliott said. Adam buttoned his shirt. The muscles on his hands rolled to his forearms with each finger movement.

"Although Gilgamesh is dying now, our mother still faces danger by coming here."

Adam moved closer to Elliott and Albert for the first time. They looked up at the man they once feared and were now beginning to understand. His words were strong. His tone was firm. His face was on the edge of transforming into the Butcher. He said, "Gilgamesh tried to kill my mother and Kayne in Texas. I protected them. Nothing changes when she comes here."

The three stood in silence in the dark, dirt room thirty-feet underground. The reality of the gathering storm grew with Adam's words. It was clear more people were going to die, and failure was a real possibility.

Albert dropped his head like a marathon runner unable to finish the race. *I don't know how I survived these horrific tragedies. How can I live through what is coming? I've lost everybody dear to me. All I have left are my two sons and Betty, the only woman I ever loved. Their lives are in jeopardy . . . as are the lives of many others swept into this nightmare.*

Elliott watched Adam place his hand on Albert's shoulder. *You too can hear the thoughts of others*, Elliott thought. *You're not an empty vessel. I'm beginning to know the man inside. Can you hear me? If you can, thank you for comforting our father. He is overwhelmed with pain. He fears for us. He is searching for strength.*

Adam's eyes moved to Elliott—*I understand*. Only Elliott heard him.

A flash of light swept over a distant dirt wall. Elliott turned off his light and they watched it move closer and grow brighter. Then they saw its source.

Like a wild animal preparing for a kill, Adam shifted weight, lowered his head, and leaned forward. With eyes focused on the shadow behind the light, his left hand dropped to his side, leather coat opened, and the blade of the butcher knife caught the scant light in the black soup. It flashed the familiar, shivering shape. Albert and Elliott backed to the wall. They would soon witness the horrific skills of the Bluff City Butcher.

EIGHTEEN

"Elliott Sumner? God, I hope it's you."

Marcus Medino. Elliott touched Adam's left arm. His coat closed. "Marcus. Over here." He clicked his penlight and moved it in a circle.

Marcus walked to the tiny light looking back. "I was a bit apprehensive. Thought I heard others down here. Thought I found them instead of you. That would have been a problem." They embraced. "Good to see you again, Dr. Sumner."

"Albert, this is Marcus Medino."

Marcus extended a hand. "The Bell patriarch. It is a real privilege to meet you, sir."

"And it is very nice to meet you too, Dr. Medino. Elliott shared with me your harrowing escape from Nashville, Patterson House I believe."

"I would have been taken for sure. Dr. Sumner came into my life at precisely the right time. I suppose miracles do happen after all."

"Then sir, I believe you've had a few," Albert said with a serene smile.

"Father's discovery. Yes, sir. Of course. And please call me Marcus. 'Dr. Medino' is reserved for my father."

Albert nodded as Marcus's eyes found and climbed the most intimidating shadow in the tunnel. He never forgot the eyes. With a respect and familiarity, he dipped his head. "Hello, Adam. I see you found my note."

Adam nodded once.

"It has been a long time," Marcus said.

"You left him a note?" Elliott said.

"You asked me to invite Adam. I had no idea where he would be, but I knew he was somewhere down here, this giant ant farm for grownups. I left a note—time, place, and some other relevant details. You see . . . we have a chalk board my father used. It's in one of the chambers, the tissue culture lab. Years ago we dedicated a corner of it for messages. It worked well because we were often in different parts of the catacombs or out of town."

"I got your message," Adam said. Marcus jumped.

"You can talk. I've never heard you talk." He turned to Elliott. "I didn't think he could speak. Not that I ever asked. But Adam never spoke when I was around so I assumed . . ."

"I suspect there's a lot we don't know about Adam," Albert said with a smile.

"We need to get busy." Elliott pointed his pitiful light up the tunnel. "Marcus, we've got time constraints. It could already be too late."

"What's this about?"

"International authorities are hunting the three surviving Gilgamesh board members. They are wanted for their connection to eighty-six deaths over five decades. Suffice it to say the evidence against them is substantial."

"I know some of the Gilgamesh board members through my father. They tried to recruit him to head up their research program in the 1960s and 1970s. He mentioned some of them."

"Did he tell you why he did not join Gilgamesh?" Albert asked.

"He wanted his independence. And, he didn't trust Mr. Bella." Marcus slid his hands into his pockets and stared into the dark tunnel. "Mr. Bella ordered my father's death. Mr. Bolivar led the effort. My father would have died years ago if it were not for Adam." He flickered his eyes at the intimidating figure and then back to Albert and Elliott. "Who are the three . . . left?"

"Mobuto Ali, Robert Armstrong, and Francisco Bolivar," Elliott said.

"Mr. Bolivar sent more than a hundred trained assassins to kill my father. Each one was stopped, but Mr. Bolivar never did. He was relentless."

"The three are somewhere in Cape Town."

"What does South Africa have to do with the catacombs in Memphis?"

"They're hell-bent on resurrecting Gilgamesh. Cape Town is connected."

"Do they have anti-aging biotechnology?" Marcus asked.

"Not yet," Elliott said. "Alberto died trying to steal your father's research. The surviving board members are wasting no time. They've already tried to kill me twice, and they've attacked the Bell mansion. So far we've been fortunate."

"After they eliminate us they will take your father's breakthrough," Albert said.

"At the moment, however, they seem to be focused on securing the Gilgamesh global information control center—the GICC. There are two, one in Memphis and the other in . . ."

"Don't tell me—Cape Town."

"Precisely," Elliott said. "We have a small window, Marcus. Bolivar is waiting for GICC access codes. Once he has them, the Memphis portal will go down—game over."

"They regain control of their stealth global network," Marcus mumbled. Elliott's eyes left Marcus. He looked deeper into the tunnel. Adam turned slowly.

"If they retake control of the GICC, they regain all the advantages lost when Alberto and the other seven board members perished. My dissolution efforts would come to a halt, and the three in Cape Town would be unstoppable."

"They disappear with a global operation. They complete their mission," Marcus said. "You think the Memphis GICC is down here, Mr. Bell?"

"I'm certain it is in the catacombs," he said.

"Can you help us, Marcus?" Elliott asked.

"I don't know." The four stood in silence. "Mr. Bell, you attended board meetings."

Adam and Elliott turned to their father. "Yes," he said. "I am a board member."

"I'm sorry about the way that sounded. I was processing. There's no need to explain your involvement. Dr. Sumner educated me on our way from Nashville."

Since his arrival, Marcus had watched how Adam and Elliott looked at their newfound father. He knew they could not fake the admiration and trust they felt for the Bell patriarch. Even if Marcus had some doubts, they would be gone now. The bond was true, and Albert Bell's presence tamed the genius monster.

"I recall very little about GICC," Albert said. "I remember Alberto ranting over the importance of protecting it. The catacombs were mentioned as a potential site."

"Marcus, your knowledge of this place can help—can narrow down our search area. We must find it and install shields to block Cape Town."

"It's been so long, and this place is complex. I spent all my time in a small part, always afraid of getting lost. I did not want to die underground—not the explorer type."

"I understand. Just do the best you can."

Marcus walked several tight circles. When he stopped, he shook his arms and high-stepped in place as if ready to run a race. "Sorry, not good with pressure," he said. "Okay. I had a system, my way of navigating this dark, cold, miserable place."

"That's a start. Now relax," Elliott said closing his eyes. "What was your way?"

"I found a map," Marcus said.

Elliott's eyes popped open. "You found a map of the catacombs?"

Marcus pulled the eight-inch paper tube from his coat and unrolled. Elliott aimed his penlight on the glossy document. There were thick black marker lines, dotted lines, fine squiggly lines, letters, and some symbols—a solid black square, a square with diagonal lines, a pyramid, sets of double bars and circles, and the letters "M" and "D".

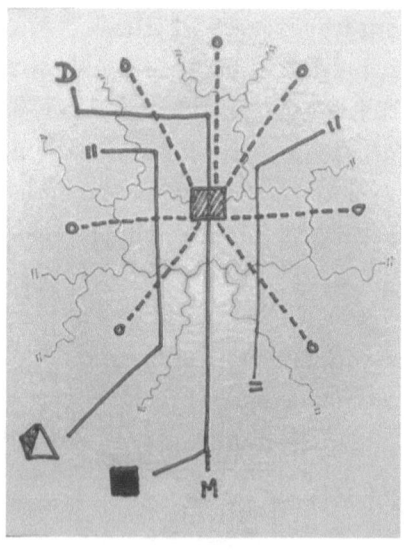

"Where did you find this?" Elliott asked.

"One day, waiting for my father to arrive from Nashville, I

ventured out on my own. For years I stayed in the three chambers where we worked. Beyond those chambers and associated tunnels things got unsafe and confusing fast. On that day I got up the courage to explore some. I felt my way down one of the large tunnels, maybe a hundred feet or so. I stayed close to the wall dragging my hand. I felt a crevice. I reached inside and found this map. I don't know who it belongs to, but I took it. Last night I remembered where I hid it."

"What can you tell us about the lines and symbols?" Elliott asked.

"It's not to scale, but the relationships are close. The square in the middle of the map is the Brent mansion—the hub of the catacomb universe. These dotted lines emanating out from the mansion are the drainage pipes—there are seven." Marcus put his finger on the north pipe. "You and Albert came here by way of this one. We are standing here."

"This helps," Elliott said.

"There are three main corridors. One is the western corridor, one the central corridor, and this is the eastern corridor. These squiggly lines are naturally formed tunnels. They are most of the catacombs. Those on this map are charted majors. Most are uncharted. The double bars means the tunnel continues."

"I assume 'M' is for Memphis."

"Yes. The solid black box is the break from the central corridor to downtown Memphis."

"And the western corridor's southern leg goes under the Memphis Pyramid Arena?"

"According to the map, it goes across that geography beneath the Wolf River and to Mud Island. This is an old map. The Memphis Pyramid Arena was not constructed until the 1990's."

"What does 'D' stand for?" Albert asked.

"Dyersburg. The northern leg of the central corridor goes up the Mississippi River Valley fifty miles. I read about tunnels and underground rivers," Marcus said.

"The evolution of the Mississippi River is incredible," Elliott said. "The subterranean changes are as astounding as the surface changes over millions of years."

Marcus passed the map to Elliott. "All natural tunnels appear to connect to the three major corridors. Is that a correct interpretation of this map?" he asked.

"Yes. And there are more than shown here. I got lost in some."

"What else is missing?" asked Elliott.

"The chambers—or dirt rooms—are offshoots from the tunnels and corridors. Some have large, obvious entries, others are hidden. One time I counted thirty chambers in a fifty-yard diameter circle under the Brent estate. They have an entrance and an exit. Some were used by Gilgamesh, some by me and my father, and others were never used."

"How do you know?" Albert asked.

"Look down."

"This powdered dirt is everywhere."

"In places it is deep. Footprints are swallowed in a day."

"Then how do you know if a chamber has been used?"

"I got good. I shine a light over the soft dirt bed and interpret irregularities. It takes years to eliminate all signs of activity."

Elliott passed the map back. He memorized every detail and would revise with real time experience. "I've got it. Anything else you can tell us before we get started?"

"There is one thing about this map you need to keep in mind. It does not show the levels of tunnels and chambers. It's one dimensional. I learned the hard way."

"Where would Gilgamesh put the GICC?" Elliott wondered aloud.

"We stayed in the northwest sector of the catacombs, off the central corridor fifty yards from the Brent mansion. Gilgamesh stayed in the other two corridors. They avoided our corridor."

"Why, because it was uncharted?" Albert asked.

"Because bodies of Gilgamesh assassins were stacked there."

"You would think with all their resources they could have stopped Adam," Elliott said.

Adam stared.

"It was not from a lack of trying," Marcus said. "I suspect the risk got too great. They did not want to jeopardize the rest of the operation."

"I suggest we first look in the western and eastern corridors," Albert said.

"Good idea. Makes sense," Marcus said. "Would be the heart of the operation—want accessibility and a location they could protect."

"And it would have Wi-Fi. Could be close. Albert took a phone call down here."

"There are some chambers a few hundred yards out."

Elliott raised his hand. "And we may not be alone. They could be guarding the GICC, even in hibernation mode. Guards may be oblivious to Gilgamesh's deteriorating situation."

"Would explain, if it's not destroyed," Marcus said.

Albert muttered. "Or, access could be limited."

"The three board members can't come to Memphis," Elliott said. "Alberto could be the only one here with codes—now he's dead. Stephen Grendel—the IT Officer in a London jail cell—is the last man standing with codes. Gotta find the GICC before Grendel and Bolivar connect."

Floating particles in moving beams led their way down the irregular passages. Sudden drops, steep climbs, and tight narrows made the short journey more than strenuous. When the tunnel leveled and straightened, they neared the Brent mansion and target zone.

Marcus led. Albert was next, and then Elliott. Adam trailed the threesome thirty yards behind in the black. When their light found stacks of dust laden boxes lining the carved dirt walls, Marcus knew they were near chambers that could hold the GICC.

* * *

After a week of waiting in the dark, the five Gilgamesh special ops hunkered down in the uncharted tunnel connecting the western and central corridors. The environmental-controlled chamber twenty feet below the Brent mansion sat twenty yards behind the guards. Inside the dirt room, under a dust-laden tarp, the Wi-Fi modem flickered by the Memphis GICC.

Wearing specialized, underground combat gear, the five guarded the asset with strict orders to stop anything that moved. When the GICC initializing process began, the soldiers did not see the green lights pop on, or hear the soft hum of the primary cooling fan. They were too busy monitoring the bouncing light coming their way. Their commander counted three and signaled lights off, night-vision goggles on, and earpieces in. They unlocked AK-47 assault rifles. Now there was one path. The five slid behind the wall of boxes and raised their weapons.

NINETEEN

"Suspicion is the courageous side of weakness."
Unknown

Cape Town, South Africa

"Eduardo, how much farther up this damn mountain," Tony barked. The South African guide was provided by a trusted friend of Maxwell's, a counter intelligence specialist on assignment during the Soweto uprising in '76.

"We have three hundred meters to go." He pushed forward up the steep, narrow trail with the Memphis homicide detective close behind. Farther back, Max labored next to two others with automatic rifles on their shoulders. The moonlight broke through the trees enough to light the trail, but the climb proved to be more treacherous than either imagined, especially Max.

"Anthony. Stop. I need a moment. Take a smoke break." Max sat on a rock.

"I guess a short break won't hurt." Tony went back, lit two cigarettes, and passed one to Max. Eduardo and the two rifles moved further up the trail and waited.

"You okay with these guys?" Tony asked.

Max took a long drag and exhaled slow. "I am okay with Eduardo. Keep your eyes on the other two," he whispered. The two looked back. Max held up three fingers. They nodded.

"Shit, I had the same bad feelin'. Keep your gun safety off. Don't hesitate to shoot the bastards. If I was hiding up here, I'd keep an eye on this damn trail. You said Devil's Peak is the last place your people saw the three assholes."

"On the plane I had an opportunity to study satellite images and maps of the region—changing topography, history of the place."

"Gee, sounds like fun, Max."

"I think the board members are hiding in the mountain, Anthony."

"No kidding. I'll be damned. What makes you think that?"

"Satellite images over the last three decades. Looking five years apart I see changes in the exposed mineral deposits. They're isolated . . . the southwest base of the mountain."

"What the hell does it mean?"

"Could mean nothing. I'm no geologist. However, it could mean someone's been digging and spreading the debris. Based on what I see, it appears there's a lot of debris fanning out from the focal point on the ridge, the Dutch church we've all heard about."

"Let's get going. We need to get up there. If they live in the damn mountain, their front door is somewhere in the church. I read six dead people were found in that church—some bullshit ghost story, legend of Dutch djinn."

"Someone could be manipulating the local populous."

"Tryin' to keep them stirred up and away from the place."

Tony jumped to his feet and helped Max off the rock. They climbed to Eduardo and pointed *go*.

Eduardo looked back and said, "We reach top in twenty minutes. We rest end of trail. We then go to church. Is good for you, Maxwell Gregory?"

"Yes, is good for me. Please proceed."

"Good for me too, Eduardo," *you sneaky sons of bitches.* Tony looked back and winked at Max gasping for air.

The small Dutch Church fifty meters from the top of the trail sat on a rock ledge at the base of Devil's Peak. Tony took a knee at the edge of the trail and scanned the area. He also kept an eye on the guys with the rifles. Max raked up a handful of dirt and shined his light on the small pile, his glasses balanced at the end of his nose.

"Eduardo . . . you three go to church. Check for us. We do not know what we are walking into. You know this land. Go. Be careful. We wait here. We make phone calls. Comprende'?"

Eduardo nodded, flashing a big smile. The three moved forward through the spear grass fanning out with their rifles still on their shoulders. Eduardo held his pistol in a bent arm and looked back at Max several times. A cloud blocked the moon. The tops of the trees moved.

"What's got you nervous, boss?" Tony asked. You sent those guys off pretty quick. You left the script." He knelt next to Max who pretended to be on his cell phone. "I don't know about those two guys," Tony whispered. "They may not be the problem I thought. They don't seem interested in any of this."

"They don't appear to know how to hold a rifle either," Max said. He opened his hand. "This is TMS—hard, uniformly resistant Table Mountain Sandstone found in the region. Look close at the granules, Anthony."

"And I should see what?"

"There are chards of Malmesbury Shale and Cape Granite."

"If you say so, Max."

"Those are older rocks, geologically speaking. They weather much faster than TMS. That's why you don't see it as a surface rock. It's weathered away over eons, leaving the TMS. Malmesbury Shale and Cape Granite only exist underground . . . beneath the more durable TMS."

"And that's important why?"

"You would not find an equal volume of all three on the ground, Anthony."

"You're losing me, my friend."

"I've seen all three on the climb. A few times I left the trail and found higher concentrations of the shale and granite on top of the sandstone. They were purposely deposited off the trail, out of sight, over a long period of time. I would guess two or three decades."

"You believe it came from inside the mountain?"

"Debris from excavation. I am certain it came from the core of Devil's Peak."

"The bastards dug a hole in the damn mountain," Tony seethed.

"If Gilgamesh sought to establish a second, stealth base of operation, one as understood and secure as the catacombs in Memphis, they could duplicate it here, Anthony."

"A backup headquarters in Devil's Peak, how appropriate. Perfect name."

"Mobuto Ali is well respected in Cape Town. If he had to find a safe place for a GICC, this mountain range is perfect . . . However, at the moment, this is but a theory."

They turned to the stone church sitting on the other side of the open field of spear grass. Max dropped the handful of mixed sands and brushed his palm on a pant leg. "I believe we found them."

"Time to join our guides," Tony said stepping out his cigarette and checking his gun.

"Anthony."

"Yes, Maxwell."

"If the theory is correct, we are being watched . . ."

TWENTY

"He who controls the past controls the future. He who controls the present controls the past."
George Orwell

For the privileged, one night is unbearable. The three board members were on their third in the old, Dutch church on Devil's Peak. They had no other choice. The codes were the key. Taking back their GICC made them unstoppable.

Armstrong stood at a west window watching the shimmering lights of Cape Town on the coast. Mobuto stood at the east window in the nave. Although his view was less mesmerizing, it was the most important. Mobuto had a view of the only trail up Devil's Peak.

Above the bending bushwillows and rustling tamboti, Genadendal glowed. He remembered the sparkling town as a boy, hunting large game in the jungles of South Africa. Now Mobuto was a man with skills honed over a lifetime growing up in danger—a world where a walk in the night could be your last. Now Mobuto was a hunter of men. Now he studied the forty meters of rolling spear grass between the church and trail.

Francisco sat on an old, wood chair checking the reception bars on his cell phone. It was strong, but still no word. "Gentlemen, I have a dreadful feeling we cannot put Humpty Dumpty back together again." He sunk sliding his cell back into his pocket.

"Why would you say that?" Armstrong asked. Mobuto's eyes stayed in the spear grass.

"We may never salvage our science—decades of research gone. We were very close. And now a blasted floodlight pours over our organization as we sit in this God-forsaken place vulnerable to the common people, the masses we've avoided all our lives. And Albert Bell lives. He has never been on our side. The man knows too much. He loathes everything we stand for."

"We killed two of Albert's blood lions, Francisco. What do you expect?"

"Albert Bell will dismantle Gilgamesh and eradicate membership. With his grandfather dead and gone, everything depends on us. I don't think we can do this."

Mobuto's eyes were inches from the cracked, window pane when he spoke. His words rolled through the dark, cold room with chilling strength. "When we enter heart of Devil's Peak, we take back what belong to us." His breath fogged the glass. He wiped it with his arm and leaned closer. "We not de Humpty Dumpty."

Francisco shook his head and checked his phone again. "You know Albert is rounding up our members right now. He's demanding they be in Memphis for a meeting."

"They know nothing," Armstrong chuckled watching the lights sparkle.

"I'm worried about Dr. Sumner," Francisco said. "He's too

smart. He will locate our people around the world. I bet he's looking for the GICC in Memphis now."

"We kill Sumner and Bell," Mobuto said into the glass with a flat smile.

"Well, the Dyersburg plan didn't work. And the team sent to the Bell mansion cannot confirm kills. I suppose time will tell," Francisco said.

"The Henley twins are stupid," Armstrong said. "They need to go before they expose all of us. And using the Garrett Farm is a huge error. That place needs to stay dark."

"We must keep the pressure on. Now we are doing nothing, just sitting and waiting while our people get picked up. They're going to start talking to save themselves. The Memphis police have the TEA lists—everyone is looking for us."

"I wish they had a bead on you now," Armstrong said under his breath.

"We not do Alberto mistakes," Mobuto said. "We use all resources. We move fast like tiger. Alberto too slow. Alberto fail. Alberto dead."

"Why did he let Albert Bell get out of our control?" Armstrong said.

"Albert Bell had no interest in Gilgamesh or our mission. Alberto's plan from the start was to keep him in the dark. He wanted Albert Bell positioned to manage the new world order."

"When we secure biogenic immortality, we will decide who gets it. That is about as close to absolute power anyone can get."

"Yes. We then determine who lives and who dies. The face on Gilgamesh must be one that promotes trust, not one that generates fear. History has taught us well."

"We kill Albert Bell," Mobuto grumbled. "We find Marcus Medino and father research."

"Make no mistake," Francisco said. "With Adam Duncan

dead and gone, Dr. Sumner is our nemesis. He is more of a problem than his brothers."

"He strongest blood lion. But he not know," Mobuto said.

"We best terminate Sumner before he figures it out," Francisco said.

"I'm freezing." Armstrong cupped hands and blew. "I heard rumors Adam Duncan killed Alberto. What do we know about that? And why do you guys keep saying they are blood lions? What the hell is a blood lion?"

"Why you think Adam Duncan alive?" Mobuto asked.

"The story I got . . . Adam stopped Alberto from killing Sumner and Bell. Nobody's talking public about it, but rumors are flowing."

"Why you think Adam Duncan?"

"Alberto was killed with a butcher knife in the chest and out his back."

"There's no way Adam Duncan did it. He is dead," Francisco said.

"How can you be so sure?"

"Because I watched him die on December 23 at the Bell mansion." He got in Armstrong's face. "How is it you don't know this, Armstrong?"

He backed away. "I've been busy." He returned to the window and Cape Town's shimmering lights on the coast. "I have a life outside of Gilgamesh." After a long silence he turned around to glaring eyes. "What happened December 23?"

"We thought we had Medino's research. It was time to terminate Sumner and Bell. We manipulated Adam—he believed Albert and Elliott were responsible for Dr. Medino's death. Adam believed Albert and Elliott were Gilgamesh members. He was half right."

"But they're alive and Adam is dead. What went wrong?"

Francisco sighed. "That night in the study, Adam learned

Albert Bell was his biologic father and Elliott Sumner his biologic brother. The information overwhelmed him. Adam jumped from the balcony onto a spire—killed himself. After twenty minutes of groaning on that metal shaft, blood running down the side of the mansion, the man died. I stayed until they moved him off the roof. Watched them load the stiff corpse onto the ambulance. It crawled down Bell's driveway like a hearse in a cemetery."

"Adam dead," Mobuto said.

Armstrong rubbed his chin. "Why does everyone refer to the Bell males as *blood lions*?

"You really should attend more board meetings, Robert," Francisco mused.

"De Bell patriarch always lion—King of de jungle."

"The first male born of each generation carries the immortality gene. We have been taking blood samples from Albert and the triplets for decades, stealth of course—bogus doctor visits, physicals, blood donation, and the like. We extract the stem cells from the blood. It has fueled our research for fifty years. We are trying to replicate the phenomenon."

"Alberto Bella's stem cells never work," Mobuto said.

"How inconvenient," Armstrong shot back.

"And we have not been able to replicate the blood lions either," Francisco said. "And that is why we turned to Dr. Medino's research. He approached biogenic immortality differently. He believed the solution had something to do with creating the early stage cell environment. He believed protection of DNA promoted repair and continuous cell replacement. He was right."

"Is that why Alberto Bella was killed at the Bell mansion?" Armstrong asked.

"Albert Bell had Dr. Medino's hard drive with instructions for the anti-aging biologic. On that hard drive was formulation, raw materials, compounding methodology, dispersal parameters and administering protocol."

"How is it you know this?"

"Alberto called from the Bentley on his way to the Bell mansion." Francisco checked his phone. "He told us everything. The man was too excited. He lost judgment that night."

Mobuto held up a hand and leaned to the glass. A shadow stepped from the trail and crouched beneath the largest tamboti. It shifted and hid behind another. Then another shadow emerged from the trail, and then another. He saw a light—maybe a cell phone. Then it went out. Two shadows stopped at the top of the trail and knelt. Mobuto unbuttoned his coat and unsnapped his holster—his .357 magnum had a full load. On his belt were seven more clips, nine rounds each.

"Armstrong . . . de guards we posted . . . bring them to me now," Mobuto ordered.

Armstrong ran out the north door into the shadows. Francisco's cell phone vibrated. The letters on his screen made him smile—STEPHEN GRENDEL. "This is the call we've been waiting for." He crossed the nave to a dark corner of the church.

Eyes locked on moving targets, Mobuto waved behind his head as Armstrong approached with the three, tall, skinny South Africans holding rifles—contract killers. Two would position low on the east windows and find targets. The third would climb into the rafters.

Across the room Francisco held his phone to his ear with his back to the action. Mobuto pointed outside. "I see five." He eased away from the moonlight pouring through his window into the dark church.

Armstrong watched Mobuto's thumb rub the steel barrel of the automatic and asked, "How are you going to do this? We don't need a crazy shootout that attracts attention up here."

Mobuto smiled and turned to the shooters. "Three spread out

—de stand in de spear grass. Two sit at top of trail. Like de lion wait for prey, we let come to us."

As they screwed silencers onto their rifles, the South Africans smiled at the pathetic man named Armstrong. Mobuto stepped between them and whispered, "First, shoot three. Put bodies by back door—no leave in field. Then we wait for clear shots, the two at top of trail. They not move until must."

The white eyes of the dark Africans danced as barrels slid out windows and scopes adjusted. Many years ago, a single pane of glass was removed from each window of the old church. The oddity never appeared in a Cape Town police report . . .

TWENTY-ONE

"What the f . . ." Tony yelled as he pulled Max down. Three bullets zipped by clipping the blades inches above their heads. "Stay low. They've got us in their sights."

"Did not hear the first shot. Silencers. Good eyes, Anthony," Max said with the calm of one meeting for drinks after a long day at the office. Life with the agency had dulled his senses.

Tony popped his head up three times before another bullet zipped by. "Bastards. Couldn't make out much but got enough." He looked back at Max. "We're getting close to something, my fearless warrior."

Max pivoted on his belly. If he was going to get hit, he preferred the butt instead of head. "It appears they're not inclined to welcome visitors this evening. Too soon after they lured locals for the removal of their dead tourist from beneath the upside-down cross."

"Wonderful. We're battling Satan." Tony pointed to the woods. "Follow me." He pivoted on his stomach, pulled with his elbows, and pushed with his legs. "I saw a gully along the edge of those trees. We need to get into it now."

Max followed like an old walrus on dry land. "I'm not as physical as I once was. My last decade with the agency was cerebral." Two more bullets zipped overhead.

"Well, tell your brain to tell your ass to get into gear and stay low."

"Silencers in the wilderness, a strong indicator we're dealing with Gilgamesh or some derivative thereof," Max grunted between pulls, his face touching the ground.

"Pretty clear they don't want to create a ruckus up here, something that could spill into Cape Town and attract attention. They don't want people poking around tonight."

"Their desired outcome, in these wee hours, is termination and disposal."

"They'll grind our asses into little pieces and spread us like Malmesbury shale and Cape Granite—the billionaire bastards." Tony reached the gully and dropped a couple feet below field level. "This is deeper than I thought—perfect. Hurry, Max."

"Good that you picked up on things quickly back there, Anthony."

"Saw the flash and pulled you down. Not a big deal. Thank God the assholes can't aim worth a shit. They had three opportunities to hit one of us sittin' there big as you please."

Max flopped into the gulley. His long, gray hair flipped forward onto his sweat and dirt covered brow. He pushed it back, and then glasses up the bridge of his nose, and brushed his filthy suit. "Did you get a look at our shooters?"

"Saw two guys. Didn't look like ours. These projectiles humming by are high velocity hollow-points—got that telltale whistle. I checked our boys' ammo before the climb. They don't have hollow-points."

"Very good, Anthony. On occasion, your intellectual capacity surprises me."

"Well CIA man, if you live long enough you might learn a lot of shit."

They ducked more bullets zipping through the spear grass and into the woods. The flurry disturbed a covey of sandgrouse and stirred some critters in the jungle.

"The bastards are fooled—must not have night vision. They think we're still back there at the top of the trail—idiots."

"I suspect our three friends did not survive." Max wiped his face with an arm.

"You may be right. They didn't get a shot off." Tony pulled out his gun.

"Have you devised a plan, or are you waiting for me?" Max asked.

"I have a multiple choice. Plan A—charge the sonsabitches with guns blazing. Plan B— crawl our asses up this gulley, and sneak up on the sonsabitches. Plan C—retreat. Get back down that trail and get reinforcements. Come back and kick their asses."

"You've noticed our cell phones are dysfunctional?"

"Yes. Jammed. And that pisses me off more. That's why I have proposed Plan A."

"Well then," Max removed his glasses and blew the lenses. Another bullet buzzed inches above his head. He didn't move. "I'm not up for charging with my gun blazing. I'm afraid those days are over."

"Didn't think you'd go for plan A, but I had to try."

"If we depart Devil's Peak we lose the opportunity to neutralize their GICC take-over effort. Therefore, I'm choosing Plan B—the gulley strategy."

"I concur. Enough discussion. Let's start crawling. We may get ten minutes before these snakes slither out here looking for bodies."

They crawled the winding gully pushing through low-hanging limbs, animal feces, nesting reptiles, and a wide assortment of African insects. Ten minutes later they reached the most advantageous stopping point. They watched the first scout leave the stone church low into the spear grass. Seconds later, the next holding a machete entered the grass. They both moved toward the trail like lions hunting caribou.

"Shall I dispose of the two?" Max whispered.

Tony sat up in the tall brush in the shadow of a thick yellowwood tree. Thirty feet away he saw a window of the church and a large black man in the shadows. Tony leaned out as if to assess the progress of their scouts.

"We don't randomly kill people, Max. Take off your CIA hat. We don't do covert, illegal shit. Put on your law enforcement hat. We do things according to law—you know, innocent until proven guilty." He pulled a pen from his pocket and held it to his eye. "We are honorable Americans."

"Is that one of those new, high powered pen-scopes?" Max asked. "I do believe it is. Yet again, you surprise me, Anthony."

Tony acted uninterested, but relished the accolades from the CIA veteran. "I came prepared. I would have thought you'd have a bag of tricks." He crouched and studied the layout.

"What do you see?"

"One fathead inside the church, moving. Nothing outside, yet." He aimed the small scope to the north end of the stone church. "I just found your buddy and our guides . . . back of church." Tony froze. They were in a pile. "They're dead, Max. Bastards killed them . . . all three."

"Now may I dispose of the two who desire to toss us on that pile? It is in our best interest they not return to the church with news of our absence."

"It's them or us. How are you going to dispose of them? They're forty yards out."

Max screwed a silencer on his gun. He attached a mini-scope with a soft click and winked. "Night vision . . ."

"Nice."

Max raised out of the spear grass, shot twice, and squatted back down. In two seconds the two scouts dropped—headshots, base of the spine, immediate paralysis—dead. Max removed his scope and used it to study the church. Without a word, Tony looked through his scope at the church.

"We need to get inside," Max whispered.

"I don't see cameras," Tony said. "I'm sure there are some. Nowadays they can hide shit anywhere. Could look like damn head of a nail or a bug. By the way, that fathead I saw at the window is gone. Haven't seen movement inside for a while."

"I suggest we stay in the tree line shadows on the northeast— the most options with minimal risk of detection."

"Excluding motion detection devices," Tony muttered with his eye to his scope.

The three-quarter moon provided ample light and shadows to navigate. Tony and Max left the yellowwood tree on a direct path to the rear corner of the stone structure. Their line passed one window. They stayed low in the spear grass and moved in concert with the night winds that swept the grounds between Lion's Head and Devil's Peak.

The three guides were shot in the back of the head—with contact wounds. They were captured and executed. Pockets were pulled out and belongings gone. The blood trail led to the north door. With backs to the wall, Tony and Max waited for stillness and quiet except for the rustling treetops.

"I'm checking windows," Tony whispered. "You wait here for me." Max nodded, raising his gun to his chest.

There were three windows on each side of the church. Tony went first to those in the shadow of Devil's Peak. From an edge he could see inside to the front of the church. It was dark and still.

But Tony failed to look up in time to avoid boots crashing down. Dazed, he rolled over to the barrel of a gun and looming shadow.

The gun dropped to the ground and the man fell on Tony. "Need to always look up, son—textbook," Max said as he lowered his gun and helped Tony up. He wiped blood off his hands with his dirty handkerchief. They backed to the church wall.

Tony whispered, "That guy is not the guy I saw in the window. Different head shape."

Max nodded. "We're still not alone."

"Need to get inside the goddamn church . . ."

"I suggest the north door."

Fresh blood on the stoop and grass led to the stacked bodies. Tony stepped over the pile and reached for the knob. He turned. "Unlocked," he whispered.

They entered with guns out. Tony went right, Max left. With backs against the walls they spread out and studied the room. It was thirty feet wide and a hundred long, no ceiling, rafters and the underside of a slate-covered roof. There was no chancel, because the Dutch church never had a choir. The altar was a rickety table with warped legs. The dust-covered, splintered top had a fat candle in the center, and a box of stick matches. Tony picked up the one match on the floor beneath the altar. He smelled it, set it down, and backed into the shadows.

The nave took most of the hundred feet. Except for the front and back rows, a dozen wooded pews laid on their backs, scattered, and with missing legs. A thick layer of disturbed dust covered the floor. Debris from the paramedics and police mixed with the rat droppings, spider webs, and wild animal feces.

"This is not what I expected," Tony whispered forcefully across the nave. "I don't see shit that tells me Gilgamesh has been here . . . except one goddamn match. This looks like just an old, abandoned church in the boonies."

"The first pew and those three chairs have each been sat in," Max said. "The dust on this table has been recently disturbed."

"Could be tourists or paramedics or Cape Town PD. I don't see anything that tells me this is a Gilgamesh asset, except for the welcoming committee."

Max holstered his gun and went to the heavy wooden lectern beside the altar. He ran his hand over the top edge, backed away and studied it from multiple angles. "This is peculiar."

"What're you thinking?" Tony asked looking around the room.

"This is a substantial piece of furniture in an abandoned room of debris."

"It's a goddamn old abandoned church, Max. What're you expecting?"

Max lowered a shoulder and pushed against one side. It did not move. He went to the next side and pushed. Still nothing. Tony joined him on the third side. They pushed, it moved. They looked at each other with eyes darting around the room and reaching for their guns. They pushed more. The lectern slid three feet. When they stood, it returned to its original position.

"What do we have here?" Tony asked.

Max sat in the front pew rubbing his chin. "I do believe we've found a portal into the mountain. And I'm certain it is monitored, Anthony. When we open the trapdoor under this lectern, it will sound an alarm somewhere . . . if we have not already done so."

"That's not a very positive thought, Max."

"Once down the hole they can do just about anything they want—trap us, gas us, shoot us, electrocute us, drown us, or something horrible and painful I have not fathomed."

"Are we being just a little negative tonight?" Tony mused. "Look, we don't have a whole lot of time or options. We gotta go down there to have any chance at shutting down this GICC and maybe finding three rats. We can't let these freaks get up and running, Max."

"There's a very good chance we will not get inside this mountain."

"And there's a chance we will."

Max walked over to Tony. Their eyes met. "This could be our last assignment."

"I understand that, Max. And I say, we create as much hell as we possibly can."

Max smiled. "I concur, Anthony."

They repositioned their shoulders on the lectern and pushed. Max reached down and opened the trapdoor. Tony's gun was ready. Max lifted the door the rest of the way, and they looked into the dark hole. "There's a goddamn metal ladder."

Tony descended. "It's a tunnel, Max. I see dirt walls like the catacombs back home."

Max followed. Halfway down the ladder, the trapdoor closed. Max could hear the lectern sliding back into place.

"Anthony . . . Where are you, Anthony?"

TWENTY-TWO

Memphis, Tennessee

The catacombs were quiet beneath the Brent mansion. They were close. Elliott's light bobbed up and down as they neared the potential site for the GICC. "Something's not right," Elliott whispered. He stopped.

"What's the matter?" Albert asked as Marcus looked for irregularities.

"Where's Adam?" Elliott asked. They pointed the lights back. Nothing.

"He never said he would stay," Marcus said. "Matter of fact, he didn't say anything."

"I should have included him. I didn't ask him about the catacombs. Adam knows this place better than anyone alive." Elliott took a few steps back in the tunnel and called for him. His voice died in the cold, dark tunnel.

"He's not talking to anyone yet," Albert said. "He's beginning to trust. Adam's been living in a world we'll never know. He's been alone a long time."

Elliott stared into the darkness. Albert walked up and gripped his shoulder. He whispered, "Adam would have said something if he had something to say. He understands the importance of stopping Gilgamesh. He will be back when he's ready. We need to be patient with him, son."

I feel you, Adam, Elliott thought. *You're nearby. Why did you leave . . . ?*

"Let's move forward."

Elliott nodded. "Marcus, this place feels different. Where are we right now? And how far are we from our target destination, the chambers?"

Marcus left them and walked to a cluster of dust laden boxes along the wall. He moved his light up and down the side of the stack and touched one box. Rubbing dirt from a corner, two red circles were revealed. He counted boxes forward inspecting each corner.

"We're less than a hundred meters from ground zero, beneath the Brent mansion."

"And why is that important?" Elliott asked.

"Our theory is to look at the chambers offering convenience and defensibility. Under the Brent mansion are what I call spider tunnels—a network of small passages. Because there are so many in all directions, it's easy to get lost around here. It's also the sector with the most connects between the three primary corridors on my map. There are a dozen chambers, too."

Elliott looked down the tunnel one more time for Adam. The *connection* he felt before evaporated. No he felt only a presence.

"Adam would not leave unless he had a good reason. I now know that much about him."

"Do we have time to wait for him?" Albert asked.

"We gotta keep going."

They moved the next fifty meters. Marcus inspected another

set of boxes confirming their location. The tunnel split into three. They took the center one.

What are you doing? I feel your rage. The intense feeling shot through Elliott like an ice spear. *Adam. Don't kill. Please.*

"Turn out the lights now," Elliott whispered.

"I hear something too," Marcus said.

"We keep moving, but no lights. Stay close to me." Elliott led the way. Albert stayed close enough to see him. Marcus followed. They dragged hands on the dirt wall.

Why am I thinking about Barcelona now . . . the dark climb at Aragon and the horrific kill? Elliott forced his eyes to work in the dark. *Are those thoughts a message? Is this a new thing I've not yet experienced—extrasensory perception? Why would Aragon have anything to do with the catacombs and now?"*

The grunts and muffled cries filled the tunnel and vanished so fast one would question if they even happened at all. The sounds of leather scraping across rock, and metal hitting metal, and plastic shattering turned into an eerie silence as if an invisible door closed, or a part of the world broke away.

Marcus's voice broke. "What should we do, Elliott? We're not alone."

"Stop here," Elliott ordered. "I go alone."

Albert grabbed Elliott's arm. "We're going together. You cannot protect all of us anymore. We must do what we came here to do."

Elliott looked over his shoulder knowing Albert's words were reality. He could no longer do it on his own—he tried and failed. He looked back at Albert and nodded.

They moved single file along the dirt wall like blind men until they rounded a bend. Ahead a faint light defined the tunnel and the sloping floor leveled out. The soft layer of dirt covering the floor showed signs of recent disruption—as Marcus described before. Spider tunnels branched in all directions from the main corridor, and more stacks of boxes lined the wall ahead.

As they neared the boxes, sounds came from several locations. Was someone whispering orders? Could Gilgamesh soldiers be talking unaware of their presence? The three froze at the edge of the soft light. Did they walk into a Gilgamesh camp? Were they too deep to turn around? Maybe no one saw or heard them approaching?

The large shadow stepped form the wall into the light and stood at the center of the main corridor. Albert and Marcus knelt down behind Elliott . . .

"You can use lights now," he said motioning them to come forward.

Elliott recognized him first. "You never left," he said under his breath.

"Adam," Albert said. "There you are."

Elliott and Albert stopped at Adam. Marcus walked by aiming his light up the tunnel. He found a body lying next to the boxes. "God, Adam. Did you kill this man?"

"Did you need to kill a man, son?" Albert asked. Adam did not move.

Elliott went to the body and knelt down. Marcus shined the light. The man in black fatigues and body armor didn't move. Elliott lifted an eyelid and passed his penlight left to right. The pupil dilated.

"He's alive. Unconscious." He examined the body. Both shoulders are dislocated. He is bound at the wrists and ankles.

"There's more over here," Marcus shouted. Adam's eyes followed Elliott and Marcus to each. There were five. Night vision goggles were broken. The straps were used to bind them.

"They're alive," Elliott announced. "All of them. One has a broken leg and crushed fingers. The one over there has a broken arm and fractured tibia—he won't be running away. These two over here got off lucky—dislocated shoulders. Oh, and the one on top of the boxes in the tunnel over there, he has a hip dislocation and a few fractured ribs. None of the five Gilgamesh soldiers are dead or in danger of dying . . . just broken up and unconscious at the moment. When they wake up, they will not be too eager to move."

"And they're tied up," Marcus said. *I'll be damned. He didn't kill this time . . .*

"Elliott." Heads turned. Was that Adam? He pointed to one of five cave openings around them. Adam said, "The GICC is there—first chamber, right."

After getting over Adam talking like a normal human, they ran to the room. Inside, Marcus yanked off the tarp. The computer system was running—the hard drive engaged, cooling fans humming, and panel lights flashing in a rhythmic sequence.

"Data transfer is a work in progress," Marcus said. "We don't know how long this has been going on. We need to do something fast."

Elliott found the keyboard. Marcus turned on the giant monitors.

"Should I unplug things, smash the Wi-Fi or something? Tell me how aggressive you want me to be, Elliott. I can stop this transfer now."

"If we unplug, we trigger security software and lose everything on this system. They may have most of the data now—there's no way to know." Elliott pounded basic system commands on the keyboard. Nothing happened. The GICC continued to hum.

"You're right. We can do forensics on the hard drive and recover vital data to stop Gilgamesh later. We need to get inside to protect the hard drive, Elliott."

"We can't allow them to keep this information from us. Alberto Bella had to have a password we should be able to figure out. The man was 165. He was old school, not a technical man at all. The password should be obvious."

"Alberto hoarded information," Albert said. "Computers were a nuisance but a necessary part of his life the last twenty years. I agree with Elliott."

"You knew him all your life, Albert. People choose passwords they can remember, one that means something to them. We have little time to get inside to protect data and disrupt the Cape Town transfer. Start talking, and I'll start entering passwords."

Albert nodded. "Okay, he was born in Italy. He started the cotton merchant business at the turn of the century, was wildly successful. Alberto changed the family name from Bella to Bell. He wanted to be an American. He purchased *The Memphis Tribune* in 1905. He faked his death in 1925 and took the name, Rudolph Kohl . . .

Elliott kept punching in potential passwords, each with half-dozen permutations. At any time, the process could trigger lockdown or release a security virus—but they had no choice. Cape Town was ahead of them. Elliott's worst fears were taking shape—they were losing the battle.

"He worshipped Teddy Roosevelt. Alberto was a democrat all his life, leaned Libertarian. The man loved his powder-blue Bentley convertible. Gilgamesh consumed Alberto's life. He loved the *Epic of Gilgamesh*, the oldest written story—came out of ancient Sumer. The story is about a demigod and his lifelong search for immortality, the historical King of Uruk, 2500 BCE. Alberto took the name for his dream . . . now a nightmare."

"You're doing good, Alberto. Keep going," Elliott said as he entered passwords.

"What else . . . ? Alberto's first male born son was my father, Robert T. Bell, born in 1895. My father was the second Bell patriarch—1925. I was born in 1932. My father died in a plane crash—in the Gulf of Mexico off the coast of Galveston. Oh God!

That day in February of 1956 devastated me. I recall Alberto could only think of one thing. He demanded I take over as the next Bell patriarch, and take my father's seat on the board."

Marcus went around to the back of the massive computer. "I can unplug any time," he said.

Albert rubbed his head. "I don't know what else to say."

Elliott kept pounding the keyboard. "Think. What one thing is the most important in Alberto Bella's life? There's gotta be one thing, Albert. Was it his dynasty? Was it his family name? Maybe a girl or relationship or possession or child . . . ? You know what it is. Open your mind." The lights flashed faster and rolled faster as other hard drives initialized and cooling fans came alive. Elliott kept pounding password iterations as the others watched their mission fail.

"I know it. I know the password," Albert declared. "It is *blood lions*."

Elliott typed in *blood lions*.

The screen popped on. A picture of the Gilgamesh demigod flashed.

"We're in," Elliott declared.

Marcus ran around to the keyboard and stared at the monitors. Elliott pounded commands and opened the master file. "Take over, Marcus. This is your field of expertise, doctor."

Marcus slid his hands on the keyboard as Elliott slid his off. The flurry of commands Marcus delivered with precise and darting strokes were a blur. Marcus performed like a concert pianist as the numbers and letters poured across the screen and files opened and closed.

"Each file Cape Town accessed and transferred has been deleted from the Memphis GICC system. I'm sorry to say, we are too late to stop them."

"Can't you do something . . . send a virus . . . launch security software?" Elliott said.

"They just took the last file, Elliott."

The massive computer powered down as they all watched. The flashing lights popped off. The monitors flickered. Marcus pushed the keyboard back and rubbed his head.

They have it all, Elliott thought. *Now it's up to Max and Tony*

. . .

TWENTY-THREE

Cape Town, South Africa

"Now what?" With his lighter Tony walked the length of the chiseled room ten feet beneath the Dutch church. "Damn place's cut out of sandstone and granite like a hot knife through butter. There's gotta be a damn door somewhere."

With his penlight next to his nose, Max moved up one corner of the ten-by-thirty-foot room. "I don't like this, Anthony."

"And I don't like that tone."

"We may have been tricked."

"That's just great," Tony said. He casually reached for his gun stuffed under his belt.

Max scraped at the wall with his pen. "While you've been looking for a door down here, I've inspected the walls and each corner for an irregularity. I now have my doubts this is a reception area. This may be a bogus entry portal into their operation." He leaned back and whispered, "I suggest we depart expeditiously."

Tony missed the sense of urgency. "Why not poke around

some more? We know these idiots are down here somewhere. They have to get into their rat hole. Seems like a big production for it to be just a dead end."

Max pointed to a dangling root above his heads. "This, my good man, is a nozzle. Not a root. Gases or fluids come out of nozzles, sir." Then he pointed to the opposing corner. "And that is a lens. I do believe we are on a monitor somewhere."

Tony chewed his gum faster. "Well, ain't that just hunky-dory." He backed up to the lens no bigger than a pencil eraser. Tony stuck his gum on it. "See any more?"

"No. Just the one."

"So ya think they know we're here?" Tony whispered as he closed his lighter.

"I would assume they do. There is a very good chance we will be gassed soon."

"I've never seen you so negative, Max. They could very well be busy screwing with the GICC. Billionaires are not multi-taskers. It's not like they have a staff."

Tony returned to the ladder. "I'm gonna open that damn trap door if it's the last thing I do. I will not be gassed." He started climbing.

Max followed. He gripped the railing and started up. The ladder vibrated. Max let go, and it stopped. "Don't move, Anthony." Max grabbed the railing in the same spot. The ladder vibrated again. He let go, and it stopped again. "Something of a hydraulic nature is activating."

"What the hell?" Tony said from his perch five feet above. "Can I move?"

"No, sir . . . Be very still."

Max moved his penlight over the back of the metal railing. "A compression pad," he whispered. Max investigated further. Seven rungs from the bottom he found another and turned off his penlight.

Tony whispered, "What the hell are we doing, Max? I can't just stay on this damn ladder."

"I believe I've found the key for entry. This entire ladder must descend into a receptacle. I assume it opens into the primary chamber or another level with surveillance."

Tony started back down the ladder.

"Stop moving, Anthony," Max ordered. Tony froze, recognizing the tone. "The question before us—what do we do with this knowledge?"

"What's your concern?"

"If we activate the entry mechanism on this ladder, there's a very good chance we reveal our presence to the enemy. They will have the advantage."

"Right. The bastards could kill us—tell me something new," Tony said. "What's the chance the three rich knuckleheads don't know how to work half the shit down here?"

"I would hazard to guess a twenty percent probability on a good day."

"There ya go, Mr. Negative. Look, it's after midnight. I'm not near as smart as you, old boy, but I'll bet you those billionaires don't pull all-nighters. They're probably snuggled in their little cave-beds snoring up a storm. I'll also bet half the security shit has not been turned on. I say squeeze those damn compression pads and let's ride this ladder into hell."

Max got on the ladder and squeezed. It vibrated as a crescent of light appeared at the base and grew into a large circle. The ladder descended. Max found his reflection on the stainless steel wall of the cylinder and brushed his jacket. When it reached the floor twenty-feet down, the ladder locked in place and the cylinder resealed above.

At the far end of the stainless steel room an elevator door opened. Max went inside and waited for Tony. "I do not see camera lenses anywhere. It is feasible to omit security apparatus on a secured level."

"Like after you get through security at an airport?"

"Precisely." The doors closed. They felt the elevator descend, although a sense of depth would be impossible to assess. The doors opened seventeen seconds later.

"We're in, Max, and still kicking."

They entered the tunnel. The elevator door closed behind. "This is not a stealth fortress, Anthony. It is a research facility. This could be where they hold their advanced biogenic work. I doubt Mr. Bella intended anything more for this location."

"Means they didn't have other hiding places."

"I'm sure the backup GICC is here," Max said.

"Getting control of the GICC was not a bad plan."

"I would not underestimate these people, Anthony. They are wealthy, educated men."

"I understand. The battle above ground and nothing below ground supports your theory this is a research facility. They don't have fighting capabilities down here."

"I'll hazard to guess those above ground know nothing of this operation. They were contracted to keep people out of the church."

Max and Tony proceeded down the tunnel. It opened into a larger chamber with polished stone walls. Five wide steps dropped into the hundred-foot square room with lines of laboratory counters. Laminar air flow hoods, microscopes, incubators, tube racks, centrifuges, and sinks were at two dozen work stations. The far wall had shelves and cabinets from the floor to the ceiling fifteen feet above. Unopened boxes of laboratory and medical supplies were stacked around the room— sterile beakers, tissue culture flasks, chemicals and cleansers, lab coats, gowns, gloves and masks.

"You think anyone else is here beside the threesome?" Tony asked.

Max stared at the nearby work station. "I doubt it. This facility is new. Close to operational but not yet on line." He turned on the water. It popped and gurgled and spat out dirty water. "This has never been used."

They moved to the wall and stayed in the shadows, away from the recessed light fixtures overhead. There were two archways into halls away from the chamber. Before proceeding, they knelt behind a row of file cabinets. "Up until now we've had a series of fortuitous experiences," Max pontificated. "I'm quite surprised we're still alive." He removed and cleaned his glasses on the one not-filthy section of his shirt.

"Although you are the smartest man I know—outside of Elliott—Max, you can be an annoying, pompous twit. We make our luck, my friend." Tony peered over the file cabinets and got his bearings. "The three blind mice are down one of those two halls. We've got a fifty-fifty shot at picking the right one. I have twelve bullets left. The way I figure, I only need three."

Max checked his gun. "I believe these men are civilized. I do not expect a battle with anyone but their protectors. Remember, we must find and disable the GICC."

"Oh gee, I forgot," Tony chided. "If we're really lucky, first I can shoot the bastards, and then you can take your time disabling the GICC." Tony slid his gun in his belt. "I think it best we stay together—splitting up never works in the movies."

Max rolled his eyes and checked his gun. They eased down the first tunnel. After fifty meters they knew it was the wrong choice—minimal lighting, unpolished granite walls, a ten-degree drop in temperature, and a wet floor sloped into the dark abyss.

They wasted no time getting into the second. Every twenty meters they came upon glass doors on each side of the polished granite corridor. Etched on each was a designation—Tissue

Culture Lab, Operating Room, Labor & Delivery, Clinical Research, Genotyping, Histology. They rounded an arcing curve. Double glass doors at the end of the hall came into view. As they approached, the etched words came into focus—Gilgamesh Global Information System.

Light poured from glass doors into the dimly lit corridor. They saw the large black man and middle-aged Caucasian standing over a third man typing on a computer keyboard. The three stared into the same monitor.

"The trifecta," Tony whispered as he reached for his gun. When he touched the handle, the three turned heads in unison. Max and Tony froze. "The bastards see us," Tony said without moving his lips. *What are they going to do about us?*

Mobuto Ali smiled. Oblivious to the guns pointed at his head, he pointed to the ceiling over Tony's shoulder. They looked. A flat screen descended and flickered to life.

"What the hell are they doing," Tony muttered.

The screen displayed four camera field quadrants—one in the nave of the Dutch church, one in the room under the lectern, one inside of the elevator, and one with a view behind the file cabinets in the main chamber. The picture faded. Another full screen picture came into focus, one of Max and Tony watching the monitor.

They turned back at Mobuto Ali. "They knew where we were every step of the way."

Max smiled. "We're exactly where they want us."

Mobuto reached for the panel out of view. Tony shot three times. The three billionaires jumped. "I knew the glass would be bulletproof . . . just wanted to scare the shit out of those rich bastards." Max smiled and shot three more times. "Bastards jumped again," Tony mused. Where did those candy-ass smiles go?" Tony raised his gun and pointed it at Mobuto. "Bet that son of a bitch thinks I'm crazy enough to shoot in the same place and it just might penetrate their magic glass. Oh look, they're getting all busy now . . ."

"I believe you've sufficiently motivated them, Anthony. They are about to show us why they wanted us in this tunnel at this location."

A trumpeting siren blasted at a deafening volume and pitch. Although it would not reach the surface forty feet above, it would force Tony and Max to drop their guns to save their eardrums. Holding the sides of their heads, they watched the billionaires get to their feet with new smiles. The granite wall began to descend from the ceiling. The four-foot-thick slab of stone made a harsh, grinding noise as it inched its way down.

Tony tapped Max's shoulder. "What now?"

When the first descending wall reached three feet from the floor, the second stone wall emerged from the ceiling. To avoid being trapped between the walls, Max and Tony ran to escape. The first firmly seated as the second reached three feet from the floor. Then the third stone wall started to drop at the entry to the corridor by the main chamber.

"We gotta fly, Max. Keep up with me, partner," Tony said.

They ran and slipped on the floor, wet from the spray lubricant on the sliding granite slabs. Tony slid under and into the main chamber. Max went head-first into the narrowing gap. Max stopped halfway, the bottom of the slab touching his head.

Tony reached in. "Give me your hand goddamn it."

Max reached as far as he could, his head pushed down by the two-ton slab inching its way and old muscles too weak to care.

Tony had seconds, or Max would not make it. He turned his head sideways and dove into the narrowing space. He found Max's arm and yanked him out. When Max's foot cleared, the slab seated and the grinding stopped.

The two sat on the wet floor watching the sheet of water from the ceiling slow to a trickle. The trumpeting sirens stopped.

"I sure as hell didn't see that shit coming," Tony said, lighting two cigarettes. He passed one to Max. They sucked a few deep ones.

"Think we need to get out of here?" Tony asked.

Max examined his bent frames and broken lens. He threw them against the wall.

"Let it go. I'll buy you a new pair if we live," Tony said.

"Those were my favorites."

"Max, a little CIA guidance here would be nice. Us city homicide detectives don't run into a lot of underground research facilities and sliding walls and shit."

"Sorry, Anthony." He sucked a long one. "I saw a possible alternative exit on the way down here. I didn't think it important at the time."

"What the hell did you see?"

"Another ladder. I believe it goes all the way to the surface—possibly a work portal less traveled. Likely opens in the little stone church, or an inconspicuous rock formation, or behind a clever bush arrangement."

"You had me at 'the little stone church.' You think they got any more surprises for us?" Tony looked up to make sure they weren't sitting under anything remotely troublesome. "Any chance they would flood this place?"

"Logic says we've seen the extent of their protective apparatus."

"Okay. How does logic speak to you, Max?"

"Clearly they needed us in that tunnel. If they had other, more formidable options, they certainly would have taken them. Why risk us reaching their GICC? With the correct weaponry, we could have gained access. No. They needed to get us in a position to capture us—between walls. It would eliminate the immediate threat, and it would maintain the secrecy of this location. We would simply go missing, sir."

"Sometimes you're damn brilliant, Maxwell." Tony lit another cigarette. He removed the short one from Max's trembling fingers and replaced it. "At least we trapped the three bastards. We can get a team down here and blow through those walls in no time."

"Wrong again, Anthony. You're not chasing common criminals."

"What am I missing now?"

"They did not paint themselves into a corner. They would never design a billion-dollar underground facility with but two exits. This site is not designed for a group suicide mission."

"They've got their emergency exits . . ."

"Suffice it to say they have multiple ways to depart Devil's Peak without notice, and in comfort."

"But their GICC is here. They can't leave it behind."

"They needed access to the Memphis GICC to regain control—complete data removal and render the site impotent. They can now transfer this data anywhere in the world. This GICC will be useless to their enemies."

"Shit . . . They have another mother ship?" Tony mumbled.

"Precisely."

"We're screwed."

"Let's hope not." Max said with smoke drifting from his nose. "We must get topside and call Elliott. Maybe they've had better luck at their end."

"At least we've made the Cape Town operation useless," Tony bellowed as he kicked a file cabinet on his way out the main chamber. "Let's go damn it. . ."

"They'll have to move now for sure," Max shouted—hollow encouragement. He dropped his cigarette to the wet floor and watched it sizzle. *This is not Alberto's backup site. The old man resists change and thrives on control. It's near Memphis . . .*

Max watched Tony climb the granite steps and disappear

into the tunnel with his new limp. Tony had to put the Devil's Peak failure behind him—his way. He needed a new assignment before he exploded. The top MPD homicide detective's frustration grew from a lack of understanding. The Gilgamesh board members were a criminal breed unfamiliar to him. They lived outside his typical crime world. Tony preferred the heinous serial killer—they were something he could understand, motives and behavior. He could never get his head around a billionaire criminal with a worldwide mission.

All his life Max had pursued white collar evil across every continent and untangled countless sinister plots. Although beaten often, Max had his share of victories. And the retired CIA operative learned something Detective Wilcox had not—the battle against evil is never over.

Max had watched evil die many times. And he had watched it take on a new form on a new day. Evil finds a way to bubble to the surface. It launches new battles with new soldiers. Like the four seasons, evil is a predictable part of the human experience.

But this time it was different. Max knew the day he connected Gilgamesh to the Bluff City Butcher and the twenty-five-year secret war. It was not a religious war, or a quest for a geographic place or wealth. The Gilgamesh evil was the ultimate battle, the one that would change the future of mankind. The sinister few would control the lifespan of the human race. If immortality was real, the few would control the universe for an eternity. They would steal personal freedom from every living soul forever.

As Max struggled to his feet on the wet granite floor, he stared at the wall that had almost crushed him. *Today, you three harnessed a weapon needed to complete your century-old plan. Today, you gave yourself a chance to prevail where Alberto Bella failed. I never understood the saying until this moment. "God has a reason. All men must die."*

TWENTY-FOUR

Memphis, Tennessee

Albert and Elliott sat in the last car to pull up to the south entry. Constructed in 1990, the Memphis Pyramid Arena loomed thirty-two stories high, and the 600-foot base swallowed their Bentley. The replica of the Great Pyramid of Giza—sixth largest in the world—closed its doors to the public in 2004. Now only used on occasion for private events, the unique venue north of the city had become the most viable option for Albert's impromptu meeting. William made all the arrangements a week in advance.

The 20,000 seats were not needed—the controllable isolation was. Inside the dark arena, the only lights washed over the small stage on the south edge and the four hundred chairs arranged in ten rows of forty. Two hundred members of Gilgamesh attended with personal bodyguards. The full parking lot had lines of empty limousines with motors running and drivers standing by opened doors. The billionaires inside the arena were impatiently waiting—they were not used to doing anything they did not want to do. This time, the Bell patriarch gave them no choice.

Although their accumulated wealth equaled the GNP of a European country and could attract the criminal element, their collective egotism and paranoia put a hundred additional bodyguards on the grounds at One Auction Place. It did not go unnoticed that the venue sat close to Mud Island, the place where the heads of seven Gilgamesh board members had been found on ghastly display. If Albert Bell had wanted to send a chilling message, he was successful.

An overpass at the south end of the property provided an opportunity for an elevated, mobile assault. And the Wolf River running along the west side of the pyramid presented a quarter-mile of black water access. Both risk areas got the attention of the private security team. The north and east borders outside the ten-foot chain-link fence were managed by off-duty Memphis police. They were paid well to ensure Albert Bell's guests were not disturbed during their short visit, and to look the other way—there were enough illegal assault weapons and mercenary combatants on the grounds to take the city.

The polished, black and silver Bentley idled in front of the south doors. No one approached. The host of the mandatory meeting would signal when ready.

"I gave Marcus the leather case," Albert said as he leaned forward and looked under the trees at the moon's reflection on Wolf River. "We were alone. I believe it is safe now. He can begin his work."

"Good. Yes, he can get started. Every minute counts." Elliott's thoughts returned to the catacombs left hours ago—and their failed mission to secure the GICC. His mind raced. He evaluated the variables and assessed the decisions. *Losing control of the GICC is a game changer. The resurrection moves this to another level. The focus and desperation of the three is intense. They will eliminate everything in their way.* He forced a smile.

"I know you better than you think, Elliott."

"What do you mean?"

"You're thinking about *them* getting the GICC." Albert straightened his French cuffs and meticulously rotated his gold/diamond studded cufflinks so the tops of the triangular design aligned with his arm. "We had a narrow window."

Elliott looked out the side window. *First Carol, and then Adam telepathically, and now Albert gets inside my head. I've been alone with my thoughts forty years—alone with my demons. I don't know about this, letting people inside. No. I won't encourage it—I'm not ready.*

"Actually, my thoughts were on this meeting. Disbanding the members of Gilgamesh is another way to reduce assets, cripple their network, and diminish their chances for success."

Albert nodded, accepting Elliott's comment. He would remain in the car a while longer. The nervous billionaires had never been told what to do until now. They needed to sit in the dark arena, waiting and thinking and wondering. They would become more malleable with time.

"What about the five men Adam stopped?"

Elliott smiled. *Adam is a warrior.* "You mean the five he *politely* allowed to live? The five he deposited on the front steps of the Brent mansion?"

Albert chuckled. "That was nice of him. He showed great restraint, don't you think? Adam is attempting to change or adapt."

"He left before I could thank him . . ."

"I'm sure he knows you were appreciative."

Yes. I am sure he does . . . telepathically speaking.

"After I creatively explained to the Memphis police how they came to be neatly packaged on the steps of the abandoned mansion, and why we were at the Brent estate in the first place, the five NRA advocates were hastily hauled away with little discussion. I knew they would not be talking to anybody."

"Among your many gifts, 'creativity' is certainly one."

Bodyguards walked under trees looking into the Wolf River with dancing flashlights. "It helped that Tony called the MPD from Cape Town. He got a hold of his partner—Detective Harris —a good man, first to the scene. They're booking those guys for interstate transport of illegal firearms—a felony. Brings in the Feds—antiterrorism concerns."

"Should take them out of circulation a while," Albert said.

"Not long enough. We're pressing charges—attempted murder. That'll put them in a cell a bit longer. I doubt Gilgamesh is in any position to send lawyers to represent one of their hit squads in Memphis. I expect they'll distance themselves. These five may be holdovers, a contingency force contracted by Alberto Bella before his death."

"To guard the GICC, of course. It makes perfect sense." Albert removed a silver flask from his coat and unscrewed the cap. He took a swallow and closed his eyes. "Abandoned. That could provide an opportunity for us. Maybe one will talk."

"These are the type that takes the poison pill. They're not talking. Detective Harris had to take off to another homicide— Tom Lee Park. We'll know more about those five after Tony gets back in town and stirs that pot. I wouldn't want him interrogating me."

Elliott looked across Wolf River at the black strip of land— Mud Island. *So much has happened here over the last year. Now I'm a stone's throw from the people that fueled the twisted organization. Although they were unaware of the diabolical workings of their chairman, their greed and detachment from the world made all the carnage and pain possible.*

"I'm ready." Albert returned the flask inside his coat and gave his son a warm but stately wink of the eye. "Don't worry. The blood lions will find a way."

Elliott smiled at the man he admired most in the world, even before he had known Albert was his father. Thoughts drifted to Gilgamesh. "Do you believe in the immortality gene?"

Albert leaned back in the seat and waved off the hand reaching for the door. "The immortality gene? I've never thought much about it." He smiled briefly. "I have heard it discussed within the family, but I'm not quite sure I ever knew what it meant."

"We've never discussed it. Maybe it's time to start that dialogue."

Albert removed his flask and took a swallow. "Very well. I'll tell you what I know." He passed it to Elliott. "The story is the Bella family—later the Bell family in America—possessed a peculiar history going back as far as we have family records. The first male born of each generation lives a very long time. It's said they do not die of old age, only injury or disease."

"The blood lions . . . ?" Elliott asked.

"Alberto's term—the past, present and future Bell patriarchs. A ridiculous term, I think."

"Tell me the history you researched."

"I've gone back to my great, great grandfather—Angelo Armand Bella. He was the first male born I could investigate and cross reference. He lived to be a hundred-twenty-seven. Died falling off a bridge. Went for a walk one night. I suppose he could have been pushed."

"What about his brothers and sisters?"

"Two younger brothers. One died of natural causes, age seventy-one. The other was killed in a house fire. Angelo had three sisters. They died of natural causes, according to the notes in the family bible. Angelo's first son was Giulio, my great grandfather in Italy. He lived over a hundred years. His brothers and sisters died in their sixties. And you know Alberto Bella. He was Giulio's first male born. Bible notes say Alberto was born in 1850."

"And your father?"

"Robert T. Bell was born in 1895. As you know, he died in a plane crash in 1956. That year I was installed as the Bell patriarch, age twenty-four. My father was an only child. I have a brother and three sisters in Florida, all alive but in poor health."

"What is it about the genetics of the blood lions? Has there ever been a legitimate medical assessment? Surely the rare genetic trait attracted attention before it was looked at as an advantage to be covertly developed for less than savory purposes."

"I don't know, Elliott. Alberto was the one determined to find out what it was all about. The covert aspects were never discussed." Albert shook his head. "My grandfather would be alive today if he had left it alone and enjoyed his privileged life."

Knuckles wrapped on the window. Albert pressed the button and it dropped with a soft hum. "Yes, William."

"I'm sorry to interrupt, sir. Will you be much longer? Your guests are restless. Some want to step outside to stretch their legs, sir. It might be difficult to herd them back into the arena."

"I'm on my way. Pass it along. Three minutes."

"Very well, sir." William disappeared as the window closed.

"I suppose I should not refer to us as 'blood lions'. I am a carrier of the family genetic anomaly. You and Adam possess it as well. It is ironic Alberto managed to create the men who would bring an end to his dream."

"Do members know about the Bell genetics? Do they know the term—blood lions?"

"They've heard the term, yes. But I doubt they know what it

all means. Maybe we should go inside now." He turned to Elliott and saw the distant look. "Are you ready?"

"More important, are you ready?" Over his shoulder the pyramid doors opened. Elliott's brow dipped and eyes focused. His face hardened.

"Try not to think of this as a nest of vipers. They are not going to strike with deadly force." He gripped Elliott's arm. "They're rich people with many interests. For most, their membership was inherited. Most know little and are now frightened to be in the middle of a mess."

"That crossed my mind." *But I'm thinking about the few deadly snakes in the room.*

Albert ran a finger under his collar and pinched his knot. "They had a dream. Gilgamesh was—shall I say—the dream weaver, another place to park money." Elliott nodded. To continue the discussion would be fruitless. Albert had not yet fully grasped the magnitude of the gathering storm or its worldwide implications.

But why would you get any of this? Elliott thought. *The concept of people living forever is beyond bizarre. It's fantasy. And the thought that one entity could control it is incomprehensible. No. You've been misled all your life, masterfully manipulated by your family and the Gilgamesh board. And you did not have my experiences battling Gilgamesh, or my gifts.*

Since the catacombs and loss of the GICC, Elliott had reprocessed the facts and reconsidered their strategy to stop a resurrected Gilgamesh.

When Alberto died, I allowed myself to believe it could be over. Now I can feel the hell on earth growing stronger. The three surviving board members, somewhere in Cape Town, are more dangerous than Alberto Bella could ever be. They are desperate and focused and determined. They've secured the GICC and will implement their plan.

We don't have a chance . . .

"Let's go." Albert patted Elliott's leg and tapped the window. William stepped up and opened the door.

PART THREE
THE BIOLOGIC

TWENTY-FIVE

He handled a lot of dead people over the last three years. But this case he would work alone, and the chilling crime scene looked oddly familiar.

The call came in at 23:45. Alex Harris approached the bench in Tom Lee Park. The first patrolman on the scene stood with a small flashlight in his mouth, writing in a notepad. The second on the scene ran yellow tape and kept onlookers back. The ambulance sirens echoed above the city. Harris watched the spinning lights break from the black buildings onto Riverside Drive. They would hop the curb and roll down the sidewalk along the Mississippi River like before. And, like before, they would not be needed.

Taking the lead role made Alex nervous—Wilcox was out of the country. Alex preferred the number two position. He liked being the quiet guy in the crowd, the one in the back of the room or at the end of the line. As a third generation cop, he didn't even consider any other profession. But he had never thought he would be promoted to detective.

No one expected the chubby, balding guy with glasses from

Bartlett to graduate at the top of his class at the police academy. They were shocked when he cleared all the hurdles and aced all the tests. They assigned him to homicide at the age of twenty-eight. No one thought the Director of the MPD would put a rookie with the top homicide investigator in the city.

If they made a movie, it would be about Clint Eastwood and a Radio Shack employee working heinous crime scenes in Memphis. Tony Wilcox was the tall, lanky, in-your-face, disorganized, hard, top investigator in the city with no rule book. Harris was the introverted, detail-oriented, by-the-book rookie. With his partner halfway around the world, he had to handle a few days of Memphis homicides on his own. Up until 23:46, Harris did okay.

The dead man had been positioned in the one shadow draping across a park bench and sidewalk on the east bank of the Mississippi River. Alex stood with his arms folded and hand on his chin taking it all in. Standing alone ten feet away, the first responder pulled the flashlight out of his mouth and approached. Harris ignored him and walked up to the deceased and felt the carotid artery. The cold skin gave him something. He stepped back and resumed his stance.

"I'm Officer Bailey Holmes, badge 2866. First here. Called it in immediately and my partner chased everyone off except them." He pointed to an elderly couple sitting on the park bench south of the crime scene. "Who are you?" he asked, his pen ready to fill in a blank.

"Harris." He studied the chilling picture in front of him—a black man tied to a bench in a casual posture. The right arm stretched across the back and the head was propped to look like any other river watcher.

"Are you Homicide, Harris?"

"Yes." The shadow covered his face, and the eyes.

"The victim's stabbed in the chest," Officer Holmes said as a gust of wind shot off the river and took his hat. He grabbed it in flight. "I'm no ME, but I think he's been dead a while."

Harris didn't turn. "Cold and stiff . . ."

"What's your full name for my report?"

"Alex Harris." He held up the flashlight he squeezed under his arm. He clicked it on the dead man's face. Holmes pocketed his pen.

"I removed the wallet. Have an ID."

"Wish you hadn't touched anything," Harris grumbled. "You never know where we're gonna find prints or DNA or something helpful." He moved the light around the head.

"I was careful. Only thing I touched. Just a corner. It stuck out his back pocket through the slats—almost dropped out. I set it over there." He pointed to the end of the bench. "Name's strange, but sounds kinda familiar."

Harris moved the beam down the dead man's chest—no blood. The shirt was unbuttoned and flapped closed. He would wait for the ME, but knew Wilcox would take a peek without disturbing the crime scene. Harris leaned in with his pen and opened the shirt. "What's his name, Officer Holmes?"

The ambulance pulled up. The headlights poured over the park bench, sidewalk and them. "Tell 'em we don't need 'em." Harris stared at the wound. "You hear me, Holmes? Tell 'em now."

Holmes met the paramedics at the front of the ambulance. They stared at the crime scene. Squad cars approached from all directions. Traffic was rerouted. Police on foot with dogs unloaded onto the grounds. Pedestrians were herded out of the park and off Riverside Drive.

The paramedics set down their trauma cases and one approached Harris. "I'm Mike Hinton. You sure about this? You don't want me to take a look?"

"The man's been gone a while—stiff as a carp. There's

nothing to do unless you're going to bring him back from the dead."

"I hear ya, detective. Looks like he's in rigor."

"Right now I need all the physical evidence I can get. No need to get your DNA in the equation, Hinton."

"Not a problem. We'll back off and hang around a while in case you need paperwork or he starts talking to you." Hinton returned to the ambulance and set his report on the hood. They had to wait for the ME to cut them loose.

Holmes joined Harris at the bench. "You said you had a name," Harris said.

"Yes sir. Panther McGee . . ."

That's what I was afraid you'd say. "What kind of ID are you looking at?"

"This one." Holmes handed him a driver's license as the ME's van hopped the curb and crossed the grounds, the shocks squeaking all the way. Alex's cell rang—Wilcox.

"I got to take this. Tell the ME I'll be back in a minute."

Harris got out of earshot studying the driver license. "How did you know to call now, sir?"

"What the hell are you talkin' about, Harris. It's seven in the damn morning in this God-forsaken jungle. I'm about to depart South-damn-Africa and these wild animals and devil mountains. I'm boarding a plane with Max, one of Bell's private jets. I'm getting my American ass home as fast as possible."

"Well, sir, I'm working a homicide right now. We need to talk." Alex waved off the police officers approaching him. They stopped and turned back. He could see Deputy Chief Cottam talking to Officer Holmes and the two witnesses fifty feet away. Cottam kept looking back.

"You don't need me to work your homicides, Harris. You're a smart guy. Take care of business. I'll be back in Memphis in seventeen hours, give or take. I hate flying."

"You need to hear this," Alex said with the tone Wilcox learned not to ignore. Max boarded the plane. Wilcox waved him off. They would wait.

"What's got your underwear up your ass, Harris?"

"Are we one hundred percent positive the Bluff City Butcher is dead?"

Only a few know Adam's alive, Wilcox thought. *We agreed it was best we not talk about it. Best people think him dead, especially with all the Gilgamesh shit going on.* "Why in the hell would you ask me a stupid question like that, Harris?"

"You remember the Panther McGee homicide in 2008?"

"Hell yes, of course I remember that sick-ass case."

"I'm standing in Tom Lee Park at the very same park bench."

"Okay and . . ."

"There's a black man tied to it, sir. He's been dead a while. His ID says Panther McGee."

"That's impossible, Harris. Someone's playing games. Someone killed a black man and tied him to the park bench and used the name to screw with the Memphis police—simple as that. Panther McGee's dead."

"But I . . ."

"No buts, Harris. Granted, I have no idea what some sick bastard is trying to prove using the name and park bench, but it's not the work of the Bluff City Butcher."

"There's more," he whispered as Cottam approached the body and the ME stepped out of his white van. "There are things about this case that . . ."

"Stop beating around the bush. Tell me what's got you all worked up," Tony bellowed.

"There are things never shared from the 2008 case. This is an exact duplication."

"I'm listening." Wilcox turned his back to the plane.

"This young black man is tied to the bench with the same knots the BCB used."

"That's not near enough, Harris."

"He's been bled out somewhere else and brought here."

"No damn blood . . . ?"

"It's worse. His heart is gone. I looked close at his chest. It sinks in where the heart would be. It's all stitched up just like the BCB."

"Tell me about the sutures."

"Just like Panther McGee's. I did not count 'em, but I think there's fifty individual stitches. Packers' knots."

Tony changed ears. "What about each end of the sutured incision?"

"It's there, too."

"Say it."

"Knots of Isis are at both ends. That information never made it into a police or ME report."

This is not looking good. "And the edges of the incision, anything noteworthy?" *Don't tell me neatly trimmed . . .*

"Neatly trimmed, sir. This looks like the Butcher's work. Since the BCB is dead, we may have another one running around out here. Maybe Kayne's alive. We don't have his body." Harris turned his back to the death scene and the deputy chief. "What do I say? Mr. Cottam is coming my way."

Mother of God! The exsanguination and removal of heart could have gotten out there. And the surgical closure, maybe. But the packers' knots and Knots of Isis, no way.

"Mr. Cottam is going to be here any minute," Harris whispered.

"Under no circumstances do you parallel this to the 2008 case. Just let people get there on their own—it'll give us time. Don't say a goddamn word about stitches or the Knots of Isis. I'm flying out of this stinkin' jungle in a few minutes. I'll be in

Memphis tomorrow. Have everything ready for me. I want you at that autopsy takin' notes."

"I'll be there."

"Bye." Tony disconnected and looked at Max standing next to the jet with his hands out. "What do you want?" Tony yelled, as he yanked his bag off the tarmac and marched to the plane.

I've gotta talk to Elliott. His brother may be losing it again, reliving his past or some shit I don't understand. I can't let the BCB kill people in my town. Never trusted that psycho . . .

Harris pocketed his cell and turned around. Deputy Chief Cottam stood inches from his face. "It's Detective Harris, correct?"

"Yes, sir. Harris." He stared at the bruise on Cottam's face. He knew the story.

"Who were you talking to, Harris?" He leaned closer.

"A personal call, sir." He squeezed his flashlight. Cottam's eyes flashed down and back, long enough to see the white knuckles.

"Are you okay, Detective Harris? This is your first important case solo. Your partner is on some secret mission . . . I mean taking some well-deserved vacation time."

"I don't know what Detective Wilcox is doing, sir. He's supposed to be back in a few days." Harris leaned to the right to watch the ME walk up to the deceased. "I need to get over there."

"First, what are your thoughts about this homicide, Detective Harris?"

"Well, sir, I need some time to pull those together."

"Surely you have first impressions," Cottam pushed.

"I don't think my first impressions are relevant, sir."

"Oh, I think you're wrong. I want to know what they are."

"Are you taking over for Director Wade, sir?"

"Yes. Why do you ask?"

"Director Wade never came to a homicide scene in the first

hour. And he never asked us to guess what happened. He didn't think it helpful. I tend to agree with him, sir."

Cottam stepped closer as if sniffing for alcohol or a girl's perfume. "Fair enough. But I am curious about something. Maybe you can help me so I can get out of your way."

"I'll try, sir."

"Do you think there's a connection to the 2008 Panther McGee homicide? Does Detective Wilcox think the Bluff City Butcher is out there somewhere . . . ?"

TWENTY-SIX

"Immortality is not a gift. Immortality is an achievement; only those who strive mightily shall possess it."
Edgar Lee Masters

Memphis - Catacombs

"Marcus, did you just say your father's research is *not* on the hard drive?"

"Yes and no." He moved the mouse to wake the system. When the screen came alive, he started pounding the keyboard with a two-finger blur. "Hold on. Let me get inside. It's easier to show than tell. Father was a very clever man."

"I'm starting to see."

Marcus continued entering data. "How'd the Pyramid meeting go last night?"

"As well as could be expected. Most got the message."

"You don't want to talk about it?"

"Not much to say. They came and Albert helped them understand the significance of the moment. He set forth a case for each to abandon Gilgamesh or be prosecuted for mass murder."

"Mr. Bell has a way with words," Marcus said pounding away. "Guess they're on their way back home to their life of privilege few will ever know."

With hands in his jean pockets, Elliott looked around the cold dirt room deep in the catacombs. "You see Adam lately?"

"No. But that's Adam. Always been a man of few words. Could have stopped by a few times. I'd never know it."

Elliott leaned over the computer monitor. The constant flow of coded instructions was met with a flurry of entries launching new screens. Elliott watched Marcus type a cascade of back and forward slashes, numbers, colons, stars, and upper-lower case letters. "I'm starting to see how important you are to our little project." He smiled as he lifted a folding chair over an exposed power line running across the dirt floor.

"Thanks for not unplugging me." Marcus played the keyboard like a piano. "While I was down here waiting for our infamous hard drive—thank you Albert Bell—I hunted for a power source. Found a live outlet in the basement of the Brent mansion and the old conduit leading to my favorite room—here."

"You worked in this room before?"

"Yeah. This was where we did data entry." He pointed over his shoulder. "Those boxes are full of computer hardware. Old, but I found enough stuff to build this baby." He patted the side of the outdated, dirty white monitor. Dust puffed into the air by the flickering light of the small kerosene lantern.

"We need to get an electric lamp and new tower and monitor."

"I'm good for now." He kept responding to the parade of prompts. Completed screenshots minimized and lined up with flashing red borders. "I knew then about the conduit. Took a while to find it. Caked with dry mud and god-awful spider webs and dead bugs. I reamed the pipe with some stiff cable. Found a roll in the basement. Fed a line this morning."

"Impressive." Elliott kept looking over his shoulder as if he expected someone. "We need a talented man down here."

"I'm through the first partition. Did not trigger my father's favorite security virus—the Chernobyl Viper. One missed entry stoke unleashes that bad boy."

"It renders the hard drive useless?" Elliott asked.

"Exactly." Marcus's fingers explode into rapid fire. "Sorry. Had a time limit on that one. One error and the viper eats up the data so fast it melts the casing on the hard drive."

Elliott straightened in his chair. "Shouldn't you slow down? You're only trying to access the secret formula for the greatest evolutionary leap for mankind."

"Thanks for the added pressure. The trouble is, everything's timed. If I slow down, I can miss windows and screw up for sure. The faster I type, the more accurate my work." Marcus pounded the keys at an even faster rate.

"Your father tutored you on this access process?"

"It's been three years." Marcus kept pounding the keyboard. "I have to focus now."

Elliott explored the dirt room with his penlight as Marcus typed. There were tables on one wall with boxes of computer hardware and stacks of files. On the table nearest him were smaller boxes and a stack of notepads. He picked up one and fanned through.

"Those are some of my father's notes," Marcus said with his eyes on the monitor.

Elliott smiled and opened it. Inside were scribbled notes, drawings of molecules, sketches of the double helix DNA with labeled nucleotides, and cryptic notations on certain sequences:

their composition, the associated organic chemistry, and proteins. There were pages and pages of endless equations. When Elliott returned it to the top of the stack, something fluttered from its pages and settled on the dirt floor—a fifty dollar bill.

"Whose fifty?" Elliott asked.

"I suppose a gift to me from my father."

"A gift?" He started to put it back in the notebook.

Marcus kept entering with his nose inches from the monitor. "Well, I say a gift. I found it in the leather box Mr. Bell gave me. It was under the hard drive."

Elliott took a closer look by the lantern. "Why would he put a fifty-dollar bill in there?"

"Great . . ."

Elliott turned back to Marcus. "Great what . . . ?"

"We've reached the pivotal point I wanted to show you." Green numbers and letters streamed spanning the width of the monitor and raining down.

"Don't pay any attention to this. It's a trap." Marcus pointed to the left side screen. "We wait until this margin moves right. It must cross the fifty percent vertical. When it does, I hit the delete key and we are in."

Elliott scratched his head watching the thousands of characters flow. "I don't see how anyone could know that. And even if they got this far it seems like you'd hit 'enter' not 'delete'."

"This program's full of traps. Most security software geeks know a lot of this stuff. That's why my father has his own twists on things. As a rule, never do the obvious.

"We are in . . . now."

"So you've been here before?" Elliott asked.

"Yes, but . . ." Marcus watched the screen. Elliott watched Marcus. Marcus entered more codes. "Although there have been countless attempts to override the biological clock, no one ever got there until now, Dr. Sumner. I know your medical knowledge keeps you from embracing this incredible possibility."

"Let's just say I'm not a believer. I'm waiting for the science."

Marcus leaned back from the monitor. "We have three minutes." He checked his watch. "I also know by now you've done your homework, looked at the most current research, and read the most current publications on the matter. I know you've seen the emerging biotechnology and the progress made on understanding the human genome. I'll bet you've read the latest in genetic engineering, therapeutic cloning, stem cells, and cryogenics, just to name a few."

Elliott stared at the monitor. "I always do my homework. It doesn't take me as long as others, and never forget what I learn. Sometimes it's not a good thing."

"My father was an active member of the American Academy of Anti-Aging Medicine. He tried to share his work but no one would listen, or they didn't understand. That's how he found Jack Bellow, the one man willing to sit down with him."

A menu popped up onto the screen.

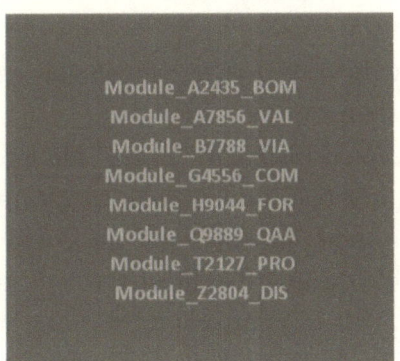

Module_A2435_BOM
Module_A7856_VAL
Module_B7788_VIA
Module_G4556_COM
Module_H9044_FOR
Module_Q9889_QAA
Module_T2127_PRO
Module_Z2804_DIS

"This is the main menu—eight modules. Each opens to a set of security hurdles. The first module is a bill-of-materials . . . the component parts needed to produce the biologic."

"And the other modules?"

Marcus ran his finger down the screen stopping on each. "There are extensive work files: validation, viability, compounding, formulation, quality assurance, production, and what my father calls dissemination. I call it distribution and administering."

"When we started, you said there were problems."

"I can get into seven modules. I cannot get into H9044."

"The formula module," Elliott said. "The most important one."

Marcus moved the cursor over module H9044 and clicked. A picture of the U.S. Capital filled the screen.

"This is as far as I get. I'm not sure what to do with it. If I make the wrong entry, the formula is destroyed and all other modules are useless."

Elliott leaned closer. "Let's think. What is Dr. Medino telling us with this picture? And is that blinking box waiting for your next entry?"

"Yes, it is."

"How long can you stay on this screen without triggering something bad?"

"Don't know. Best we not test it. Should exit and discuss." Marcus reached for escape.

Elliott intercepted his hand. "Wait." He looked at the fifty-dollar bill. *This is a Series-2004 gold certificate,* he thought. *It was minted the year Medino and Jack started the LIFE2 Corporation.* "Didn't your father break the code in 2004?"

"Yes. March." Marcus stared at the flashing box. "He tested it on himself in June. He almost died. Not from the biologic, but from his chemo for pancreatic cancer. When he got off it the benefits of his biologic became evident." Marcus turned to the monitor. "I really think we should . . ."

"I saw the video files of your father in October and December

—miraculous. Jack walked away from four successful business ventures to invest everything he had in your father and his biotechnology. Jack's participation is why I'm in this now. I know he saw something."

"Why's all the history important now?" Marcus asked.

"Because your father and my brother were on a path. We need to get on it so we can start thinking like them and figure this out." Elliott turned the fifty over and held it to the lantern. "This is the same picture of the U.S. Capitol that's on the screen. Go ahead and exit."

Marcus hit escape. The file closed and computer powered down. "Our family never had a lot of money. If a message is being sent, my father would not make it too obtuse."

Elliott pulled a fifty from his wallet and set both on the table. "Your father's fifty has serial numbers on both sides of the bill. There shouldn't be any on the U.S. Capitol side. Those numbers have been added. One is eleven and the other is twelve numbers long. Some are in bold print."

"What could it mean?" Marcus asked as he studied the bills.

"Letters in a sequence are supposed to tie to one of twelve Federal Reserve Districts."

"Is this the photographic memory I've heard about?"

Elliott nodded. "Twelve Federal Reserve Districts. I won't

bore you with the details, but for example 'A' is Boston, 'B' is New York, and so on."

"I see an 'N' and 'E' and 'W' in these fake serial numbers. What districts are they?"

"None. Those letters are never used by the Federal Reserve. And something else, there's a negative sixty-two in front of the words 'U.S. Capitol'."

"What could all this mean?" Marcus asked.

Elliott slid the Medino fifty into an envelope. "We need to think about this. I'm having dinner tonight with someone good with puzzles . . ."

TWENTY-SEVEN

"I believe in the doctrine of meliorism." Carol held the Ulysses S. Grant by the light and moved a slow magnifying glass.

"Really. You're going there tonight?"

Elliott got up from the sofa with his drink and stood by the window. From the twelfth floor apartment he could see up Second Avenue and down Union almost to the river. The night mist turned into a steady rain—from the Peabody, the city of Memphis sparkled even more. But the spectacular view, the scotch, and his plan for an intimate evening would not deter him. He would not lose this argument. Elliott would not risk losing Carol again. He could not expose the woman he loved to the unpredictable dangers gathering around him.

"You can't keep thinking this way, protecting me from the world, Elliott."

"Meliorism—the world can become a better place with human effort—is nice, but not my reality. Evil is around every corner—I attract it. Why do you think I've been alone all my life?"

"Because you had not met me," she teased. "Elliott, this is what life's about. You find someone and fall in love. You don't stop living. Life is full of risks."

"I understand, but I'm not your typical guy, darling. I'm a genetically engineered being created by bad people. They're trying to kill me, Carol. They're very powerful, well resourced, and determined. I can't expose you to that incredible risk."

"First, you're not a creation of men. You have a mother and a father."

"You know what I mean."

"Genetic engineering enhances traits. You are not a Frankenstein."

"Still, I didn't know my mother or father until I was forty, and Gilgamesh monitored me my whole life. My point. They want more and will do anything to get it. People around me die. I am at the top of their list. I cannot put you in the middle of this hell storm."

"After the death of seven board members and the chairman, Gilgamesh can never be the same. I don't care if the survivors got control of their GICC. This time the whole world's looking for them, Elliott. They can't hide long. They're not a stealth organization anymore. The FBI, CIA, Interpol, and every law enforcement agency in the world has their pictures. We know where they live. Their assets are frozen. They are hunted men. And Albert just met with the two hundred members and ended their participation in the sick little club."

"Darling, I could never forgive myself if anything happened to you because of me."

"And that's how I feel about you." Carol went to the window and wrapped her arms around his waist. "Ell . . . Love makes everything in this world feel different. It's supposed to expand life, not put limits on it."

They kissed.

"I've never loved before, because I'm different," Elliott whispered. "I took my biological assets and tried to help make this world safer."

"There you go—meliorism."

"But I'm surrounded by death, Carol. I'm hunted by people who want to control the world. These three monsters are more dangerous and unpredictable than Alberto Bella."

She spoke into his warm chest. "Before we met I lived in danger too. My life as a freelance investigative reporter, and a single woman on the west coast, put me in harm's way on a regular basis. To get to the bottom of the stories that mattered, I had to take many risks. Ell, nothing's changed. I think we are a lot alike. We just need to trust we both can handle the world."

Granted, Memphis is where I escaped the Butcher's knife three times, Carol thought. *And Gilgamesh did use me to lure you. I gotta find a way to remove this burden. I can handle the risks, but I put you in danger . . . you are now vulnerable and they know it . .*

.

"Let's not spend all evening on this," Elliott whispered. "I had other plans." His hand slid down the curve of her back and pulled her close.

Carol looked up. Her long, blond hair fell from her face revealing her soft neck and moist lips and big, round, sensuous eyes. But the amorous look was replaced with a serious one. At the moment, Carol had something very different in mind.

"Coordinates!" she whispered when Elliott's lips touched hers.

He froze, still unwilling to abandon his mission. "Coordinates . . . of course."

She kissed him, not the way he hoped, a peck. "The bogus serial numbers on the gold certificate, I think they are coordinates."

Elliott followed her to the sofa. They sat close. "You said there were serial numbers added to this bill."

"Right . . . the side with the capitol building."

"I thought about it all during dinner. It's been percolating and just dawned on me. What if those numbers are longitude and latitude coordinates?"

"N2958453183E," Elliott recited from memory. "The N and the E could be north and east. The letters don't tie back to a Federal Reserve Bank. I can see them as degrees, minutes, and seconds." He set down his wine glass. "Where's your laptop?"

She pulled it from under a stack of newspapers on the coffee table. "So we're goin' to a longitude/latitude site, right?"

"Google something simple like—find a latitude and longitude."

"Gee, there's only four-million sites." She picked one and scrolled. "Here we go. Okay photographic-memory-man; give me numbers to put in the boxes."

"Latitude box 29.5845. In the longitude box 31.0803." The U.S. map disappeared and the Mideast loaded. A red circle marked the location of the new coordinates. The two stared.

Carol reached blindly for her wine glass and took a sip. "Egypt? What are we looking at? I'm gonna zoom in on this location."

"The Great Pyramid of Giza," Elliott whispered.

"Why would coordinates of a pyramid be on Dr. Medino's fifty-dollar bill?"

"Put in the second bogus serial number," Elliott said.

"You already know. Okay, give 'em to me, smart guy."

"Latitude 35.0920. Longitude 90.0307." The map changed.

"Memphis, Tennessee?" She zoomed. "This is very weird. Those are the coordinates for the Memphis Pyramid Arena. Did you know? My God, Dr. Medino connected the Memphis

Pyramid to the Great Pyramid of Giza. Okay, I'm Googling Memphis Pyramid Arena."

Elliott rubbed the pain climbing the back of his neck. Carol went to the Wikipedia site. Elliott scanned the screen taking in everything in seconds.

"What's important here? They built it in 1991, at a cost of $110 million. The official name is the Great American Pyramid. It is a sixty percent replica of The Great Pyramid of Giza."

Elliott pulled out a pen and grabbed a file off the coffee table. "Give me the height of the Memphis Pyramid"

"It is 321 feet."

"And the pyramid in Giza?" he asked, as he drew a grid with several columns.

"Giza is 455 feet," she said. Elliott labeled two columns—Memphis and Giza—and inserted the numbers and asked for the bill. Elliott's cell phone buzzed, Marcus.

"I've just been in touch with Max about a meeting tomorrow with some LIFE2 researchers and a Dr. Vince Vanlandingham. This is follow up to my request for help."

"Yes, getting the biologic ready for global distribution . . . assuming we get to your father's formula, and assuming it works." Elliott watched Carol pour wine. "I heard this Vanlandingham guy is a lead geneticist fully vetted."

"I'm uncomfortable. Why be with Gilgamesh in the first place? Why trust him?"

"The story is one of desperation. Years ago, Vanlandingham needed money to take care of a sick family member who later died. Gilgamesh made him an offer he couldn't pass up. They took care of everything. Later, Vanlandingham realized he made a mistake. He could not get out."

"He couldn't pay them back and leave?" Marcus asked.

"No one leaves Gilgamesh, Marcus. They stay or disappear. The dissolution of Gilgamesh should set free a lot of good people.

Vanlandingham appears to be one," Elliott said. "Regarding the meeting, it's at LIFE2 downtown at 6:00 a.m. tomorrow morning. The handpicked scientists have been vetted, too. They don't know the reason for the meeting. I want you in another room. I'll bring you in if it's right."

"Okay. I'll be there. Before I hang up, have you gotten anywhere with the fifty-dollar bill?"

"We think so. I'll tell you in a minute. Right now we're considering the negative sixty-two. It could have been inserted anywhere on this bill. Your father put it in front of the words 'U.S. Capitol', and positioned it under the picture of the government building. I'm putting you on speaker. Carol's with me."

"My father did everything for a reason," Marcus said. "If he and Jack Bellows were killed, I know he wanted the hard drive to get to me—I would understand the formula and synthesizing processes. He put the fifty-dollar bill in there for me to find. I know how he thinks."

"We're listening."

"The sixty-two ties to something under the U.S. Capitol building," Marcus said.

Carol leaned to the phone. "Are you saying something's buried there?"

"No. That would be impossible—government security and all. My father spent all his life in Mexico, Texas, and Tennessee. Today I studied the U.S. Capitol building looking for something to tie to these common places."

Elliott stared at his grid, the two headings and numbers. "In your notes, do you have measurements for the capitol building?"

"Sure do. It's 288 feet tall."

Elliott wrote the number in the third box and labeled the column—capitol. "Sixty-two is twenty-one-point-five percent of 288," Elliot mumbled.

"We connected the bogus serial numbers to coordinates— longitude and latitude. One takes us to the Great Pyramid of Giza. The other coordinates take us to the Memphis Pyramid Arena in downtown Memphis."

"He often talked about the pyramid downtown," Marcus muttered.

"Now we have a third location—the U.S. Capitol building." Elliott ran calculations, comparisons, and concepts as he scribbled notes.

"Your father lived in Memphis the last twenty-five years of his life," Carol said. "He experienced the building of the pyramid arena downtown. Why is he taking us there? Is he using Giza and the U.S. Capital building to take us to a place in the Memphis Pyramid?"

"You're right." Elliott filled the boxes of his grid with numbers.

Marcus whispered, "The password for the formula module is somewhere in the Memphis Pyramid. It makes perfect sense, but where?"

"Giza has a subterranean chamber ninety-eight feet under the pyramid," Elliott said. "That's twenty-one-point-five percent of the 455-foot height."

"Sixty-two is twenty-one-point-five percent of the U.S. Capitol building's 288-foot height," Marcus said. "It's an exact connect."

"If the figures hold, we need to find a subterranean chamber under the Memphis Pyramid."

"God, you think they built a subterranean chamber?" Carol said.

"I doubt it. Probably a preexisting structure. If our calculations and assumptions are correct, it's sixty-two feet down." Elliott poured wine into their empty glasses. "Your father gave us everything we need. I think you're right, Marcus. The password we seek is down there."

"It's in the catacombs . . . or those old drainage tunnels under the city. I'll bet one or both pass under the pyramid sixty-two feet down," Marcus said "It's on my map."

Carol smiled as she and her wineglass barefooted over to the window and view of the city. *Now all we need to do is find it,* she thought, listening to Elliott and Marcus bounce thoughts.

A pair of lights in the parking garage across the way moved down each dark, empty level. In an almost hypnotic trance, Carol's eyes followed, the wine taking hold. When the lights reached the quiet streets of Memphis, she glanced over at the First Tennessee Bank building on the other side of Union. Now late, the dark building loomed over the lighted streets.

She closed the curtains each night before bed because in the morning she could see into each office, and they could see her. On this night she did not see the eyes on her. They were not from an office window. Carol missed the large shadow on the rooftop, the one that had been there the last three nights. It hunkered down, leaning over the edge two stories above the Peabody's twelfth floor.

"Remember I don't have experience in the catacombs more than a few hundred yards away from the Brent mansion," Marcus said. "But we know who does."

Carol closed the drapes and returned to the sofa. She turned off the only light and sat next to Elliott with a soft smile.

"Leave a note on the board for Adam. Tell him I need his help. I'll meet him at nine o'clock tomorrow night on Mud Island, our usual place."

"Why Mud Island?"

"I prefer minimizing my underground experience. Adam will know a nearby entrance into the catacombs or city tunnels."

Carol's hand slid up the inside of his pant leg and she nibbled on his neck. He turned to her. She had the look in her eyes he could not resist.

"Marcus, I think we're done for tonight. I will see you at LIFE2 tomorrow morning." He set down the phone. Carol wanted him now . . .

TWENTY-EIGHT

The text message came from Harris's phone—IF WANT SEE ALIVE COME TO MEMPHIS LIBRARY FOURTH FLOOR.

Only Harris knew Wilcox had landed late Sunday night. When the cell phone vibrated as the plane touched down, Wilcox expected some lame attempt to welcome him home. The text message changed everything. He hit speed dial. Harris's went straight to message. Then he called Memphis homicide.

"This is Wilcox. Where you got Harris tonight?"

"Harris didn't come in today," Bedford said.

"He had the weekend. Did you talk to him?"

"He wasn't answering his phone. We sent Thomas to his place to check. No one came to the door. Car was gone. Figured he was running around."

"Didn't you think it the slightest bit suspicious, Bedford?" Tony changed ears, staring at Max in the opposing seat.

"Yes, we did," Bedford barked back. "But Harris called in sick before we could get all crazy, Wilcox. Said he wasn't home because he felt like shit. Went to his mother's for some tender loving care. Look, I gotta go."

Harris never cusses. "Did Harris say—feels like shit—or is that you talkin' Bedford?"

"He said it, Wilcox. Verbatim."

Did anybody call his mother to check on him?"

The Dassault Falcon taxied across the tarmac and neared the dark hanger. Wilcox stared out the small window, waiting for Bedford to say something to explain away the text. He saw his car and felt for his keys.

"This ain't no babysitting service, Wilcox. Where the hell are you, and why don't you check on your partner? I gotta go. Got my own shit to deal with . . ."

"Mrs. Harris. Tony here. Sorry to call so late. Just got back in town. Alex's not picking up his phone. I need to talk to him. Is here there?"

"No. If he's not working, he should be at his apartment. Have you tried there?"

"No ma'am. I'll do that. Thank you."

The Falcon rolled to a stop in front of the hanger on the wet tarmac. Max did not ask Tony why he jammed his cell in his pocket and checked his gun. He got enough when they stared at each other as their small jet navigated lumbering commercial airlines crossing runways at Memphis International. Max had seen the look before. He pieced together the phone conversation —Harris missing. He watched Tony read a text before he called MPD. It couldn't be good. But who would harm Detective Harris? Max knew whoever it was, Tony would go it alone. There was nothing he could say or do to change that.

Before the turbines stopped spinning, Tony popped open the door and landed on the wet tarmac. Max stayed buckled. "Call me if . . ." Soon he heard the squealing tires. He leaned to the small, oval window. Tony's car fishtailed out of the parking lot onto the access road and accelerated. Headlights passed cars and disappeared over the horizon.

Raymond Munson died on October 17, 2000. The retired English professor was an unlikely homicide victim. The old man's days were a predictable balance between reading, napping, and fishing. Why would anyone slice him up and hang him from the ceiling on the fourth floor of the Memphis Public Library? Then they learned Munson had touched the Bluff City Butcher's life in a bad way twenty-five years earlier.

When Tony turned off Poplar into the dimly lit parking lot, he saw Harris's car in the fire lane in front of the four story glass building. He slowed and jumped out. His car hopped the curb and butted up against the metal bike stand on the south side.

Looking inside, Wilcox pulled his gun and moved across the front of the dark building. The only light inside poured down the glass staircase from the fourth floor. The rest of the nightlights were off. The first door was open. He went in and hugged the wall. He saw blood. A few feet into the darkest shadows he found the night watchman—dead—throat cut. Next to the body he saw a bloody message on the tile, an arrow and one word—UP.

He had to assume they knew he had arrived, even though he had traveled a twenty-minute distance from the airport in eight. Wilcox suspected they would be upstairs waiting. He climbed slow. Listened after each step. The Munson case had prepared him for the layout.

Five minutes later at the top, he lowered his gun. He saw what he refused to accept. Harris and he were alone. The naked body hung from the ceiling like Raymond Munson, arms outstretched, hands dropped at the wrists like a man trying to fly, an incision where the heart used to be. The sutures were small and tight, and the wound neatly trimmed. Harris' lips were gone. His nose, eyes. And ears, too, and each orifice had been stitched closed like a rag doll. Wilcox did not see any blood. Harris had died somewhere else. The three-word message carved on Harris's stomach made Wilcox gag—*I am back . . .*

Elliott's cell vibrated. He reached for the nightstand. Carol sat up in bed, the sheet dropped from her breasts and her hair draped over her shoulder. "Is it Tony?" she asked. He nodded.

"Tony. You back from Cape Town?" *Something bad happened. You never call me unless . . .*

"I'm at the Memphis Public Library on Poplar. You remember the place. Alex Harris has been killed, Elliott."

"Alex killed!" He watched Carol put on his T-shirt and throw her hair out of the way. This time her beauty did not register. She came to him and sat on the bed rubbing his back. She heard the two, terrible words.

"I'm here alone," Tony whispered. "Got a fucking text when the plane landed. Got here as fast as I could. It said if I wanted to see Alex alive, come alone." He turned from the carnage. "He's been tortured, Elliott. It's a recreation of the Raymond Munson killing."

Elliott slid out of the bed and reached for his pants. "Recreation? What does that mean?"

"A fucking perfect duplication, Elliott. I don't need to be a forensic expert to see."

"I'm sorry, Tony."

"Harris bled out. His goddamn heart's been cut out of his chest. He's stitched up exactly the way the Butcher does it. The bastard took his lips, eyes, nose, and ears—sewed up all that shit. He's naked, just hanging here in the same place we found Munson." Tony's voice broke. "I'm looking at my dead partner, Elliott. Fucking Adam did this. He is sick. We gotta stop him."

"I'm coming now. Are you sure you're alone?" He stepped into his shoes as Carol helped him with his shirt.

Tony looked around for the first time. Harris hung from the

ceiling in the only lighted area. Tony leveled his gun and aimed in each direction, hoping for a target to kill. "I think."

"Have you called it in?"

"Not yet." He turned the opposite direction and looked deep into the rows of bookshelves. "I don't see the bastard anywhere. I pray to God I do. I will kill that fucker this time, Elliott. I will empty my gun in him and then jump on his carcass and beat the living hell out of him until he stops breathing."

Elliott stopped dressing and looked at Carol. She too had the look on her face. They both believed the Bluff City Butcher killed again. "Tony. Adam did not kill Harris. It's staged."

"Are you blind? Elliott. That sick bastard kills people."

"Listen to me, Tee."

"Just because he talks to you doesn't mean he's cured. He's a psychopathic freak and you know it. I'm looking at his work right now."

"Adam only killed Gilgamesh soldiers trying to kill Dr. Medino or him."

"Munson was not a Gilgamesh soldier. He killed him."

"No, he did not. Gilgamesh killed Munson along with other innocent people to perpetuate the legend. We know this now. Gilgamesh set them up to get law enforcement to hunt their nemesis. You know Adam has not been tied to killing innocent people, Tony. You're smarter than this."

Wilcox leaned against the table looking at his young partner. "Adam killed more than a hundred people over twenty-five years. You just don't do that without being crazy. Pull your head out of the sand. Come out here and look for yourself. I'll call it in after."

"I'm sorry about Alex, Tony. But you know me. I don't make mistakes on matters like this. I promise you, Adam had nothing to do with Alex Harris's death. Adam is no different from one of our soldiers fighting on the front lines. He's not a monster. None of this is important right now. What is important is learning from this tragedy so we can stop Gilgamesh once and for all. I'm on my way."

"I guess he had nothing to do with killing the *second* Panther McGee—another duplication. Last night. Same park bench. Same bloodletting. Same heart removal and same suturing skills —the *Knot of Isis*, Elliott. You know we never told anyone about that damn knot."

"Something's not right."

"You're not opening your eyes. Your brother's killing again. He can't stop. He's reliving something. It won't be long before this city is crawling the walls again and the brass is all over us. They'll know the Butcher is doing this. It'll take all our attention off the resurrected Gilgamesh shit. Hell, we won't have time to mess with Medino's formula or any of this *saving the world* shit . . ."

"While you were out of the country I got a call from Deputy Chief Cottam."

"Oh yeah. So what did he have to say?"

"Boris Tanner escaped the holding facilities downtown."

"So you want to put this on Tanner?"

You're gonna have to catch up on your own. I'm done talking about this. "I'm leaving now." Elliott pocketed his cell and turned to Carol. "We've got to be at LIFE2 in five hours."

"Go without me. Killing an MPD homicide detective will turn this city upside down."

"They'll sit on it as long as they can," Elliott said.

"The *Tribune* won't let it alone. If these cases look like BCB work, they'll develop it."

"I think it's important you be at the LIFE2 meeting in the beginning," Elliott said. "You may see something we all miss."

"When Tony calls in the homicide, I need to be at the *Tribune* to keep it on the rails as long as I can. You know they'll connect the obvious dots. People will want to take another look at the night Adam died. There's gonna be questions and speculation. Tony's right about one thing. Our effort to get the Medino biologic to the world just got harder."

"I can get enough forensic evidence to show this is the work of a copycat. Henderson Bates and Collin Wade are recovering. Bates may be ready to resume his role. He can help deflect the mob tendency."

"Bates is a good medical examiner, but they won't listen to him for a while. He's still struggling with injuries, Elliott. And he'll never overcome the memory of the night when you kept the Butcher alive in the attic at the Bell mansion. Regardless of his pledge to you, it haunts him. And Director Wade is in complete denial, almost a mental case. The mayor never liked him. They'll never let him resume his role as the director.

"Elliott, don't underestimate how the unbridled fear of the Butcher legend will change priorities in this town. People will demand time and attention from the top forensic investigator in the world—you. They will put Albert back under the microscope."

Gilgamesh is orchestrating these kills, a calculated diversion strategy. They can stay in the background and kill each of us, build fear and chaos, and hide their mission.

They walked down the quiet hall to the elevator. Carol pressed the button. They embraced. Elliott whispered, "Albert's been through a lot. He's lost everyone. Now he's afraid he'll lose Betty and me. I need him to take lead at the LIFE2 meeting. He knows international business. He must figure out how to get this biologic into the world. I hope he's up to it."

"His patriarch skills will kick in, Elliott. Albert is a strong man, like his son."

His finger moved a few strands of hair from her eye. *I hope you're right.* He looked down the empty hall. "Max is good with the vetting process, too. Said he has five scientists for us to look at in the morning. Marcus is the one who needs to be comfortable."

"Having an investigative reporter from the *Tribune* there sends the wrong message."

"Not any more than a forensic pathologist."

Carol pulled him close. "It's all happening, Elliott. If Dr. Medino's breakthrough is real, I can't imagine what it'd be like, living hundreds of years. What kind of a world is that?"

"I don't know. But I do know we've been given the responsibility to get it out there. And if it's real, I wouldn't mind hanging with you a few more centuries." He pulled her closer.

"Ell, without you we don't have a chance." She rubbed his neck and looked into his eyes. "The next time you question your life and your incredible gifts, think about us." She kissed him and pushed him onto the elevator. "And I know it wasn't Adam."

He winked. The elevator doors closed.

At the end of the hall, another door closed . . .

TWENTY-NINE

The old Cotton Exchange Building downtown sat vacant more than a decade. Jack Bellow, an acclaimed biotech entrepreneur, purchased the property without fanfare, and one year later the global headquarters of the LIFE2 Corporation was announced. On that cold January day, no one could have known the attention Memphis, Tennessee would get as the home of a revolutionary healthcare company introducing biogenic solutions that would change everything.

Over the ensuing years, LIFE2 developed their first product —human cartilage regeneration. As the FDA clinical investigation progressed, it became clear the noninvasive biologic could slow and often reverse the osteoarthritic disease process. The advance would benefit an aging world population and cripple the orthopedic medical device industry dependent upon profit streams from total joint replacement surgery.

The threat of massive change in the treatment of orthopedic degenerative disease would start the healthcare war—LIFE2 pitted against the orthopedic industry, physicians, and healthcare providers. Battles would be waged on all fronts, most covert and some lethal.

Jack Bellow and Dr. Medino understood the war. And only they knew the Ossi2 orthopedic product was only the beginning. The decoy product was the least disruptive way to build a global distribution network that one day would take their veiled life extension biologic to the world. It would be the product the FDA would never be given access to approve. It would be the single medical advance to change more than healthcare. Living forever changes everything.

At six o'clock on Monday morning, the LIFE2 Corporation doors would open in two hours. The skeleton staff of the innovative biotech company in hibernation would begin another workday with questions and doubts about their futures. Inside, the sun cut through the vertical blinds transforming the boardroom into a long, narrow prison cell. Every few inches the blinding bars of light climbed the walls and crossed the ceiling in a sea of floating dust, forever choking the old building by the river. Squinting, the tall, silver-haired patriarch entered from the CEO's office.

Impeccably dressed—a charcoal pinstriped suit, white shirt with French cuffs and diamond studs, and a brilliant red and gold paisley tie—Albert walked to the chair at the head of the twenty-foot conference table. He paused and looked at the five pairs of eyes. A thin, travel worn, leather satchel dangled from his left hand as he greeted each with a professional nod. Albert's confident smile and calm demeanor projected a rare sense of wisdom and put the room at ease.

"Good morning, my friends," Albert said.

His eyes found Dr. Vanlandingham, the large man in the tight-fitting lab coat. He looked more like a heavyweight boxer than a gifted bench technician and geneticist. Dr. Vanlandingham had been instrumental in the selection of the other scientists present, the four sitting in a covey at the far end of the long table. They were unsure of Albert, the interim COB appointed by the SEC following stockholder fraud and a failed takeover. They did know Albert Bell was the only reason LIFE2 continued to exist after the deaths of the founders and investor improprieties. Albert pulled out the tall leather chair. He smiled when he saw the steaming cup of coffee. Vanlandingham closed the blinds and set the room free.

Albert sat and sipped his coffee in the silence. He unzipped his satchel and removed a single sheet of stationary. After setting it before him on the polished cherry wood, he placed his Mont Blanc horizontal to the first line of notes only he could decipher—there were five lines.

How shall I begin? he thought, as he settled into his chair and considered the task before them and the risks facing all who joined their mission.

The cramped and stuffy room possessed a musty mix of old dust, new mold, and too much Pine-Sol. The muffled honks in streets three floors down mixed with the whir of the ceiling fans stirring the respiratory mess. Albert had to move forward. They needed the people at the table involved.

"Today LIFE2 employs eighty-four people, including twenty-nine of the most highly skilled geneticists, cell biologists, physiologists, biochemists, and physician specialists in the world. You've been selected to be here based on specific criteria that has less to do with scientific credentials and more to do with character."

Albert leaned forward and clasped his hands on the table. He cocked his head and leveled his steel blue eyes with an intensity that made the timid uncomfortable. "This will be the most important meeting of your life. By the close, you will understand why. And you will know what you will do. You are invited to be a part of an important mission. Your decision to participate is yours alone. There will be no questions asked of you. There will be no judgments made of you. And there will be no repercussions. Am I clear . . . ?"

The five looked at each other and then back to Albert. They nodded as one.

"Should you decline, I ask you honor my one request." Albert sipped his coffee and set the cup down as he made eye contact with each person at the table before his next words.

"You need sign nothing. You verbally agree to comply. Your word is what binds you. Regardless of your decision, I require you to never discuss what you are about to hear in this room—not any part, not ever. If you cannot give me your word, please excuse yourself now."

He waited. No one moved. Then each scientist spoke one after the other. Each of the four gave Albert their word. Dr. Vanlandingham stood, gave his word of honor, bowed, and sat down.

The door opened. Elliott took the seat by Albert. Max patted Vanlandingham's shoulder and sat next to him.

"You know Maxwell Gregory from the vetting process," Albert said. Max tapped his forehead. "And this is Dr. Elliott Sumner, physician and consultant . . .

"No doubt the last year of disruptions, tragedies, and the unknown has made everything suspect at LIFE2. After receiving a meeting invitation from me, I suspect you stayed up much of the night thinking like scientists think, running scenarios and solving problems. What could Albert Bell want with me? The terrible stories about the founders and the uncertainty of the science, are they true? Maybe I need to leave now."

Max poured coffee into Albert's cup and moved around the table like a bee to flowers. When he sat, Albert slid his Mont Blanc to line two. Elliott watched with approving eyes.

"Dr. Medino has discovered the secret to immortal life, continuous cell renewal."

Albert touched his cup to his lips and allowed the words to settle in. When wide eyes and whispers moved to elbows on the table, he continued.

"You're smart people, brightest in the world at what you do, or you would not be here. You've always known the possibility existed—from your work with Ossi2, of course. If Dr. Medino can regenerate a cartilage cell, he understands a mechanism. We can do this with other cells.

"It is true. Dr. Medino has found a biogenic secret to continuous cellular replication. As you know, this is a common occurrence in all organisms. We've never understood why the process slows with aging, and then stops. Something I'm learning firsthand . . .

"Dr. Medino believed *life* to be a miracle, extending it a far less ominous feat. But his discovery is more than life extension. Dr. Medino's efforts to protect DNA and promote continuous cell renewal had an unexpected side effect, one never thought possible. Diseased and damaged cells were replaced with healthy cells. This biogenic breakthrough may cure disease. Rather than relying on an immune response, the elimination and replacement of damaged or diseased cells may be the answer we've been looking for. Time will tell"

Albert moved his pen to the third line. "I've said all I'm qualified to say about the science. I shall stop here. Suffice it to say we asked you to come today because we believe we have in our hands a world-changing biogenic solution for human health and immortality.

"Rumor . . . Dr. Medino and his family were killed. It is true. The one car 'accident' in north Memphis was *not* an accident. It was intentional." Each scientist squirmed.

"Rumor . . . Jack Bellow was my son. That is true. Jack

Bellow, Elliott Sumner, and Adam Duncan are my sons. And yes, Adam Duncan is the Bluff City Butcher of Memphis urban legend." The room reeled. Albert waited. "But that too is not as it seems. Adam is not a monstrous serial killer, randomly preying on innocent people. We have discovered Adam has been fighting a secret war against a sinister force for many years, protecting Dr. Medino. I tell you this because knowing the truths will help you understand our mission and the associated risks . . . should you decide to join us."

Albert poured more coffee, walked to the window, and opened a slat. The room waited. He looked at the street three floors below—the endless stream of cars, and the business people and tourists crowding the sidewalks, and the horse drawn carriages. The city was bright and alive. He smiled inside, thinking of Jack and the view he had experienced many times as the CEO of LIFE2. They shared a moment. It was all Albert would ever have with the son he never knew. He pushed back the surging emotion and turned back to the waiting eyes.

"Gilgamesh is a century-old secret society of the very privileged—billionaires—pursuing the secrets of human immortality. Somewhere along the way, their mission broadened. Not only would they seek immortality, they would want to control it. Gilgamesh would determine who lived forever. These men lost their way—drunk on a dream. In their world where everything is possible, it made perfect sense they would control the greatest evolutionary leap for mankind. Their dream became an obsession, and turned into a nightmare.

"Gilgamesh embarked on secret, unsanctioned research and illegal human experimentation in the 1960's—genetic engineering, cloning, stem cell transplantation, cryogenics, pharmaceuticals and more. They used my DNA without my knowledge. They used me and the woman I love. It led to the birth of triplets, three sons I would not know existed until forty years later. This unimaginable behavior is but one exhibit of their demented nature and evil ways.

"My sons benefitted from the most advanced science in the world at the time. They are gifted in many ways—sensory perception, genius intellect, physical advantages and much more. But they lived alone in the world. They were monitored like laboratory rats. They were the unknowing specimens under the Gilgamesh microscope, used and manipulated.

"Imagine being alone in the world, not knowing who you are, where you came from, and why you are different. I did not know my sons existed. Their mother was taken from me and forced into exile. The three were separated at birth and dispersed for random adoption and constant observation. Then the day came. Gilgamesh no longer viewed my sons as assets—they had minds of their own. They could not be controllable any longer. Their genetic-engineered advantages presented an untenable risk—one Gilgamesh would be unwilling to accept.

"My sons became liabilities. Gilgamesh released termination orders. Their stealth army of trained assassins eliminated hundreds of innocent people over a half a century. They terminated Dr. Medino and his family. Now they had to remove the last obstacles to achieving their mission. They had to terminate my three sons, their mother, and me.

"Dr. Medino crossed the finish line before Gilgamesh. He found the secret to life extension. It is why they killed him. They believed they commandeered his research. They were wrong. We have it. And unlike Gilgamesh, we will take it to the world, or destroy it."

"Excuse me, Mr. Bell," Dr. Vanlandingham interrupted. "You may have Dr. Medino's research, but we scientists understand too well one man's research can be another man's unsolvable puzzle. Without intimate knowledge of how Dr. Medino thinks, we can lose ourselves in his equations. We can miss his key assumptions and interpretation of a very complex science. A simple notation can be an impenetrable barrier for the smartest geneticists."

"May I?" Elliott interrupted.

"Please." Albert leaned back, relieved he did not have to field the question.

"What you say is a correct, an astute observation, Dr. Vanlandingham. We agree, of course. Without intimate knowledge of Dr. Medino, his methods and approaches, we are lost."

"You and Mr. Bell are smart men. Knowing this, what brings you here today? What makes you believe any of us can begin to navigate Dr. Medino's ground breaking research?"

Heads turned back to the renowned forensic pathologist. Elliott smiled. "He had a son . . ."

THIRTY

They thought they saw a ghost . . .

When the CEO's door opened and Marcus Medino walked into the boardroom, the scientists pushed back from the table. Elliott realized for the first time how much Marcus looked like his father. The room quaked as if Dr. Enrique Medino had returned from the dead.

Dr. Vanlandingham recovered first. He rushed up to Marcus. They shook hands and embraced. The moment meant their success equation changed. Marcus Medino could navigate his father's groundbreaking research.

Each scientist greeted the son of the man they had long admired, the reason they left promising careers with established companies. Dr. Medino had given them what they needed to risk a startup company with an unproven biotechnology. Now, they mourned the death of a great visionary and attempted to complete the Ossi2 clinical trials. Most had begun a search for a new opportunity, one far away from LIFE2 and the pain.

They could see his father in his face, and the way he moved in the room. They saw the same penetrating eyes and gentle smile. They heard the confidence in his soft voice. They had missed the way Dr. Medino shared his findings and described the possibilities. As each scientist shook Marcus Medino's hand, they wondered if he was special, too.

"We worked at a private laboratory, our farm outside Nashville," Marcus said. "Later, I came to Memphis—college and medical school—and I continued assisting my father at another secret location. I did so until the day Gilgamesh killed my family."

"A terrible day," Vanlandingham said. "Where did you go? What did you do?"

Marcus blinked back the painful memories. "I returned to Nashville. The newspaper reported a single car accident . . . I knew differently. No one knew Dr. Medino had a son, but I had to go into hiding in case. I worked at the Vanderbilt Medical Center, under an assumed name, and did basic research. I thought I would be safe.

"Although the family plan was always for me to takeover where my father left off if anything ever happened, *reality* set in. I needed time. My family's execution crippled me. I was lost, didn't know if I could go on.

"After a year I felt stronger, but still wounded. I thought I could return to Memphis and work with Jack Bellow, like my father wanted. But they killed Mr. Bellow, too . . .

"I stayed in Nashville—more frightened and unsure than ever before. Then the people that hunted my father for decades came for me. They discovered I existed and decided I too needed to go. Gilgamesh sent trained assassins." Marcus turned to Elliott and smiled. "This man came for me the night Gilgamesh decided to make their move."

Marcus leaned on the table and looked into the eyes of each scientist. They hung on his every word. "Dr. Sumner saved my life. He got me out of Nashville minutes before Gilgamesh henchmen arrived. If not for him risking his life for me, I would not be here today."

Heads turned. "We were lucky that time," Elliott said.

"Marcus's terrible story illustrates the cold realities of this mission. If you join us, you enter a very dangerous world. As we attempt to take Dr. Medino's biologic to the world, we must fight sinister forces determined to stop us. The Gilgamesh mission is clear. They want to control life extension, use it in their own nefarious ways. If they win this battle, the few will dominate the many, and the future of mankind will be forever changed. We can't allow that to happen. Yes, there is a lot at stake. If you join us, there is a good chance you will not survive.

"However, I will promise everyone at this table that we will do everything humanly possible to keep you safe, and to keep our activities secret. We realize Gilgamesh has people everywhere— we cannot be sure anybody or any situation is free of their grasp. Even now, it is possible one of you is a Gilgamesh operative. Everyone here and everything said in this room could find its way back to them. Although you've been vetted, nothing is guaranteed."

Dr. Vanlandingham said, "We understand the mission, but what is the strategy? How can we keep the Medino biologic from ever falling into the hands of diabolical entities? They will multiply in numbers and always seek to control it for their own purposes."

"Our strategy is a simple one; we take the Medino biologic to everyone in the world as fast and as efficiently as possible. When accomplished, the anti-aging gene will be a common part of the human genome, like eye color. The biologic will be a commodity like the air we breathe. Only then does it lose its value to depraved entities like Gilgamesh."

"That is logical, but impractical," Vanlandingham said. "Even when it is readily available, the covert groups could interrupt the flow into parts of the world and next generations. They could still find a way to take control. The task of maintaining worldwide distribution channels indefinitely seems unlikely, I'm afraid."

Marcus cleared his throat. "We only need to get the biologic to a person one time. Once they are exposed, it becomes a part of their DNA. It is passed down like any other genetic trait. There will be variations as with any other genetic trait, but not significant. The infusion of the life-extending trait is molecular and permanent. Our challenge is to find the best way to disperse the biologic."

The door opened. An attractive woman leaned her head in. "I'm sorry. I didn't know the boardroom had been scheduled." Her eyes moved around the table and stopped on Albert. "Hello, Mr. Bell. Please forgive my interruption."

"Hello, Miss Reese."

Dr. Vanlandingham stood. "Miss Reese, I posted this meeting in the company calendar Sunday. I think you need to refresh your screen. Regardless, we intend to adjourn soon. Please see we're not disturbed."

"Of course, doctor." The door closed.

Albert removed his pen from point number five, and slid the single page into his leather satchel. "This meeting needs to be over. I want each of you to consider all that's been said here today. You may let Dr. Vanlandingham know your decision. I remind you of your word—confidentiality. On behalf of Dr. Sumner and Dr. Medino, thank you for your consideration."

The Asian scientist lowest in the chair stood first. He held his hands behind his back. His white lab coat had no wrinkles. "Mr. Bell, I am Dr. Kim Sorokin," he said in a warm voice and then bowed. "I want to tell you today my answer, sir. I tell you now because you must not wait on your important mission."

"Yes, Dr. Sorokin, please continue," Albert said. *A decision this fast cannot be good. We need all five. Dr. Vanlandingham assembled the best in each discipline necessary to move forward. We will lose precious time if even one passes.*

"First, I give you my word. Second, I join your mission accepting all risks. I knew Dr. Medino and Mr. Bellow. I here because of these great men. We not told all, but we understand genetics. We know how Ossi2 work," he giggled. "We cognizant of vast implications of a life extending breakthrough. The socioeconomic impacts cannot be ignored. We also know battles for control never far behind all significant discoveries. Dr. Medino want you complete his work. I join you. I do what I can to help. This important to world."

Albert sat up, his eyes wide and smile growing. "Thank you Dr. Sorokin. Thank you for your trust, loyalty, and willingness to. . ."

The next scientist jumped to his feet. Pushing his bushy, black and silver hair back with one hand and wire glasses with the other he boomed, "I'm Dr. Robert Stubs, molecular biologist and geneticist. I wish to declare my intentions." He tugged at his sleeves and brushed the lapels of his lab coat. "I commit to you gentlemen and this world changing project. I accept the associated risks. All breakthroughs come with risk." He dropped his hands deep into lab coat pockets and looked at his feet. The room got still. "Mr. Bell, Dr. Medino, and Dr. Sumner, I dreamed of a day like this my whole life. Thank you for asking me. I am honored."

"I am on board as well. I am Dr. Jean Flanders. I have no big statement to make. I concur with my colleagues. My expertise is biochemistry and the human genome. I think I can be of help and will do whatever is needed to achieve this lofty mission. And I too accept the risks."

Before Dr. Flanders finished, the fourth scientist got out of his chair. Dr. Flanders helped him with his cane as he leaned against the conference table. "Dr. Leo Stark here." The old gentlemen with the short-cropped white hair and red face struggled to get the weight off his right hip so he could talk with less pain. "Being last has no bearing on the level or intensity of my commitment to people like you gentlemen—patriarch Albert Bell, the world renowned forensic pathologist Dr. Elliott Sumner, and of course, the gifted son of a giant, Dr. Marcus Medino. A true scientist would be a blithering idiot to pass on an opportunity of such unprecedented magnitude. My years in anti-aging medicine and genetic engineering may help, gentlemen. My knowledge of global logistics and bio-delivery mechanisms will be useful as we look for the most effective way to inoculate the planet," the scientists chuckled . . .

The door to the CEO's office opened a few inches. As Dr. Stark continued his acceptance speech, Elliott watched the two fingers retract and an eyeball move in the crack. When his curiosity neared concern, he recognized a portion of William's long, narrow, gray face. Then he saw angst and despair. *Why are you here?* Elliott wondered. *You didn't drive Albert. Max did.*

Elliott felt he had to leave, but he did not want to disrupt the positive meeting. He pulled out his cell phone and held it to his ear so the room could see. Standing and leaving the table, he whispered, "Memphis police." Dr. Stark's emotional bloviating continued undeterred, as Elliott eased across the boardroom and closed the CEO's door behind him. The blinds in Jack's office were closed. Elliott found William by a small lamp in the corner.

"William, what are you doing here?" Elliott approached inspecting the tall, slender man who had served Albert for over four decades. "I've not seen you like this before. You're trembling."

"I am sorry, sir. I do not know what to do. I do not want to . . . to do this, sir." William dropped his head into his long skinny fingers, his hair falling forward like a mop on its way to the floor.

"Calm down, William. Whatever it is, we will deal with it."

"You and Mr. Bell have been through so much, sir."

Elliott grabbed his shoulders. "What, William? What is it? Talk to me."

William lifted his head. His eyes were wet and face broken. "Betty Duncan is dead . . ."

Elliott let go of William as if a baseball bat had hit him between the eyes. His hands dropped to his sides and his head flew back. Everything left him—his air, saliva, muscles, vision, hearing. *My mother is dead? No! God no! Not now. Not ever . . .*

"I am so sorry, sir. I don't want to tell Mr. Bell, sir. I cannot tell Mr. Bell."

Elliott tried to return. After several short breaths and uncontrolled blinking, sound returned and he saw William again. His mind raced. He had to react.

"Are you certain of this, William? Are you positive my mother is dead? We cannot put Albert through this if we do not know for sure. Tell me you are certain before he walks into this room. Tell me everything you know, William. Tell me now."

"I received the call from Detective Wilcox. I got here as fast as I could, sir." William wiped his eyes and closed them. "He called me because he did not want you to hear on the phone."

It is true, Elliott pined. *Tony would know. He would not act if it was not a fact. He would not let me find out any other way.*

"Detective Wilcox wanted to come to tell you himself, but he's in transit to New Orleans. He must meet with the NOPD. He said there is a window. And he's going to recover the body. Mr. Wilcox did not want Miss Duncan to fly to Memphis alone, sir."

Tears rolled down Elliott's face. They dripped from his jaw until his head caved forward. He exhaled. "William, did Tony tell you what happened?"

"Yes. Miss Duncan died on a commercial airline, on the runway, sir. The plane was hijacked."

"Hijacked?" He lifted his head in shock.

"Mr. Wilcox said her throat was cut on the plane. Miss Duncan bled to death in front of the passengers. There are witnesses, sir."

Elliott's face went cold. "How many people were killed?"

"Just Miss Duncan."

"Who did it, William?"

"The police do not have a name, sir."

"One name? Are we talking about one hijacker?"

"Yes sir. He is described as an unusually large man, over seven feet tall, sir."

Elliott closed his eyes and rubbed his forehead. *Gilgamesh. One of the twins . . .*

"A passenger has video, a cell phone. Mr. Wilcox said to tell you he would send what he had when you were ready, if ever."

Elliott straightened up and wiped his face with a shirt sleeve. He tugged his coat sleeves and brushed his arms. His voice shivered—a mix of heartbreak and rage. "I want you to listen to me very carefully, William. We will not tell Albert how Betty died. He will only be told she is a casualty of a plane hijacking."

He gripped William's shoulders and pulled him close. "For now, when he asks, you will say there are no details. That will be enough. He won't ask. William, Albert cannot handle the details. Leave them to me, understood?"

Elliott felt his headache growing. This time, the pain rained down from the top of his skull and shot into the core of his brain like a hot knife. Pressing his temples gave him some relief. This time the pain throbbed. Elliott's inner demons stirred.

"Yes sir. Are you going to be okay, sir?" William asked as Elliott fell back a step and caught himself. "The hijacking, Miss Duncan's death, it happened yesterday."

"Yesterday?" He shook his head and refocused. The pain subsided. "It did not make the news. It would have been on the national news." Elliott blinked the double images out of the room. "And why did it take so long to notify next of kin?"

"Hijacker demanded no press or more people would be harmed. Miss Duncan traveled under an assumed identity. The police and airline had trouble identifying the one missing passenger."

"Missing? You mean the one dead passenger."

"Missing . . . sir. The hijacker took the body with him. Detective Wilcox said that's why he's going down. Miss Duncan's body would only be returned to you or Mr. Wilcox."

"This makes no sense."

"It is why police knew to contact Mr. Wilcox."

Before Elliott could react to the bizarre information, the door to the boardroom opened and Albert entered, hands clapping in the background. He met Elliott with a broad smile, William still out of view behind the door.

"Excellent meeting. They're all on board. Wonderful people. Dr. Vanlandingham and Max are to be commended. And they all took to Marcus. We just might have a shot. It's about time we had something positive."

Albert followed Elliott's eyes. He turned and found William with his head down. Albert's smile faded. His face melted as fear and concern took over.

"William. Why are you here?" Albert asked. He looked back at Elliott and saw his son's red eyes and wet cheeks for the first time. "Elliott, what is it son?"

"Albert, something terrible has happened . . ."

THIRTY-ONE

*H*ow do *I tell my psychopathic brother someone killed our mother, and then accuse him of killing two innocent people? After that, how do I ask him for help?*

Elliott sat on the bank of the Mississippi River. The moon draped a fog blanket over Mud Island and the rolling turbulence of the river a few yards away. *If he has lost control, he will kill me tonight . . . put me out of my misery.*

Elliott scraped up a handful of rocks and tossed one into the churning water each time his thoughts moved from one crisis to another. *My mother is gone, killed by the monsters hunting her from the start. She never should have attempted to come, but I cannot blame her. She had every right to be with Albert and to see her sons. She had sacrificed enough.*

Albert had to be medicated at LIFE2. *I lost you in the first sentence—Betty is dead. You didn't need to hear more. You collapsed.* Carol would stay with Albert. *She calms him like she calms me. Now, there are no words. Nothing can be said . . .*

The Panther McGee and Alex Harris homicides were perfect recreations of staged Bluff City Butcher kills. Although

Elliott did not personally examine the body, he knew what to ask. The kill presented Adam's unique skill sets, his trademarks. The wounds were sutured in ways Elliott had never shared. *But why would you kill now? Why would you relive the past? Is it because you've killed so many for so long, been alone for so long? Is it unbridled anger, uncontrollable rage? I don't understand the mental workings of a psychopath. How can I ever understand one genetic engineered into a superhuman state? I cannot allow you to kill people, Adam . . .*

Elliott sorted the small pile for the largest stone in his hand and threw it as far as he could. He couldn't see or hear where it hit, but it went way out there somewhere in the swirling water. The splash would be a mile away in another minute. The physical release felt good. Elliott threw another, this time harder. *Does any of it matter? The world is enormous and we are nothing. The universe is in a constant state of change. We live. We die. Our existence is soon forgotten by those who knew us, but unknown to most forever. For the eternity after our life, it's as if we never existed. Why should we care about anything? Why should we fight for anything? We should live, be happy, and avoid pain . . .*

This time when Elliott reeled back his hand met something hard, unmovable. He turned. The shadow took shape—Adam. He said nothing. He sat on the bank next to Elliott and gazed upon the majestic river, something he had done a thousand nights before, but alone.

"Thank you for coming," Elliott said. He threw the stone. *I can't just put it out there,* he thought. *But I can't wait. I can't delay the bad news. It could be misinterpreted as lying. I don't know how he'll take it. I must choose my words . . .*

"Who killed our mother?" Adam asked, his eyes leveled on the river.

"We don't know," Elliott sighed. He felt Adam in his head.

Don't run with my random thoughts on any of this, Adam. And don't go to New . . .

"New Orleans? I'm not going there. I don't need to. They will come here." Adam crushed the rock in his hand. The powder exploded between his fingers. He let the gravel and sand drop from his fist like sand in an hourglass.

"I know who," Adam said with a chilling tone.

"Who?" Elliott asked.

"Tanner or a Henley twin. I will kill all three bad men. The three board members, too."

He could not go there with Adam. Elliott's life had been dedicated to bringing criminals to justice. Even they had rights. Only the law made sense to Elliott in his dark world. Gilgamesh had turned Elliott's life upside down. They had killed hundreds of innocent people. They had killed Jack, and now they had killed Betty. They continued to be unstoppable without their leader or most of their board, unstoppable without their members and with frozen assets.

Adam flipped his hair over his shoulder with a head turn. His black crystal eyes swallowed the night light like an animal's. "I did not kill those men," he said.

You did not kill Panther McGee or Alex Harris? Elliott thought as he looked into his brother's dark eyes for more than words.

"And I did not kill the first Panther McGee," Adam said. "I have no interest in Detective Harris or these others. They've done nothing to me or my family." Elliott dropped a rock. They watched it roll down the bank and jump into the river.

"There are people who believe you did, Adam. I must prove to them you did not."

"Few know I exist," Adam said. "Deep down, they believe you. They are with you. The others do not matter. They are not in this war."

"The forensic evidence points to you, Adam. No one has your skills with a knife or your suturing technique—the tight stitching, the packers' knot, and Knots of Isis. It is how I tracked you. It is how law enforcement knew you were involved. How do I get past it?"

"You have been misled. I have never sewn a wound in my life. It is Gilgamesh. They created a monster—the Bluff City Butcher —to enlist support to hunt me so they could kill Dr. Medino and take his science. Dirk Henley killed both Panther McGees, two men randomly taken, their identities changed. They were invented by Gilgamesh and planted for MPD."

"What about the knife skills?" Elliott asked.

"The Henley twins were spawned in Gilgamesh labs after us. They are like me except for one thing, Gilgamesh can control them."

"How do you know this?" Elliott asked.

"Gilgamesh sent many to kill me and Dr. Medino. I stopped them. They had to die or they would come back. I had no choice. Many talked. I listened. I remember everything, too." A slight smile flickered across Adam's lips. "I followed Henley twins twenty years because I knew one day they would come for me."

"Is Boris Tanner genetically engineered?" Elliott asked.

"No. He is a freak of nature. Unpredictable." Adam threw his last rock.

"I didn't see that one coming," Elliott muttered.

Adam got to his feet and looked east. "Someone is coming. We go now."

"You've been in my head. Do you know where I need to go?"

Adam did not answer the question. He ordered, "Follow me . . ."

They went to the dark water's edge and stepped into the thick line of wild bushes and river birch saplings. Staying in the shadows, they moved south down Mud Island thirty yards. Adam stopped. They both knelt in the thick scrub. Seconds later, a large man appeared on the bank where Adam and Elliott had sat before. He touched the ground with an open hand and looked up and down the river. He paused and raised his nose like a dog smelling the wind. He got up and walked to the sandy clearing. There, for the first time, the moonlight fell on his face.

Yes, I know where you want to go, Adam thought.

Do you know who is looking for us now? Elliott thought.

Boris Tanner . . .

THIRTY-TWO

How did they know to send Boris Tanner—*the freak of nature*—to Mud Island to kill them?

Adam and Elliott waited thirty minutes by the water before Tanner lost interest in his hiding place, the tall grass at the edge of the small clearing, the place where seven heads of Gilgamesh board members had sat atop seven poles. The Memphis police had removed the heads and combed the area for physical evidence. After they were certain they had everything they were going to get, Mud Island was reopened to the public and the wild weeds reclaimed the crime scene. In days, evidence of the macabre carnage would be swallowed by a greater force.

The incline of the river bank and the night shadows provided enough cover as they waited to make their move. Elliott stayed by the water as directed, his head below the horizon and out of Tanner's view. Adam's night moves were undetectable. Whenever Tanner moved, Adam led them to a new position.

"Shouldn't we stay in one place?" Elliott asked.

His glistening eyes and dipping brow confirmed Adam was in the predator mode. His methods made no sense to Elliott. But when Adam turned to him with controlled rage, he made himself very clear. "Do not question. This is my world. Stay close and do not speak."

They moved south along the bank toward the Hernando de Soto Bridge. When they reached a point west of the Memphis Pyramid, Adam led Elliott up the bank. There they knelt in a cluster of saplings on the edge of a field, the narrow part of the island. They had to cross.

He pulled Elliott's shoulder—his head followed. "We crawl. There's a trail." Then Adam pointed northeast. "Tanner, forty yards." He pointed east. "We go to woods other side of island."

They crawled along the beaten path in the three-foot weeds. *Do you know where I must go tonight?* Elliott thought.

Yes. Focus, or I will need to kill Tanner now, Adam thought.

When they reached the stand of trees, they could see moonlight reflecting off the west wall of the Memphis Pyramid on the other side of the Wolf River. While Elliott took in the view, Adam returned to the edge of the field.

When he came back Elliott asked, "Problem?"

"Tanner moved. Follow me."

They went deeper into the woods and stopped by a pile of twisted timber and stumps, and clumps of asphalt. Adam pushed through tall bushes and pulled Elliott in. He saw a two-foot high, circular stone wall. On top he saw rotting plywood and a large rock. Adam slid the board over a few feet and revealed the old well. He reached inside and pulled out a rope attached to the inside wall. "We go in here," Adam said sitting on the wall looking in Tanner's direction.

Elliott stared into the black hole and sighed, "I hate wells. I hate tunnels and tight places." He moved his painful look to Adam. "How far down? Is there water?"

"Thirty feet. Don't think water. You go first. Shake rope at bottom. I come. Do not leave bottom. Get lost." Adam put the rope in Elliott's hands. He slid over the side.

Adam patted the top of Elliott's head and said, "Go. Tanner comes."

The descent into the cold, dark abyss was as miserable as he imagined—breaking spider webs, brushing crawling things out of his hair, the whining rope threatening to snap, and the dank smell of a stagnant hole next to the largest river on the North American continent.

The dry part of the inside wall lasted ten feet. As Elliott descended, it went from damp to soggy to slimy. Disturbing squeaks grew louder. At thirty feet, he could not see the bottom. Elliott wrapped a leg in the rope and dug for his trusty penlight. But the tiny beam for examining gunshot wounds and pupils proved pitiful for exploring wells or caves. The dark soup under his boots swallowed the beam.

After another thirty feet, Elliott reached bottom—soft mud under a foot of water. He sank to his ankles. Holding the sticky rope, he moved his light around the five-foot circle. Vermin were in the four tunnels that branched off the base of the well. He looked up at the small crescent light and shook the rope. Adam dropped over the side. All went black when he reset the plywood over the opening. The rope shook each time Adam's grip changed, his legs never touching. What had taken Elliott three minutes took Adam seven seconds. He dropped the last fifteen feet, landing on a rock ledge avoiding the water and mud—he had been there before.

"Is this the only way to the pyramid?" Elliott whispered.

Adam steadied the rope against the wall. He turned off Elliott's little light and pointed up. The plywood moved. Moonlight poured in. A head leaned over the side. Adam stepped into the east tunnel, pulling Elliott with him. The muddy water covered his boot holes and settled before the light filled the well.

They stood a few feet inside the tunnel as Adam watched the last bubbles emerge from the mud. And he saw the rope sway less than an inch against the wall.

Adam pulled Elliott's arm. They moved deeper into the tunnel. The light behind went out when they rounded the first curve and went down a slope. Logic said the tunnel had to drop to get under the Wolf River. If not deep enough, it would collapse and become part of the river bed.

The irregular cave structure created eons ago revealed the once-active underground water route carved in sedimentary rock before the Wolf cut its path to the Mississippi. Although the old well stayed full of water most of the time, Adam found it dry when he scouted potential routes to the room beneath the Memphis pyramid. The others were impassable.

The steep incline made for a difficult climb down—narrow sections, poor footing, and jagged rocks. When it leveled, they found the water. The tunnel was flooded. "We swim a short way," Adam said. Elliott moved his light over the surface of the crystal clear water.

"Once on other side, we climb to . . ."

"Adam. Your idea of a 'short ways' is not always my idea of 'short'. I'm not as physical as you. I could get into real trouble if I need to breathe and can't."

Adam paused in Elliott's light. It was the first time Elliott saw frustration in his face. He knew rage and thinking. The new expression touched Elliott in a way he never expected.

"You can do this," Adam said.

Elliott saw the man—not the monster. Adam had had to figure out the world and how he fit into it alone. He was no monster. He was a man fighting a war waged by evil men. Elliott knew Adam had not killed Panther McGee or Detective Harris, because Adam said he did not, and Adam never lied. He feared no one. Consequences of actions meant nothing to him.

Adam wet his face. "*Short!* Then we climb. The place you seek under the pyramid is not far. It is where I took Dr. Medino a month before they killed him." Adam waded into the water.

Elliott grabbed his shoulder. "Wait. You know of this place? You've been there with Dr. Medino? There is a subterranean room?"

"Yes." He turned back to the water and went deeper.

"But why didn't you tell me before?"

Adam turned, chest-deep, and squinted into Elliott's light. "You ask me, I tell you." Before Elliott could respond, Adam went under.

He put his cell phone and penlight in a plastic bag and stuffed it in his pants. Like most forensic investigators, he carried a lot of useful things—a hazard of the forensic profession. He would never be caught in a situation where he could not collect and preserve.

Please only be twenty feet. Elliott sucked in his last air and went under the cold water. He felt his way along the jagged rock wall, finding outcroppings to pull forward—each time he propelled himself deeper into the dark tunnel with hope the end was near. The exertion soon drained him. His wounded shoulders still ached and limited his upper body strength.

Elliott kept pulling forward in the dark, silent, boundless world with no sense of progress or time. His fear turned into desperation. He reached his limit, the edge of mind control over his body. His lungs would explode in a frantic search for air. Elliott panicked. He froze.

Then he heard Adam in his head—*you are here*. The massive hand grabbed his arm and pulled him the rest of the way. Elliott broke the surface on the other side. For twenty seconds, there was not enough air on the planet. Between gasps in the black stillness, Elliott heard Adam breathing. The hand pulling him through the end of the tunnel now pulled him from the water like he was a child. *How can you be so strong? You don't look that much bigger than me,* he wondered, but blocked the thought from Adam.

"I hope we can take another way out of here," he muttered as Adam pulled him onto the rocks. In silence and darkness, they climbed the rest of the way and reached the primary tunnel. After several selections between several tunnel options, they stood at the entry of the subterranean room. As Elliott expected, it sat sixty-two feet under the Memphis Pyramid, a depth calculated and now confirmed as his penlight passed over the number carved into the stone above its entry.

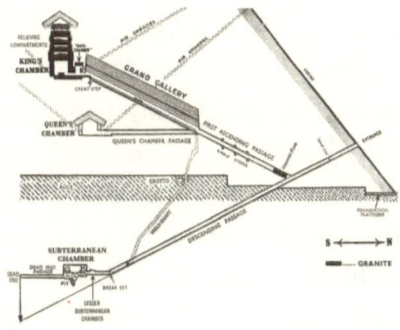

"This is the subterranean chamber, like in the Great Pyramid of Giza," Elliott said. They stepped inside and looked back. "And this rock slides. It may be intended to seal the room." He followed Adam's eyes into the depths of the tunnel.

"We need to be careful with this, Adam. It looks like it rolls into place with a firm push. I don't see how to get her opened again. I'd hate to be trapped in this place." Elliott ran his hand over the edges of the honed stone door, and looked around the empty room. It was manmade; fifteen feet long, fifteen feet wide, with a ten-foot-high ceiling. Two walls, the floor and the ceiling, were solid stone. Two walls were brick. Elliott walked the perimeter with his penlight, sliding his hand over the surfaces. Adam stood in the shadows by the entry.

"When you came here with Dr. Medino, did he say anything about a secret code, his research, his biologic . . . anything?" Elliott asked. "Did you see him do anything in this room, Adam? I don't see anything. I don't see carvings on the walls except the number above the entry. Did you see him do anything, Adam?"

"No. I left him here a half a day. He said don't stay. Come back for him."

"He wanted to be alone?" Elliott sat on the stone floor in the center of the room and studied the layout. *What am I supposed to see? Where would you leave the password to access the formula module? Is it to be derived from the dimensions of this room, fifteen by fifteen by ten? Does it have something to do with the brick walls or the sliding stone at the entry?*

"Did Dr. Medino bring anything with him? Did you help him carry something?"

"A chisel and hammer," Adam said as he left the room and disappeared into the tunnel. Elliott found himself alone underground with his penlight and another puzzle.

A chisel and a hammer . . . You hid it in the brick wall, but where? I need to find a loose brick. Elliott jumped to his feet and inspected the wall. *It is forty bricks tall and thirty long. That's 1,200 bricks. There are two walls. That's 2,400 bricks. I'll never find the loose one.* He examined one wall, his trusty penlight losing strength.

The password for the formula module had to be in the subterranean room. It had to be hidden behind one of the 2,400 bricks. Examining each brick would take days and he could still miss it. He returned to the floor at the center of the room and ran through everything known about the gold certificate, the alterations of the bill, the calculations tying Memphis Pyramid to the U.S. Capitol Building and the Great Pyramid of Giza. What have we learned from opening several of Medino modules already?

What is the unique tie between this room and Dr. Medino's research? The fifty-dollar bill got us here. Something else gets us to the password.

Elliott looked up. Adam stood at the entrance with his predator face. "Problem?"

"Tanner," Adam said.

"He's out there now?"

"Will take some time to get here. I need to stop him." He turned to leave.

"No, Adam. We need to stop the killing. How much time do I have?"

Adam stepped back into the shadows of the room and whispered, "Minutes."

Elliott studied the brick wall. *How would Dr. Medino direct me to the brick? I know behind one is the password to gain access to his life extension formula, module H9044.*

"Movement," Adam said, pointing to the doorway.

Elliott jumped to his feet. "Module H9044." He went to one brick wall. "It is coordinates to the brick. Maybe *H* is for high. I start counting from the top." He went to the corner where the two brick walls met.

"I'm going to count nine down, four over and four down." He checked the brick. It did not move. "Okay, from the bottom I will count nine up, four over and four up." Again the brick did not move. Elliott stepped back and rubbed his neck, thinking of the possible combinations.

"Okay, I'm going to reverse it. Dr. Medino would not be obvious. This time I'm counting four down, four over and nine down." When he touched the brick, it moved. "I found it . . ."

Elliott turned from the wall with his hand on the brick. He thought Adam filled the entrance. Boris Tanner smiled. . .

THIRTY-THREE

E lliott had never considered the possibility of dying sixty-two feet under the Memphis Pyramid Arena. A day ago he had not even known the subterranean room existed. Now he stood in it looking down the barrel of a gun fifteen feet away . . .

They thought he was the last lethal blood lion—Adam Duncan and Jack Bellow were dead, and Albert Bell was impotent. Dr. Elliott Sumner's knowledge of Gilgamesh, his genetic gifts and advanced, investigative skills, posed the last great threat to the operation. With the forensic pathologist out of the way, Gilgamesh could focus on the Medino hard drive and achievement of their mission. But Boris Tanner knew something he would not share with his employers—the Bluff City Butcher lived.

He had not died on the snow-covered roof of the Bell mansion in December. Tanner had seen him several months later, the night Alberto Bella had died. If Director Cottam's bullet had not stopped Tanner, he would have killed the overrated local legend on the balcony. If Gilgamesh knew Adam was alive, this time they would send armies of assassins. Tanner could not allow that to happen. Killing the Butcher was his only dream.

Now, standing in the entry of the subterranean room, he thought he could see everything. His plan was simple. He would shoot Sumner in the head, prop up his body, and wait for Adam to return. The bait and labyrinth of dark tunnels converging gave Tanner the perfect setting to surprise his nemesis.

But Adam Duncan was not a typical man. He was a master of stealth. His hulk merged with the surrounding shadows and stone walls by the massive, sliding rock. When Tanner's gun entered the room on extended arm, Adam moved with the hideous swish of legend. Before the trigger could be pulled, the butcher knife whispered through the air, severing Tanner's hand at the wrist. After the hand gripping the gun flopped on the floor, the bloodcurdling scream erupted from the mouth of Boris Tanner.

Adam moved in for the kill, his coat fanning the air as he pivoted to land the final blow, his ten-inch blade implanted in the baneful heart of a horrific killer. But in mid-flight Elliott pleaded, "No. Adam. Don't kill him. Please."

Tanner fell backward into the dark tunnel. Adam froze and his black leather coat dropped to his sides. He turned to Elliott. "Tanner dies or we die." He raised his knife, ready to lunge.

"No, Adam. You don't have to kill anymore. It's time to stop. It's time to find other ways." Elliott stayed at the brick wall and spoke to Adam's back with a raised arm and a blood-dripping butcher knife. Elliott spoke to him in his head so Tanner would not hear: *There are more important things in life than getting this password, Adam. Your life matters to me. Your life will change when you find other ways to deal with evil in this world, ways that don't make you evil.*

In excruciating pain, holding his bloody stump, Tanner yelled from the tunnel floor, "I'll kill both of you with one hand." He started to get up . . .

Adam did not turn to Elliott. He kicked the large stone. It rolled into place and sealed the room. The two-ton door sunk into the wall, leaving only a paper-thin crack. Elliott stood with his mouth open. He walked up to Adam and touched his rock-hard shoulder and smiled. *It took all you had to let Tanner live,* he thought.

Adam nodded. They heard the muffled rants of a wounded man outside the stone room.

Elliott ran his fingers along the crack. "Tight. Very tight. I appreciate the last minute solution, but I was thinking maybe knocking Tanner out and tying him up."

Outside, Tanner continued to kick the immovable stone.

Adam's face smiled but his lips did not move. "I'll think it through next time," Adam said.

They returned to the far corner of the chamber. Elliott removed the brick and peered into the rectangular hole. He found an envelope stuffed inside. He opened the letter from Dr. Enrique Medino. Elliott read aloud;

"Hello Son, Dr. Sumner, or Adam,

"I am quite certain one of you is holding my note at this time. And I am confident you know precisely what you have been looking for. Therefore, I shall not enter into an explanation of purpose or use. Suffice it to say you are looking for two words. Those selected are relevant to the mission because they made my discovery possible. Without them, my research would have gone in a myriad of directions and dead ends. Therefore, it is appropriate

these two words allow for movement forward. They are—
BLOOD LIONS.

Please note when using these two words in my
software, use capitalized font in all cases and a space
between the two.

"*I wanted to be present for the completion of my work*
—global infusion. However, the world we live in has risks
and a cast of unsavory inhabitants. Never did I let the
negative condition alter my quest. I am quite certain life
extension is a natural evolutionary step for mankind in
our endless universe. Although there are negatives, new
risks, and always drawbacks, the benefits are far greater
and more lasting and meaningful in the human
experience. The secrets of DNA and the genetic solutions
for substantial life extension exist for reasons not yet
understood by humanity. You must now go back to the
place you learned and PUSH onward."

"'Blood Lions' is the password to gain access to Dr. Medino's formula module. I should have known, Adam."

Elliott paused to think about the man he met briefly, the man he later saw on a gurney in the country morgue, and why he chose the words—BLOOD LIONS. *I know you selected this password for a reason, Dr. Medino. Your son said it best—everything you do is for a reason. The blood of the lions kept your research on course. This is your way to thank Jack and Adam and me. We are the lions at the gate of your immortality . . .*

Elliott folded the small paper square and slid it into his pocket. "How we gonna get out of this place, Adam?" he asked.

Adam took Elliott's penlight and shined it into the hole. He stuck his hand inside and pushed. A section of the adjacent brick wall popped open a few inches—a door. He pulled it open. The dark, musty tunnel was quiet.

"How did you know to . . . ?" Elliott asked.

"Last line, Dr. Medino's letter," Adam said. He stepped through the opening and looked back. "Let's go . . . now."

The Memphis Tribune: Mutilation Kills in Memphis —Is the BCB back?
Staff Reporter

Memphis, TN May 11, 2010: Memphis police release information on May 8 homicide in Tom Lee Park, but hold details on May 9 homicide at Public Library. Both deaths have similarities to those caused by the Bluff City Butcher.

At 11:30 p.m. on Saturday, May 8, MPD was called to Tom Lee Park where they found a 28-year-old black male dead and tied to a park bench. The deceased was identified as Panther McGee. Cause of death was ruled multiple stab wounds to the chest, and manner of death was ruled a homicide by interim Shelby County Medical Examiner, Dr. William Kramer. "I have seen this before, but will not jump to any conclusions. Much more work is necessary," said Kramer. The ME report has not been released to the public. The name and circumstances of the death are identical to the Panther McGee homicide in September of 2008.

On a related case, MPD was called to the Memphis Public Library at 11:50 PM, Sunday, May 9 where another homicide took place. The name of the homicide victim and details surrounding the death are being kept confidential. Unnamed sources close to the investigation say the victim was mutilated and hung from the ceiling of the fourth floor of the Memphis Public Library, a duplication of the Raymond Munson homicide—October 17, 2008. The time has not yet been set for the Memphis police press conference.

Both homicides are similar to homicides committed by the serial killer of Memphis urban legend, the Bluff City Butcher, Adam Duncan. Duncan died on December 23, 2009 attempting to escape police at the Bell mansion. Over a hundred eyewitnesses watched Duncan die on the rooftop of the mansion. "To speculate that Duncan is somehow responsible for these homicides is unfounded in fact, preposterous, and distracts from a legitimate effort to solve these two homicides," Deputy Chief Henry Cottam said. Cottam serves as the director of the MPD. Collin Wade recovers from injuries received in April at the Bell mansion.

Dr. Elliott Sumner, world-renowned forensic pathologist, pursued the BCB for over a decade. Interviewed at the Memphis Public Library Sumner said, "I understand the tendency to link cases. It is obvious someone is attempting to mimic past homicides. When we find out why, we will catch them."

Anyone with information on the homicides at Tom Lee Park and Memphis Public Library are asked to contact the Memphis police department.

PART FOUR
ARCANUM

THIRTY-FOUR

Arcanum (ɑːkeɪnəm): *a profound secret or mystery known only to initiates.*

M arcus entered the password—*BLOOD LIONS*—and the formula module opened. The screen went black. "Oh no..."

"Problem?" Elliott asked, watching white triangles form in the four corners and converge. Soon the black screen went white and flickered.

"I think we're about to lose it to a virus," Marcus muttered.

"How can that be? We used the password. We know it's correct."

"I don't know, Dr. Sumner. Maybe it's an entering error or the wrong password. Maybe BLOOD LIONS is another clue." The screen flashed and went blood red. "Now that's weird."

"We did everything we could. We broke the code of the fifty-dollar gold certificate. We found the subterranean room. I found the loose brick and letter from your father. Let's see what happens here. Don't give up on it."

"This is what happens when things shut down." Marcus pounded the keyboard. He entered *alt-delete* several times. He moved the mouse. Nothing. "This is not good."

Elliott kicked over his metal chair. "You know what? Maybe this is a good thing. Maybe it's all for the best, Marcus."

"What you mean?"

"We need to stop all this craziness. No offense, Marcus, but I don't think your father found the secret to immortality. I've been down this rabbit hole for a year now. It is preposterous to say the least. It is fiction at its best. Good guys and bad guys chasing the impossible dream. Billions spent, hundreds dead, a series of stupid puzzles. It is a farce, Marcus. What am I thinking?"

Marcus stared at the screen. "Maybe you're right. How could anyone believe this nonsense? When you think about it, seems ridiculous and impossible."

Marcus got to his feet knocking over his chair in the dirt room. He turned to Elliott. "But, you know what—it's true, Dr. Sumner. I saw it work. I understand the science." He picked up his chair and mumbled, "But I guess it won't matter now." The screen faded.

"I understand and respect your loyalty to your father, Marcus. But it is not real. Your father beat cancer. It happens. It's rare to beat pancreatic cancer, but it happens, Marcus. You wanted to believe he found the anti-aging biologic. I get it." Elliott turned from the dying monitor to the dark tunnel looking for answers not there. Everything in the dirt room was useless, just pieces of an endless and impossible puzzle.

"Your comments have no bearing on the validity of new science. I've been around crazy people all my life. My father never let it stop him from his work."

"So you think my words are frustration, disappointment, and

anger?" Elliott walked to the opposite end of the dirt room. He leaned his head into the darkness. "These catacombs have been nothing but trouble, Marcus. Used by Gilgamesh for decades, it is just a cold, dark, dismal place where people die." Elliott dropped his head and kicked the dirt.

"Oh my God . . . We're in," yelled Marcus.

Elliott looked back over his shoulder with nothing left. The brilliant green letters and numbers rained down the screen in a sparkling shower eating the red. Letters flashed, exploded, and vanished. Text emerged.

"This is a good thing," Marcus whispered with a smile. "It is calibration."

Elliott reluctantly approached the monitor. "What does it mean?"

"The doors of the eight modules are now open, Dr. Sumner. They are connecting and setting up a new order of protection. It means *BLOOD LIONS* can access the master file and has the ability to navigate all modules. We don't have a long, convoluted, risky initializing process anymore." He turned to Elliott. "We now own it. We can change the password and export data."

The formula menu popped up. Marcus scrolled down and selected *infusion*. Like a kid opening presents Christmas morning, he leaned into the monitor with dancing eyes. "This biologic inactivates a negative control system in our genome." The field populated.

They read the summary narrative written by Enrique in 1984. When they reached the bottom, Marcus turned to Elliott. "The simplicity is profound. It was always about finding the biogenic needle in the haystack. My father searched endlessly. He knew it was there. He never gave up, Dr. Sumner. He lived in another world."

"Explain the negative control system to me." Elliott leaned

closer to the monitor, his pupils narrowed like an eagle targeting a rabbit a mile away. He would analyze and remember everything.

"We know DNA is a molecule that encodes genetic instructions used in the development and functioning of all living things. My father dedicated a lifetime to understanding deoxyribonucleic acid, because it was the center of life."

"Your father's science...it's time I learn about what we have." *I doubt the existence of unlimited life extension . . .*

"My father was one of the first to understand the concept of a genome and that genetic information is held within genes, units of heredity. He discovered a small percent of a genome sequence actually encodes proteins that make things happen. The majority of the human genome is composed of non-coding, repetitive sequences. That is where he focused his research. He theorized the non-coding sequences had a structural role—like keeping things running smoothly, the genetic maintenance department, so to speak."

"Like telomeres and centromeres, they have few genes but are vital components in the management and stability of a chromosome," Elliott said.

"Research can go in a thousand directions. My father focused on two paths. Path one—DNA over time is damaged or becomes senescent, making it dysfunctional. God gave us a DNA repair system. Unfortunately, it can't get around and fix everything. It is logical to conclude that protecting the integrity of DNA can only extend life. My father's strategy was to find a way to restore and maintain the cell environment as close to the inception state as possible. He believed it was the optimum environment for the maximum protection of DNA."

"And what was his second path of research focus?"

"Inactivation of that negative control system I mentioned earlier. When he worked it out, he found the key to continuous cell replication . . . immortality."

"Tell me his thinking."

"Cells replace themselves all the time. A cell gets old, damaged, and dysfunctional. They are replaced naturally with new, vibrant cells at a robust rate from conception to birth and often into adolescence. At some point in life the cell renewal process slows down—we call it aging. When it stops, we call it death. My father hypothesized the cell renewal process was the natural state. Something turns that process off."

"So his research looked for and hypothetically found the genetic on/off *switch*? He rewired it with his biologic to stay on."

"Yes. That fed directly into his theory that a newer cell environment better protects DNA, the essence of all life. The benefits translate from the individual cells to tissues and organs and to life systems preserving the organism. The Medino biologic triggers a lasting genetic trait that keeps the cell renewal process from turning off . . ."

Marcus reached for a box next to the screen. "I have something you should hear. Jack Bellow's first words when he witnessed my father's recovery from pancreatic cancer, 2004, the year they started the LIFE2 Corporation."

"Your father was not expected to make it to the end of the year," Elliott said.

"Their first meeting was in Las Vegas, June that year. Chemotherapy and the end stage of cancer were tearing down my father. Just getting to the meeting almost killed him."

"I understand," Elliott said. "He was determined to attend the Anti-Aging Medicine Conference. I know the story well. My brother met with him. He was not buying any of it. It's a bit difficult to sell a secret to immortality when you're dying."

"And I understand Jack Bellow's position then," Marcus said.

"Jack expected your father to be dead in a week. Out of empathy and respect, Jack agreed to a second meeting six months later, one he did not expect Dr. Medino to make."

"And he was blown away at the Crescent Club six months later."

"That's right," Elliott reflected, lost in the moment, remembering his brother and the profound experience caught on video.

"Would you like to know what you brother said the night he realized the strong, vibrant man he met in the bar was the man dying from cancer six months before?" Marcus reached into a box by the monitor. "My father taped the meeting." Marcus pulled his head out with a small recorder. He set it on the table like a precious gem.

"I found this. It is incredible. My father explains his science to your brother. Rummaging through these boxes, I found a bunch of tapes—only listened to a few so far."

"I can't believe . . ."

"This tape is the best synopsis we'll ever have of his work. You will hear your brother. I believe this is when he regained consciousness."

"He was unconscious?"

"Blacked out when he realized my father and his science were for real."

He turned on the recorder. Jack Bellow spoke first. *"Promise me you won't ever do that to me again, Dr. Medino."*

Marcus hit pause. "Jack was coming out of a stupor. My father was holding him up."

Marcus hit play. *"Now that I have your attention, I can make that promise."*

Jack said, *"Did you find what every man has thought about in their life? Some have searched but all have dreamed. Did you find a way to stop the biological clock?"*

"Yes," Dr. Medino said. *"1984, after decades of genetic testing —stem cells and somatic cells—I had enough information to formulate a compound-mixture with a goal; stabilize the human*

cellular environment to optimize protection of DNA and maintain the cellular replication process indefinitely—keep it from being turned off. I call my life extension biologic LIFE2. Then the real work began; assess 3,457 phase one formula variations to achieve TGO-STASIS."

"What is TGO stasis?" asked Jack.

"Keys for DNA protection are telomere maintenance, oxidative stress reduction, glycation and helix supercoiling. From there, to understand me, you must learn a new language . . ."

Elliott reached over and turned off the recorder. "How many tapes do you have?"

"More than fifty. Why? Should I destroy them?"

"No. Put them somewhere safe. We don't need Gilgamesh getting hold of them."

"Like the subterranean room . . . ?"

"I'm not going back down there. You don't need to be that creative. If your father's biologic is real—I'm not saying it is—one day the world will want to know about Dr. Medino."

Marcus turned back to the monitor and entered a flurry of commands. "I have good news. Infusion is a molecular process. Infinitesimal amounts of the biologic are needed."

"You mean infusion of one person?"

"Yes, and more. According to this, the infusion options are numerous—transdermal, respiratory, intravenous, intramuscular, and oral."

"Are there multiple transport substrate options or one required?"

Marcus entered the new command. The screen changed. He scrolled. "Once compounded the biologic is stable." He scrolled. "If I'm reading this right, it can survive all transport mediums short of molten lava."

"It is similar to durability of DNA," Elliott muttered.

Marcus wiped dirt off the screen. "The static electricity is a magnet for the floating dirt down here. It acts like this biologic."

"How do you mean?"

"The biologic is attracted to DNA like dust to this screen. It bonds immediately. But unlike the dust, it integrates with the host DNA, becomes part of the genome."

"When will you know you can produce it, and how much of it we will need to infuse a world population? That sounds ominous," Elliott muttered.

Marcus flipped through several screens. "I need a week to figure it out. Right now it appears we will need a comparatively small amount. It starts the ball rolling globally."

"How small?"

Marcus punched numbers into his calculator. "What's the population of Mexico?"

"120.8 million," Elliott said accessing his photographic memory.

"A two-gram ampule is sufficient to infuse sixty million—half the population of Mexico."

Elliott rubbed his face trying to wrap his head around the concept. "How's that even possible? How do we spread two grams of anything over sixty million people . . . ?"

"We put it on our finger and run around touching as many as we can," Marcus teased.

"Seriously, we can't touch sixty million people without running into Gilgamesh."

"One infusion spreads in the population like the common cold," Marcus said. "Two grams properly dispersed can infuse sixty million people or more in a relatively short period of time."

"Are you saying we need to infuse hundreds of people, then they will spread this biologic?"

"Yes, but it assumes our targeted regions are right," Marcus said. "If we include people on the fringe of a target region—where there's little or no contact—they will not be infused."

"So we need to select the right target regions and produce ample quantities of the biologic to launch a global epidemic." Elliott walked in a tight circle. *Is this something we should be doing?* He thought. *Is this our right? Some people will not want to extend their life. We're making that decision for them.*

"No one asked me if I wanted to be born," Marcus said.

"What are you talking about?"

"I know what you're thinking. There's no difference here, Dr. Sumner. We're not taking anything away from anybody. We're giving them more of what they already have—life."

Am I that obvious? He's not Adam. I know he can't read my mind. "Maybe someone lost a loved one. Maybe they look forward to seeing them again in death."

"And maybe people who live several hundred years will be more open to suicide as their right to depart this world. Maybe the right to decide when you die will become an accepted medical practice. Maybe some people will want to live because someone that was going to die is now going to live . . .

"Really Dr. Sumner, we can do this all day. For every negative, I can give you a positive. It's no different from anything else new in the world. There are always going to be two sides. But regardless of all the changes and all the debates, the world goes on. We adapt."

Elliott stopped circling and sat on the dusty stool. "Okay. Go back to the science. You said infusion occurs at a molecular level. What's in the file on that?"

"My father talks at great length about how his biologic finds host DNA via molecular charge and recognition. His biologic does not behave like a foreign body—it does not trigger an autoimmune response. On the contrary, the biologic is a completing entity. It is a missing piece of our genetic puzzle. It fits in one place and galvanizes the genome. My father believed modern humans are a derivative of an immortal, bipedal hominine. Immortality was once part of our genetic fabric. It was lost. He is restoring what we once had billions of years ago."

"Genetic material lost in the evolutionary process, returned? That makes some sense," Elliott said under his breath. "Once reincorporated in the genome, it cannot be taken away any more than someone can take your eye color."

"That's how I read it. And Mr. Bell's global dispersion options are many," Marcus said.

"Albert may not be participating. Betty's death devastated him. I don't know if he will ever recover. He's been through too much. He has no more reasons to go on. His world is crushed."

"But he's the one with all the international ties, the global distribution network and experience. If Albert Bell cannot help us, we will fail. You know Gilgamesh is closing in. We could be in their crosshairs right now."

"Your father has shown us this biologic's future does not rest with one man." Elliott held up a hand and looked toward the tunnel. "Did you hear that?" he whispered.

Marcus turned off the monitor. "Yes. Someone's coming."

"Throw a tarp over that." Elliott ran to the edge of the room and leaned into the tunnel.

The echo of shuffling feet and buzz of undefinable dialogue grew louder. He backed up to Marcus and pulled him to the wall. "If we get out of this, we are relocating." They knelt behind the stack of dirt covered boxes. The growing light danced in the tunnel.

"If they come in here they're gonna see our tracks," Marcus whispered. His hands trembled. "That tarp's not big enough. And the monitor is hot." He would never feel safe in the world that took his family.

The light stopped at the entrance to their dirt room . . .

THIRTY-FIVE

N*obody knows about this place,* Marcus prayed.

The light turned into the dirt room, cut through floating debris, and danced off the walls and across the wrinkled, brown tarp draped over the monitor. The seats of the swivel chair and stool were missing the typical thick layer of dirt. A trained eye would see.

If you come in here, Elliott thought, *we wait until you reach the computer table. You'll pull off the tarp and see the monitor. You will feel it—hot. You will turn it on and sit down at the keyboard. That's when we ease out and disappear in the tunnels. We must avoid a conflict that could result in capture, injury, or worse. The chances of you looking behind these boxes now is slim. We can do this . . .*

Elliott's hands found Marcus's head. He pulled it to him and whispered in his ear. "Wait for me to move. Just follow. Do not look back. Do not knock over these boxes."

Marcus nodded in Elliott's hands.

"Goddamn it, how many of these rooms are we gonna look

in? No offense, but we've been poking around down here for two hours now. Does anything look familiar, Max?"

"Tony?"

"Elliott? Shit!" Tony pushed through the narrow entrance scraping dirt. More lights followed him inside. The room got brighter as beams merged. "I hear you, but don't see you."

"What're you doing down here? This place is supposed to be top secret." Elliott and Marcus stepped from behind the stack of boxes as Max entered and then Carol. "Hey, Max. Carol—I never thought I'd see you in the catacombs again."

They embraced as the last light entered the room. "This place still creeps me out," Carol said. "We brought Albert with us."

"Albert!" Elliott went to him. "I didn't think . . ."

"I wasn't sure I could get us all here, but had to try." He found Marcus in the shadows and smiled. "Hello, Marcus. And thank you for your patience, Detective Wilcox."

"Patience? You are too kind, Albert," Max said wiping the sweat and dirt off his face with his filthy handkerchief. "This man is the most impatient person on the entire planet."

"I heard that, Max-man," Tony shot back, pleased to find his best friend.

"Albert, you don't need to do this," Elliott whispered. "You've been through enough."

A day ago they had buried Betty Duncan on the grounds of the Bell estate.

Albert looked at the five standing with him, thirty feet underground, attempting the impossible. There was fear on their faces and determination in their eyes. He reached for Elliott's shoulder. "Now, more than ever, I must do this. We must do this. It can be no other way." He looked upon the group. "My strength comes from my sons—Jack, Adam, and Elliott—and from the woman I love." He took a deep breath.

"Betty's life matters. Her death further emboldens me. I was blind all my life. Now, I can see." Elliott pulled Carol closer to his side.

"Gilgamesh forced her into a lifetime of hiding," Max said. "Those people hunted her. They never stopped. I don't know how she avoided them for so long.

"Being out there—somewhere in the world—was the only way Betty could protect her three sons and me. Now it is up to us," Albert said.

"The documents found in these catacombs tell us Betty was a colossal problem for them," Carol said. "Her threat was terminal exposure."

"What turns a billionaire into a monster?" Tony muttered.

"The Bell triplets were a milestone project," Elliott replied.

Max sat on the swivel chair. "When you three were born, they believed they could reproduce the coveted genetic trait of the blood lions. They became monsters because they believed they could live forever and would not let anyone get in their way."

"'Blood lions', my grandfather's favorite term," Albert said. "When we thought Gilgamesh had fallen, Betty did not waste a day before trying to reunite with her family."

"I failed to measure the resurrection—their renewed strength. I was too disconnected from the growing risk. If only I could have warned her," Elliott said.

"Do not blame yourself." Albert pulled out a handkerchief and wiped his eyes. Max lifted the tarp as Marcus put the stool next to Albert and Carol helped him sit. He was weary but they drew from the old patriarch's inner strength.

"We cannot shoulder the blame for the evil in the world. I'm not stepping back, or slowing down, or giving up," Albert said. "I'm pushing forward. Anything else is a distraction from what we must accomplish now."

"We must move this operation. If Tony can find us, Gilgamesh can," Elliott chided.

"I'll shut things down," Marcus said. "Get the portable drive out of here and a couple of boxes with my notes and stuff."

"May I suggest my place," Albert offered. "Max has people everywhere. The security is formidable."

"I don't know, Albert. A secret location is far more secure than a line of machine guns. And Gilgamesh is getting desperate."

"I have a place on the premises I promise will meet everyone's requirements."

"And what might that be?" Tony asked.

"If I were to tell you, it would no longer be suitable, now would it?"

Chuckles moved around the dirt room. Relocation preparations got underway. Certain boxes were set by the entry. Marcus pounded the keyboard, with Max breathing over his shoulder. Carol's flashlight found the box of tapes.

"The catacombs are no longer safe. I have no idea why all of you came down here."

Tony lit a cigarette and stepped up to Elliott. "I'm here for Adam."

"I've been over this with you, Tee. You need to drop it. Adam is not responsible for those staged homicides."

"You saw the newspaper, the return of the Bluff City Butcher," Tony barked.

"I saw that article. We know it is Gilgamesh. Everything's designed to confuse, mislead, and distract us from our counter mission. You've got to see through it, Tee. And this discussion is not one for the whole group. It is between you and me. You are being stubborn."

Carol slid her hand around his waist. "Elliott, you need to hear what Tony has to say."

"What, you too . . . ?"

"Two of the five LIFE2 scientists were killed last night," Carol said.

"*My God!* They already know who's working with us." Elliott leaned against the boxes as if he had taken a blow in the stomach. "Who?"

"Robert Stubs and Jean Flanders," Carol whispered.

"These people were killed unmercifully. They were cut up with the precision of the Butcher. Hear me out," Tony demanded. "Dr. Stubs was decapitated, Elliott. One pass of the knife, like the cases we worked on the Hernando de Soto Bridge last year. We've seen that kind of strength and accuracy before."

Carol took over. "Elliott, Dr. Jean Flanders was dismembered. The medical examiner said it happened so fast, she was alive for all of it."

"This is terrible," Albert sighed.

"The severing of the limbs—swift and singular passes. That's not something we see unless it's the work of the Butcher."

"I've listened," Elliott said, wiping dirt from his eye. "I'll examine the bodies. I believe you will agree, I am the only one standing here qualified to assess the forensics."

"There's more," Tony said. "We can place Adam at the scenes. We have him entering and leaving both residents around the time of death."

"What do you mean, you have Adam?"

Tony passed his cell to Elliott. "We have video."

Elliott watched Adam enter and leave both locations with a time log on each event.

"This is pretty damning information. You know, as an expert in the field, we have too much here to ignore," Tony said. "You cannot ignore this, Elliott."

"The video is viral. *The Tribune* is going on this," Carol said. "I can't turn it off. People believe the BCB is alive. Some think he's a demon. Unstoppable. The community is demanding the Memphis police do their job and stop stonewalling."

"Adam is not a well man," Tony said. "He needs help. He may not even know he's doing this shit. We can't ignore the evidence."

"Thank you, Dr. Wilcox. I'm sure your diagnosis is accurate since you've been practicing medicine for so many—seconds." Elliott straightened up and rubbed his aching neck.

"What's wrong, Elliott?" Carol asked. She knew his inner demons were stirring.

"Nothing. A splitting headache Tony's giving me." He squeezed his eyes tight and leaned over with a grimace. Carol steadied him.

"I need your help to bring him in, Elliott, before he kills more people," Tony said.

"Maybe we need to consider the possibility," Albert said. "If it's true, Adam needs our help. We can't leave him alone. We need to be there for him."

Elliott blinked several times. His brow was wrinkled, eyes dilated, and nostrils flared. "I'm not doing this with any of you. You need to believe me. Adam is not responsible for these killings. To blame him will only push him away, and we lose precious time."

"Then I'll do it myself," Tony said. "You're his brother. You're blind to the facts."

Marcus dropped the hard drive into his satchel. Max picked up a box from the table. Carol took the one with the tapes. "Okay, everybody. We should go," she said. "We can talk about this later, when cooler heads prevail."

They filed into the tunnel. Tony led the way, then Elliott, Carol, Marcus, and Albert and Max took the rear. Their lights moved down the dirt walls in silence as they headed for the main corridor and the dim glow, light leaking through the floorboards of the Brent mansion.

When Tony stopped, the line stopped. When Tony pulled his gun, all eyes found the formidable image standing in the center of the tunnel twenty yards ahead.

"Don't move a fucking muscle, Adam. I'll shoot you where you stand . . ."

THIRTY-SIX

"**P**ut your gun *down*," Elliott commanded as he grabbed Tony's shoulder.

Tony pulled away. "Adam, do not do something you will regret. I cannot let you go. Four people are dead. We have you on video leaving the scene of two." In one hand, Tony held a flashlight, the other his gun. Adam lowered his left hand. His coat opened. Tony's light found the butcher knife in his belt.

"What are you doing?" Elliott leaned closer to Tony. The others froze. "This is not right. You can't shoot Adam even if you *think* he is guilty."

"I can, and I will if he moves, Elliott. He's a dangerous man even if you can't see it." Tony raised his flashlight. The beam was too weak. Adam's face was dark. His large frame and long coat filled the tunnel.

Albert pleaded, "Not this way, Tony."

Adam crouched down like a lion ready to pounce on its prey.

"He's not going to make this easy," Tony said under his breath. "He's getting ready to charge me. He knows I got him. He killed those people."

Elliott grabbed Tony's shoulder again. "You and I have a history. You know I get these things right. It may look bad. Everything's telling you Adam's the killer. All your instincts say you have your man.

"Tony, I've never asked you to trust me before. I'm asking you now. Trust me completely. No matter what happens in the next fifteen seconds—*do not shoot Adam.*"

Tony looked back over his shoulder. "Fifteen seconds . . . ?"

Eyes locked on Tony's, Elliott whispered to the group. "Everyone get against the right wall—now! Tony! Look at me! Do not shoot Adam, no matter what happens next . . ."

The others leaned against the dirt wall. When Tony looked back, Adam was in a dead run closing on them. Tony raised his gun, but Elliott pulled him down and forced him to the wall. Tony's gun fell from his hand.

Adam flew by them at a speed unnatural for any man. Dropped flashlights rolled on the dirt floor and beams crossed in the rising cloud.

"Breathe through your shirts." Elliott yelled. "Close your eyes." Elliott held Tony down, but the homicide detective was no longer wrestling to break free. In a pile they listened to sounds of a battle echoing from the depths of the tunnel—muffled grunts, stinging yelps, leather coursing over jagged rocks, and the pounding of flesh.

"What the fuck is going on down there?" Tony asked as Elliott loosened his hold.

"I'll explain in a minute, I hope."

A deathly quiet fell over the tunnel. Carol moved to Elliott as he rolled off Tony. Max picked up the flashlights and passed them along. The dust cloud that filled the tunnel thinned. Max raised his light and pointed it into the depths behind them.

"What're ya doing?" Marcus whispered. "Now is when we turn lights out." He scrambled to his feet. "Now is when we disappear into one of these rooms, Max. Come on everybody. Get up. Let's get moving. It's how it's done down here."

But it was too late. They turned to the sound of heavy breathing. They saw the eye glare towering over them. A few feet away, the massive form emerged from the dark dirt cloud. Marcus slid back down the wall and tried to melt into the floor.

"He was coming for you," Adam said between explosive pants.

Elliott scanned Adam for blood. Some dripped from his hand, coming from under his cuff. And there was fresh blood on the side of his head, a gruesome gash under his right eye.

Albert started to stand. Adam reached down and helped him to his feet as if his father were a toy.

"Who was coming for us?" Max asked.

He did not look at Max. He looked at Tony. "Boris Tanner."

Elliott went to his brother. "Is this your blood?" He shined the light on the left arm. There was an open wound beneath the slashed leather. Looking for more, Elliott moved his light over his brother's chest and neck. Elliott checked Adam's head and returned to the arm. "I need something to stop this bleeding now. Anything. Somebody."

Carol jumped up, pulling off her windbreaker. "Use this." Adam's eyes moved to her. His brow relaxed. Then he looked back at Tony—his face hardened and eyes narrowed. Elliott watched the transition as he pulled Adam's arm from the leather coat sleeve. Albert steadied the light on the wound—it was long and deep, to the bone, caked with dirt. But it had already stopped bleeding.

"Anything else I need to look at?" Elliott questioned, knowing Adam would be of no help. For him, wounds were nuisances. They healed on their own.

"You killed again," Tony said. "You want us to believe this time you killed to protect us."

"Tony, what's the matter with you?" Elliott scolded.

"Maybe Tanner had no intentions of hurting anybody. Maybe Tanner was hiding. He watched you kill his boss, Adam. The man broke out of jail and came for you. Maybe Tanner was not a threat to anyone but Adam."

"Stop, Tony. You're way off base," Elliott said.

"Why? Because he's your brother? Because we think he only kills Gilgamesh soldiers trying to kill good people?" Tony got to his feet. "I remember that night . . . him in my condo, torturing me and watching me die. I saw the look in his eyes. I know Adam like no one else in this goddamn cave. Go ahead. Ask him why he tried to kill me, Elliott. Ask him."

"There had to be a good reason for that night, Tony." Elliott looked at the others. He could see they wanted to know the answer to Tony's question, too. "And, you should add that Adam did not kill you, Tony. That means something, too."

"He can't explain his sick actions, Elliott. He's a monster."

Albert put his arm on Adam's waist. "Leave him alone, Tony. I've put up with your arrogant judgment long enough. You should know more than anyone else that we are in an atypical war. Things are not as they appear. Wake up, young man. Listen to Elliott. He's no fool.

"Most of my family has been systematically eliminated by Gilgamesh over the last twenty years. Every death looked like an accident. My sons were kept from me for forty years. They were unwilling and uninformed subjects of a ghastly experiment that defined their life.

"Adam and Elliott are all I have left. They are fighting for the right things. I believe in Adam. He has been alone and faced with all of this all his life."

"I understand your feelings, Mr. Bell, but that doesn't put them above the law. Adam has killed more than a hundred people. In anyone's book, he's a homicidal maniac. At least Elliott is not some kind of pathetic killing machine."

Elliott tied the tourniquet with an angry yank. Adam winced. "Sorry," he said as he eyed Tony and emptied his water bottle on the dirty wound. No one spoke as Elliott folded a handkerchief and applied pressure.

"You've never gotten past that night, have you?" Elliott said. Tony looked at the ceiling.

"What night?" Marcus asked.

"The night Adam visited him at his condo. The night Memphis thought Detective Tony Wilcox died at the end of the Bluff City Butcher's knife." He turned back to Tony. "The night he believed the serial killer of legend was an unstoppable beast. The first night in your life that you were as frightened as a child. You have still never dealt with it, Tony."

"I will tell you," Adam said. No one moved.

Tony's angry eyes left Elliott and moved to Adam. He looked up and down the massive hulk daring him to kill now. Tony's face was filled with the rage he carried from the night he met the Bluff City Butcher.

"Now you speak. Tell them why you cut me open, filleted my gut, and watched me bleed. You sat there and waited for me to die. Tell them how you reveled in the sick moment."

Adam didn't move. "I stayed so you would not die."

With gritted teeth Tony lunged forward and grabbed Adam's coat. "What the fuck are you trying to do, play some sick game? Do you expect me to swallow that bullshit?"

Adam stood solid, like an iron pier in a storm. He looked down at Tony—he could crush him with one hand in one second.

"They wanted you dead. You were a problem. If I passed on the assignment, you would be dead by another."

Tony let go of the leather coat with a flicker of doubt in his eyes. "You're a liar. That makes no goddamn sense."

Adam's face didn't change. Controlled rage was in every line, streaming through every muscle. "They killed Dr. Medino," he said. "I could not protect him. Twenty-five years, but they came for him." Adam's pupils contracted to pinpoints as he relived the painful memory. "I would find a way to get inside—go to them instead of waiting for them to come for me."

"They always wanted you working for them. You used that," Elliott said. "They knew you were wild. For it to work, they had to believe you were manageable."

"Dr. Medino was gone. They thought I was lost," Adam said. "Gilgamesh would try to use me one more time, to see if they could control me."

"Tony was a test," Carol said. "Gilgamesh wanted to see if you would take direction."

"I was a test! That is pure bullshit. You are all crazy if you're buying this," Tony huffed.

"It fits," Elliot interrupted. "Gilgamesh was making their final moves. They thought they had Medino's research. It was time to terminate the Bell triplets. And if Albert could not be manipulated, he would be eliminated too. Ideally, Adam would do it all. Gilgamesh could count on it being done. And they could hide behind the urban legend they had created."

"A serial killer everyone would hunt. And one day, destroy," Carol said.

"From an old CIA guy, this makes perfect sense. All the key elements of a calculated plan are in place, Tony." Max pushed off the wall and limped over to Tony. "Damn hip. Tony, we've established that Adam stopped operatives sent to kill Medino. You and I know Gilgamesh sent their best people. And they lost their best people. They recognized Adam was a superior force. It makes perfect sense they wanted to use him for their end game."

Tony leaned into Adam. "Why not just kill me that night? Why let me live?"

Heads turned to Adam. Adam's eyes stayed on Tony. Adam's face softened as the reason for the truth bubbled up forcing the rage out. "Because you are important to Elliott. . ."

Tony froze. He thought, and then looked away in the awkward silence. Elliott and Albert smiled—Adam was not the wild animal of urban legend. Everyone there could see. Tony turned away and walked to his gun. He picked it up and approached Adam. Tony slid the gun back into his holster. He'd heard the words, too. They were real. They connected everything. Tony was mad and afraid, but he could not dismiss truth or logic. As a homicide detective, that's how he lived life every day.

"Someone better check on Tanner. Can't leave him down here," Tony said.

Max tapped Tony's shoulder. "I think you should go. You've got the gun."

With his eyes still on Adam he asked, "Do they need my gun?"

"No."

Max and Marcus went down the tunnel. Tony leaned closer to Adam. "Tell me why you were coming out of Dr. Stubs' and Dr. Flanders' homes. We have you on video."

Adam's face hardened. "I was too late for them."

"Too late . . . ?" Tony asked. "What's 'too late' mean?"

"Sorokin and Stark, I was on time for them." Adam pushed his bandaged arm into his leather coat. "Gilgamesh, they were stopped."

"Who are these other doctors? Elliott, Albert, someone?" Tony asked.

"We met with them at LIFE2, geneticists," Elliott said. "Max vetted each over the last week. We had to recruit specialists to help Marcus take the biologic forward."

"MPD did not tie the two dead doctors to a group. I got the

calls—routine homicides. Only connection I saw, they were LIFE2 employees . . . and the way they were killed—a knife." Tony turned to Adam. "How'd you know about these doctors?"

"Heard Marcus on phone in the catacombs. I don't forget things."

"Why did you go to them?" Tony asked.

"Gilgamesh will not allow LIFE2 scientists to defect—puts their mission at risk. When they got the information, termination would be immediate."

"Adam, you didn't say Dr. Vanlandingham. Did you check on him, too?" Elliott asked.

"Yes. No one came for him."

Elliott looked at Marcus and Albert. *Why did Gilgamesh leave Dr. Vanlandingham alone?*

"We must move the scientists to Albert's place immediately," Max said.

Albert nodded and got on his cell. "I'll make arrangements, now."

"Hello, William. Please get with Max's people and gather Dr. Vince Vanlandingham, Dr. Kim Sorokin, and Dr. Leo Stark at once. They are in grave danger. I will explain later. Only time for an overnight bag. Max will arrange for their security. William, please proceed with the upmost caution. This must happen rapidly."

Carol grabbed Tony's arm. "Have the Stubs-Flanders homicides made the news?"

"No, we're keeping it under wraps. We have twelve hours before leaks."

"Should we assume Gilgamesh knows?" Elliott asked.

Tony turned to Adam. "Do they?"

"Yes . . ."

THIRTY-SEVEN

Marcus emerged first from the catacombs. He stepped into the abandoned ruins—the basement of the Brent mansion—and held the tattered shelving unit open for the others. Tony pulled Elliott aside. Two hours had passed since his confrontation with Adam. There were loose ends.

"When I had my gun on him, you said fifteen seconds . . . trust me . . . don't shoot."

"That's right."

Tony waved by an approaching Max and turned Elliott from the others emerging from the catacombs. "How did you know he was going for Tanner?" He whispered.

With his back pressed against the basement wall, Elliott watched over Tony's shoulder as each came through the wall. Adam emerged last. He had Tanner's corpse draped over his back. The bloody stump swinging reminded Elliott of Tanner's intentions.

Like the time Adam had deposited the five injured assassins, he would leave Tanner on the front steps of the Brent mansion for the MPD and disappear.

Elliott looked back at Tony's confused face. "What's our story here . . . about Tanner? We have a dead body to explain, Tee."

Tony straightened up and stuck a cigarette in his mouth. "We keep it simple. We found him down there, dead."

"And why were we in the catacombs today?"

"You asked for help. You wanted to get some boxes of documents you set aside. You thought it would help with the TEA investigation. I came along to help. Albert wanted to get out of the house. Carol's your girlfriend. Marcus is . . . just keep him away from everybody. I don't know what he is."

"Good. That'll work. I needed time for my shoulders to heal. Finally ready to get back to work. But, we don't have boxes."

"Shit, Elliott. You've always been a piss-poor liar. Go with the flow. We don't have boxes because we tripped over the damn body. Ya see how easy it is to lie. I didn't even have to think."

"Those videos of Adam are going to be a real problem," Elliott sighed. "We've got to do something, bury them. How many people have seen them?" Tony looked away and brushed his sleeves. He patted his pockets for his lighter. "You don't have videos, do you?"

"The one of him at the gates of the Bell mansion . . . a year ago," he muttered, his cigarette wagging in his lips. Elliott reached in Tony's coat pocket, pulled out his lighter and lit his cigarette. "Thanks."

"You're pitiful. You never had those damning videos of Adam. You made it all up."

"Look, Elliott. I've got four dead people—butchered. I had to put Adam at a crime scene to see how he'd handle it. I can tell when people are dancing around the truth."

"So how'd he do, lying master interrogator who has no problem lying?"

"Cute," Tony puffed. "Turns out he was at both. I did not expect him to look me in the eyes and say what he said. And I sure as hell didn't think he'd be intelligent and direct. He told me the truth. Like I said, I can tell—is that what you wanted to hear?"

"Sometimes you miss the obvious, Tony. You're the best homicide detective I have ever known. But when you miss something...

"We're in a war. When it comes to Gilgamesh, you've got to set aside the book. It's tying you into predictable knots. They want you and the rest of the MPD chasing your tails. They use your investigative procedures and police policy to take you out of the game, Tony. It's time you trust the team like you trust me, including Adam."

"Look, I'm not there yet with Adam. That night was ..."

"That night you were more scared than you've ever been in your entire life. That night you were a child in the room with a monster, Tony. Maybe you were so afraid of that night coming in your life you became a policeman. All I know is, the monster in the room was the man trying to keep you alive in a very complicated world.

"Adam never lies. I don't believe he knows how. He grew up alone and never experienced the need to lie. Adam is chillingly honest, Tony. He will tell you anything you ask him. You need to see for yourself. His ways are more like you than you think— black and white."

"Answer my question, Elliott. In the tunnel, how'd you know Adam was going for Tanner? How did you know he wasn't coming for me?" Tony leaned in closer and whispered, "You asked me to trust you, now you to trust me."

"Adam and I ran into Boris Tanner three days ago. We were in a subterranean room under the Memphis Pyramid to get something relevant to the Medino software. Don't ask. It's a long story for a later time."

"Guess that explains the missing hand. I'm surprised Adam didn't kill the guy then."

"He wanted to," Elliott said. "I asked him not to."

"He can restrain himself? Good to know. Now explain the fifteen seconds."

"We talk to each other, communicate with thoughts."

"Like mental telepathy?" Tony asked.

"By definition it is the transmission of information without the use of known sensory channels or physical interaction."

"Right. Mental telepathy," Tony rolled his eyes. "Did Adam tell you Tanner was coming?"

"Yes. He saw Tanner thirty yards behind us."

"It was pitch black in that damn tunnel."

"Adam has incredible night vision—like a wild animal. He can also smell like a bloodhound and hear like a bat."

"You and your genetic toys," Tony sighed.

"I had to get you out of the way," Elliott said. "Tanner had his eyes on the gun. You were going to die first, Tony. If Adam had not stopped Alberto and Tanner the night Alberto came for the Medino hard drive, none of us would be alive today."

"He knew then. That's why he came to the Bell mansion."

"That's why he came down here today, Tony."

"Shit . . ." Tony kicked the dirt.

Carol approached. "Okay, you boys have whispered long enough." She put her arm around Elliott's waist. "Are you two on the same page now?"

"Gettin' there," Tony said.

Carol smiled and continued. "Adam put Mr. Tanner on the porch and left. And William picked up Albert, Max, and Marcus. Everyone's moving into the Bell mansion today."

"You should, too," Tony said.

"You should, Carol," Elliott agreed.

"I'm not as important as you guys and the scientists. I'm just a newspaper girl."

"That's not true, and you know it."

She shrugged off the debate. "Anyway, I've got to go by the *Tribune* to find out who knows what. I'll update you later tonight, Elliott. I've got a journalist meeting in New York City tomorrow morning. I'm flying up this afternoon. Will be back tomorrow evening."

Elliott would talk to her about her trip—alone. Traveling now was not acceptable and she knew it would not sit well with him. "Did William say anything about our three doctors?"

She could hear it in his voice—he was not happy with her. "They're at the Bell mansion. Tony, I suggest you get over there today to talk to them about their friends. I'm sure they have questions and the MPD has not made the connection."

"Regarding Tanner's body on the front porch, if you're asked any questions, we tripped over it when we were retrieving boxes of documents for the ongoing TEA investigation."

Tony waited for Carol to nod favorably. "Okay. We're good. I'm calling in the hounds now." Tony pulled his cell and hit speed dial—MEMPHIS HOMICIDE. "Since all the boys are gone, our story is a lot easier."

The front steps of the dilapidated structure were shattered and warped, and the hand-carved stone supports eroded and crumbling. The first Bell mansion, once the center of southern class and sophistication, now melted into the north woods of Shelby County. From the front steps of the tired stately manor and abandoned sheriff substation, the group watched spinning lights turn onto the gravel drive overtaken by weeds. Elliott sat with Carol on one side. Tony sat with Tanner on the other.

"Talk to me, Elliott?" Carol whispered.

"Tell me about New York . . ."

Six squad cars slid to a stop in front of the Brent mansion. With guns in the air, they emerged from the growing dirt cloud. Behind them, an ambulance pulled onto the property with lights and siren.

"Well this is just fucking great," Tony barked jumping off the porch waving his hands. "I told you the guy is dead—damnation to hell. I said everything's under control. Holster your goddamn guns, people." Tony kicked the ground. "And why all the back up? Screw this!"

As the herd of police surrounded the body, Carol and Elliott moved to the far end of the porch and stood behind a pillar. They kissed and held each other close. "I'll be careful," she whispered. "I know you don't want me to go. But I must."

"I don't like it. They killed Betty. You're important because they know you are with me."

"We can't do this, Elliott. We can't let them control our lives." She put her hand on his chest and smiled. "It's going to be fine. I'm meeting other newspaper people at the airport. We're sharing a taxi to the Omni. I'll call you when I get there. It's just one night. Meeting's in the morning. Got one connection—DC—then home. I've done this trip many times."

"I want you to cancel," Elliott said. "Just until we get control of things."

"You remember Richard, my government source?"

"Of course. I remember everything. He's the guy you asked to look into Gilgamesh government ties. He disappeared. Why, is he back?"

"He left me a message on my disposable phone, Elliott. He's in hiding. Richard has something for me. He could not leave details, but said it was about Gilgamesh."

"You can't meet this guy alone. You have no idea what's going on with him. He could be followed. He could even be working for Gilgamesh now."

"Richard is harmless. I've used him a dozen times over the last ten years."

"People change, Carol."

"Richard's going to meet at my layover gate in DC."

"It could be a setup to get you."

"Not at a busy airport, Elliott. This is what newspaper people do. Not everything has to do with Gilgamesh. I talk to unnamed sources all the time. Don't over think. Gilgamesh is focused down here, in Memphis. They want Dr. Medino's research. I'm the one who should worry. They want to get rid of you and Albert, the two most important men in my life." She pecked him on his lips. "I trust you. Now go focus on the hard drive. Help Marcus. I'll be back in no time."

The Taxi pulled up behind the patrol cars and honked. "There's my ride." Before Elliott could respond she kissed him hard. "I'll see you tomorrow night. I love you."

"I love you. Be careful," he said under his breath as she left. Director Cottam pulled up in an unmarked police car and got out, watching the taxi pull away.

Elliott saw her blond hair in the rear window. She turned and smiled. The taxi disappeared down the gravel road.

I don't feel good about anything anymore, Elliott thought. *Why does this feel like the last time I'll ever see you? Is this my paranoia . . . or is this another . . . gift?*

THIRTY-EIGHT

Washington DC

Richard was the only one alive who knew Medino had made three hard drives. The man with the third was now floating in the Chesapeake Bay, if the crabs hadn't found him. Richard's deal was with Gilgamesh. He needed an insurance policy—Carol Mason.

It was rush hour in DC. He wore a black raincoat under a black umbrella, jumping puddles and pushing his way down Pennsylvania Avenue like everyone else. Blankets of rain folded into the city as legions poured from office buildings. Like a colony of army ants, the bulging sidewalks of marching masses spread throughout the nation's capital.

Richard broke from the anonymous crowd and turned down Thirteenth Street. He moved at a steady pace, keeping his head down inches from a sea of sizzling hoods, tinted windows, and flapping wipers. Travel on foot proved to be another correct decision—he was brilliant. *Nobody gave me the credit I deserved. I was invisible to them,* he thought.

At the end of the first block, he turned the corner and looked back over his shoulder. Staying on the inside edge of the narrow sidewalk, he grazed brick walls and wrought iron fences and manicured shrubs, and he inspected each shadow approaching. Richard would know if one was out of place, the one walking with no purpose, trying to blend. Or the one staring, or looking a little too long, or the one not looking at all. Richard classified himself as an expert in the field even though his career as a government employee failed to compensate him appropriately. But everything would change soon.

Leaning into the stiff, wet wind, he slid a hand into his pocket to take control of his flapping raincoat and to confirm the presence of his portable hard drive he knew was there. Thinking about the new life he deserved, Richard rubbed the soft leather case with a fat thumb. The transfer of funds would set him up for life. He would live like royalty, anywhere in the world. Richard kept rubbing the magic box as he trudged forward, eyeing each sliver of darkness for the unexpected. In his other pocket he had his .38 Glock. He controlled his life, at last.

His turned into the alley to assess the pedestrian flow. Did they continue without interest? He watched as he backed deeper into the black rain between the buildings. When he reached the lone dumpster, he slid to the wall and pulled out his throwaway cell. It had one number on speed dial—Carol Mason's. For years, she had used him—her mole. It was his turn.

"Are you at Reagan National?" Richard asked, pressing the phone to his ear to hear over the pounding rain on his black umbrella. Water flowed off the brim of his soaked fedora.

"Delayed due to weather," Carol said. "But I'm here, now. Where are you? I'm at the gate."

"Change of plans."

"What now?" Carol asked, looking around the terminal for anything suspicious.

"You need to meet me. I'm in the city."

"That's impossible. My flight could board any time. I need to get back to Memphis."

"Do you want the third hard drive? Dr. Medino's research?"

"Is that what you have for me, a hard drive?"

"Yes. There were three. Everyone thought two. It's why I had to disappear."

"I find it hard to believe, Richard—a third hard drive?"

"Have I ever steered you wrong?"

"No."

He leaned out from the dumpster and watched people file by the alley. "I've been moving all day to be certain I'm alone. I had some close calls. I don't think I can risk the airport now. Some bad people want this thing. They killed a man, Carol. I got away. They're looking for me. They are watching the airport and train station."

"Richard, hide it somewhere and get out of town. Take a taxi to Alexandria and get a bus out of there. Go to a small town somewhere. I'll make arrangements to get it, or meet you next week. It's the best way. I know about these people. They are dangerous. You need to go now."

"I can't let this out of my sight, and I can't risk carrying it around when they're hunting me. I'm only dealing with you. I've been hiding for a year. These bad people are everywhere. They are inside the government, Carol."

"You need to . . ."

"If I give this thing to you, I'm hoping you can get me some financial help from your friend Mr. Bell. I need to go away for a long time."

"If you have what you claim, I'm certain Albert Bell will be very appreciative."

"Meet me now. It is best. It will take an hour out of your schedule. I'm not far."

"I can't miss this flight, Richard."

"Right now, this is yours. I can't make any promises after tonight. They have flights to Memphis all the time. I'm pretty sure this hard drive is important. If Gilgamesh gets their hands on it, I don't think that's good for anybody."

Carol looked at her watch. *I can't tell Elliott. He'll go ballistic.* "Where are you?"

"The address is in a note taped to the bottom of a seat at your gate. It's the third row from the walkway under the third seat from the end."

"So you've been to the airport?" *What are you doing, Richard? What are you not telling me?* Carol thought.

"Last week, before I had the hard drive, I used a disguise. I needed a backup plan. I sensed this could get dangerous for both of us. Take a taxi to the brownstone on the note. I'll be there. I'm alone. Our only risk is the phone. I'm destroying mine now . . ."

Richard disconnected and stepped out of the alley, blending into the pedestrian flow. When he rounded his last corner, a blast of cold water hit his face like a wet hand. Startled, he walked six more blocks from Pennsylvania Avenue—four for show. The three-story brownstone had one light in the top corner window. It meant they were ready.

Gilgamesh had agreed to deposit $50 million into Richard's Cayman account for the third hard drive upon confirmation of authenticity at the designated location—the brownstone. Delivery of Carol Mason meant another $50 million. The deal was $100 million, or nothing. Mason had to be part of the deal. She was leverage for the access codes.

Richard studied the brownstones and parked cars lining both sides of the quiet street. Mason's taxi arrival before proceeding would be ideal, but he had a timeline. When the first $50 million hit his Cayman account, he had ten minutes to deliver the hard drive—not eleven. As they confirmed authenticity, Carol Mason would arrive. The second $50 million would go.

Richard pulled out his cell phone and checked his Cayman account. The funds had not transferred. Backing into the hedges, he watched with an even more critical eye and considered all the possibilities. Had they lured him to a discrete location for nefarious reasons? Had he accepted the wrong deal? Should he hide it and go? Why didn't he mail it?

Each time he felt paranoid, he remembered that billionaires in a ridiculous club had made the deal. Their immortality pipe dream was a joke. And they had enough money. What was $100 million when you had billions? For all he knew, they hadn't killed anybody. Richard had killed the man with the third hard drive. He was more dangerous than Gilgamesh.

From the wet hedges and beneath his dripping fedora, Richard looked at the brownstone. *Someone could hide between any of the parked cars*, he thought. And every thirty feet he saw a fat oak tree. *There's a ton of hiding places. There could be a small army out there, waiting for an opportunity to grab me and steal my future—the one that made me kill a man and dump his body in the Chesapeake . . .*

Richard backed deeper and winced when the sharp branches poked his sides. Then he felt for the leather case and smiled. He remembered his training—the obvious threats were rarely problematic, mere distractions. But his heart kept pounding and he continued to hyperventilate. Then he checked his Cayman account again. This time, he saw the $50 million deposit.

He'd made the deal of a lifetime. He was invincible. The money was in the bank, and the pot would only get sweeter when Mason's taxi pulled up to the brownstone. Another lucky break— the deposit delay would work to his advantage. Mason or no Mason, Richard was already a wealthy man. He had more money than he could ever need.

Scanning rooftops, alleys, hedges, and the fat oak trees, he approached the brownstone. The place looked haunted—dark and dead. But Richard had the money now. The rest of his job would be like delivering the mail. The only remaining risk was intervention by an unknown, covert entity. He moved forward in measured steps, his black umbrella dipping from time to time to send the message—*just try to make a move on me.* He felt for his gun.

To the world, the brownstone looked like another rundown apartment house undergoing endless renovations. To a few, the government property did not appear on any record or official document. The hidden asset in a complex operating budget only appeared on city residential rolls as leased apartments. The tenants, an importer and European antique dealer, traveled year round. Their mail and newspapers were picked up daily.

On the dark landing at the top of wide cement steps, Richard stopped. The rain continued to beat down as he closed his black umbrella and tilted his head to allow water to run off his brim. Richard leaned back and took a last look up the street, hoping to see the headlights of Mason's taxi. There were none, so he texted her—*Come inside, I'm waiting.*

The seven-foot, black iron door seemed excessive. He leaned forward and felt under the tin mailbox for the plastic cover he knew would be there. He lifted the shield. The keypad glowed. Richard paused for one last look up the street. He punched in the five numbers given him. The last one released the door with an electronic grind and whirring whine. It popped open an inch. One last pocket check, one more smile, and one more thought of his fat Cayman account. Richard grabbed his sopping wet umbrella, pushed open the heavy door, and went into the dark entry with the last gust of miserable weather whirling behind.

Maybe if he had waited to shake his umbrella, his spine would not have been severed. Maybe if he had turned one more time, he could have gotten to his gun. Or maybe he could have talked his way out of the impossible situation. But Richard stopped thinking on the porch. Why would anyone want to bother with him now? The money had been deposited in his bank account. He now delivered the crown jewels, as promised. They could never get back the $50 million.

His failure to tend to *all* the details explained his lackluster government career, and greed, and will to kill for personal gain. Richard's failure to operate at a hundred percent at all times would be the cause of his death. On the most critical night in his life, he missed the one shadow tracking him in the rain. He missed the large man pressed against the brick wall on the porch where he fumbled with the keypad and an umbrella. And Richard missed the man following him into the dark entry—the wet gust of wind. He missed the man who sank the butcher knife into his back and cut across his spine like a steel plow shearing through soft dirt.

His legs buckled. He dropped to the wet stone floor. Paralyzed, he lay in the dark as the iron door whined closed. A hand grabbed his cheeks and pinched open his jaws and lifted him by his head. He dangled helplessly as hands rifled through his pockets.

Richard felt life leaving his body. He stared at the empty, deformed face of the stranger who handled his crippled body like a bag of dirty laundry. When the stranger found the hard drive and Glock, he dropped Richard to the floor to finish dying.

Lying there, everything that mattered one minute ago meant nothing. He would soon be dead, an unfortunate condition he placed on Carol Mason and the poor man floating in the Chesapeake. A thousand thoughts rushed through his dying brain, but one kept returning; *what have I done to her. Please don't come. Please don't . . .*

Richard would leave the world believing he died a

millionaire. He would never know the deposit into his Cayman account had been reversed minutes after his digital log out. He would never know such arrangements were possible if you were a billionaire with connections. Gilgamesh never intended to pay for the hard drive or Carol Mason. They would do what they always did—take them.

He watched the stranger clean his knife and pocket the cherished hard drive. And he watched the stranger leave the brownstone without looking back—Richard meant nothing to them. And before he closed his eyes for the last time, he watched the black iron door stop inches ajar, and felt the cool rain on his hot face.

He prayed for forgiveness . . .

THIRTY-NINE

C arol tossed her bag into the backseat and got in. "Just drive." When her door closed, the taxi fishtailed into the chaos of Reagan National.

The skinny man had one hand on the wheel and one on a water bottle. He maneuvered like a Daytona 500 driver hell-bent on taking the lead before the next curve. Seconds later, they blended into the metal and lights and smoke.

She studied his face in the visor mirror. The rangy, dark-skinned man from India wore a neatly pressed, white cotton shirt under his frayed Washington Redskins windbreaker. His large, angular nose dominated a narrow face with sunken temples. He had small black eyes and a persistent, toothy smile.

"I drive you until you say stop." He hit the meter and moved over to the airport exit lane.

"That'll be good, for now." Carol looked at her phone and swayed with the moves of the cab. *If I call Elliott, he'll worry*, she thought. *He's got enough on his plate. I know Richard. He's cautious—over-worries. I'll pick up the hard drive—probably a fake but can't take the chance—and hop on the next flight out.*

Elliott's working with Marcus and Albert on the dispersion plan. They don't need this distraction. She unfolded the note Richard had left her. Holding it out of view she studied it and her driver. *This is a random taxi driver. I gotta risk it . . .*

A picture hung from the visor—made at Disneyland. He had his arm around a woman, his wife. They were standing behind four kids, all with his nose and smile. Mounted in plastic in the center of the dash she saw the picture-ID: again the smile, a registration number, and name—Ray Penndel.

"How long have you been driving a taxicab, Mr. Penndel?"

"I drive nineteen years October. I drive eight in capital city. I meet wife here." He points to the Disney picture, "You see family, my children. We like America very much."

"Nice family," she said as she studied his face in the mirror. "Where are you from?"

"India, Naharastra on the Arabian Sea."

"Ray's not an Indian name."

"Ray for Rahul. I like better. You worry, Miss. You want Ray to lose somebody?"

"What makes you think I want to lose someone?"

"I see look many times. I drive. You be alone."

Carol smiled. "That would be nice, Mr. Penndel."

"Yes, and you call me Ray." He hit the accelerator and snaked across five lanes of bumper traffic, forcing the risk-averse to open holes only he could navigate in fractions of seconds. He shot off the next exit and reversed direction. Three blocks later, he turned down a quiet street, slid to the curb, and turned off the car. "We lay down in seat, Miss."

Headlights turned onto the street and crawled. When they passed, Carol peeked over the seat. The black Suburban turned at the stop sign and accelerated. Then she saw they parked in a line of a dozen empty taxicabs. She whispered, "Where are we?"

"This place they fix taxi. I always come here, very good

price." Ray looked over his wheel and in his mirror. "We good. Where you want to go?"

"I'm Carol Mason. I need your help tonight, Ray."

"Okay." He hopped the curb, crossed a field and went down an alley. "You nice lady." He popped on the lights and took the next ramp back onto the highway and they got lost in traffic.

The rain stopped by the time they pulled up to the brownstone. Ray gave Carol his cell number. He would stay in the area and wait for her call. She forced him to take two one-hundred-dollar bills. He forced her to take one back.

"I may need you fast, so don't get too far away. And Ray, be careful you are not followed." Carol reached for the handle.

"I come back for you when you call Ray. I know area very good. If you leave, tell me where and I come. I find you, Miss Mason." She stepped out and the taxicab sped away.

Carol stood under the oak tree looking at the brownstone. If all went well, Richard would be waiting inside. She would get the hard drive and call Ray.

The place seemed abandoned, one light in the third floor corner room and no porch light. *Maybe this is not a good idea,* she thought.

A year had passed since Richard vanished. She had used the reliable government source for ten years. He had strong credentials, a Penn State CPA satisfied with a low-stress job. The tedious number cruncher took care of the financials for a dozen senators—spreadsheets, consolidations, taxes, and spending validations. After thirty years, he became invisible, like an old house cat nobody fed. Richard had access to mountains of classified information. He navigated the government, the numbers his guide. Nobody had his skills. He connected the dots and found all the secrets.

There would be no turning back now. She went up the sidewalk and stopped at the steps. *One day you'll need to tell me what you learned about Gilgamesh, Richard. And how you got your hands on a Medino hard drive, one nobody knew existed.* The door was ajar.

Carol climbed the steps and pushed. It whined. "Richard?" she called out. She flipped the light switch—nothing. *I don't like this.* She took a few steps. Her foot bumped something on the floor. It didn't move. She froze. All her alarms went off as she reached for her keys and the small light on the chain. She pressed. "Oh my god. *Richard!*"

His eyes were open and glazed. He lay in a pool of coagulated blood, his pockets out and shirt untucked. One arm clung to his side, the other was outstretched, his finger pointing to a hallway going to the back of the brownstone. She knelt, clicking her tiny light off and turning back to the door. The menacing shadow climbed the steps. Carol kicked the door closed, jumped up and slid the deadbolt over. She had no time to use her cell. She had to escape, hide, and then get help.

"Open this door," the man yelled as he pounded and rattled the knob.

Carol ran to the end of the hall ignoring the pounding on the iron door. She would not have long before the rear exit would be unavailable. She left the brownstone and ran down the wood steps. When she got to the ground, she pulled off her heels and ran down the alley looking for a way out. The fences were tall, the gates closed and locked, and the hedges thick. She kept moving. *Don't go where they would go. Don't do the obvious. Elliott's gonna kill me . . .*

The back of the abandoned two-story warehouse could work. The boarded windows and crumbling brick looked like a place she would avoid—it was too perfect. She found a loose board and went inside. The gritty, oil smell and laced through stacks of rusted car parts—fenders, hoods, bent wheels, torn car seats, piles of bald tires, and rows of metal drums. *This is not a warehouse. This is not a warehouse. It's a garage.*

Carol felt her way to a corner and doorway into a small room packed to the ceiling with cardboard boxes of motor oil. Inside, she found little space to stand. From there she watched the larger room and got on her cell. *Maybe Ray Penndel knows about this place . . .*

"Ray," she whispered. "I'm in trouble. I'm hiding in an abandoned garage with car parts and tires two streets behind the brownstone."

"I come get you Miss Mason."

"No, Ray. I'm being chased by a bad man. I think he killed a person. He's coming for me. Call the police." She heard something. "I need to go." She disconnected and leaned an eye.

God . . . he's as big as Adam. Could he be one of the Henley twins Elliott ran into in Dyersburg? He's enormous . . .

She leaned back and hit speed dial. Elliott's name filled the screen.

"I was just thinking about you. Are you getting on a plane darlin'?" Elliott teased.

"Just listen. I'm in trouble. I agreed to meet Richard."

"Carol, where are you?"

"I'm in an abandoned garage somewhere in DC. I'm hiding. I think one of the Henley twins is looking for me. They killed Richard. I'm sorry Elliott. I didn't think . . ."

"Call police now. Leave phone on to find you."

"Elliott. He's here," she whispered. "He's coming toward this room."

"*Carol!*" he yelled into the phone. He held it tight to his ear. Boxes were falling. Glass shattered. Carol screamed. He heard the fighting, and then Carol screamed a second time. This time it was a bloodcurdling shriek he could never imagine coming from the girl he loved. There was wailing and crying...and then, nothing.

"Carol. *Please God.* Are you there?" he whispered. *But I know . . .*

He recognized the raspy breathing on the other end of the phone. Henley spoke with no emotion. "Dr. Sumner. Do not go anywhere. Do not talk to anyone if you want to see your lady again in one piece. It would be a shame to dismember such a pretty girl . . . We will call tonight."

Elliott dropped to the sofa and stared at the cell phone . . .

FORTY

"I successfully produced the first batch," Marcus said.

Albert sat at the head of the long table in the rich dining room. Unlike the first meeting at LIFE2, the three scientists sat close to the patriarch, Max and Marcus across from them.

"May I assume the facilities have proven adequate?" Albert asked as he looked over at Max—the man who knew every square inch of the estate his people now guarded 24/7.

"I believe 'adequate' is an insufficient word, Albert," Max crowed.

The bunker—one level below the well-stocked, Bell mansion wine cellar—was a defensive fortification intended to protect the billionaire under the worst possible conditions. The thick stone walls, iron doors, and independent ventilation and power sources defined the acre room with multiple escape routes and was equipped for five years of independent survival. Now it made for a perfect location to produce the coveted Medino biologic.

After leaving the catacombs, Tony Wilcox—taking Carol Mason's advice—met with the three scientists and explained the deaths soon to be released to the public. No one wanted to talk about the horrific tragedy again. The pain was too great.

Marcus opened the top file on the stack. He flipped through inches of documents like a stamp collector looking for the perfect specimen. When he stopped, holding up the single page, he remembered others were in the room.

"My father's formula has been surprisingly easy for me to follow. My father was a genius." Marcus set down the page and sat behind the stack with the face of a man who had just witnessed a true miracle. His eyes danced.

For the most observant in the room, Marcus looked different. His jet black, curly hair no longer had gray strands crowding the temples, and the pronounced wrinkles at the corners of his eyes were gone.

"The apodictic answer to biogenic immortality is in our hands," Marcus proclaimed.

Max looked closer, as did Albert and the three doctors. Had Marcus taken the biologic further than agreed? Did he do more than synthesize? Why would he use such a word? 'Apodictic' was a specific, descriptive term. It meant 'incontestable because of having been proved'.

He continued. "Mr. Bell, my colleagues obtained the quality and quantities of ingredients required. I located the completing components not shared." Marcus's smile faded as he turned to the three doctors. "Not shared for your own protection, of course," he stuttered. The horrific killings flashed in everyone's head. Dr. Flanders and Dr. Stubs never had a chance. They had not even had time to pack an overnight bag—how had Gilgamesh known so soon?

Max broke the awkward silence. "Albert, the equipment is helpful to the team. I'm quite sure they have utilized much of the kitchen gadgetry to produce the first biologic."

Marcus agreed. "The blenders, rotary whisk, mortar and

pestle, cocktail shakers, and assorted ovens have been great. The industrial dishwasher serves numerous purposes. We did need to purchase desiccation equipment. William found it in a day, allowing for smooth and time-efficient formulating, compounding, and decanting processes."

Albert nodded as if he knew what they were talking about—he had no clue. He never visited the bunker or the well-stocked wine cellar. But the patriarch knew people. He saw the pain and confusion in their eyes. He saw broken spirits as the white lab coats sunk in the chairs.

"Doctors." They lifted their heads. Albert leaned forward, opening his hands on the table as if reaching for each. "We must deal with this. I am sorry you lost your associates, your respected colleagues, your dear friends. I wish there were words to help explain the madness, to make sense of the wrongs in this world, but there are none.

"You are engaged in an epic battle between good and evil. To have any chance, we must honor those lost and find a way to draw upon their end to renew our strength. We must reach deep and find a way to transform pain into focus, determination, and courage. Each tragedy we experience cannot be a burden, or we will die beneath its weight. Each tragedy must strengthen our resolve to achieve victory." Albert's steel-blue eyes touched each.

"If immortality is the next evolutionary step for mankind, I believe we are to deliver it to the world. Only when it is received can all of humanity determine its course—for better or worse. I believe . . . for better. Each of you must find your reason to be here. You must hold onto it. We must confront the evildoers. And we must prevail."

After a long silence, Dr. Vanlandingham pushed hair from his forehead in a boyish manner and said, "Dr. Flanders and Dr. Stubs—may they rest in peace—were exceptional scientists and dear friends. I was not prepared for what happened so soon. I will be next time."

"You met the wrath of our enemy on the first day we met," Max muttered.

"I am sure I speak for my colleagues when I say we join this important mission without reservation," Vanlandingham said. "We stay the course. We honor our friends."

Dr. Sorokin nodded. "We may fail scientists . . ."

". . . but we will not be diverted," Dr. Stark said.

Marcus was last to speak on the painful topic. "We have all lost people close to us. My father told me his research would first cause death. I did not understand. I thought it ironic—how can a secret to extending life cause a premature death?"

"Your father was more aware of the realities of our world than most," Albert said.

William entered the room with a silver service tray. He distributed the cups and saucers and poured coffee as the room reflected in silence.

"Where are we, Marcus?" Albert asked.

"The biologic is synthesized in adequate quantities to begin global dispersion. Because the substance seeks host DNA at a molecular level, a relatively small amount is required. We must infuse a minimum of one hundred million people with the biologic. Based on our targeted population center dispersion strategy, in one hundred days the seeding program should infuse ninety-four percent of the 7.2 billion world population."

"7.2 billion, how is that possible?" Max gasped.

"Allow me to explain," Dr. Stark said. "In the simplest of terms, when one person is infused they transmit to others. It's like spreading the common cold."

"It is an exponential transmission process," Marcus said.

"Infusion—or inoculation—can be tactile, airborne, or ingested."

"Interesting. How much of the biologic do we have?" Albert asked.

Marcus looked at Max. Max nodded. He turned back to Albert. "We have three suitcases in powder form ready to go."

William moved through the room refilling coffee cups. Albert set down his cup. "I suppose it is time to discuss the global dispersion plan," he said. "Our family is very fortunate. Although cotton is our mainstay, we have engaged in a wide variety of international business ventures over the years. Those we liked, we now enjoy controlling interests. That being the case, I can say we have several, excellent dispersion routes to consider. The challenge we face—as Marcus has already shared—is to reach as many people as possible in the shortest amount of time. Without taking everyone through the details of the analysis, I have determined a commodity product is the best avenue to take."

"Commodity as a marketing term, please expand," Dr. Stark said.

"Allow me, Albert. It can be a confusing term for scientists who apply it differently in the laboratory. Dr. Stark, a commodity is a class of goods in demand supplied without qualitative differentiation—wheat, cotton, water, copper, petroleum."

"Well said, Max. A commodity reaching most people at all economic levels in all countries is the ideal vehicle to deliver the Medino biologic," Albert said.

"I understand. As in science, there will be exceptions in all models. But we must start somewhere," Dr. Stark said.

Albert signaled William. A giant flat screen monitor lowered from the ceiling and the dining room lights dimmed.

"This is a panoramic view of the world. Note the red boxes in each country. They represent primary business sites—I will explain. The arrows show product flow, and on each continent you see triangles and stars.

"The Bell family owns an international chain of bottling

plants, over seven hundred. These operations bottle everything from purified water to soft drinks, teas, and sports drinks, to name a few of the beverages. They bottle for all major brands. Each facility participates in humanitarian endeavors. The triangles depict bottling plant locations and market hubs. The stars depict secondary markets and smaller distribution hubs. As you can see, the movement of products—glass and plastic containers—reaches most of the world. We have holes in South America, parts of the Pacific Rim, and the poles."

"How are you getting the biologic to the people without triggering regulatory hurdles? Surely the governing bodies in each country would have a problem with a business introducing unknown agents into an approved process, especially a drink," Dr. Stark said.

"You are quite right, of course. We will introduce the biologic at the last stage of bottling, the seal. I've met with the director of global operations for Bell Bottling Enterprises. Infinitesimal amounts of the biologic will be introduced to every unit over the next thirty days. The mode of infusion across the consuming population will be either by tactile or ingestion."

"I still don't see how you get around the regulatory bodies. I'm certain every country has rules and inspectors on site."

"The sealing processes are standardized at our facilities. Please excuse my butchering of the terminology. There are sterile coupling devices—my words—in the bottling machinery. They are delicate. Changed on a schedule. Cleaned and sterilized. The biologic will be incorporated via this off-line process sterilizing these coupling devices. They are shown to be sterile and then reinstalled. The treated couplers introduce the biologic to every unit sealed."

"Three suitcases of the biologic, is that enough?" Dr. Sorokin asked.

"The short answer is yes." The flat screen retracted into the ceiling. "Max will take a morning flight to New York City. At the airport he will be met by my director of global operations. Max will have with him the three suitcases of the biologic. The handoff will be made at the airport."

"It's been my experience the most obvious is the least risky. It's the creative that gets you in trouble," Max said with a chuckle. "I travel with the global director to all sites and ensure the proper execution of the dispersion program. We are handling the powder as a proprietary antimicrobial developed by Bell Pharmaceuticals to enhance long-term sterility."

"In the morning, each of us will depart the estate grounds beginning at 5:00 PM. We will be followed. Max will leave last. He will go to the airport and fly commercial, the least interesting method of travel and the best way to move the biologic to the staging area in New York City."

William leaned in the door and waved to Albert. He acknowledged. "Excuse me," Albert said. "I have a matter to attend to. Please continue." He left the room.

"Your telephone, sir. Mr. Wilcox. He's distressed, sir." He passed the cell phone

"Detective Wilcox, Albert here."

"Carol was taken in Washington DC. We're sure it's Gilgamesh. They killed her, Albert."

"*No!* My god. Not Carol . . ." Albert fell back against the wall.

"DCPD gave me the details. They described the place where they found her cell phone, shoes and purse. It was goddamn terrible—like the airplane with Miss Duncan. They killed Carol the same way. The DCPD said the blood pool—nobody could survive losing that much blood."

"Are we certain it is Carol's blood, Detective Wilcox?"

"She's AB-positive. It's a very small percent of the population. We're sure. And like with Miss Duncan, the bastards took her body to taunt us. We're waiting for the phone call now. I don't know what they're gonna ask for to return her body. Do you?"

"I'm sorry. I'm not thinking clearly right now. Does Elliott know? Oh my god. This will kill him. He loves her so. He didn't want her to travel this week."

"Elliott knows something. Exactly what, I don't know. He was on the phone with Carol when they killed her. He's lost it. I'm at his place now. He's gone. I'm worried. Carol was everything to him. He could hurt himself. This may take him over the edge. We're looking for him now . . ."

FORTY-ONE

"An injured lion still wants to roar."
Randy Pausch

Somewhere in Arkansas

In the cracked mirror, Elliott stared at the drunk with the gun in his mouth. *They killed Carol. They killed me . . .*

He closed his eyes.

I've been nothing more than an experiment my whole life. They manipulated my genetic makeup. They gave me genius intellect and enhanced my senses beyond what any man could bear. They threw me into a sick world to figure out what I am . . .

I can't stop it now. The evil is eating me from within—the monsters I've hunted, the victims I've mourned. It's too much to feel . . . too much to ever heal. Without Carol, my demons will now overrun me. Their malevolent ways will unleash the anger in me, Adam's anger.

He pulled the trigger. The metallic click lingered. No explosion. No smoke. No bullet. No blood. He opened his eyes.

Is this death? Did I cross over seeing, hearing, and feeling nothing? No . . . !

He closed his eyes and pulled the trigger again—nothing. He took the gun from his mouth and threw it across the room. The cracked mirror hopped off its nail and crashed to the floor. He stared at the empty wall in the sleazy hotel as the pain washed over him. Emanating from deep within the core of his genetically engineered brain, it exploded inside his skull and shot down his spine. Every muscle screamed as raw anger stirred.

It had always been there, but this time he let it out. This time his demons were set free, the monsters living in his perfect, photographic memory. Elliott fell into the sea of heinous acts and ghastly killers. He felt all the sickening details of all the homicides. He drowned in the visual carnage and haunting eyes of the madness. His anger grew. He became Adam. He had to kill.

The bottle of scotch sat on the nightstand. *But I can't even kill myself.* He grabbed it and drank until he saw the bottom of the bottle. He threw it against the wall and watched it shatter and rain down in a thousand pieces like his pitiful, tormented life.

They said they would see me in Memphis? They said they would kill me next . . . then the rest of the Bell family. They would take Medino's research. They will kill Marcus and Tony and Max and William. They will kill everyone in the way of their demented mission. This will never be over unless . . .

Elliott slid off the bed, his legs unsteady but his mind crystal clear. He had a new mission—he would end it all tonight. Now he understood. He had always been the only one who could.

Carol was dead. His demons were back. He had no more reasons to be civilized. He would do what he did better than any living man—assess the pieces of the century-old puzzle, consider every word ever spoken by the enemy, relive every experience and look at every clue and every pattern. He would apply his genius intellect and advanced logic. Elliott would use all his assets to find and kill the Gilgamesh leaders tonight.

Where would you go? he thought.

You're on the run. You're hiding from law enforcement—the FBI Most Wanted. Assumption #1—you went to Cape Town to retake the GICC. Assumption #2—you went to Cape Town because you had no other place to hide in the Eastern Hemisphere. Assumption #3—you need to coordinate the Memphis kills and acquisition of the Medino hard drive. Assumption #4—you know the hard drive is at the Bell mansion. Conclusion—you must base in the midsouth.

Assumption #5—Alberto's residence is not a suitable hiding place, watched 24/7 by the MPD investigating the TEA homicides. Assumption #6—the catacombs under the Brent mansion are no longer suitable, watched by Shelby County Sheriff's Office 24/7 . . .

Elliott left the dingy hotel room. He stared at the foggy, gravel parking lot lined with empty semis and used cars. At three o'clock in the morning, the rain stopped and the storm crawled northeast, leaving Arkansas. The weather reminded Elliott of the tornados he battled on the edge of Dyersburg, another night when Gilgamesh had almost removed him from the equation.

He leaned on the hood and watched lightning flashes outline the pile of clouds descending upon west Tennessee. Swirling winds whipped across his face and stirred his memories.

Dyersburg. The Garrett Farm. The place where I met the other set of genetic engineered freaks. The Hansen twins were a lot like us, misfits and alone, but different in that they were manageable . .
.

He opened the passenger door and popped the glove box. Sitting on the edge of the seat, he grabbed the box of .38 caliber hollow points and took out a handful. He held one to his eye and rotated it in the flashing sky, unleashing his photographic memory—*the .38 caliber hollow point offers controlled expansion where six serrations divide the bullet into six symmetrical sections that weaken the jacket to allow expansion at low velocities and ensure fragmentation does not occur at high velocities. It delivers deep, terminal penetration with every shot. It has a swaged core and drawn copper jacket, diameter 0.357, weight 125 grains, sectional density 0.140, and ballistic coefficient 0.151 . . .*

"Stop, brain," he whispered, rubbing his forehead. He shoved the carton back in the glove box, slammed the car door behind him, and froze. His brain had been working without his knowledge. It spat out something important.

The abandoned farm, why lure me there? The Garrett Farm was not a random site. Nothing about Gilgamesh is random. It has something to do with control and convenience. Is it another Gilgamesh base, a regional backup to the Brent mansion catacombs?

He sat on the steps to his hotel room and looked at the moving storm. *I know this feeling. It comes when I'm close to solving a homicide or catching a killer. It comes when facts and logic merge and a path tightens. The Garrett house sits on prime real estate surrounded by flourishing farms. Why the dead corn crops and dead trees and dead brush? Why the beaten path from the barn to the rear of a collapsing structure? The abandoned Brent mansion is a portal to the catacombs. The old, Dutch church is a portal to another underground operation. The map of the catacombs references a corridor to Dyersburg.*

Elliott loaded his gun and got in his car. He knew where they were.

FORTY-TWO

"What is play to a cat is death to the mouse"
Danish Proverb

S omeone is going to die today . . .
Max would fly commercial with the biologic. Checking the three bags at the curb of Memphis International attracted the least amount of attention. Transporting with armed guards on one of Albert's private jets posed too great a risk.

Max stayed up all night—the news of Carol's horrible death rocked him to the core. And concerns for Elliott weighed heavy on his mind. Elliott had been missing for twenty-four hours, and thoughts of Elliott's suicide paralyzed Max. But Max knew sticking to the plan and staying on schedule had to be the focus. Even though their chances of survival were nonexistent, their attempt to disperse the Medino biologic had to go forward.

The tap on the door came at 4:30 a.m. Max sat on the edge of his bed in the dark. "Come in," he said in a scratchy voice, followed by an old man's hacking cough.

William entered and closed the door behind him. He turned on a small lamp and found Max. "I see you've decided to stay with the stout, twilled cotton suit," William bantered.

Their relationship had grown in the shadow of Gilgamesh, a mutual respect for their accomplishments over the last half-century. Although most knew about Max, few knew William was a decorated fighter pilot and cloaked CIA asset. He worked on commission. Fewer knew William was Albert's closest friend and confidant, responsible for executing enormous business deals around the world for Bell Enterprises. They successfully disguised their relationship beneath the male servant persona.

"Something wrong with khaki?" Max mused, as he moved to the long mirror and swept wrinkles from his arms.

"On the contrary . . . casual and appropriate. Projects vacation. Brilliant." William parted the curtain an inch and looked outside. "Your limo and driver are in stall number five. You'll leave last. Suitcases are in the trunk. We need you in place at 05:00."

"And the others?"

"They'll be ready as per schedule. We are being watched." He let the curtain close.

"Gilgamesh is moving to their end game," Max muttered. "Always knew this day would come. No way to avoid it." He checked his breast pocket for cigars and found his plane ticket. He held it at arm's length under the lamp and squinted. "United Airlines flight 4532, departs 6:12 a.m. Let's see here, arrives Newark 10:00 a.m. Two hours forty-eight minutes. Maybe I'll get some sleep up there above the clouds," he chided.

"I'm quite certain you will, sir."

Max smiled and turned to the door.

William approached. "If I don't get the opportunity, it has

been my personal pleasure to know you, Maxwell." He extended his hand. "Both professionally and personally . . ."

"Yes, my friend. Me as well." They embraced. Max passed William the leather satchel.

The first garage door opened at 5:07 a.m. The limo left the Bell estate west on Walnut Grove and would go through downtown Memphis to I-40 and into Arkansas. Being the first out of the gate, they anticipated Dr. Sorokin and driver would take two or three Gilgamesh tracking vehicles to Little Rock.

Dr. Stark and driver were in the second black limo. They departed at 5:11 a.m. going east on Walnut Grove and then southbound on I-40 to I-55. Dr. Stark would be followed by one or two Gilgamesh vehicles to Jackson, Mississippi.

Marcus left in the third black limo at 5:12 a.m. eastbound on I-40 to Nashville. Based on a week of surveillance, the last Gilgamesh vehicle would be forced to follow. Backups would be racing to observation points by the Bell estate. Drones would be employed.

At 5:13 a.m. Albert's Bentley passed through the gates and got on I-40 to Wilson Air Services at Memphis International Airport. There, his private jet would be fueled and on standby. A flight plan would be filed from the Bentley. Max departed the Bell estate last. Two minutes after Albert's departure, Max's black Tahoe turned west onto Walnut Grove and south on Perkins Extended. He went to the airport with plenty of time. Four Spyglass associates traveled in separate cars disrupting traffic flow. Upon arrival, Max checked the three suitcases curbside and walked to his gate with nothing but a folded newspaper under his arm.

United 4532 landed seven minutes ahead of schedule at Newark Airport. The tall German standing at the gate with a folded newspaper under his arm wore a flowered shirt, Bermuda shorts, and sandals with white socks. Max emerged. They greeted like lifelong friends.

"Richard Kamholt. Is that you?" Max said so others could hear. They shook hands. "How long has it been, my dear man?"

"Maxwell, you haven't changed a bit. It's been at least fifteen years."

"Still young and vibrant like you, I suppose." They laughed and talked, selling it to whoever watched. Max scanned the surroundings for anyone with more than a casual interest. Although there were no guarantees, it appeared they were alone on the first leg—Max could nudge Kamholt toward the baggage area.

"Are we ready?" Max whispered while maintaining circumference surveillance. A move by coverts before claiming the bags would be unlikely, but experience taught him to avoid the knife in the back or needle in the neck when moving in crowds.

"We will go to my home. This afternoon we begin our travel —seven cities in the U.S., eight in Europe, five on the African continent, three in Australia, and then our route back home goes through South America and Latin America. The five-week plan provides the best opportunity to deliver and incorporate in seventy percent of our bottling plants."

"We're going to seventy percent of the plants?"

Kamholt laughed. "No. Twenty-five facilities. They are the primary hubs serving dozens of other sites. What we do in the hub gets implemented in the subsidiaries in days."

"I see. And how's it going—directives, questions, cooperation?" They stepped onto the escalator and descended. Max saw two suspicious men back out of view on the lower level.

"No questions. We do this all the time. Government regulation of consumables is an ongoing challenge. Costly and often ridiculous, but most necessary."

"I see." When they reached the lower level, Max scanned for the two men. They were gone.

"We're constantly implementing improvements," Kamholt said, pointing to the baggage claim area for United. "Anything we can do to reduce cost and increase quality gets priority attention. It is good business and my job to oversee."

"Good to hear. Albert Bell will be pleased. This improvement is important to him. One of his research facilities has worked hard to reduce all risks of contamination in mass production environments. I'm no expert, but he tells me the last thing to touch the product must be the first place to guarantee sterility."

"I've been in the bottling business for Bell Enterprises fourteen years, now. Prior to that, I worked in the cotton side of the business. Offline antimicrobial processes are the easiest places for change without stirring up regulatory agencies. All they want us to prove is our production machine parts are clean. This new program makes them sterile. No agency's gonna squawk at that kind of improvement. We hope they demand our competitors do it too, but they don't have our magic dust."

"Can you count on your line management to faithfully implement when you're not around?"

"Guaranteed. Everyone gets paid on performance. Reducing contamination rates increases yields and improves profits, and all with no more paperwork," Kamholt mused.

They reached the baggage area and took a position behind the crowd at the mouth of the conveyer belt. The expansive layout was designed to efficiently serve, but it was bastardized by human nature—a hundred pushing bodies merged when the bell rung.

Max kept his back to a concrete pillar managing potential lines of attack. The emergence of the three suitcases in Newark would be the next logical target. And the two suspicious men seen on the way down were still missing.

Max did not see the last person to board flight 4532, and the first to get off. The seasoned operative often fooled her targets. An overweight, sixty-two-year-old woman with a hairnet and overstuffed knitting bag sat in first class. Although the plane was full, seat 1-A opened at the last minute—a no show. Thelma Birnbaum flew on standby and got the seat—the sudden death of a sister in the Bronx. They moved her to the top of the list. United was pleased to accommodate.

The three bags dropped onto the conveyer. Kamholt grabbed two and Max one, and they walked to short term parking. Birnbaum got in the car parked next to Kamholt as they tossed the bags in the trunk. The presence of an old lady gave Max a sense of security, another thin layer of defense. If they stuck with past methods, Gilgamesh would not risk exposure in a public parking garage in broad daylight with witnesses. But he underestimated their desperation.

Max lit a cigar and smiled at the old lady as she started her car. When he slid into the front seat she nodded and smiled back. He closed the passenger door. The silencer popped once, an inch from the back of his head. Kamholt leaned Max back in the seat and put out the cigar. He casually stepped out and returned to the trunk. Kamholt transferred the three suitcases to Birnbaum's open trunk. When her lid went down, Birnbaum put a bullet in Kamholt's forehead and pulled him forward, guiding his fall between the cars. Looking around and unscrewing the silencer from her gun, she dropped both into her knitting bag and got in her car. Her departure was uneventful.

* * *

"Marcus, Albert here." The cell phone connection went in and out.

"Yes sir."

"Max did not check in. His plane landed thirty minutes ago."

"I don't know what to say. Have you heard from Sorokin or Stark?"

"Nobody," Albert said with an urgent tone.

"We should have done something about Vanlandingham. I don't like this."

"Max said it was best we leave him alone to mislead Gilgamesh."

"I hope you're right. At the moment I'm being followed by three cars. We better get off. They are listening."

"Be careful," Albert said.

FORTY-THREE

Dyersburg, Tennessee

In a drunken stupor, Elliott drove all night until he found highway 181 and signs pointing to Dyersburg. When he got close, he took Bradley Road toward the River and turned up Chic Road; it ran behind the luscious tracts of farmland and was quiet except for the occasional tractor.

He parked off the road in a cluster of trees and went the rest of the way on foot. He could see the Garrett farm less than a mile away, it had the rotting cornfields. He walked through the clouds of flies and stench of animal carcasses decaying in the morning sun—the flood had left a blanket of victims. As he neared the farmhouse and the scotch wore off, Elliott's altered state took hold.

You tortured her, he grumbled as he moved through dry stalks, breaking webs and stepping over what the buzzards had picked apart and left for the insects. *Mobuto Ali, Robert Armstrong, and Francisco Bolivar . . . like Alberto, you are swine . . . savage demons . . . ghastly excuses for human beings. I should have killed all of you in the beginning. I should have helped Adam and Kayne. Carol and Betty and Jack would be alive. I've been such a fool.*

Elliott knelt at the edge of the field behind the last line of brittle stalks. The farmhouse looked even more surreal in daylight. A hundred feet away, enclosed in a tangled knot of barren trees and stick shrubs, the broken structure sunk into dead hay. As Elliott took in the Gilgamesh lair, he fought the battle inside. The forensic sleuth told him to take it slow, study his surroundings, gather the clues, be patient and methodical, and only move with knowledge and purpose. But the Adam growing inside spoke louder, the powerful voice pushing back the relentless demons living in his head. Elliott's Adam grew stronger and said to abandon all caution and trust his instincts. Be the beast today. Fear nothing. Create the horrific advantage and kill the enemy without delay. Forget justice. Take revenge.

Ten days ago, he had escaped the Henley twins and seen the path from the barn to the house. Standing on a crossbeam out of the reach of killers, Elliott had pushed the loose board from the barn wall. Before he had jumped into the rain and lightning, beneath the flashing skies he saw that the bald trail went to the back of the old farmhouse. That night, the trail was just another observation stored in Elliott's photographic memory. He would carry it forever. But now, in the light of day, it had meaning. From the cornfield he saw the trail from the barn across the brown brush to the old, cellar doors.

You always hide your sick hobby underground—under the Brent mansion and the old church on Devil's Peak, Elliott fumed. *Here, this desolate piece of ground, you travel down a hidden gravel road and park in the old barn. You wait. You watch. When you are certain you are alone, you slither the same path to your miserable hole—the basement of a crumbling house.*

His muscles hardened. His eyes narrowed. His nostrils flared.

Elliott could see the tips of the broken hay and smell human flesh. He could feel the river air cling to each hair and flood every pore. *I will kill all of you in your nest . . .*

He left the dead cornstalks and ran to the back of the farmhouse. Elliott dropped to the ground and leaned against the crumbling wall. Without caution he moved to the cellar doors. There were no padlocks, no barriers to entry. He pulled out his gun and lifted one door enough to lower his head into the dark, musty hole.

I've killed before, he thought . . .

But the men he had killed were serial killers trying to kill him. Even under the most horrific and heinous circumstances, Dr. Elliott Sumner rationalized his actions. He always hesitated risking his life, reluctant to take even a monster's life. Each time he almost died. Each time something took over in the final seconds.

In the end I do what I must. I stopped horrible people before— serial killers. Today, I stop three more—mass murderers. Today I crush the last of the Gilgamesh brain trust. Today I bring an end to the last of the real monsters in this world.

The cellar door settled behind him as he descended the steep, stone steps. Darkness grew and the temperature dropped. Ten feet down, his feet found the stone floor. Concerned he would not be alone he slid to one side of the dark cellar and clung to the wall where his eyes could adjust to the darkness and ears to a new silence.

Lines of daylight leaked through the floors above. The basement was larger than the footprint of the dilapidated structure. Elliott felt the cold, rock walls and saw the steel-reinforced wood pillars. Like in the catacombs, there were stacks of cardboard boxes, empty barrels and crates, and piles of broken furniture and junk. Puddles covered most of the stone floor— remnants of the flood. At head height there were three windows of broken glass on three sides. The south wall had none—it was black. And the path of wet newspapers led the way.

Elliott assessed his new obstacle course. Now certain the cellar held a portal into another Gilgamesh base, he knew his presence had to be known. There would be cameras, motion detectors, and maybe a guard.

"Talk to me," Elliott tested. But his words fell dead.

The sun streamed lines across the wet, stone floor and chest-high mounds of debris. Holding his loaded gun he drew more strength. Elliott could never be as physical as Adam, but he had the enhanced senses, and he could handle a gun. He moved toward the dark wall in the bitter smell of rotten cornfields and dead animals. The site had been carefully selected. Although some water had found its way into the cellar, the house and barn had avoided another rising Mississippi river.

Come to me, he dared. *Slither out of your hole. I will cure this cancer in mankind . . .*

Elliott raised his gun, stepping into the dark end of the cellar. He listened for any sign of movement—nothing. When he reached the south wall, he found an empty bookcase like the one in the basement of the Brent mansion.

Surely you're more creative than this, he scoffed. Elliott pulled. It opened like a refrigerator door. He entered the hole in the wall. The tunnel reminded him of the catacombs under the Brent mansion. There were pipes to the surface—the barren trees —allowing light into the tunnel every twenty feet. And there were rooms cut in the black dirt. They were empty. Elliott went deeper with one hand on the wall and the other pointing his gun straight ahead—the attack would come from there. *Maybe my presence is undetected. Maybe they are overconfident fools.*

The dark, musty tunnel ended at a brick wall with a metal door. He felt along the edges and pulled. It opened and lighting popped on, revealing a long corridor of smooth stone. Every twenty feet were frosted-glass doors, and at the end of the long hall, frosted-glass double doors. He could see the gold emblem, the gothic profile of a demigod—Gilgamesh.

Elliott proceeded with less caution and more anger. At the halfway point, the lights behind him popped out in sequence. He stopped and backed to the frosted-glass door and moved his gun from one end of the corridor to the other—still no sign of another's presence. Then the lights ahead started to pop out in sequence, the farthest first working to him. In ten seconds, ten lights were out. Elliott held his gun, standing in the only light—vulnerable. But he had a fifty/fifty chance of stopping an attack. It had to come from one of two directions—ahead or behind. Elliott weighed the odds and selected 'ahead'. He aimed his gun. He could pull the trigger in a fraction of a millisecond, more than adequate to get a shot off and redirect for the next. Elliott froze by the glazed-glass door in the only light and waited and listened and called upon all his genetic assets. Now he was a killing machine like his brother. The devils that killed his Carol would die, and Elliott was ready to die with them. *Where are you . . . ?*

The hand exploded through the glazed-glass door and grabbed Elliott's throat. Another hand slapped his gun to the floor as if it were a melting Popsicle falling from a child's hand. It skidded to the opposite wall as fat fingers tightened around Elliott's neck and lifted him off the ground, kicking and holding onto the iron wrist of a Henley twin.

"Saw you comin', Dr. Sumner," he said with a hideous sneer. Henley held him out from his body like a writhing, poisonous snake. "Been a while, but we knew you couldn't stay away."

Elliott kicked and struggled to pry the fingers from his throat. "Stop kicking. I'll do you now," Henley said as he dropped his other hand on the top of Elliott's head and squeezed. Elliott reached for Henley's grotesque face and went limp . . .

FORTY-FOUR

The explosion echoed down the stone corridor from the dark.

Elliott dropped to the floor. Henley turned to the source. Blood spurted from his neck onto the polished stone. He covered his wound with his giant hand, but it did not matter. Blood poured through his fingers in a steady, massive red stream. Henley's eyes rolled into his head. He fell backward through the shattered frosted-glass door from where he came. His feet kicked and shook and trembled. Then they were still.

"Goddamn it, Elliott. Come on now," Tony yelled as he listened to Elliott's chest. He was no doctor, but there was nothing—no beating heart. Elliott was turning blue before his eyes.

"I don't know this shit, Elliott." Tony clasped his hands, raised them high above his head, and brought them crashing down on Elliott's chest.

"Damn, Elliott. Don't do this, buddy. Come on."

Tony did it a second time. Elliott coughed and sucked in air. "There ya go. Give me some more of that sucking. Breathe baby breathe," Tony said as he shook Elliott by the shoulders. "Wake up. Come on, you're doin' good. Breathe brother."

When Elliott opened his eyes, Tony's face was three inches away. "You're not going to do mouth-to-mouth are you, Tee?" Elliott smiled as he patted Tony's cheek.

"Nope. Would not do the mouth thing, Ell. I'd have to let ya die," Tony chided looking back at the broken glass door and the behemoth lying in the pool of blood. "Who is that son of a bitch?" He picked up Elliott's gun and squinted at the dark end of the hall.

Elliott sat up, rubbing his neck. "That's a Henley twin. I think he was the one I watched kill the old farmer ten days ago. He wanted to put me out of my misery."

"I remember the story." Tony kicked Henley's foot. "Fuck him. He's dead. When I saw you guys, I thought the bastard already killed you. He held you like a rag doll. You were not moving."

"We better check him, Tony." Elliott tried to stand and fell back.

Tony stepped over the broken glass and through the door. He felt Henley's carotid. "He's dead. No pulse." Tony checked pockets for a gun or knife. "Nothing here but a freak."

Elliott got up and leaned against the wall, his head aching from the Henley grip. "Where'd you come from, Tee? How'd you find me down here?"

"You never think I listen to you." Tony put a cigarette in his mouth and pulled out a lighter. "You're not the only smart guy. Honestly, Dyersburg was my last option. Looked everywhere."

"Don't light that," Elliott ordered.

Tony froze. "Why not?"

"More people are coming. I need to clean this up and find a place to hide."

"No, damn it. I'm calling for backup," Tony said as he pocketed his lighter.

"No you're not," Elliott puffed.

"You're one bossy bitch after I saved your life."

Elliott got serious. "Thanks for that—I think—but I'm going this one alone. It ends today, Tony. I don't expect you to do this with me. Leave now."

Tony turned his back to Elliott. "Right. Like that's gonna happen. Screw backup. What are we doing today, genius?"

Elliott nodded. "Well, I don't exactly have it all worked out. I've been improvising."

"So what do you think's gonna happen next . . . and what would you like to do about it?"

Elliott rubbed his head looking at Henley lying in blood. "I know this sounds crazy, but the three Gilgamesh board members are coming here. It could be today or a week from today."

"They're coming to Dyersburg? Okay. I'll go there with ya. Continue. I love this shit." Tony hung a cigarette in his mouth and leaned against the wall with a hand on his gun.

"This place is another Gilgamesh base of operations. It could be a backup for the Memphis operation. When they lost the catacombs under the Brent mansion, they went to Cape Town to activate their GICC. Now they lost Cape Town—thanks to you and Max."

"You're welcome," Tony sighed.

"I think they've gotta come here. There is a lot to this place."

"I don't know. It's a big world and they got a lot of money, Elliott. Why not South America where the Francisco weenie lives? Or another place in Africa where Mobuto-man is king of the jungle? Or Chicago, Armstrong's stomping grounds?"

"They've been moving around Africa for ten days. After every sighting, they move. I don't think they have a secure location over there. If they did, they would disappear."

"Okay. Makes sense. I'm listening."

"On the way here I passed a door with GICC etched on the glass. Gilgamesh had three. We just found the third one. It makes perfect sense. Alberto Bella had to put it somewhere close so he could keep an eye on it. This place is an important backup to Memphis."

"The damn GICC is their nervous system."

"And without it their mission is doomed."

"You said these people have unlimited resources. They can adapt. Setup shop anywhere."

"They may have unlimited resources, but they don't have unlimited time. Gilgamesh was not ready to lose their chairman, most of their board, all their members, and most of their assets."

"This place may be their best and only option at the moment," Tony said.

"After they killed Carol . . ." Elliott froze. His eyes filled. His head dropped. He took a deep breath and whispered, "The man on the phone told me they were coming to Memphis for me." Elliott's voice broke. He held his face and tried to recover. The raw feelings tore at his insides. Not only losing Carol killed him, knowing the fear and pain she suffered hurt too.

"Elliott." Tony put his hand on his best friend's shoulder. "There's nothing I can say that can possibly help you. It is killing me, too. I know you are a thousand times worse. But you gotta get strength from that great lady who feared nothing and loved you more than I thought a woman could love a man. She will always be in your heart, my friend. I am so sorry."

Elliott lifted his head and looked down the hall and another hundred miles. "That's why I must do this, Tony."

"If you think those rich bastards are coming here, then there's a good chance they are. We need to be ready," Tony said.

"We're not taking them back to Memphis."

"What are you talking about?" Tony asked.

"This is where it ends," Elliott said. "Gilgamesh dies in Dyersburg. I take full responsibility."

"That's not you, Elliott. It goes against everything you stand for. Taking the law into our own hands never fixes the pain. You know that. You're not thinking clear. You are nothing like these monsters. You would not be able to live with yourself after killing them."

"If I don't stop them here, they will never be stopped, Tony. I am the only one who can stop them. I know that now. These people are not your typical criminals. They threaten the future of all humanity. There has never been anything like this before."

"They can die in prison, Elliott, or the electric chair after conviction by a jury."

"No. These people would buy their way out of every court in the land."

"You can't do this, Elliott. I know you."

"The Gilgamesh board is comprised of the most dangerous people to ever live. The three remaining are worse than any serial killer I've ever hunted. They are mass murderers, Tee. If they get control of biogenic immortality, they'll determine who lives and dies."

"That shit's still science fiction to me. Like I said, I know you. I'm staying with you. When push comes to shove, you are a good man. You will capture these assholes before you kill anyone. You are built that way, my friend. So let's move on." Elliott pushed off the wall and looked down the hall. "How do we turn on the damn lights down here?"

"I think they're motion activated," Elliott said. "I got in trouble because I stopped walking. The lights behind me started going out and rattled me." He moved three feet down the hall. All the lights popped back on.

"These doors," Tony pointed to a half-dozen on each side of the hall. "Let's see what else they've got goin' on down here. And let's put the jolly green giant in a dark room and clean up this blood."

"Just be careful. We don't need to trigger anything."

One room, filled with laboratory equipment—ovens, dryers, blenders, and packaging materials—had plastic drapes from the ceiling to the floor around work counters. Elliott recognized the laminar airflow vents and environmental control panels. "This is where they will produce their version of the Medino biologic."

Tony scoffed, "I hate Dyersburg."

Elliott opened the GICC door. "Here she blows . . ."

The modem lights were rolling. Codes streamed across three monitors. Fans were humming. "I'll be damned if they didn't transfer everything from Cape Town," Tony said. "Should we destroy this GICC?"

"Leave it alone," Elliott ordered. "You will need it to find Gilgamesh operatives around the world." Tony followed him to the end of the hall and double doors. "I want to see what's behind this Gilgamesh image." Elliott opened the door and leaned inside. "So it is true. The catacombs reach Dyersburg."

Tony opened the other door. "Whoa! That's part of the Memphis catacombs? I'll bet they got a lot of bad things going on in there—their own little hell. Let's check it out. We can confront the bastards in the catacombs."

"No. There are too many variables. And they'll see our mess . . . know we're here. Surprise is our only advantage. We need a smaller, more controlled space." He closed the double doors.

"The cellar," Tony said. "There's one entrance. They've gotta come down those stairs behind the house. They'll make a beeline to the bookcase . . ."

FORTY-FIVE

The cellar doors opened at midnight. Tony got to his feet, pulled out his gun, and stood to the left of the hole in the wall. Elliott pulled his gun and stood to the right behind boxes.

"Where're the Henleys?" one intruder asked. The question rolled down the stone steps into the cellar as shuffling footsteps got louder.

"They're unreliable. We don't need them for this," the second voice said.

"It doesn't matter much, right?" a third voice asked.

Four shadows entered the dark cellar. The first two each carried a suitcase. The fourth was holding the shoulder of the third—and smaller in stature—silhouette.

Before they went deeper into the cellar, Tony stepped out and raised his gun. "You can stop moving or you can die. It makes absolutely no difference to all of us." He cocked his gun. They stopped at the bottom of the steps.

"You can drop what you're carrying and raise your fucking hands. Spread out so we can see you. Men, hold your fire unless they try something stupid. Then empty your guns."

Elliott stepped from the boxes and squinted at the four. He only saw shadows.

"Who are you?" one yelled. "Are you here to rob us? Because if you are, we will give you money and you can leave us alone, no police and no hassles."

"No, you idiot. You're dealing with the Memphis police and FBI. We don't make deals with international criminals. Raise your fucking hands or it will be our pleasure to shoot you for resisting arrest and causing me undue stress. I'm sensitive."

"Excuse me, but do you know who we are?" the second voice asked.

"Shut up asshole. I'm starting to count. When I reach three, I will take it you do not intend to cooperate and wish to do us harm. It will be recorded you made an attempt on my life. That is why you are dead," Tony growled. "One . . . !"

"Don't count. I pay everyone in this room one million dollars each to let us go."

"Two . . . !"

"We don't want your money, Mobuto Ali," Elliott said. Instantly, muffled squeals came from the silhouette behind the board members. "Francisco Bolivar and Robert Armstrong, we know you too. Number four is a mystery, at the moment."

"But we will shoot number four, too. Sure you're as sick and twisted as the other three," Tony chided. "Are we ready? And a three . . . !"

The crashing blow to Tony's head knocked him against the wall and his gun into a pile of broken furniture. He slid down the wall and slumped to the floor. He did not move. Before Elliott could react, the giant arm wrapped around his chest and squeezed so hard his gun fell to the ground as he gasped for air. Again a massive hand gripped the top of Elliott's head.

The board members smiled as they watched their friend

retake control of the room. The second Henley twin might have arrived late, but this time his tardiness would be overlooked . . .

FORTY-SIX

"Cowards die many times before their deaths—the valiant never taste of death but once."
William Shakespeare

"You're a fool," Mobuto bellowed, watching Henley ready to break Elliott's neck. A single bulb hung from the ceiling. It flickered on. In the weak light, Francisco removed his hand from the wall and returned to his suitcase next to Mobuto.

"Not yet, Henley," Francisco said. "I will tell you when you snap the neck of the world-renowned forensic pathologist."

In the penumbra behind Mobuto and Francisco and the suitcases, a struggle and muffled squeals intensified. Elliott could not see the board members. Henley pressed Elliott's head tight against a sweaty, rock-hard chest. But Elliott saw Tony on the floor, dead from a crashing blow. He saw the closed eyes and the blood on the side of Tony's head.

"We stopped everyone, Dr. Sumner," Francisco gloated. "They're all dead now. They won't be in our way anymore. Your brothers are dead, and your mother, but that is old news. You may not know Maxwell Gregory is no longer with us. We left the old CIA man in a parking garage today, Newark Airport. He never should have tried to move the biologic that way. It was much too easy to intercept. I thought Gregory to be much smarter."

"And your doctor friends from LIFE2 have been terminated," Armstrong said. "We didn't want to do it, but they knew too much about our program and the new science—Sorokin, Stubs, Flanders, and Stark are gone—maybe you should have left them be."

Francisco brushed his sleeves and picked lint off his coat as he spoke. "That is a correct observation, Mr. Armstrong. I must say Dr. Vanlandingham has been more than helpful this week. The man's been on our payroll for decades, Dr. Sumner. How did you not know? He helped us follow your infusion program," he boasted. "Now he will help us dispose of Albert at the right time, our remaining loose end."

"Alberto, he never do what he must," Mobuto said with hate dripping from each word.

Elliott struggled to turn his head. He reached deep for new strength. He had to find an opening. *This can't be the end,* he thought. *Monsters can't win* . . . "Why tell me any of this? Are you demented barbarians?" Elliott poked to buy time.

The three laughed. "Demented barbarians? Such subjective words," Francisco said. "We're like you, Dr. Sumner. We are educated, gifted, and very privileged men. We simply have different objectives. We are not any more demented barbarians than you or Albert Bell. You two killed Alberto Bella. And you must know your brother Adam killed more than a hundred of our best men."

"They were sent to kill. You could have stopped the carnage at any time, but you did not."

Francisco ignored Elliott's accusation. He continued as if the doctor had never spoken. "And Jack Bellow, he and Dr. Medino stole from us. They took the DNA of the blood lions, the secret to biogenic immortality. It belonged to Gilgamesh."

Armstrong joined Francisco's rant as if to justify his participation in the killing about to happen. "None of this had to happen, Dr. Sumner. Gilgamesh invested billions of dollars and thousands of hours advancing the science. We sat on the doorstep of the most significant breakthrough of all time when Dr. Medino decided to tell the world everything. Immortality was our dream. The biogenic key was our patented biotechnology worth billions. Medino had no right to give our secret to the world. We would lose all we worked for and our dream."

"That we not allow. That not right and we stop it," Mobuto growled.

"Our closest friends—our board members—were slain by Adam's offspring with your help," Francisco accused. "Kayne, polluted with Adam's lies and enabled by you, was set loose. You follow this madman around the world and watch him take our heads. You are the first to visit them—their heads on poles. No, Dr. Sumner, you are the demented one, sir."

"Let's not forget you and Albert Bell want to destroy Gilgamesh. You ran off our members and stole our assets," Armstrong said. "You brought this war upon yourselves."

Mobuto held up a hand signaling to stop. "Enough said." They parted. Armstrong pulled Carol Mason into the light. Henley turned Elliott's head to see the bound and gagged prisoner.

"Carol! You're alive!"

"Yes, Dr. Sumner. Miss Mason is alive," Francisco sneered.

"But the blood on the floor in DC, I saw it myself. There was too much for anyone to . . ." He struggled with newfound strength to break Henley's grip.

Mobuto pulled out his gun and smiled.

"The blood pool was staged," Armstrong said. "We wanted you to believe Mason died like your mother. That's why we bled out Betty Duncan and took her body. We planted the pattern in your mind, Dr. Sumner. We know the genius forensic pathologist prides himself on finding morbid patterns to solve crimes. Betty Duncan's death set our trap—if we needed it. If you believed Mason died a horrible death and one day learned she was alive, you would be desperate to comply with our every wish. You would do anything we asked."

The three chuckled. "And here you are," he said. "We have you and the first production run of the Medino biologic. And soon, we will have the hard drive."

"We didn't need Carol Mason after all," Armstrong said.

"Don't hurt her," Elliott pleaded. "Let her go and I'll see you get the hard drive. Then you can kill me. If you kill us now, there is no guarantee you will ever have the Medino formula. It has eluded you for decades. There are passcodes you must have or you lose everything."

"We have a hard drive, Sumner. There were three. We will get the passcode on our own."

"There were never three hard drives. You're being fooled again. There are only two," Elliott said. "You destroyed the first because you didn't know how to get through Medino's security virus. It's more complicated than that. Don't be fools again and lose everything. Let Carol Mason go and you have me to realize your dream this time. She's never been in this war. Make the right decision."

"You're a very persuasive man," Francisco said. "It is a shame you never worked with us before. Alberto wanted you from the start—the blood lions made biogenic immortality possible. It started with Albert's stem cells, then his progeny. The Bell triplets possessed the genetic trait, but we could never reproduce it. Now we can do so without you. Two of the blood lions are dead. It is time for you to join them. When we are done with Albert, he will join the rest of his family. Only then can Gilgamesh control its destiny."

"We terminate you now," Mobuto barked. "Enough talk." He raised his gun. "It has been a long war, Dr. Sumner. We win. You watch Mason die first. Then we make sure your friend dead. Then you die this night. It be over . . ."

Mobuto cocked his gun and put it to Carol Mason's head.

But on Mobuto's last word Henley's arms dropped to his sides and Elliott fell to the floor.

"You idiot," Francisco yelled. "Did you kill Sumner before my order?"

Mobuto looked up from Mason. Henley did not reply to Francisco. Instead, his face hung cold. He stared back at the three with an open mouth. They waited for the words. Henley's eyes rolled into his head. The three board members froze as Henley dropped to the floor and a larger shadow stood before them.

In the dim, musty cellar, the Bluff City Butcher stood with his eyes leveled on the three and the blood-dripping knife in his left hand. The man they had feared from his beginning was now the grown, hungry lion outside his cage.

"You alive!" Mobuto bellowed. The big game hunter raised his gun and fired until the deafening explosions were replaced with feeble clicks and the light bulb went out.

In the darkness more shots were fired and darker shadows moved. Boxes fell and wood barrels crashed against stone walls. Then quiet and burned gunpowder and fresh blood moved through the room, promising death.

He never saw Adam—the light went out and the battle ensued. His only thought was to rescue Carol. Elliott crawled the wet floor climbing debris until he found her. He kissed her head and pulled her bound body away. They hid behind another pile unsure of their situation—did one or all of the board members survive? Were they now hunting Elliott and Carol?

Elliott whispered in Carol's ear, "We will get out," He untied her. "Please stay here. I need to find my gun." He moved to another stack and slowly stood to assess the situation. Then there were more explosions—more gunfire. It was not over. In the smoky haze and the flame from the muzzle of a gun, Elliott saw a shadow descending . . . then there was silence.

Was that Henley? Why did he let me go? Elliott wondered. *Or, was it . . . Adam? How would he know to come here?*

Elliott stayed low and moved to where his dropped gun could be. He moved in the quiet cellar, feeling blindly for their only chance. *Maybe one or all three alive waiting for a new target. If Adam came, maybe he needs my help. And Tony may be alive. I've got to get to him.*

Somehow Elliott got turned around. He crawled through the maze and bumped into the wall with the only light switch. He reached up and flipped it on. Through the layers of gun smoke he saw the three board members were dead, stacked in a blood-drenched pile by the steps. Elliott could see Henley on the floor. He had not moved from where he let go of Elliott.

"Adam," Elliott yelled. He found his brother covered in blood and leaning against a pillar.

Carol saw Tony and ran to him.

"He's breathing," she yelled. "He's alive, Elliott."

"Use his phone. Call for help," Elliott yelled over his shoulder as he examined Adam's bloody wounds.

Carol propped Tony up against the wall and punched 911. "He's unconscious."

"I've gotta take Adam," Elliott yelled back. "He's been shot too many times. He's in bad shape, even for him. He needs help."

She finished giving directions to the DPD and dropped the phone. "They're coming. Elliott, we can't leave Tony here. He's . . ."

"Yes you can, goddamn it," Tony growled spitting blood.

"You're back with us," Carol said holding his shoulder.

Tony rubbed his head as he said, "Someone needs to be here to explain all this shit." Carol helped steady him as he struggled to get to his feet.

"You need to stay on your butt, Tee," Elliott ordered from across the cellar, working on Adam's wounds.

"You guys gotta get Adam out of here. Anyone else hit?"

"Just the Gilgamesh board," Carol sighed.

"They're all dead, Tony. By the steps out of this place. We need to hide those suitcases." Elliott helped Adam get to his feet. "Hold on now . . ."

"I'll take care of that," Tony said, rubbing his head and approaching the man who had saved everyone's life. Adam reached to steady the injured homicide detective. "This time I wish you had been a minute early . . . *my friend*," Tony mumbled with a wincing smile.

Tony held onto Adam's good arm for balance. He saw blood seeping from Adam's abdominal wound. "Elliott, ya gotta take him now."

Tony looked up to Adam. "He's a good man . . ."

The face of the Butcher had left the dark cellar when the last Gilgamesh board member died. Now, Adam smiled the only way he knew—two blinks and a nod. Elliott threw the massive arm over his shoulder and propped the infamous monster of Memphis urban legend—the man he had hunted for a decade, his biological brother, and the man who fought a world war few would ever know and fewer would ever understand.

Elliott helped Adam to the cellar steps with Carol at his side. They climbed and sucked in the night air. Tony watched the three disappear into the dead cornfield as sirens and flashing lights turned onto Garrett's farm.

Maybe now this nightmare can be over . . .

EPILOGUE

"I don't believe this is the end of the nightmare." Albert's words left the brim of his coffee cup and were lost in the morning gust and rippling bugleweed and wild dagga.

The west patio of the Bell mansion was inviting this time of year, especially in the early morning hours. Cool shade amidst sunbathed lawns provided the perfect setting for the reunion. It had been eleven days since Dyersburg.

Across from Albert, Marcus Medino stared at the water beads rolling down his orange juice glass. He had eaten little since the day he lost his research team and Maxwell Gregory. "I hope you're wrong, Albert," he said under his breath.

"The FBI reports Mr. Kamholt had ties with Gilgamesh going back twenty years." Albert set his empty cup on the saucer with a soft clink. "They have video from the Newark parking garage," he whispered. "The man shot Max from behind."

Marcus shook his head. "Who shot Kamholt?" he asked.

"An old woman parked next to them. After he shot Max,

Kamholt transferred the suitcases to her trunk. She shot him point-blank. The NYPD pulled a Miss Birnbaum out of the Hudson River days later. FBI didn't piece it together until yesterday. I got a call."

"I'm responsible for Max's death," Marcus said. "I never should have gone along with the New York plan. The trip was too dangerous and I knew it."

"You can't second-guess," Albert said. "It takes you nowhere. I know it for a fact, young man. I've been doing it most of my life."

The new maid—an attractive Bolivian woman—filled Albert's cup and replaced Marcus's orange juice with a fresh glass. She smiled dutifully and left the patio.

"And it was Max's plan . . . a very capable CIA man. He wanted them to follow him to New York. Max understood the risk better than anyone." Albert reflected. "I think he knew he would not be coming back."

"That may be true," Marcus shot back. "But Dr. Sorokin and Dr. Stark were not equipped for any of this. They were pawns in a death match. They were simply driving around to confuse Gilgamesh and . . ."

"None of us thought Gilgamesh would stoop so low—they did not have to execute the doctors. Marcus, I suggest you find a way to let it go. You must focus on outcome. In the end, Maxwell's plan worked. All of us faced danger and some of us survived. Honor those not here by living to the fullest."

The backdoor opened. Tony emerged. "Hello, gentlemen."

"Good morning, Detective Wilcox." Albert pointed to a chair. When Tony sat, his coat opened, revealing his .44.

Marcus watched it sink under the table. "You carry on weekends?"

"I carry every day." The Bolivian maid poured his coffee. Tony winked and watched her disappear into the mansion.

"Wow, Albert. It's about time you got some good-looking help." He unfolded his napkin and dropped it on his lap. "That said, where's William? For that matter, where's everybody? Thought you said eight o'clock Saturday morning."

"William is out of town. He checks in every day." Albert pointed to the speakerphone at the center of the table. "The others should arrive any moment. I've not talked with you or Elliott since Dyersburg. I believe you were the last to see him."

"You are right, Albert. I've been unable to talk to anyone since that night. They've kept me sequestered—Cottam's wearing my ass out. Lots of stupid questions and wild accusations come your way when you climb out of a cellar on an abandoned farm with four bodies covered in blood."

"I can't believe the three board members were in Dyersburg of all places," Marcus said. I guess it makes some sense. I always wondered why Dyersburg was on my catacomb map."

Albert held his butter knife, feeling the edge with his finger. "Your message was appreciated—'Elliott alive'. But I've not heard from Adam. I suspect he was involved."

Tony avoided the open-ended question. Managing emotions was not a strength. He'd leave the heavy lifting to Elliott.

"How you holding up, Marcus?" Tony asked to divert the conversation.

"Not so good."

"Maybe you'll feel better someday." Tony reached for a blueberry muffin and the back door opened. "You've been through a lot more than many of us."

"Albert," she called out.

When he saw Carol Mason, he could not stop the quiet tears. Albert got to his feet. She ran across the patio and held the father of the man she adored. There were no words to say or needed. Elliott walked up from behind and watched with a serene smile.

Another breeze swept across the west patio. Elliott found Tony and Marcus and humbly nodded.

When Albert opened his eyes, he saw his son for the first time since the day Elliott could have taken his own life. Holding Carol in one arm, he reached for Elliott.

"We thought we lost you, my dear lady," Albert said. "Washington DC left all of us in an abyss we could never climb out of."

"I'm sorry, Albert. I was lured into a trap. Elliott tried to warn me. I should have known better." Elliott rubbed her back as she smiled at Tony and Marcus.

They sat at the table with only one empty chair. It was next to Albert, but he did not know.

She reached for Albert's hand. The days together after Betty's death completed their bond. "I was taken by Gilgamesh people. They needed a way to get to Elliott. They faked my death to create an opportunity for when they were ready."

"Misguided people to say the least," Albert muttered.

"It almost worked," Elliott said.

The servants delivered plates of scrambled eggs, bacon, biscuits and white gravy, grits and fresh fruit. The five ate and bantered about everything but what weighed heaviest on their minds. After empty plates were taken and coffees refreshed, Elliott tapped his water glass with a spoon.

"Thank you, Albert, for opening your home for this important time together." Elliott turned his attentions to the others at the table. "Why are we here today?" Carol's leg touched his. "We are here because we each have pieces of a century-old puzzle to share," he said. "And I should start first . . . with complete truth.

"Something happened to me when I thought I lost Carol. It crushed me. I had no desire to live in this world anymore. I was a broken man. The headaches came that night. They were so severe I cannot begin to describe the pain. I've had them before, but this time something new happened. This time, I started to change inside.

"I carried anger all my life—just under the surface. I worked to hold it back, to control the beast within. But when I lost Carol, the anger took over. It consumed me. That rage took me to Dyersburg."

Elliott looked down. "I'm not proud to tell you I went to Dyersburg to find and kill the three Gilgamesh board members . . . and anyone who got in my way."

Carol reached for his arm and squeezed. "That is understandable," Albert said. "You've lost so much, son. To have the one you love taken . . ."

"I would have felt the same way," Tony said.

"I appreciate your words, but the rage inside me was not normal. It was monstrous. It had complete control of me. I felt the rage I've seen in Adam's eyes."

"You're not a monster, Elliott. Nobody is a monster because they are fighting evil. There's a difference," Carol whispered.

"I understand, but what I'm trying to say is I could not reason with the world. I had to kill even though it went against my core beliefs. Something owned me."

Tony said, "When I shot Henley, he let go and you dropped to the floor, Elliott. When I got there, you were not breathing. Your heart stopped. You were dead. You did not kill Henley or anyone else in Dyersburg. They killed you! They were the monsters. How you felt means nothing. Your feelings, from uncontrollable rage to unbridled love, are human."

"You saved my life, Tony. You brought me back. For that I will forever be thankful. But the point I am trying to make is . . . I felt Adam's anger and rage inside me. Granted, I did not have his strength or skills, but I felt the internal battle he faces every day. I went to Dyersburg to kill bad people. It is something I never contemplated doing before."

Tony lit a cigarette. "And then the Gilgamesh trio arrived. We had the drop on them. Next thing I know, the lights go out."

"The second Henley twin came out of the catacombs behind us," Elliott said. "He knocked you out, Tony. He got me under control before I knew what happened."

"What changed?" Marcus asked. "How did you get out of there alive?"

Elliott backed his chair out and stood up looking toward the west wall of the estate. The others followed his eyes. Adam crossed the sunlit field—he looked different. Instead of his long, black leather coat, he wore a white cotton shirt. His long, black hair was draped over his back. He had a bandage around his forehead.

Elliott left the table and went to him. They spoke on the lawn as the others watched and then both walked up to the west patio. Albert was the first to greet Adam. They could see the wide abdominal bandage through the shirt, and another wrapped around his large bicep. Adam said nothing. He simply looked at each present and stopped at Carol. Then he smiled his way.

Adam took the chair next to Albert. They sat quietly as the maid started to pour his coffee. Adam gently touched her wrist and pointed to the empty glass. "Water, please."

Adam's eyes went to Elliott as he entered his head. *What do you need from me?*

Elliott responded, *Your presence.* He turned back to Marcus. "I want to answer your question. What changed everything in Dyersburg was my brother, Adam . . .

"Your map shows the catacombs reach Dyersburg. I needed help that night. Adam heard me. He came through the catacombs. He got there just in time."

"Mobuto Ali said the three of us had to die," Carol said.

"Adam stopped Henley from hurting Elliott, and then he faced three guns."

"When it ended, the three Gilgamesh board members and Henley twins were dead. Tony was unconscious and Adam was severely wounded—he needed emergency medical attention."

"I guess I woke up when it was all over," Tony said. "Told them to go—get Adam patched up and leave the mess to me. It was gonna be hard enough to explain. Adam didn't need to hang around. He's been covering our backs a long time and we didn't even know it. I'm still tryin' to wrap my brain around all that stuff. Now he needs to know he's not alone anymore. We've got his back now . . ."

"Adam has a family," Albert said.

"Although we stopped Gilgamesh in Dyersburg, we lost our good friend Max," Tony said.

"And we lost a suitcase," Elliott said. "Someone has the Medino biologic."

"The suitcases were decoys," Marcus said.

The table leaned in. "But the plan . . . you produced enough biologic for a major infusion event. Max was to get it to Albert's bottling plants for distribution and infusion."

Marcus shook his head allowing Elliott to finish so the others at the table could keep up. "The three suitcases contained plastic bags filled with a concoction of flour, refined sugar, and a protein powder in case someone did a quick test for organics."

"So this immortality stuff has been nothing but bullshit all this time?" Tony scoffed.

"I assure you, the biologic is real. It is the decoy concoction that is bogus. I also synthesized the biologic in adequate quantities to infuse one hundred million people."

"Are you saying success does not require infusing every person?" Carol asked.

"Yes, provided my father's theory is correct. The model is

quite simple. We infuse subject #1 and they acquire the life-extending genetic trait. However, they also become a vector."

"What the hell's a vector," Tony asked.

"A vector is an agent acting as a carrier. In our case, the vector spreads the life extension trait to others like a common cold. We inoculate one. They inoculate hundreds and so on . . .

"Maxwell transported bogus material to misdirect Gilgamesh. It was a change in the plan only a few of us knew for security purposes."

"Who moved the real Medino biologic?" Carol asked.

The speakerphone chimed. "This will answer that question." Albert tapped the bar.

"Mr. Bell. William is on the line."

"Thank you. William, can you hear me?"

"Yes, sir."

"Good morning. We are all here on the west patio. You may speak freely."

"Thank you, sir. I must first express my heartfelt praise for those with you today and my deepest condolences for those we've lost."

"Thank you, William. It has been a difficult time for all."

Albert lifted his head and looked around the table. "Before William begins, I should tell you two things. First, William is an accomplished pilot—that is relevant now. Second, William has discretely conducted business for Bell Enterprises around the world for many years. He is far more than my butler. William is my closest friend and confidant. We go back to 1965 when we met. He was my private pilot in the beginning. From there our friendship grew immensely.

"I share this background with you now because these little-known facts were of enormous importance to Maxwell, the architect of our global dispersion strategy. That said, William, please carry on."

"Very good, sir. On the morning of May 16, five cars left the Bell estate. All were followed by Gilgamesh operatives. Max's was the last car to depart. That provided me with the opportunity to cross the grounds on foot—undetected. I climbed the stone wall, possibly the most dangerous aspect of my journey, and located the four-wheeler hidden earlier in the woods.

"My travel was, as expected by Max, uneventful. Upon locating a small, unassuming house in an east Memphis neighborhood, I traded my four-wheeler for a nondescript van I drove to the Olive Branch Airport. From there I flew a crop duster to Jackson, Mississippi. From there I flew commercial to Atlanta. I won't bore you with the details of my convoluted route that brought me to my final destination the next day, London."

"You carried the Medino biologic?" Elliott questioned.

"Yes, Dr. Sumner. Max gave me the leather satchel with the biologic that morning."

"Three test tubes held enough biologic to accomplish our dispersion objectives," Marcus said. "Our infusion number leaked to Gilgamesh through their mole, Vanlandingham."

"Goddamn Vanlandingham is with Gilgamesh?" Tony bellowed.

"He's now in FBI custody, complicit in the termination of Max and four LIFE2 scientists."

"He won't last long in the federal pen," Tony mused.

"Regarding the biologic, our infusion needs misled Gilgamesh. They were looking for suitcases moving, not test tubes. Max saw the disparity as a major advantage."

The speakerphone crackled. "Upon arriving in London, I met the appropriate personnel. I am pleased to report the biologic has been dispersed according to plan. Sir, this might be the time to educate the group on the delivery substrate and dispersion mechanism."

"No need. Heard all about the bottling plants," Tony said as he lit another cigarette and leaned back in his chair.

Albert smiled. "I'm afraid you're operating under another false assumption, Detective Wilcox. The bottling industry has always been a most inadequate route for our purposes—too many variables. Not enough control. However, it did serve as a credible decoy to the uneducated."

"Reeled in Gilgamesh," Elliott said.

"Cotton has always been the mainstay of the Bell family, a century of strong relationships and specialized knowledge. We are well-connected with the textile industry around the world. Our business interests are fully integrated, from cotton seed to finished goods. This afforded us the opportunity to select the best avenue within the business to incorporate the biologic."

Marcus inserted, "Best infusion avenue, minimal risk, and fewest questions."

"Quite true. And we have access to all major population centers. We reach the economically privileged through direct sales, and third world countries through well-established humanitarian outreach programs."

"How is the biologic dispersed?" Carol asked.

Albert smiled. "Cotton! It is the most widely used fiber known to man. A single cotton boll contains 500,000 fiber strands. After every strand is processed, it must be washed. In the business we say 'desized'. Last time I looked, our company enjoyed a ninety-five percent share of the global desizing reagent market."

"I like," Tony mumbled.

"We manufacture this reagent outside London. The biologic is introduced as a proprietary ingredient, a performance enhancer. Marcus can explain infusion best."

"Anyone who comes into contact with a textile product desized by Bell Enterprises is infused. The biologic works at a molecular level with DNA—that means we require a minuscule amount to successfully bind with host DNA."

"Hey doc, how does this biologic work in layman terms?" Tony asked.

"Damaged cells naturally repair and replace themselves from conception. Something slows or turns off the process for unknown reason. Cells fail and die; a precursor to disease, aging, and death. The biologic, once introduced, neutralizes the process. The cells simply continue to repair and replace like before, but indefinitely. I'm not sure my father knows the exact mechanism that turns cell repair *off*. Somehow his biologic codes the DNA and keeps the switch *on*."

"Can someone be overexposed to the biologic?" Carol asked.

"No. Once a person is infused, all future exposures are ignored. And the biologic remains active on the textile for a long time and only effects those not infused."

"If I'm no longer needed, I will say goodbye," William said.

"That will be quite all right, William. Thank you. Goodbye." Albert tapped the speakerphone and leaned back, cradling his coffee cup as another breeze swept across the patio. The five sat mulling over the information and totality of life-changing events. Servants refilled coffee cups and disappeared into the mansion.

"My grandfather's dream of immortality became a nightmare," Albert said. "But not all is bad in the world. Some good has come. I'm thankful for my two sons—blood lions," he said with a wink. "And I am thankful for all of you, my new family."

Elliott set down his cup and reached for Carol's hand. "Gilgamesh is gone and the biologic dispersed. I wonder if this nightmare is over or just beginning."

"People living a long time, that may not be a good thing," Tony said. "This is big."

"My father believed *life* was the miracle. Extending it is not new. Each generation has hygiene, antibiotics, vaccination, medicine, surgery, and diet."

"That said, if the biologic works, Dr. Medino simply accomplished what our generation's science allowed—a genetic path to extending life," Elliott said.

"How will we know it works?" Carol asked.

Marcus stared at his glass rubbing the new beads with his thumb. "Disease as we know it will decline. They won't be able to explain it. Demands on healthcare systems around the world will decline. People will be more active. Then—in time—people will realize they are living longer. Maybe at around 150 they will wonder what happened!"

"This evolutionary leap could be lost for centuries. Eradication of disease will lead to years of head-scratching." Elliott said.

"Maybe the nightmare can be over after all," Carol said.

"Yes, maybe it can," Elliott said. *But even the simple things in life are more complex than we know.* He watched the wild dagga at the patio's edge, the orange flowers leaning in the gentle breeze.

How long did it take before you could bend in the wind?

"*Leonotis leonurus,*" Adam said.

All eyes turned to the man they least understood. At that moment Elliott knew his brother understood far more than anyone.

Albert smiled at his two sons. "Better known as the lion's tail —a survivor."

ABOUT THE AUTHOR

STEVE BRADSHAW is a forensic field agent and biotech entrepreneur writing his unique brand of mystery/thrillers. Steve's training and experience investigating thousands of unexplained deaths for the medical examiner's office, and as the founder-President/CEO of an innovative biomedical device company enables him to put his readers on the front row in the fascinating worlds of fringe science, modern forensics, and the chilling pursuit of real monsters.

Steve enjoys sharing his experiences and perspectives as a forensic investigator, President/CEO, and mystery/thriller author. Visit his website and join MEMBER GUEST so you can interact with the author, get insider information and updates, arrange for an author visit, and to be the first in line for new releases.

For more information:
www.stevebradshawauthor.com
steve@stevebradshawauthor.com